"Reloaded Version 2013"

®©

TIME TO LEARN-RELOADED
TIME WILL REVEAL PART 1©

BY

BLACK COFFEE©

TIME TO LEARN-RELOADED-Time Will Reveal-part 1

Published by: True's Relate Publishing
Time to Learn-RELOADED- (Time will reveal: Part 1)
Library of Congress Control Number: TXu 1-126-243

REGISTERED TRADEMARK-MARCA REGISTRADA
ISBN:978-0-9844701-0-5
Printed in the United States of America
Set by: Createspace
Cover design by Gregory Spencer of Misvision Graphics info@misvisiongraphics.com
Logo design: JayRocOne [age 15] JayRocOne Designs
Requests for information on ordering, scheduling the author for signings and appearances should be addressed to: truelovelybrown@gmail.com

Black Coffee's websites
http://www.blackdollone.com
www.truesrelatepublishing.com
http://twitter.com/AuthorBlkCoffee
On Facebook: Black Coffee Books {Fan Page}
Facebook group: Black Coffee's Crew Nation-The Movement

Manuscript Preparation: Black Coffee
True's Relate publishing company
P.O. Box 2911
Gulfport, Ms. 39505

[PUBLISHER'S NOTES]

[REVIEWS]

"Ebony Brown is discovering that life doesn't always work out the way that she'd like. When her grandmother falls ill, her family decides to send her to Houston in order to help take care of her. For Ebony, this is a drastic change. She'll have to leave her home, her crew and Ajay, the boy she's come to love very much. ----------------But the family's plans are delayed when several unexpected and somewhat upsetting, events take place. -------Time Will Reveal is,---- a coming of age novel. Overall, the story is entertaining and often emotional. --------- is interesting and very much like a real family unit."

Reviewer: C. Noël Rivera, Allbooks Reviews

"I am very interested and I look forward to reading more and more!!! Keep up the good work and keep it coming."-Venetia Crawford-Aisola, Admin of True's Relate

---

DEDICATED TO THE MEMORIES OF:

MY MOTHER

BIG MAMA

CLARA

APRIL

Nuunk Nuunk

Sometimes you win, sometimes you lose, sometimes you miss the game because you're singing the blues.

I'd rather be in the game, as the time gets diminished. For it's not how you start it but it's how you finish.

And if you're looking for support and it seems you're at war. First try being the same friend that you're looking for."

-Author Black Coffee {off the dome} 3/21/2010

CHAPTER 1

DADDY'S HOME-THE INTRO

TIME TO LEARN-RELOADED-TIME WILL REVEAL 1

As the sun dawns on another day, all is still quiet in the house. The crew is still resting while outside, the birds begin to sing. It's another beautiful day in Cleveland Ohio. Pearl opens her eyes, looks to the ceiling and thanks GOD for another day of life. Today is Monday, the 3rd day of July and the 1st day of her long awaited vacation. She makes her way into the bathroom to start her morning routine of brushing her teeth, washing her face and whatever else she needs to do to help her prepare for a new day. She brushes her silky hair away from her face. As she gazes into the mirror, she reflects on the life her and her husband John are managing for their 4 children. Thoughts of the news, her and her sister Brenda received from their mother in Houston, causes her eyes to well-up with tears.

"What's the matter, mama?" a voice from behind her asks.

She turns to see her only daughter Ebony, standing in the doorway of the bathroom with a look of concern on her face.

"Oh it's nothing, baby girl," Pearl replies with that smile big John says could light up a room. She adds, "It's just nerves, baby. Mama's fine."

Emotionally, she's far from fine. Just 3 days ago, she found out her mother had been diagnosed with breast cancer and has to start treatments, very soon. The family talked things over with big John, over the phone. It was decided *someone* has to be there. Pearl knows it would be impossible for her to go to Houston and stay, because of her job at the hospital, her home and her children. It was decided Ebony would go and stay until the treatments are done. Big mama insisted it be a female and Ebony *is* her oldest granddaughter. This is 1 of the toughest decisions of Pearl's seasoned life and 1 of the hardest to digest. Ebony has been told of the trip. Though she doesn't want to leave her friends and family, she wants to be there for

big mama. Her big mama really needs her and she's also the 1 person whom Ebony credits with teaching her the most about being a little lady. Big mama has been teaching Ebony how to recognize husband material since she turned 6 years old.

"Is big mama doing worse?" Ebony asks.

"No, baby girl," Pearl answers softly, "There's been no change. I'm just worried about having to send my baby girl away from home."

"I know, mama," she says, "Daddy said that to me, when we was on the phone. He said he can't be there to protect me from the mannish boys."

Ebony is the 3rd of Pearl and John's 4 children and their only girl. She's thirteen, 5 years older than the baby boy Jesse, who's eight. Their oldest, John Jr, is better known as Jb. He's fifteen and set to start his junior year at MLK high school, this fall. Their 2nd oldest child is Jeremy. He's better known as Tank and he's fourteen. He's only 11 months older than Ebony. They were both born in 1975. Tank was born on the 25th of January. Ebony was born on Christmas day. They always tell people, who don't know any better, that they're twins. That's because they are the same age for 1 whole month, each year. The 2 of them are extremely close. So of course, if Ebony has to go to Houston, Tank is planning to roll too.

"Go and get your brothers up, baby," Pearl says to Ebony, "I'll be finished in here in a few minutes."

"Yes ma'am," Ebony says.

***"I'm already up,"* Tank says as he stammers into the bathroom, rubbing his eyes and stretching.**

"Son, *don't* you know better than to walk into a bathroom with ladies in it?" Pearl asks with a frown on her face.

"Oops. Sorry, ma," Tank says.

He looks down now, as he backs out of the bathroom. He's still half asleep. He quickly removes himself from the bathroom and to a more respectful position, then asks, "Do you want me to go get Jb and Lil man up, for you?" He asked from just inside of Pearl's bedroom door, where he now stands.

"Yes please," Pearl answers him with a smile.

He can't see her face but he can hear that she's smiling. He's happy just knowing she isn't angry with him over his ill mannered interruption.

"Okay," he says as he heads back toward his room. But he has something else to tell his mother. From the hallway, he yells, "Oh mama!"

TIME TO LEARN-RELOADED-Time Will Reveal-part 1

"Yes dear? What is it?" Pearl asks as she continues to smile.

"Ajay and June spent the night!" Tank says.

"Okay, sweetheart. I want you to get them up too. And I want all of you to get ready and come down for breakfast," Pearl says as she dries her hands.

She turns to Ebony and says, "Baby girl, the bathroom is all yours. Don't you camp out in here either, okay? Your brothers had company that spent the night. So I want you to make sure you dress *completely* before you come out. And please hurry. I want you to come on downstairs and help me out in the kitchen. You know how much your brothers and the rest of those boys can eat. So don't you lag around for too long. Or there won't be any breakfast left for you to eat." Pearl laughs as she exit's the bathroom.

Ebony smiles as she says, "okay," then closes the door after her mother leaves.

Ebony uses the master bathroom in her mother and father's room, on a daily basis. She has 3 brothers who use the main bathroom, in the hallway and she hated how they always left the seat up. With 3 of them and 1 of her, she was the *minority*. So she always had to put the seat back up when she finished. But after she started her menstruation period, 4 months ago, she insisted and everyone else agreed, her and Pearl should share the master bathroom because that's where Pearl keeps all of their personal products. Anyway, the boys was seriously conflicted with having those types of products in the bathroom they used. And once again, Ebony was the minority in the discussion. But in the master bathroom, her and Pearl are the majority. So eventually, John, who's away most of the time driving his rig, started using the hallway bathroom with his sons when he comes home. That's the best solution for all involved. Ebony still has to help her mother clean the bathroom in the hallway. She doesn't like that part, at all. But that isn't up for negotiation.

Big June and Ajay stay at their house often or Jb and Tank stay with them. They all attend school together and are very close. But last night's sleepover was different. Anthony or Ajay, as he's commonly known, had stayed the night, indeed. Only this time he had slept in Ebony's room, the entire night. He had gone back to the boys room, only an hour ago.

TIME TO LEARN-RELOADED-Time Will Reveal-part 1

It wasn't unusual for Ajay to come into Ebony's room. He *is* her boyfriend and has been for 3 years. Only their parents don't know about that part yet. When Ajay comes to her room, in the night time hours, they always talk but they do *other things* too. A couple of years ago, they kissed for the very first time. Ajay told her then that she was the only girl he had kissed and she was the only girl he would ever kiss. They have kissed a lot since that first kiss. She likes the way he kisses her, a whole lot. They progressed to touching, a little over a year ago. She loves the way he touches her too. He touches her face, so gently with 1 of his hands, while his other hand explores her developing breast and body. Eventually, he graduated to the point to where he would end up caressing her most private spot. He would roll his tongue around in her mouth and over her breast and nipples. *She thought* it was him who was responsible for the growth of her breast. At least that's what he has said for the last year since her breast started to form. He's always telling her that. When the fact is, she's just going through puberty, the adolescent changes a female's body takes on leading up to menstruation and the transformation into womanhood. Ebony never liked how it felt when he placed his finger inside of her. But he would always try it. As soon as he felt her squirms of discomfort, he would stop immediately.

Ebony is a very intelligent girl. She's just very naive when it comes to sex. Ajay is the opposite, sex wise. He's very experienced, at his young age. Ebony had been a virgin until just a few hours ago. With touch from only Ajay, for the last 2 years. Ajay, on the other hand, has been sexually active since he was 8 years old. Knowing she was leaving in 3 days, made Ebony eager to feel the real thing Ajay was always talking to her about. He has never pressured her to have sex. But it was Ebony who knew, 1 day they would go all the way. In her heart, she knew Ajay was the only boy for such an honor. He hadn't tried to go all the way before, though he's deep in the street game and known throughout their community for his heartless ways. But he has always shown a certain respect and compassion for Ebony "baby girl" Brown. They grew up together. Their parents are best friends and their homes on next door to each other. Ajay and Ebony use to fight and argue all of the time when they was younger. She'd say, *"I can't stand him".* Their parents figured that would eventually change and they would start to get along. But they had no idea of how much that would change. Or how soon it would change, either.

TIME TO LEARN-RELOADED-Time Will Reveal-part 1

Their extended families have been very close for 3 generations. Their oldest living generation fled north, prior to and during the infamous civil rights movement which had infamous battlefields in the south. Their families are rich in history and have always had an entrepreneurial spirit. The first and second generations are raising this 3rd generation to be no different than them.

But for now, Ebony is struggling with how she will tell her mother about her and Ajay's relationship and especially, last night. She's afraid her mother will be disappointed in her. Before last night ever happened, she wanted to tell Pearl that her and Ajay had kissed and touched. Only she hadn't found the courage to do so. She knows her mother will say she's too young for that sort of behavior, without even hearing her out. She has to find a way to tell her mother before she leaves for Houston and she has to tell her face to face. That's the way things are done in the crew family. They all have to live by the honor system. Ebony has only 3 days left to come clean. She has to find a way to tell Pearl about her intimacy.

Ajay will turn 15 in 8 days. Due to his experience, he seems a lot older to Ebony and most teens, their age. He hangs out with Ebony's brother Tank, Tank's 1st cousin big June and Ritchie Rich, who is Ajay's 1st cousin. Being that Ajay and Tank live next door to each other, they spend mostly all of their days together. While Big June and Richie Rich, who both live down the street, spends at least, half of their day with them and the rest of the guys in the crew. These 4 boys are all 14 and they keep the scene hot, along with the rest of the males in their crew.

Ebony has been sheltered by everyone, to a certain extent. Most of their circle still treats her like she's a *little* girl. And her parents, Pearl and big John, still buy her baby dolls at Christmas time. Her oldest brother Jb, acts more like a father figure than a brother. Which is what their father demands from him. Jb and Tank are very close with Ajay. So close in fact, they act more like brothers than *just* neighbors. All of the guys in their crew have a similar bond and being that Ajay lives in the house next door to them, they stay at each others home, most nights. Jb and Tank knows he likes Ebony and they know she likes him too. They're both cool with their union because they know the fathers and grandfathers would approve of

the 2 of them having a future together. In this crew, the male opinion matters, a whole lot.

Their father John Sr, who is best known as big John, is a heads up street smart, charming and smooth brother. He has bridged many gaps for his extended family which they *collectively* call, *The Crew*. John wasn't afraid to go tripping through white neighborhoods, if it meant a chance to earn some money. Though he would never lay down his pride or his dignity, he always kept the crew on solid ground. He always put it down. He did things which he knew would benefit him, Pearl and their kids, as well. He drives commercial trucks for a living and he loves his job. Only it keeps him away from home for 2 week intervals. He had gotten this job in the early 70's, just before his 17th birthday. That was made possible with the endorsement of a fair minded integration supporting, white mogul named Jeb Baker. Mr. Baker always told John he wanted him to have his own branch of the company, someday. So for years, John has saved a lot of his earnings while investing some. He was more than able to start a sister company, years ago. He loves driving the open road but the fact that it keeps him away from his home and family, is the only drawback because the earnings are above average. Big John has many trades but his truck driving job holds the greatest promise. He set a goal of driving long haul for 25 years. Once he reaches that goal, he'll set up his own company. He's a hard worker and he takes no shit from anyone.

Pearl always told their 4 children stories of how they grew up and came to be husband and wife. She told them about the marches they participated in as young children, along with their parents, for civil rights and voters rights. If there was a viable protest in the south or mid-west, this crew rallied in it. They were known to be involved in matters that mattered. Solid bonds and life long friendships were formed back then. Many of those bonds still exist today. As teenagers and young adults, they protested the Vietnam conflict and the draft. Pearl explained how their young lives was about peace and love in the midst of wars. Both foreign and domestic. When she was an adolescent, her and her crew had taken the strength they'd drawn from their parents struggles and mistakes. And pushed forward to try and make a change in the world. Often times they did this through groups they formed with good Caucasian Americans. Together they all

sought to end separatism. It was what would later be known as the yippee hippie, smelly bearded and free spirited, free thinking era of *Jimi Hendrix, Woodstock* and rock-n-roll. The era in which today's R&B legends was recording and performing the *real* love songs of the modern day. The days of *Black love, Black Pride* and *Black power* was the 2nd generations coming-of-age era. Smoking reefers and tripping off of psychedelic drugs was the norm. Young folks wore Tye-dyed t-shirts, *Afro's*, Afro puffs, micro mini's, bellbottomed jeans, clogs, knee boots and flip-flops. She also told them they didn't always stay on the right side of the law, themselves. She told them of how John and his crew brothers ran their neighborhood, back in those days, just as they still do today. You could ask anyone around town nowadays and they would agree. The 2nd generation was as strong as the 1st generation. Only they were a bit more reckless, many would say, as well. This 3rd generation with big Chill at the helm, seems to be even more reckless than their predecessors. And they are even more fearless and head strong when dealing with similar injustices.

Jb is just like his father, big John. At 15, he's already a made man. He hangs out with all of the *big dogs*. Namely; Kenneth "Big Chill" Payne, a kingpin in the mean ass Cleveland streets. Big Chill is 20 years old. He has any connection one would need for daily street survival. Nearly everyone knows and respects big Chill. He is the only child of his deceased parents, Paul and Willamena Payne. They was apart of big John Sr's crew, the 2nd generation, where everybody had their own specialty. Willamena had been killed in a car accident before Chill was even double digit in age. His father Paul was killed, just over a year ago. His parents were power brokers in the street hustle. Although they had degrees and many other money outlets, the streets was their niche. They owned lots of property which was passed on to big Chill. But that isn't all that passed on. Their power and muscle, in the streets, passed on to him as well. He had learned the street hustle just as well as he'd learned his books. Only Chill could combine the 2 niches, sprinkle them with common sense and break bread like no one this crew had ever known.

Ajay's parents are big Chill's Godparents. Chill, being an only child, took Ajay, an only son, as his blood brother, early in life. Chill had money, power and respect, in Cleveland and the Tri-State area, before he

reached the age of maturity. Now he's looking to expand southward. He's young, powerful and the leader of the 3rd generation of this strong willed crew. Being leader of the crew, brings on even more power and respect, just on the legacy alone. But in this *dog-eat-dog* world of money, power and respect, also comes jealousy and envy. There is always somebody trying to take what Chill has. That's when he has to show *why* he's the king. And that's also when the crew has to and do, flex their unmatched authority. They're heartless when dealing with anyone who disrespects Chill or any other member of their crew, for that matter. Chill is not blood kin but he's family, in all of the ways that count. Ajay's parents had taken total responsibility for him, a year ago, when Paul was killed. Just like it was with Paul, whenever 1 of the crew families fell on hard times and needed some quick cash, 1 of the sons would come up with it. They knew it was Chill, who had put them onto something so they could make some *change*. It may have been ill-gotten but when you have needs, meeting those needs is all you want to do. No matter what the means are of meeting them.

But of all the guys in their crew, Ajay is the most intriguing. At least to Ebony he is. He's usually quiet, laid back and most of the time buzzed from weed. Though he's an awesome basketball player, he loves to smoke marijuana. As a matter of fact, the whole 3rd generation loves to smoke it too. They know some of their parents use to smoke and some of their parents still do. Ebony smokes with the crew when they allow her too. But most of the time they don't share with her because she usually has to watch Lil man while Pearl goes to work. But it's mainly because Ajay doesn't want her to smoke unless she's with him or about to be with him. Ebony is friends with all of the true homeboys and home girls in their crew. It wasn't until she turned 13 that she became a legitimate member of their *active* crew. Thirteen is a very significant age in this family of strong willed soldiers. It's significant and sets a separate milestone for each generation.

It was the age when their grandparents, the 1st generation, had to have jobs to earn money and help out on whatever land their families sharecropped on. Most of them had been forced to leave whatever little schooling they were getting, to marry and have children. Offspring who would be able to help out in the fields and such.

TIME TO LEARN-RELOADED-Time Will Reveal-part 1

For the 2nd generation, 13 was the age when they were allowed to join protest, freedom rides and marches without their parents at their sides.

But in this 3rd generation it signifies the age when they have to accept that whatever they do, they're going to be held accountable for it. Maybe not according to the laws where on paper, 18 is the age of maturity. But they will certainly be held responsible for their actions by their elders.

They had started to witness young black men, much younger than 18, being sent to prison with grown men. And they were being tried as adults before they turned eighteen. This family which always prided itself on staying a step ahead, reared their young to think mature, act with respect and be accountable. Thirteen years of age, give or take a year in some cases, is when they had to show their stuff. Because at that age, they would become an active member of their crew. A crew that could stand separate from the crews before them and survive, if need be. But that need to stand separate would never arise. The crew just keeps getting stronger, just as it was intended to do from the onset.

Tank is a player but there is 1 special female in his life. Her name is Nina Jackson. Nina is Ajay's younger sister. Her and Ebony have been best friends since birth. They are half of a quartet which is collectively known as; *The Foursome*. There is a 3rd girl named Rebbie and along with Ebony's 1st cousin Latrisha or T-baby as she's called by the family, they make up the foursome.

T-baby is big John's niece. She's also the only girl in her family, just as Ebony is in hers. These 4 girls got the nickname; *The Awesome Foursome* because they are inseparable. Nina is the oldest in this quartet by only 3 days. She's 13 like Ebony. Her birthday is 3 days before Christmas. T-baby is 7 months behind Ebony with her birthday being on July 24th. Rebbie's birthday is August 2nd. Her and T-baby was born in 1976. These 4 girls sing in their church choir and they enjoy singing at home or anywhere else, for that matter. The guys can sing too. But they would get high and then flow with a sound and rhythm that no one could touch.

Another girl in the 3rd generation goes by the name of Jan. She is T-baby's, maternal 1st cousin. Jan can sing too. Her and her best friend Breanna or Bre, who is Rebbie and Nina's 1st cousin, prefer to flow like the

guys do, instead of singing with the foursome. They are all talented, very close and have each others back in every situation. Their loyalty is the same way for each other as their parents and their grandparents have always been in their first 2 generations.

****

"Ebony, do you hear me calling you?!" Pearl yells from the bottom of the stairs.

"Yes ma'am. I'm coming," Ebony replies.

"Well, hurry up!"

Ebony is finally dressed. She's a very pretty girl. She's tall for her age and a good basketball player, just like her boyfriend Ajay. Her and T-baby are on their 7th grade team where Nina and Rebbie are cheerleaders. The 4 of them always talk of going to college together and it doesn't matter what college they attend, as long as they are there, together. Most of their parents went to college. Education is 1 of the things they were raised to take pride in. Not just education but a college education. The sacrifices made in the past for them to be able to be educated is what has been instilled in them all of their lives.

"It's not a privilege to go the college. It's expected. Many of your ancestors were killed for trying to educate themselves."

Ebony walks into the kitchen, joins her mother and begins to help set the table.

"Baby girl set seven places, so June and Ajay can have some breakfast too," Pearl says.

"Okay," Ebony replies as the guys stroll into the kitchen.

Jb has lil man across his shoulders. Lil man is screaming and giggling but he's not really trying to get free. Big June goes straight for his seat while Tank grabs a cup or a glass for each of them. Ebony and Ajay's eyes meet for a second. Her sudden shyness of him causes her to look away. He squeezes slowly past her to his place at the table. As he does, she can feel his cool breath on the back of her neck. Tank notice them. He smiles and

looks away. He already knows what they did before sunlight. Ajay told his boys while they were all getting dressed for breakfast.

As Ajay passes behind her, Ebony stands motionless. Ajay pauses deliberately. Just long enough for her to feel his swollen manhood between the cheeks of her bottom. She can feel his breathing pattern change. She can smell his scent too. That sends her mind spinning back to the hours just before dawn, when she had given him her most precious gift and they had been joined as one. She recalls the pain of his insertion and how bad the whole act hurt. She can feel his fingertips on her face, wiping away her tears and his sweet whispers of concern for her comfort with promises that *"the pain won't last long, baby girl.*"

She tries to maintain as he works toward his climax. But the pain is too much for her to bear. She digs her short nails into his back. He has too much for her. She struggles to push him away.

Bang! Clang!

The stack of plates she's holding hits the table hard and she snaps back to the present.

"Ebony?!" Pearl shouts with concern in her voice.

Snapping back to the present, Ebony finds everyone of them staring at her. Everyone that is except for Ajay.

"Good morning, mama P. You got it smelling *good* up in here," Ajay says to Pearl, as he breaks the silence and the attention from Ebony's failed attempt at handling the morning after.

"Yea auntie. I'm ready for it!" big June adds.

"Well thank you guys, very much. And good morning to you too," Pearl says sarcastically before turning to Ebony and asking,

"Baby girl, are you alright?"

"Yes ma'am. I'm just tired, I guess," Ebony whispers as she takes the seat next to her mother.

Tank looks at Ajay and snickers quietly, then he looks at Ebony. She's staring directly at her reflection in her plate.

"Ebony go on and fix your plate, honey. Before these guys eat it all up," Pearl says while at the same time, she's reminding the guys of their manners.

Ebony puts small portions on her plate and says, "I'm not really hungry, ma. Can I eat this little bit in my room?"
Jb chimes in and says, "No baby girl. Sit here and eat with the rest of us." He and all the guys are digging in by now.

"Oh June. Brenda called for you while you were getting dressed. She wants you to call her back," Pearl says.

Pearl's sister Brenda is big June's mother. His government name is Brian James Jr. Brenda's husband's name is Brian James Sr, who's family was from Cleveland originally. Brian Jr carries the nickname big June because he was such a big baby at birth, a junior and plus he was born in the month of June.

Big June picks up the cordless phone and dials his mother while the breakfast conversation continues at the table.

"Jo doesn't even call to check on you anymore, ha?" Pearl jokes with Ajay.
She has always liked Ajay and thinks of him like a son. She's that way with all of the guys and girls in the crew. They're all 1 big family.

"No ma'am. Mama knows if I'm not at home, then I'm most likely over here or at one of the crew houses," Ajay answers with a smile.
He glances at Ebony for a split second but she won't even look his way anymore.

Ajay's mother Joanna or Jo as she's known, is 1 of Pearl and John's crew as well. Her and her husband Al have 5 children. 14 year-old Ajay is their only son. Their oldest child Lynora or Lynn is 16. She was Jb's 1st love and he was hers too. Nina is 13, Erica is 8 and Pam is seven.

More 2nd generation crew members are John's brother Greg Brown Sr and his wife Sandra, also known as Sandy. They have 3 children. T-baby is 12, Greg Brown Jr is 8 and Steven Brown is seven.

Pearl's sister Brenda and Brian Sr have 4 kids. Big June is 14 and Brittany is eight. They have a set of twins Brandon and Brina, who are 2 years old. Their twins are the youngest of the crew's *extended* family.

Sandy's brother Sam Sr and his wife Belinda have 3 kids. Janice or Jan is 14, Kim is 10 and Sam Jr is eight.

Archie Sr, Anna and Brad Sr are more siblings from John and Pearl's crew. Their last name is Wilson. Archie Sr and Rena are Rebbie's parents. They have a total of 4 children. 12 year-old Rebbie is their oldest

child. Their son Shannon is 9 and everyone calls him; Reaper. He loves rap music. Alicia, whom they refer to as Ally, is 6 years old. The baby boy Archie Jr is three.

Rebbie's aunt Anna and her uncle Richard Sr have a son and a daughter. Richard Jr known as Ritchie Rich is 14. His little sister Ruthie or Roo, is seven. They are Ajay's 1st cousin on their father, Richard Sr's side.

Richard Sr was often called a hoodlum in the late 60's and early 70's. He developed a serious drug addiction, at a very young age. It was during the peace and love era. That addiction took him down a dark road of robberies, destruction and eventually jail. He overcame it all because of his strong family. Him and Anna had separated when Roo was 6 months old. Richie Rich was 7 at the time and he has never really gotten over that separation. He has a chip on his shoulders which many of the elders see and recognize. Though his parents had a separation, Richard Sr and Anna was never far from each other. Richard Sr had moved in with his older sister Debbie and her husband Brad Sr, just down the block. So he was at Anna's house often and at all of the family functions too. They rekindled their romance after Richard Sr served his last stint in jail for armed robbery.

Debbie and Richard Sr are Ajay's mother Jo's, younger siblings. Their father Allen Saul Williams was killed during the civil rights movement. He was instrumental in trying to get blacks to register, vote and join the infamous desegregation movement. He and his wife's families hailed from Tennessee. He and Joanna Mae, whom Jo is named after, was active in marches with *Dr. Martin Luther King Jr*. This is how a lot of the original crew met. They were either fighting for voter's rights or just fighting to survive. Allen Saul was killed while trying to get blacks registered in Alabama in 1965. Joanna Mae Williams died young, in 1976. The medical reason was diabetes but many believed it was from a broken heart. She was missing her 1st and only love, Allen Saul. She was only 41 when she died. He was killed at 31. The older crew felt his murder was the reason Richard Sr was so troubled as a child. Because he was the youngest of the 3 kids, the only male and he had grown up without a father in the home.

Jo, who's government name is Joanna, met and married Ajay's father Al, who's full name is Allen, just like Jo's father. Jo said it had to have been a sign that she met him 5 years to the day that her father was

killed. They barely separated after meeting each other and they got married 2 years later in 1972.

Allen Jackson's family was pretty well-to-do to be Black, in America. He was from Massachusetts, by way of South Carolina. He had ventured to Cleveland after taking part in a protest that brought forth the *May 4 massacre*. Al was only 15 years old, at the time. He had gone there to protest with his older sister Jessica, who was attending *Kent State*. A year later, while still protesting the war, the 2 siblings joined a march at Cleveland State University. That's the day Al met Joanna Lynn Williams or Jo and since then, they've been joined at the hip. Al's big sister Jessica didn't approve of Al consorting with a girl, who had no father. But Al loved Jo, so he shunned his sister for speaking ill of his new love.

Al and Jessica's sibling rivalry would get worse before it would turn sweet again. Their family was said to have been decedents of the 7th president of the United States, *Andrew Jackson*. They was rumored to have owned slaves also. But Al had never sought to prove either of those latter 2 facts.

Jo's sister Debbie and her husband Brad Sr have 3 kids. Brad Jr, mostly known as Jr is seventeen. Breanna or Bre is 14. Bruce is eleven.

Brad Sr ran the 2nd generation of crew, initially. But a violent run-in, in 1971, with bigoted whites and the laws which supported them, left him with 2 options. Either being sent to Vietnam by 1973 or certain jail time. Jeb Baker had worked tirelessly to keep these brothers home and working. But Brad's father Charles Wilson asked Jeb if he could swing a deal for war rather than prison. Baker was a powerful man and he made it happen. Brad Sr had to leave soon after for Vietnam.

In his 1st letter from Debbie, he found out they were expecting their 2nd baby which was Breanna or Bre. On leave 7 months later, they got married in a double wedding ceremony with Richard Williams Sr and Brad's sister Anna Wilson, who are Ritchie Rich's parents and Ajay's uncle and aunt. The ceremony was held at their parents Annabelle and Charles Wilson's home. Brad Sr would spend less than 2 years in the active military. His entire service stint was served fighting with the *Vietcong*. That stint gave his crew an even more personal reason to loathe the conflict which they were already protesting.

By the end of the Vietnam conflict, all of the couples of the 2nd generation was formed but all hadn't married yet. The last to marry was Archie Wilson Sr. Again, he is Brad Sr and Anna's youngest brother and Rebbie's father. He was in love with Rena Baker. Rena was a bi-racial young lady who could pass for white. She was also the only heir to one, Jeb Baker.

Jeb Baker was an old rich white man with a lot of political juice. He owned a large national trucking company that his family had started in the late thirties. His company is the same one which big John works for, too date. Jeb Baker was also an *Abe Lincoln* prototype. He believed in equal rights for all people and he didn't approve of racism or bigotry, in any form. He had taken part in organizing and housing civil rights protest, as well as safe houses. He had helped many Black families, like John's, escape the Jim Crow laws of those days. He loved soul music, soul food and down home gospel singing. He frequented Juke joints where he heard greats like *Junior Kimbrough* and *Charlie Feathers*. That's how he came to meet Ebony's grandfathers, Jackson Brown and Percy Jones. That's also how he met big John and subsequently, got him on at his family's trucking company. Baker helped to keep John and his crew out of the draft until Brad Sr's troubles. The Baker family spawned politicians locally and state wide. Plus they had 2 state senators. 1 in Michigan and 1 in Ohio.

The Bakers, Rebbie's maternal great-grandparents, was known in those days as good white folks. Their only son had married a Black woman and moved abroad. Their union is what spawned Rena Baker, who had moved back to Ohio to live with her grandparents in 1970. That's when she met big John. He brought Pearl to meet her and they became fast friends. Pearl introduced Rena to the Cleveland crew. Pearl was engaged to John, at the time. They were planning their wedding and wouldn't actually marry until Pearl finished high school, in 1972. But they was organizing early, as they were known to do. They wanted Rena to be a part of their special day. She accepted their invitation but she needed a groomsman to walk with her in the wedding. She was yet to meet anyone in Ohio, who was her own age. John and Pearl introduced her to Archie Sr. He was 18 months younger than Rena and he needed a bridesmaid. They hit it off, instantly.

Over the next 5 years, this couple along with their crew, *literally* fought to stay together. The most news making and memorable was November 20, 1971. Mr. Jeb Baker had invited the crew to his press box seats, at Ann Arbor, to view the *Ohio State vs Michigan* game. He owned box seats at Ohio State too. Michigan won the rivalry game, that year. As the crew traveled back to Ohio and was heading towards Cleveland, they stopped off to get refreshments. At the store, they were met with resistance after Rena, who is very fair and could pass for Caucasian, was spotted coupled up with Archie. An angry white mob, who was already upset about the Ohio State loss, attacked Archie. His crew brawled with this mob. In the melee, 1 of the white attackers had been stabbed. The crew had no weapons but 1 of them was *going* to be charged. That's the way things were then and pretty much, still are now. The police wanted to charge Archie with attempted murder. His older brother Brad Sr copped to the charges. He was arrested and jailed. That was when Jeb Baker moved his hand and got Brad Sr the 2 years of military service, in a conflict that none of them believed America should've been involved in, in the first place.

Brad Sr did his service for this country. The war finally ended in April of 1975. Archie Sr waited for his brother to come home, so he could be his best man. Archie Sr and Rena married in November 1975, where her grandfather Jeb gave her away. Jeb Baker died 2 months later. He never got to meet his great-granddaughter, Rebbie Shantell Wilson, who is 1 of Ebony's closest friends, 1 of the foursome and a member of the 3rd generation of the very same crew that Jeb had helped to stay together.

****

Ebony clears the dishes from the breakfast table and cleans the kitchen. She's always been responsible, truly intelligent and a very talented young lady. Not only can she sing, dance and play sports well. She also has a love for literature. She likes reading romantic stories and she's even tried her hand at poetry and writing. Her and her girls are always writing songs. They sing them to anyone who'll listen. Which includes their entire crew. Everyone supports 1 another equally and they are all equally talented, as well. Musical talents became the foundation their crew and it's families friendship could build on with much thanks and props which go to their parents and their musical grandparents. Activism, music and true love is the glue that bonds this crew. These days, their music comes mostly through church choirs. But they do local talent shows, as well. They have a solid

music foundation to build on, if either of them decide to go that route.

It was a fact that Percy "*poppa*" Jones, who is Pearl and Brenda's father and Jackson "*papa*" Brown, who is John and Greg's father, had a band in the 50's and 60's which ruled the night spots. They had gigs, on the road with the much known; *Chitterling circuit.* The circuit toured in Chicago, Detroit and even as far away as Houston. Ebony was told this was how poppa met big mama Eloise, Pearl and Brenda's mother. Big mama is who Ebony took her middle name after. Big mama Eloise met the band when she was opening at the Night Owl nightclub, in Houston. *Jackson-Jones Revue* was Headlining. It was April 5, 1952 and big mama Eloise lit up the stage. Poppa was so taken by her that he asked her to come on the road with them. Big mama's parents didn't approve because they knew the dangers of being Black in those days. Let alone, traveling the dark highways. But big mama Eloise, being fascinated with poppa Percy plus the idea of singing in a band, ran away with him.

Poppa Percy always encouraged her to keep in touch with her family which she did. Poppa promised her parents he would take care of her and make sure she returned home. She sang in the band with Pearline "*granny*" Jackson, who is John and Greg's mother. They were closer than sisters and vowed to stick together, forever. Big mama named her and poppa's 1st born, Pearl, after Pearline. Big mama and poppa did return to Houston 20 years later, for good, before big mama's mother fell ill and later died from the complications of breast cancer. The same illness big mama suffers from, presently. *Breast Cancer* is a disease Ebony will learn is hereditary. It sometimes skips a generation and sometimes not.

****

It's the afternoon of July 3, 1989. Everyone is planning for the big *4th of July* festivities and Jb's 16th birthday. Big John is due home, any minute. Pearl is anxious to see him. She's always excited about having her family together. This holiday is especially important to her because Ebony is due to leave out when John leaves on the 6th of July, for Houston. This is the last holiday the families will all be together, for awhile. Pearl wants this to be an extra special event and holiday, for the Brown family and their

entire crew. The thing is, she has no clue of what the next few days are about to bring to her and their extended crew family.

At 9:15am when John pulls up in his rig cab. He has already ditched the trailer at the warehouse to be offloaded, reloaded and serviced for his Houston trip. He spends the 1st few hours with his 4 children. He always has to catch up on what they've done since the last time he was home. Of course, him and Pearl have some catching up to do, as well. Jb and Tank go hang out at Chill's house while Ebony and Lil man go to uncle Greg's house, for several hours. This gives their parents the house to themselves. Pearl has a special dinner for 2 prepared, along with candles and music. They slow dance to *Ray, Goodman and Brown's, Special Lady* and *Stephanie Mills, Power of love*. But it's *Rick James and Tina Marie's, Fire and Desire* which retires them upstairs.

By 6:30pm, it's time to prepare for tomorrow's annual *4th of July* cookout. Pearl and Jo live next door to each other and everyone gathers at their homes, most holidays. The women and young ladies prep all of the food, the evening before. While the men gather in the living room of the alternate house for a card games, sports on TV and to debate over who's the master grill man. They always agree to share the duties which is the best option. Because they usually have more than their share of beers and flavors before the grilling is even done. Then they end up passing barbeque tools and aprons to any man who can stand the heat of the grill, at the time.

Ebony is happy to see her father but she feels it's inappropriate to sit on his lap, like before. She feels like she's a young woman now and only little girls should be acting in such a way. Big John notices her reluctance to sit on his lap, all of a sudden. He doesn't say anything. He realizes she's growing up, rather he likes it or not.

"Mama, do you need our help in here?" Ebony asks Pearl.

"No, baby. Not right now," Pearl says, "But Belinda is bringing shrimp and we need you and the girls to clean them for us, this time."

"Yuck!" Rebbie says.

"We got the smelly job," T-baby says with a frown.

"Hey y'all, let's go see Nina," Ebony suggests and they head next door to mama Jo's house, where Nina meets them at the side door.

"I was just fixing to come over there and get y'all," Nina says, "I figured y'all would rather hang out over here, for awhile. What's up?"

TIME TO LEARN-RELOADED-Time Will Reveal-part 1

"You know what's up. Where they at?" T-baby ask and smiles.

"They're here," Nina answers, knowing exactly whom T-baby is inquiring about. "They're upstairs in Ajay's room. Let's go to my room. I got a joint," she adds with a grin.

The foursome goes upstairs to Nina and Lynn's room and locks the door. They place towels around the door crevices, then fires up the joint.

Tank, June and Rich are across the hall in Ajay's room. Along with Ajay, these boys make up the foursome's boyfriends. They hear the girls go into Nina's room and they decide to intrude.

Ajay says, "Let's go buss it up, man. Y'all know what they're trying to do up in there."

"Cool," Richie Rich says and they go to Nina's door.

Ajay knocks and quickly identifies himself. He laughs, as him and the guys can hear the girls panicking inside the room.

"Nina, it's me," Ajay whispers, "Open the door."

Ebony smiles as Nina lets them in. The guys come in and Nina secures the door again.

"Oh y'all in here trying to get high, ha?" June asks as Rebbie burst out with laughter.

"Come on," Tank says, "We'll get y'all fucked up."

He pulls out a fat sack of weed. Ajay smiles at Ebony before taking the sack from Tank and rolling up a blunt.

They smoke almost all of it with the girls. Then Ajay goes over and stands next to where Ebony is seated. He takes her hand and pulls her up off of Nina's bed.

He says, "Come go with me, for a minute."

"Where are we going?" Ebony asks.

"Just come on with me, girl. Without the questions," he says and smiles.

"Alright. But slow down some," she says.

"Are you *buzzin* or something? You can't walk?" he asks with a sly grin.

"Yes. I'm pretty high, Anthony," she says.

He leads her into his room, then closes and locks his door. After they're safely inside, he asks, "Are you gonna give me some more of that?"

"More of what?" she asks, pretending not to know what he means,

as she giggles because she's really buzzed and he knows it.

"You know what I want, baby girl," he whispers as he begins to kiss her, very aggressively.

She lets him. This is new to her. He's kissing her like she's a woman now. She knows how to kiss him back, so she figures she must be a woman. The weed certainly helps her feel more relaxed as she kisses him with fervor.

"Let me take your shirt off," he whispers while kissing her on her neck.

"Anthony, you know our dad's are downstairs," she says while trying to hold her shirt down.

"Baby girl, you know they *ain't* studying us," he says, "They're getting their party on and you know it. So what's happening wit us?"

She tells him she wants to do it again but she's afraid it'll hurt, like it did last night.

"Ah, baby girl. The first time always hurts," he says, "Remember I said *that*? But it won't be like that, this time. Okay? Trust me."

She lets him take her shirt off. He pulls her bra up, exposing her breast. Then he starts rubbing them while looking into her eyes.

He looks so damn good.

She moans.

"You like this?" he asks, sensing her moods.

"Yes."

He kisses her on her neck, then on her mouth. When he sticks his tongue in her mouth, she shivers before sucking on it. He had taught her that, a few years back. He places his mouth over 1 of her nipples. First, rolling the tip of his tongue around it, then gently suckling it. First one, then the other. Then alternating. She feels very aroused as he unbuttons her shorts.

"Oh mmm," she moans.

"Uh huh," he moans back.

He likes that she likes what he's doing. He sucks on her nipple harder and moans to her sighs of pleasure. Hearing her moan, turns him on even more. It makes his dick hard, instantly. He wants to fuck her now. He looks into her eyes as he unzips her shorts and starts to slide them down.

Suddenly they hear, *"Nina, honey!"* mama Jo yells from the bottom of the stairs, *"Belinda is here with the shrimp. Y'all come on and get started, so we*

can get everything finished up before the evening! Us ladies want to get this prep work finished up, as early as we can."

"Shit," Ajay whispers, obviously disappointed he can't finish what he was starting.
Ebony fixes her bra and shorts, then puts her shirt on. All the while, Ajay is staring at her.
After she's dressed, he says, "We need to finish this later."
"Okay," she says, "If I can come back."
"You just don't know how much I like what we did last night. Do you, baby girl?" he asks.
While kissing on her ear, he whispers, "I can't wait to feel you again. Your pussy is *so* good. I'm glad I'm the only one who knows that and we're gonna keep it like that too. Do you hear me?"
He stops stimulating her ear and looks into her eyes. He wants her response.
"Yes, Anthony," she says, "I hear you. I'm not gonna let nobody else touch me. I promise. I don't even want nobody else to touch me, Anthony. I'm only gonna be with you. You know we already talked about that."
He's satisfied with her answer, as he checks the hallway to be sure it's safe for her to walk out of his room.
Nina already has it covered. She's at the top of the stairs to answer her mother, so she doesn't have to come up.
"Okay, ma," Nina says, "We're coming."
She's looking over her shoulder to see if Ajay and Ebony had heard. Ebony finishes adjusting her clothes before she joins her girls, at the top of the stairs. She looks back at Ajay. He's still standing in his doorway and he's still watching her. She gives him a shy smile.

Ebony and her girls go back over to her house. They get the shrimp, 2 bowls and gather around Pearl's table.
"What's up, sisters!" Jan yells as she strolls into the kitchen, walking with extra pep in her step.
She had come with her mother Belinda, to help with the holiday prep.
Bre says, "Yea. What's up, foursome? Ah man! We got to clean shrimp?" she asks with a frown, "Where the guys at?"

TIME TO LEARN-RELOADED-Time Will Reveal-part 1

"Y'all got 'em this time," her mother Deb says, while laughing very hard.

Bre and her mother are really cool with each other. Bre has even told her girls that sometimes her mother allows her to smoke weed with her.

"Yea! The girls got the shrimp," Jb says as he laughs, "It's about time y'all get *that* job. We always have to clean 'em."

Jb had caught up with the guys next door and they all stroll into the kitchen, together.

"Mmm. What y'all got over here?" Tank asks while smiling at Nina.

The boys love teasing the girls, when the girls have to do jobs they don't like to do. Nina just grins because she's buzzed. They all are. To Ebony, even the parents seem to be.

Ajay is teasing Ebony, saying, "Your hands are gonna stink."

"So, somebody likes 'em," she replies.

He smiles and pinches her cheek. Pearl and Jo look at Nina, Tank, Ajay and Ebony, then they look at each other, with that look mothers have when they know something is going on. Little do the youngsters know, the mothers do know something is different about their behavior toward each other. Their parents can sense that something has changed with their children. They aren't aware of the details but they know something's going on.

For the last few years, Ebony and Ajay have cooled down on the arguing and they're actually getting along better, at each gathering. Just how much better, the parents still don't know that part yet. Though they all want to know and they are often times tempted to ask. But in this crew, they live by the honor system. In time, their kids will have to fess up about what's going on. Until then, the parents keep a close eye on them or they try too.

Shortly afterwards, the guys hit the streets, on the grind with Chill, as usual. The girls have to stay at the house and finish up the food prep.

After the prep work is done, Ebony, Nina and Rebbie leave with T-baby and her mother Sandy. They're going to spend the night at T-baby's house, tonight. This is something the foursome, often do. They have matching outfits in their favorite colors for the 4th of July. They are going to dress alike. This is something they do often, as well.

CHAPTER 2

THE SCORE

All the crew families attend the cookout, including grandparents Logan, Brown and Wilson. They phone Houston and talk with big mama and poppa Jones, first thing. They had decided to stay home, this year. Big mama wants to stay close to home and her doctor, in the event something goes wrong.

During Pearl's conversation with her mother, she tries again to convince her to move back to Cleveland, so they can all care for her. Big mama declines the offer, even when her best friend, granny Pearline insists. She says she'd rather stay with *her* doctor, the doctor who diagnosed her.

4th of July is a special holiday, in this family, for more than just the independence of America. It also marks their independence from the clutches of southern injustice, Jim Crow laws, the immoral majority who enforced it and definite freedom from the company of those who went along to get along.

Jo's father Allen Saul Williams' life had been threatened, many times. But it wasn't until 1965 that those threats were made good. He wasn't the only 1 from this crew who received death threats but he was the only 1 who died as a result. Even though he wasn't still calling the south home, he did lose his life there. He had moved Joanna Mae and their 3 kids; Jo, Deb and Richard, from Memphis and onto Cleveland Ohio, in 1961, four years before he was killed. He had moved north because of the threats he'd received of murdering his entire family. He couldn't remain there. He was ready to kill for his, which he knew meant certain death, in those days. He was willing to give his life but he wasn't willing to spare, any of his family. During that pilgrimage from 1960 to 1963, is when the Williams from Tennessee, the Logan's from Mississippi, the Wilson's from Louisiana and the Jones' from Texas, all made the move to Ohio. Ohio is where the Brown's family from Alabama had already escaped too, years earlier. It's also where the James, Bakers and Carters, already called home.

TIME TO LEARN-RELOADED-Time Will Reveal-part 1

It was in 1953 when the first crew members met and formed, initially. They were separated and communications were cut off, many times, over a decade. They never lost hope nor did they ever give up. Not on each other. Their main line of communication was through the *Chitterling circuit*. The same musical tour which Jackson Brown and Percy Jones was a huge part of. Their band name was; *Jackson-Jones Revue*. They met and befriended Jeb Baker while at a Detroit show in the early 1950's. Through his trucking company, Jeb provided transportation to their gigs but that wasn't nearly all. He helped them to keep each other informed of the goings on of the others, from state to state. Jeb was also instrumental in helping with the migration from south to north. Jackson, Percy and Jeb got the word to the others about when and where they would meet and how they would be smuggled out, never to return. They had lost contact with the Logan's and Wilson's, for more than 8 years. When they reconnected, during the civil rights marches, they had a plan to move them north for good. The crew was it's on security and protection. Protection against Jim Crow laws and the oppression. The politicians in the Baker family was their white allies. In cases where they got jammed up, they would pretend to be hired hands. An example of when they would act as hired hands, was whenever bigoted sheriffs stopped the trucks.

Once they escaped the harsh desegregation laws and threats they'd received for trying to integrate, they vowed never to be subservient to anyone, ever again. They wanted the right to run their own businesses and to be self contained. That was their ultimate goal. They raises their children with the knowledge of self. They earned their dignity, honor and respect, by refusing to bow down to oppression. They stood up against being treated like 2nd class citizens and they found a better way of life.

"It was a little safer above the Mason-Dixon line, during those days," granny Pearline says, "It was only twenty five or so years ago, when everybody got here. Our first Fourth of July celebration was in nineteen sixty three. The same year they killed *John F. Kennedy*."

"That was twenty six years ago, granny," T-baby says, doing the math for her grandmother.

"Me and Joshua had been run off from Mississippi, twelve years before we finally made it here," grandma Sally adds, "I remember they killed *Emmitt Teel,* just down the road below us. He wasn't but fourteen years old. That was it, baby. We left our farm and went from house to house until we got back up with Joanna Mae and Allen Williams, in nineteen sixty three. It was in April and they brought us, on up here."

"When they killed President *John Kennedy*," papa Brown adds, "We felt a set back, that November day. We had all moved here, by then. Horrible things was going on. But we still had to go back and help our people."

"We've been living here every since we escaped those prejudiced southern towns," papa Joshua says, "I haven't even visited Neshoba county since we left there. I had one brother who was still alive, when I left there. He already had a plan of where he was going too. He made it as far as Maryland, where my mother had gone. But they're both dead now."

"The rest of them, we don't even know if they got a proper burial," Sally says, "But when I die, I *wanna* be taken back there and buried with my mama, my daddy and my grandparents. All of you know where my family plots are and that's where I want to lay, in my final rest. So much of our family was murdered, just trying to get basic rights and for trying to hold onto our land. They was killed because they refused to roll over and stay, *literal* slaves. We don't know if they got buried with the rest of the family. But we know they got killed or run off. We had to get out of there, if *we* wanted to stay alive."

"Just in the last four years, thanks to our children, *your parents,* we've gotten back the titles to our land," grandma Annabelle says, "They took what we raised them with and they got educated in colleges."

"They learned how to fight the powers, with their *own* words and laws," grandpa Charles says, "They got the deeds to our family's land, in Louisiana and Tennessee."

"We're still fighting against what that sovereignty commission set up down in Mississippi," papa Brown adds, "We're still trying to get a handle on Joshua and Sally's, family land."

"We'll get it, though," Sam Logan Sr says confidently, "We're gonna get every damn bit of our history, that those bigots tried to take from y'all and us too. It's in the final stages, right now. Wheeler's got a team down there."

"If it takes our last breath," his younger sister Sandy adds, "We're gonna get everything our elders worked and died for."

TIME TO LEARN-RELOADED-Time Will Reveal-part 1

When the elders speak, everyone listens. Even the guest. 4th of July is independence and a day to be thankful for all of the freedoms you're blessed to have. The elders in the crew are thankful they'd all stayed alive, together and loyal. The 1st generation are proud of their children and their grandchildren too. And they expect them to carry on the crew name and the legacy too.

The elders live in what is known as; *The Point*. It's a section of Cleveland known as the retirement district because of it's quiet living. It's reserved for the elderly, pretty much. The entire 1st generation live out there.

They choose the *Shaker Heights* community, where the 2nd generation lives, to do their celebrations. It's a livelier setting with more hustle and bustle. They've held their 4th of July celebrations here, for the past 5 years. This area is where middle-aged head of households settle. It's where the 2nd generation live and raise their children, who make up the 3rd generation.

The 3rd generation, with Chill at the head, live and operate here and in other areas of Cleveland.

The 4th of July cookout is wonderful again this year. There's always more food and drink than everyone can consume. And as usual, there's a jam session before the celebration ends. For the last 10 years, there's been 3 generations of talent. The teenagers hold their own against their parents and grandparents, this year, which makes the elders proud.

Jb, Ajay, Tank, June and Rich turn it out. Ebony, Nina, Rebbie and T-baby sing and dance. They have everybody standing by the end of their routine. Jan, Bre and Lynn rap. Brad Jr supplies the beats along with Stoney and Rob, who are 3rd generation crew members as well. Lastly, the mothers; Pearl, Jo, Sandy and Rena, Brenda, Belinda, Anna and Deb, start with the old tunes and everyone turns nostalgic. The fathers get in a song or two, as well. This crew is very talented. Each generation, with it's on style. This is definitely a continuation of the best of times for this Cleveland crew. It was made possible because their elders demanded equality and a better existence. They will never let their offspring ignore or get past, that fact.

By the late afternoon, Jb and the guys are looking to do some dirt.

They are always on the grind for that almighty dollar, like the mighty *OJay's, For the love of money,* says. The song had just finished playing and they was singing it when they left and they was cutting up, as well.

They return by the early evening. Not long after their return, is when the outside girls start to show up.

All day, Ebony has waited to get with Ajay so they can finish what they started in his room, last night. He doesn't seem to be paying her a lot of attention.

During the course of the early evening, there are several girls dropping in on the celebration. They pretend to be down with 1 of the *females* from the crew. But ultimately, they are just there trying to get with 1 of the *guys* from the crew.

One of these girls who tries to blend in, bothers Ebony the most. Her name is Anita Davis. She seems to be interested in Ajay. This really makes Ebony, very edgy and uncomfortable. She wants Anita to leave immediately. Anita and her hood rat friends aren't shy at all. They like to dance to the music that big mama calls, *"shake your ass until it falls out of your clothes and shows,"* music. Ebony nor her girls can understand what, if anything, their guys would want with *any* whores. But Ebony is watching Anita because every chance she gets, she's all up in Ajay's face. Ajay is showing her less attention than he's been showing to Ebony. It's at this moment when Ebony realizes, the man she loves is a player, just like her brothers and most of the guys in her crew.

Ajay is a superstar basketball player, who has played for MLK high school since he was in 7th grade. He'll be a high school sophomore, this fall. He's *very* well known. The crew guys always have girls *and women,* hanging around wanting to get with them. But Ajay is a female magnet. He's most definitely handsome. His has smooth dark skin. His sultry bedroom eyes, look even smaller and more intense when he smokes weed. He's a slender brother with a basketball build, a killer 6 pack and shoulder length braids. Ebony loves his smooth skin and his perfect little peach fuzz which has come in, very nicely. He's a beautiful young man. Many women, literally *women,* can attest to his sexual prowess, not only Ebony. He's not arrogant, at all. But he's certainly confident and stern. And just like his father Al, he accepts no shorts and takes no losses. Ajay wants Ebony, all to

himself. He has made that clear, to his entire crew, on several occasions. But right now, he isn't showing Ebony *any* signs of what they'd discussed in his room, yesterday. He keeps a track on her location but he isn't aggressively checking for her. This only makes her more anxious. He's outright ignoring Anita. That part, she likes. Granny Pearline sends her inside to find lids to cover the food, before the adults can start their card games and relaxing. Upon Ebony's return, she misplaces Anita.
Good. She finally left.

With Anita gone, Ebony begins to watch Ajay. She tries to get his attention. She wants to tell him they can sneak away to his room without being noticed, when the bid wiz and spades start. First, she goes inside to freshen up. She's going to approach him, this time. Not wait for him to come to her. But when she returns, he's gone.
Where did he go?

She asks her girls about Ajay's whereabouts. Neither of them know. But Ebony remembers how, in the past, he would just go to his room and wait for her to sneak up there.
That's it! He's in his room!

She walks across the yard, unnoticed. Or so she thinks. She goes into mama Jo's, side door. First, she peeks into the living room where she can hear several voices. Neither voice is Ajay's. She decides to go on upstairs. If he isn't there, she'll leave a note on his lamp table. He's certain to find it when he comes in to freshen up for Jb's party, which will be at Chill's house tonight. Ebony is figuring her and Ajay can get together before the party and her curfew won't cause conflict. They have left notes for each other before, so this *seems* like a great idea. She grabs the notepad and pen which mama Jo always leaves on the little stand at the top of the stairs. She tiptoes to Ajay's door, looking back to make sure no one is coming up the stairs. She turns the knob and walks in.

This is a first, for her. She has never gone into his room uninvited but she's been in here, several times. Enough times to know her way around in the dust dark room. With his dark curtains, the room is pitch black. She feels for the lamp switch and finds it. She sits down without clicking it on.

TIME TO LEARN-RELOADED-Time Will Reveal-part 1

She feels surreal, just sitting here in her man's room in the dark. She swears she can smell his cologne, as she reminisces about the dance and kissing sessions, they have shared here, to the same tape which plays right now. She smiles to herself. Ajay, being a music lover, had left his boom box on and it's playing rather loudly. *Between the sheets,* blares from it. *The Isleys* is his favorite group. His dad plays them, all of the time, as well. She feels for the lamp switch again and this time she clicks it on. That's when she realizes why the music is playing and why she can smell his cologne. She's not alone in his room. He's in here and so is Anita! Ebony is sitting in the chair as if she has been frozen in time. She can't move.
Is this a bad dream?

They haven't seen her but she can surely see them. They're having sex!
Oh my GOD!

She can see them fucking. Still, she can not move 1 muscle.
How dare her be with Anthony! That's MY boyfriend!

Her tears won't come. There's a lump in her throat but no tears. There's nausea in her stomach but no vomit. For almost a full minute, she observes Anita. She doesn't seem to have any problems handling the forceful and rhythmic thrust from Ajay's dick, like she had, just 2 nights prior. Anita seems to be enjoying it a lot, just based on the amount of panting and porno movie type shouts she's letting off. Ebony has watched porno movies with the older girls in her crew. They've been showing the foursome what men like to have done to them. She flashes to scenes in those movies, then back to the reality in front of her. This scene seems like forever but it has only been 2 minutes since she spotted them. She begins to tremble now. The reality of what she's witnessing, seeps into her head. It creeps down to her stomach. She feels nauseated. This is her very first heartbreak and it's a massive one.
He's cheating on me, with her!

She's trembling and shaking now, as the tears finally come to her eyes. She knows she has to get out of this room, right now. She feels weak. She has to find the strength to make it to the door. She manages to stand. The notepad and pen drop to the floor. As she tries to run out of the room, she stumbles

over something, on the floor, which feels like a sandal. In her frantic state, she bumps into the dresser by the door. It makes a loud thud, as it hits the wall and the mirror attached to it, rocks back and forth. Ajay jumps up, quickly. He's panting for breath, as he witnesses Ebony just as she runs out of his room.

"Shit! Get your shit on, girl" he says to Anita, "You've *gotta* get up out o' here."
Anita crawls slowly off of his bed to get dressed but Ajay isn't patient with her, at all.
"Hurry the fuck up, girl! Damn!" he shouts.
He's rushing her to get out of his room, as he scrambles to get his pants on. He has to go after Ebony, right now.

Ebony makes it downstairs, where she runs into big Al at the bottom. Her only thought is to get out of there, as soon as possible.

"Hey Ebony. What's up, baby girl?" Al ask, as she whizzes by him. Her tears come hard and fast. She dashes past him and out of their side door. She hurries across the driveways and rushes into her side door. She hurries up the stairs and into her room. She locks her door and falls onto her bed. She's distraught.

Ajay comes downstairs and meets his father at their side door. Al is checking to see where Ebony had gone. Ajay looks too but doesn't see her.

"What's wrong with Ebony?" Al asks Ajay, "Did you see her run out o' here?"
Ajay and his father have a brotherly relationship. He could've easily told Al he had a girl in his room and suffered no repercussions. But he doesn't have an explanation as to why that would upset Ebony, so much. He decides to *embellish* his answer. What Ajay says is,
"Yea. Ah, I walked in while she was using the bathroom."

"Speaking of the bathroom. I need to get up in there, myself," Al says with a chuckle, "That Cognac is going right through me."
Al laughs as he is making his way upstairs and to the master bathroom. Ajay still stands alone, looking out of the side door. He sees no signs of his girl.

By now, Ebony has crawled up to the head of her bed. She clutches her pillow, as her whole body feels numb. She cries hysterically. Her

stomach feels like it's in knots. She tries to grasp the situation, she's just witnessed but she's unable too.

Ajay goes back to his room. Anita is dressed but still there. He tells her again to leave. This time he puts even more emphasis on his request. Thus she knows, he means it.

"You're gonna need to raise the fuck on up *outta* here," he says with a lot of impatience in his tone, "Hurry the fuck up."

She decides to make a break for it while Al is in his bathroom. Al won't see Anita slip out of their side door and escape through their backyard. But Nina, T-baby and Rebbie, having gotten word that something had just happened to upset Ebony, sure do. They go and get Lynn, Jan and Bre.

"Something happened to Ebony, at our house," Nina says to Lynn.

The 6 of them go after Anita and catch up to her in Mrs. Lou Robinson's backyard. They want answers, right now.

"Bitch! What did you do to Ebony?" Nina asks in a snarl.

"What?" Anita asks, then laughs and continues, "I didn't do shit to that lil ass girl. She just got in my business and got her lil feelings hurt-"

Before she can finish her sentence, T-baby, Nina and Rebbie pounce on her, knocking her to the ground. Anita is older than the foursome. She's Lynn's age. But Lynn, Jan and Bre decide to let the 3 girls handle her, since they're doing such a good job. None of the older females like Anita. Not since they found out she'd had sex with Chill, a few years ago. The crew ladies are very loyal to Renee. Renee is Chill's lady and she's crew too. They aren't going to stand for her to be disrespected by anyone. And definitely not a whore, like Anita Davis. They had already warned her at an MLK football game, just last fall. Anita had wisely backed off of Chill but she had since, set her sights on Ajay. Rumor has it, she's had sex with Jb, Rob and Stoney too. This further infuriates Lynn, Jan and Bre because *those crew guys* are *their boyfriends*. In their opinion, it's past time they get into Anita's ass. This is just 1 of the many whippings to come for Anita, before she'll learn to back off and leave the crew guys alone.

In the meantime, Pearl has learned that something has upset her baby girl. Immediately, she drops what she's doing and goes up to Ebony's room and knocks on her door.

"Baby girl, open the door. It's mama, sweetie."

"Ma, I don't wanna talk to anybody, right now," Ebony says as she struggles to keep her voice from shaking.

"Ebony, please open the door," Pearl insists.

Ebony wipes her face, tries to gather her composure and lets her mother in. Then she goes back and lays on her bed. Pearl enters, looking concerned.

"Sweetie, what's wrong?" Pearl asks as she enters the room and Ebony sits back up.

Ajay has come over and told Tank what happened. Tank has agreed to help him calm Ebony down. Only they have to wait for Pearl to leave Ebony's room, so they wait downstairs. Ajay sits at the bottom of their stairs, elbows resting on his knees, hands clinched together and staring at the floor.

Meanwhile, Pearl tries to get to the bottom of what has happened to her only daughter.

"Mama, I'm okay. I just wanna hurry up and leave," Ebony says as tears well up in her eyes again.

Pearl knows *something* has gone wrong and she wants to get to the bottom of it.

"Ebony, what's the big deal, baby? Is *that so* upsetting to you that you're ready to leave all of a *sudden*? It's not *that* bad. You'll get over that. I know it may be a little bit embarrassing. But really *sweetheart,* it's not that bad. He didn't see anything."

Ebony gives her mother a puzzled look as she thinks to herself.

What is mama talking about? Obviously, she doesn't know what really happened.

Ebony doesn't know it yet. But Al had given Pearl the same *embellished* story which Ajay had given to him.

Pearl continues, "He's just as embarrassed for walking in on you, baby."

Ebony is *really* confused now. She has never lied to her mother but after Pearl's next question, she knows she has too.

"Well you tell me what *really* happened," Pearl says.

She *can't* tell her mother what really happened. Not now. Not without

having to tell her, that her and Ajay have been intimate. But surely, if she tells her mother she had gone to Ajay's room, Pearl will figure the rest out. Or she'll question her until she has no other choice but to tell her the whole truth.
"Tell me what happened in the bathroom?" Pearl insists.
The bathroom? Oh no. She doesn't know.

Ebony wipes her face, takes a deep breath and she begins.
She says, "Well mama, someone was using our bathrooms, so I went next door to use mama Jo's bathroom. While I was in there, I just got depressed because I know I have to leave my girls and my crew. I got to thinking about how selfish I was being, because big mama *really* needs me."
She pauses, for a second and looks up at her mother. She needs to see if she's buying this explanation. Pearl is buying it, so Ebony goes on.
She says, "I started worrying about big mama and it all just kind of got to me, ma," she pauses again.
Then she continues, "I'm just worried about my big mama. I don't want her to die, mama. I really love her."
She bursts into tears. These are her real emotions. She knew if she thought about her big mama's health, it would justify her crying, as far as her mother's concerned. She allows herself to think of big mama in dire straits or on her death bed. She knew that would bring buckets of tears and it did.
Pearl hugs her. She knows the close relationship Ebony has with her grandmother. She's her namesake. *Big mama Eloise and Ebony Eloise.*
Pearl hugs her tighter as she says, "I know baby. But she's doing pretty good, right now. You heard how good she was sounding, on the phone, earlier, right? And you will get to see her in a few days. Then you'll be able to see that everything will be fine. Baby, don't do this to yourself. I need you to be strong for me. Mama Pearline needs your strength too. Okay? She's her best friend and she's worrying herself to death about mama."
Ebony says okay. But she feels even worse now, after lying to her mother.
"So you was already upset, before he walked into the bathroom on you, ha?" Pearl asks as she hugs Ebony again.
"Ah, oh yes. *Way* before that," Ebony manages.
She wonders if GOD can forgive her for lying to her mother. She really hopes he will because through it all, she's more willing to take the chance on

asking GOD for forgiveness, then she is of getting Ajay or herself into trouble. And even though he had crushed her heart, just an hour ago, she still loves him, so very much. In her heart, she knows he's the only one for her. One day, maybe he'll know it too.

Ring! Ring

"Pearl, come get the phone, baby," big John says while staring at his precious baby girl.
His voice sounds like thunder rumbling through Ebony's room.
John tells Pearl, "It's Lou. Trisha and the girls just beat some girl's ass, back there in her backyard."
He's chuckling as he speaks on it. He's probably already aware of what type of actions caused it. Pearl and her girls had done a lot of fighting over him and the guys, in his crew, back in the day. He would rather not even open up that can of worms. *Snakes, even.*
"Oh my Lord," Pearl says, "What is this day coming too?"
She takes the cordless phone from John and walks out of Ebony's room.
"Me and the fellows are going back there to check it out. Or maybe we can just ask the guys what happened and save some time," John adds and chuckles smugly.
Then as he looks at Ebony and asks, "Are you okay, baby girl? If you're not, just let daddy know it, right now. I'll fix it."
"Yes, daddy," she says, "I'm okay."
She isn't about to tell him what her woes are. He still views her as a *damn* toddler. She feels her father would never see her side. Not where a boy involved.
John leaves her door open, as he goes down the stairs so he can go check on her girls. As her parents leave her room, Tank comes in, as jovial as ever and smiling too. He's looking to do some damage control for his best friend, Ajay.
"Hey, twin. Are you alright?" he asks.
"No."
"My boy told me what went down," Tank says, "Twin, he don't like that bitch. That's just a *crew thang*. It ain't like you thinking, sis. Look here. See you, Nina and the girls, y'all can't take that kind of shit to heart,

right there. We *all* done had her. You know what I'm saying? She's a side piece, for any crew man that wanna hit it."
He's trying to make light of the situation and help her to calm down and not feel sad. And also, not see his homeboy as a cheating dog.
"See, Chill know a lot of ho's from when he was out there *wildin'* out and shit. They still be sweating him. But you know he ain't about to get Renee fired up. So he just turn us on to em. They do whatever he tell em to do," Tank says, "They be sweating us, *all* the time, twin. They be giving us money, clothes, weed and anything else they think can get them some attention from us."

"That's sick," she says in disgust, "Is that suppose to make me feel better?"

"No baby, it's not," Ajay says, "But it's the truth."
He had come on up the stairs to her room, after her parents went outside. He continues, "It's probably not gonna make you feel any better. But it's true. On *everything* I love. She don't mean shit to me. She ain't nothing but a piece o' ass, to me."

"And a few other acts, she likes to perform," Tank adds with laughter.

"He means, things I don't do with you," Ajay tries.

"I guess I'm a piece o' ass too, ha?" Ebony says as she is now on the verge of tears again.
She doesn't even wait for his answer. She walks right past him and out of her room. She has to go check on her girls. She leaves them in her room and heads out toward Mrs. Lou's backyard.

On the way, she's reminded of something her poppa Percy had said to her when he had first found out Ajay was sweet on her, over 3 years ago. She had asked her poppa to help her to understand, without a doubt, how she would know if Ajay really liked her and wasn't just playing games with her.
Poppa had said,
"The best way you can tell if a young man cares about you, is when he knows he's in trouble with you. If he lets it linger and don't bother to handle it with you, right away. Keep moving. But if he doesn't let the sun set on it. Meaning, if he comes to straighten it out, as soon as possible. Then he's a keeper. But you still have to let him sweat. Even if he does come to you, right away. That's

so he'll remember, if he gets another chance, not to hurt you again."

Ajay *had* come, right away. She feels a little better knowing he had gotten rid of that *trick bitch* and came to her side, immediately. Even though his explanation was cruel and blunt. But if you know anything about the Ajay type, at all, then you know Ebony has to be important to him. Important enough for him to feel any hint of remorse or give an explanation for any act he had committed.

Ebony gets out of her side door, just as T-baby and the girls are being escorted back. First, she has to know if her girls are okay and if they had gotten Anita. Then she wants to know what story they told the fathers, about the incident. But since they always know to hold up for each other, the girls automatically knew to fabricate their stories. They told their fathers, Anita had picked a fight with Lynn and they all jumped her. As usual, they all play along. Their parents don't really like their story. They would rather them only fight when provoked. The girls story sounds as if they were provoked. The parents decide to let it rest, since all involved are okay. The parents remember from their days and in this type of situation, this is the best explanation they're going to get. They spend an hour, talking about and reiterating alternatives to physical confrontations. When the girls admit they'll try not to fight, the next time this happens, the parents let up on them.

Everyone has to change gears for the night time parties. All 3 generations are having a separate one. One in The Point, for the elders. One here in Shaker Heights, at Jo and Pearl's, for the parents. Jb's 16th birthday party is at Chill and Renee's house, across the street. That's the spot for the 3rd generation of crew. Everybody, who's anybody, will be there. Crew parties are the best in Cleveland and many would agree. There is never even standing room left, when Chill throws an event. And it's the talk of the city, for days.

It's 8:00pm. The crew start to head across the street to the party that big Chill is throwing for Jb. This will be the foursome's 1st year as actual crew and they've looked forward to it, for months.

In Chill's crew, you have to be 13 before you can attend the house parties. And then, only with your older siblings present. For Ebony and her

TIME TO LEARN-RELOADED-Time Will Reveal-part 1

3 partners in crime, this is all they've ever wanted to do. Go to a crew party *with permission,* instead of sneaking over.

T-baby and Rebbie are still twelve years old. They're allowed to go to the party because, simply put, the foursome go everywhere together. Their parents aren't about to try and come between their bond. But they all have to be home by 11pm. Eleven O'clock curfew, for the 1st crew party, is also a long standing tradition. But its only been enforced on the females. That didn't just start either. All in all, the girls are just ready to get to it. They just want to show up early and get the dancing going early too.

By 9pm, their parents have gotten into the 50's to 70's music phase of their party. They are playing everything from *Otis Redding* and *Sam Cooke* to *Teddy Pendergrass*. All of the younger generation know this is their queue to clear out and they certainly do. After the foursome are done with Jb's party, they will all stay at Ebony's, since she leaves in 2 days. The youngest children are either watching TV, playing video games or already sleeping at Jo or Pearl's, just until their parents are ready to go home.

Jb's party is the place to be. Of course, anytime Chill is involved its always the talk of the set and always jumping. Ebony and her girls stick together, close to the rest of their crew. Chill gives Ebony 3, one hundred dollar bills for her trip to Houston. He knows about today's incident too.
As he says to her, "No matter how hard Ajay acts, I know in his heart, he cares for you."
He knows Ajay has love and respect for Ebony. He wants her to know, he knows it too.
He continues, "Y'all are still young, right now. And he doesn't really know how to show *how* he really feels yet. When a guy is in his teens, he always thinks that to show that he's in love, means he's soft. But he's definitely sweet on you and he has been, for about a decade. Everybody in our crew knows it and all the men, in the family, know it too. One day, he'll figure out how to manage his feelings for you. I hope you'll still be there with him." Chill finishes by saying, "But I know you will be. Want you?"
Ebony smiles. That makes her feel very good, Because she knows the guys in this crew tell Chill *everything*. And they have learned everything they know about the modern day C-town streets, from him as well. The rest, they were

just born with. She knows Chill will always be straight up with her. He would never tell her to go along with anything that would bring harm to her, either. She trusts him completely. They all do. He has been particularly protective of Ebony since she was 6 years old. She can't even remember why but Ajay's father, big Al, treats her the same way. Chill's father Paul, who was killed 14 months earlier, was that way with her also. She loves being spoiled, so she never questioned them as to why they was always so protective of her.

Big Al has been raising Ajay to be a protector. That is the type of men he comes from and big Al is driving that point home, daily. Especially after he realized Ajay wants to be with Ebony, in the future. Ajay is a natural at it too. Chill knows this but he stays in his ear about being respectful to her. And about her not understanding the ways of the streets and the crew males. Chill would never be okay with Ajay breaking her heart, either. Not ever.

Chill starts again, saying "He needs you to be there, baby girl. You're the only girl who's real for him. He knows that too. You're the only thing sane in his life, right now. As far as female companionship goes. If a brother is gonna survive in this world, he's got to have a good woman to come home too. He wants you to be *that* woman. At least, that's what he says to me, all the time, when we talk about this kind of stuff. He says you're *that* girl."

She smiles again. Chill will always tell the truth, regardless of how it affects you. He doesn't care about that part. He only cares about keeping it real and Ebony knows that too.

Ajay is the same way but she's just beginning to learn and know that side of him. In time, she will discover it.

But does she have the patience she'll need to give him the time to find his way? *Time Will Reveal.*

Ajay comes from a strong family of men. His grandfather, on his mother's side Allen Saul Williams, was a soldier. A stand up black man, who took care of those around him. He stood in the face of bigoted whites during the tumultuous 60's and took his punishment when the time came. He would never bow down to racism, injustice or oppression. *His* father had fought and died in World War II. His grandfather had fought in the Civil War. That's who raised him and was his mentor until he died. Because of the service of those 2 men, Allen Saul felt his family's debt to this country was paid in full. He wanted a better life for his children and their children. He knew the only way to get that was to fight, because freedom *isn't free*. This courage is instilled in Ajay's mother, Joanna Lynn Williams. She married Ajay's father, Allen Devante' Jackson Jr. His father, Allen Sr from Massachusetts, was apart of the railroad which helped papa Jackson Brown, Poppa Percy Jones and Allen Saul Williams to move the crew north with help from Jeb Baker. Protector's is what Ajay comes from. Not destroyers. He's a builder by nature, genetics and spirit. Things he view as important, he holds dear. For matters of the heart, he'll learn to love strong when he's set his sights on the girl for his future. Just as the men he descended from, he'll see it mentally, long before he learns to convey it to the girl. Nevertheless, he's a provider by genetics but he's still, just a boy.

The 11 O'clock hour is fast approaching. Reluctantly, the foursome are preparing to leave. Ebony and Ajay still haven't talked since they was in her room. He hasn't approached her for a dance, either. But throughout the night, she'd caught him staring at her from across the room. She loves to dance and so does her girls. She knows he likes watching her move and she knows he's watching her, right now. She can feel his eyes on her. Whenever she shares space with him, he always watches her. Tank, June and Rich, dance a lot. Ajay is usually laid back in the cut, chilling, watching and ready for anything, if something was to jump off. Ebony has watched him, watch her dance. His expression was a look of displeasure, when she danced with a guy from outside of their crew. He didn't say anything but his look assured her, he didn't like it at all. But Ebony, given the events of the early evening, feels it's time to try her hand at not being the one waiting. She stayed on the dance floor through 4 straight songs. She was dancing with a guy, who said his name was Mark.
Mark Who?

She doesn't know him and she doesn't care to know him. He was just somebody to dance with, to keep Ajay's attention on her. But when Rob slows the music down, she knows she has to come off of dance floor. Mark asks her to dance again.
She says, "Not on a slow one."
Ajay stretches his neck to see if she's leaving the floor. She felt bold enough

to dance with Mark. But she isn't foolish enough to push it, too far. Besides, she doesn't want anybody holding her except for *her man*. She calls him, *her Anthony,* for good reason. She's the only person who calls him Anthony, which is his government, first name. Everyone else calls him, Ajay. His parents call him, Ant. When she called him Ajay before, he didn't like it at all. He wants her to call him Anthony but not anyone else can refer to him as that. Only Ebony can.

He had once told her, *"My mama is the only person who calls my daddy, Allen. Everybody else calls him, Al or big Al. I want you to call me by my first name. I want you to call me, Anthony."*

He wants her, to be to him, what his mother is to his father. A Wife. She finds his request weird and encouraging, all at the same time. Tonight, he hasn't said anything about her dancing. But Tank and Jb don't feel she's moving off of the dance floor, fast enough.

"Get your ass off the floor, twin," Tank says as he laughs but she knows he's serious.

"You're not gonna be bumping and grinding with that nigga," Jb adds as he makes his way to the floor with Lynn.

He's not smiling or joking.

"It's time for you to go home, anyway," Tank says as he slow dances with Nina, kissing all over her neck while she grins and corrects Tank saying, "It's time for all four of us to go, baby."

They all know she doesn't want to leave Tank but they all know the rules also.

At the very moment when Mark is about to ask if he can walk Ebony home, Ajay steps up and grabs her hand.

"Come on, baby. I'll walk you home," he says as he gives Mark a mean look.

Ebony says nothing. She just takes his hand and they go out of the front door, together. The other crew couples pair off and follow them. Everyone else is discussing the party highlights. Ebony and Ajay are quiet.

"Hey brothers, y'all leaving?" Chill asks from his doorway.

"Nah, man. We're just walking the ladies to the crib," Rich answers, "We're coming right back."

Still Ajay doesn't say anything, as they stroll across the yard and toward

the street. Ebony doesn't say anything either. Despite all that's happened, she's still pleased to be with him, finally.

The other 4 couples are getting along well. Everyone is hugged up tight and cozy. Rich and T-baby, Rebbie and June, Nina and Tank. Even Jb and Lynn are paired up. They still love each other and they get together when everyone else pairs up. They aren't considering themselves a couple. At least, not at this time. But that will change, after tonight.

Lynn is a dedicated athlete and she loves track. She had put her sport before her relationship and Jb wasn't accepting of it. That was the reason they had broken up, last year. Ebony wants them to be together. She does whatever she can to see to it that no other girls interfere. Anytime a girl calls their house for Jb or comes by, she tells Lynn about it. Jb gets angry with her but he knows she loves Lynn, like a sister and she's loyal to her, the way crew are suppose to be. Lynn is not just her crew. She's Ajay and Nina's oldest sister. She's Ebony's sister-in-law, 3 ways. That counts for everything. Ebony dates Lynn's only brother. Lynn and Nina are dating her 2 oldest brothers and their parents are best friends. Their grandparents were best friends and soldiers for the cause which they all still represent. They couldn't possibly, be *more* family. Surely, one day, at least 2 of these 3 couples will make it official. Ebony is planning on her and Ajay being 1 of those married couples.

Time Will Reveal!

As they reach the porch, Ajay pulls Ebony to the side of the house. He wants some alone time.

"I can't just let you go inside without tasting that tongue," he says suddenly, "I hope you know that."

"Why not?" she asks, rather sassy and acting reluctant but wanting to kiss him, so badly. She adds, "It wasn't my tongue you was tasting earlier, was it?"

"Wait a minute," he says, "I don't kiss nobody but you. Because I know where your mouth has been. *Understand me?* I ain't about to be sticking my tongue inside of no dick suckers mouth. So you need to stop *trippin.* I told you before. You're the only girl I kiss. And since we started kissing, in nineteen eighty seven, I haven't put my lips on no other girl, *anywhere*. So kill that noise, alright?"

She can tell he didn't like her comment. She decides to keep it simple and

not be *too* sassy. He doesn't like that tone in her voice. Plus her big mama had told her about it too.
Men don't like a woman with too much lip!

"Anyway, I know you're not about to bring that shit back up," Ajay says, "I thought we squashed that today, in your room. You took my hand and left with me, tonight. You didn't say nothing about that. I told you what was up and we squashed it."

"Yes, well maybe we did," she says in a mildly sassy tone, "But all I'm saying is, it wasn't me you wanted today when you was in your room." Remembering her poppa's advice, she's not going to make it *too* easy for him to make up with her. Ajay stands quiet, for a moment.

Then he says, "*Damn*. Having sex sure has made you flip, at the lip, baby girl. Why don't you freeze up on that? Your man ain't *even* feeling this."

He looks unenthused. He's embarrassed that she'd caught him and he wishes it had never happened. He would rather forget about it, all together. She's never used this tone with him, before now. Suddenly, he reaches for her, pulls her to him and gently places his fingertips over her lips, so she can't speak.

"Ebony, I always want you. I've wanted you since I started grade school. I always have and I always will. Understand me, when I say that, alright?"

With his other hand at her waist, he pulls her close to him. She looks around at the others, who are minding their own business, so she loosens up.

"Huh," she pouts, "I can never tell *what* you want."

"Then come here and let me show you, please? Just give me a kiss, baby," he whispers.

He moves 1 of his fingers to the inside of her mouth, as his face grows very intense.

She sucks on his finger and says, "You give me one."

Not in sassy tone, this time. But still surprising herself that she could be so bold as to say it. Perhaps it's the 2 forties of *Old English 800*, her and her girls shared at the party, that's doing the talking for her. She surprised him when she sucked on his finger. She still doesn't know what that does to him yet, either. She had seen it done in a porno movie. Whatever it is, she feels it necessary to stand her ground and it gets a positive response out of him.

"Oh yea," he says to her demand as he moves in.
He begins kissing her. Gently at first, while caressing her face and neck. Then harder, as he rubs his hands through her hair and down her body. The force of his aggressive kiss causes her to lean against the car. She begins to kiss him back, equally as hard. He moans. That lets her know, he likes it too. She holds him close to her body as he starts to grind against her. This turns her on. He's excited too. She can feel his penis get hard. She likes how it feels when she rubs herself against it. They are definitely feeling each other, right now. She's forgotten that anyone else is even out there.
Until..,

"Hey, y'all better quit that shit before daddy comes out here and catch you, girl," Jb says as he laughs.
They pull away, quickly. This disturbs Ebony's insides. Quickly, she straightens her clothes and hair. That's when she notices T-baby, Nina and Rebbie are already inside of her doorway. She turns to walk away from Ajay. But as she does, he grabs her hand and pulls her back to him.

"Can I come see you later?" he asks in a whisper, "You know, when Tank comes home from the party?"

"My daddy's in there," she says while blushing, "And my girls are spending the night."

"I know. I know," he whispers while caressing her already hard nipple. He says, "But I'm gonna try to come and see you. I really need too."

"Alright, baby," she says, very sweetly, "Goodnight."
He smiles at her and she smiles back. He stands with his eyes trained on her and watches as she walks inside of her side door and closes it. Then he joins the others at the edge of the driveway, by the street.

They head back to Chill's house and back to the party. Ajay is still thinking about Ebony and how much he wishes they could be alone, right now.

While inside of Ebony's house, the foursome give her their take on the night.

"Whoa, girl," Nina says, "Y'all had it going on, out there, *kid*."
T-baby and Rebbie giggle as they all go up the stairs to Ebony's room. She still hasn't told them about Sunday night.

"Sshh," Ebony whispers as she giggles quietly to herself, "Be quiet before my mama and daddy hear y'all."

"Ebony, it's time for you to let mama P know that you're liking Ajay," Nina says, "I gotta tell my mama about Jeremy too. Because they're gonna know about it soon, anyway."

"I know but I don't want her to hear it from y'all," Ebony says, "So don't talk so loud."

Pearl and her crew are still having their card party. They acknowledge the young ladies when they head upstairs. The foursome continue their conversation.

"Or worse, girl. The little ones will hear it and tell on all of us," Rebbie says, "Y'all know they're asleep in mama Pearl's room."

"Who are you calling *little*?" T-baby asks, while laughing under her breath, "Ree, you're the youngest one hearing it, right now."

"T-baby, y'all are still the same status, though," Ebony says boldly, as they close the door to her room and lock it behind them.

"Oh. As if you're *not*," Rebbie states.

"Not anymore," Ebony says with a matter-of-fact tone to her voice, "Me and Anthony did it, Sunday night."

"What?!" T-baby asks, almost yelling.

"Sshh," Ebony orders.

"When was you gonna tell us?" Nina asks.

"Right now," Ebony answers as they all crawl up on her queen-sized bed and grab a pillow.

She has to tell them all the sorted details. They look directly into her face while she smiles, devilishly. Her girls want to know how and where and what took her so long to tell them.

Outside, Ajay and Jb have made it back to Chill's front yard. The others are standing on the porch, waiting for them to catch up. Ajay wants to ask Jb to bring Ebony to his house, right now. But he knows Jb wants to finish his party with him *present*.

"Ey, you ain't coming a little *too hard* for baby girl?" Jb asks while smiling.

"Nah, man. She's ready," Ajay says as he adjusts his baggy jeans to hide the obvious bulge in his pants. He adds, "She's ready. *Way* ready. I tell you what's up. See what she did to me? *Damn!* Your sister's been had my attention since first grade, Jb. I can't even front. I'm into her, a lot."

Ajay's package is also quite exceptional for his age too. They laugh loud as they catch up with Tank, Rich, Lynn and June, on Chill's porch. They go inside and back to Jb's party, where Jan and Bre are still waiting with Stoney, Rob and the rest of their crew.

"Damn, man. It's about time," Chill says, "I thought y'all took it on in or something."

"Nah, crew," Rich says, "Where the bud at?"

"Right here," Ajay says as he fires 1 up, "Come get ya buzz on." He says that while trying to hold the smoke in. They all gather around to smoke. Chill sends Renee into the kitchen to get everyone a forty ounce. All of a sudden, the doors flings open.

"What's up, crew?!" Jr yells as he strolls in with *some* honey, from across town.

A honey they'll all know, *too well,* soon enough.

"Damn, Junior. Where your ass been, all night, man?" Chill asks.

"Handling business, brother. You know that!" Jr says and laughs.

"So what's up on that work?" Chill asks.

"Oh, it's all gravy, baby!" Jr says.

The crew had been negotiating a deal with some guys from the west side of town. Chill and Stoney had reached the terms, the evening prior. Tonight was to be the exchange but Jr had left the cookout, early. Most figured he was with some girl while his girlfriend Tonya is out of town. Chill had no doubts he would handle his end of the business, though. Jr has been out all day and had just sealed the deal. Surely, at some point, he had wasted time with a girl or two. But now he can hardly wait to get the crew upstairs in the spare room to show them, *The Score*. They all follow him upstairs.

Chill's crew doesn't just dabble in the drug trade. They are heavy in the game. The 2nd generation had gotten the wheels rolling. And even though most of them have gone completely legit, Paul and Willamena never did. They thrived in the 70's and they often made big money deals. Chill learned the game, early. He took the contacts and connects his parents used and continued to make money. The drug game is more popular now, then it was when the 2nd generation was a big part it. It's more dangerous and on front street, nowadays too. *Literally*. Some guys stand out on the street corners and sale illegal drugs but not the crew. Police accost black males

daily for drug dealing. They have yet to make anything stick to Chill and his crew but that's not from lack of effort. One reason is because a lot of the police department are still on the crew's payroll from the decades before. The crew have police protection, to a certain extent. Still, there are some cops who *jack them up* from week to week. But a *bought-and-paid-for* cop usually gets the charges reduced or expelled, to save his own cut. Fortunately, today's buy had gone smoothly.

"Hell yea, baby. It's on now," Ajay says.

They're upstairs in the spare bedroom where he's inspecting the 2 keys of powder cocaine in Jr's gym bag.

"Did crew hit a lick or what?" Jr asks.

"Oh hell yeah, man. It's on and poppin now," Jb answers.

"Let me clear the house so we can get it going," Chill says.

He goes back downstairs to get rid of the stragglers and non-crew party dwellers, who still remain. Only a few guest who are truly down with the crew are allowed to stay, once the party ends. The rest have to leave now. Then the crew return to the 1st floor to process their score.

"Get the burners going, baby," Chill says to Renee.

She's definitely his lady and they live together. Renee moved in with Chill, years ago. Long before his father was killed, as a result of the crew beef. They have a son named Kenneth Ramon Payne Jr. The crew call him lil Chill or lil Kenny.

"Come on, girls. Let's do this," Renee says to her female crew.

Lynn, Jan, Bre plus Jr's friend Angie, follow Renee into the kitchen.

Once the ladies are out of ear shot, Tank has some concerns with Angie, as he asks, "Hey man, is she cool? Cause I know you don't ever let non-crew up in the mix."

"Yea, man. She's straight. I ain't slippin like that," Jr says as he smiles, "She's got mad dope in her spot. She can't tell *shit*."

Angie's cousin is the Westside connect for which the guys have been doing business. She's his stash girl, this month. Meaning she keeps all of her cousins supply, at her apartment, on the west side. After meeting her and learning this bit of information, Jr decided he wanted to get to *know her* a little better too. Physically that is and just for *this* month. For future hook ups and maybe even free product. But as a steady girl, she's no deal. He has a woman. She's just away visiting her family in Detroit, for the holiday.

In the kitchen, the girls cook the mixture and get it ready. The guys rock it, bag it and tag it for the streets. Then they divide it all up.

"Crew, it's time to get paid," Chill says.

"Hell yea," Jan agrees.

Her, Bre and Lynn can serve too. They're nearly as hard body as the guys are. Only neither of them have ever killed anybody. At least, not yet.

At Ebony's house, the foursome are still up talking at 4:30am. Ebony has told them she's no longer a virgin.

"So girl, you're a woman like me now, ha?" Nina asks.

"Yes but I hope the next time, it don't hurt," Ebony says.

"It won't," Nina assures her, "It hurts the first time. I told you that. But the second time, it's straight like that. It's all good."

"That's what Anthony said yesterday, when we went in his room," Ebony says, "I thought he was just saying that because he didn't want me to be scared."

"I ain't doing it, if it hurt," T-baby says.

Her and Rebbie are still virgins.

"Brian said that to me, tonight," Rebbie says, "He said we need to go on and get to it. But I'm scared too."

"I ain't scared of Richard," T-baby says as she looks doubtful, "I'm scared of pain."

"Ah, girl. It ain't nothing to it, as long as it's somebody you respect and who respects you," Nina says, "Just be sure you let him know you want him to be around forever, if that's what you want. And not just that day. You only get one shot to get it right, kid. So that better be who you want."

"It's got to be with somebody you love and care for. And somebody who loves and cares for you. Right, Nina?" Ebony adds, "Because we only get one man to be intimate with."

"That's right and all of our guys are crew, so you know they ain't even going *nowhere*," Nina says.

"And neither are we. Or at least, not our hearts and minds," Ebony adds, realizing she's leaving in 2 days.

"Right! Now lets get some sleep," Nina says as she yawns, "I'm tired."

They all tuck up on their pillows and say goodnight. After saying their prayers, they're all asleep, almost as soon as they lay down. Ebony goes fast asleep and forgets to unlock her door for Ajay.

They're wrapping things up at Jb's 16th birthday party. The guest are long gone. They crew have processed the score and each has received his or her share of it.

"*Damn*. I'm fucked up," June says as his voice drags.

"*Cuz,* I'm passed fucked up," Tank says and his eyes are nearly closed, as he sways from side to side while attempting to walk a straight line through the living room.

They're all feeling good and intoxicated by now.

"Let's make it," Jb says slowly.

"Hey, y'all looking like y'all need a ride across the street," Chill says as him and Renee laugh.

They're all fucked up and everybody laughs at that comment.

"Hell nah," Bre says, "But I'm staying at somebody's house, over there." She's pointing across the street as she adds, "Because a sister ain't trying to make it down the block. You *heard* me?"

"That's my word too," Jan agrees in a muffled voice.

"You know, y'all are welcome to bunk out, right here, anytime. If y'all can't make it home," Chill offers.

"Word!" Renee chimes in.

She's already curled up in their huge recliner with Chill.

"Well, y'all know I ain't trying to move nowhere," Jr says as he slides back down on the loveseat next to Angie.

Renee gives him the evil eye, while Angie isn't looking. She's not feeling Angie being with Jr. His girlfriend Tonya is her best friend and has been for more than 7 years.

"No problem, man," Chill says. Then turning to Renee, he says, "Baby, I need you to go make up the spare room for crew."

The crew ladies had only accepted Angie in their mix because of the *"stash girl"* title she holds. She would never be accepted as the girl for Jr.

"You got it, baby," Renee says as she starts up the stairs.

"I'll help ya," Angie says and follows Renee upstairs.

The rest of the crew prepare to leave.

"Alright, dog. We're gonna make it," Ajay says.

TIME TO LEARN-RELOADED-Time Will Reveal-part 1

"Everybody straight on somewhere to sleep?" Chill asks.

"Oh yea. We're crashing on Jb and Ajay, *this* morning," Rich says, "For real."

"You know it," June adds.

"Alright then, crew. Stay up," Chill says.

"See ya, dog," Jb says, giving Chill a pound.

"In a minute, homie," They all say as they file out the door.

They make it out to the street as Ajay molders over whether he should try to visit Ebony or not.

"I'm too fucked up to be trying to see baby girl," he says.

"Hell yea. Besides, all of her girls in there too," Jb says.

"I know but if I wasn't fucked up, I'd find a way to make it happen," he says as he smiles.

"Hey Jan. You and Bre can have me and Nina's room," Lynn says.

"Oh yea? Where you gonna sleep?" Bre asks.

"Ah, she's coming with me," Jb says as he hugs Lynn, real tight.

"Well happy birthday to you, dog," Ajay says, "Come on, my folks. Y'all crash at my crib and let this man have his privacy."

"My crew," Jb says, giving Ajay a pound.

"Later, bro," Tank says as him, Ajay, Rich, June, Jan and Bre go into mama Jo's house.

Jb and Lynn go to Pearl's house and to Jb's room. He had been promised the basement after he turned sixteen. He's looking forward to not having to share a room with his younger brothers anymore. The foursome are asleep when they sneak up the stairs and go into the boys room.

"Lynora, we've got some catching up to do," Jb whispers as they secure the door and he reaches over to turn on the lamp.

After he lays across his bed, he says, "I guess you know I wasn't considering us broke up, right?"

"Happy birthday, baby," Lynn says quietly, "And yes, I know you wasn't gonna be okay with us not getting back together."

She's trying not to wake up lil man. He's asleep in 1 of the 3 beds in the room.

"Then yea, it's happy now," Jb says as he rolls over on top of her and they start kissing.

They make love and fall asleep. Not even thinking about the consequences.

TIME TO LEARN-RELOADED-Time Will Reveal-part 1

It's 7:00am on Wednesday, July 5th of 1989, when Pearl is awakened by the phone ringing. She picks up, nervously. Not knowing whom it could be at this hour. She's always heard bad news comes at 2 times. Late at night and early in the morning.

"Hello," she answers, still groggy from yesterday and last night's festivities.

"Pearl, have you seen Lynn? She didn't come home, last night," Jo asks, sounding very nervous on the other end of the phone.

"Oh Lord, Jo. Let me check Ebony's room and see if she stayed here," Pearl says.

"Tank is at my house. So is Ritchie, June, Jan and Bre. But Lynn isn't here," Jo says, sounding like she's on the verge of tears. She adds, "I've never known her to stay at anyone else's house. We've already called Renee. She isn't over there either."

"Calm down, Jo," Pearl says, "Let me check my house. Okay? Don't worry. She may be in there with Ebony and the girls. Hang on."

"Okay," Jo says, trying to calm herself down as Pearl gets up and puts on her robe and slippers.

"What's wrong, baby?" John asks as he has awakened now too.

"Lynn's not at home and Jo's worried," she answers.

"Let me get up too, then," he says as he grabs the phone and says, "Jo, don't worry. We'll find her, honey. Just hold on while we check the house."

He gets out of bed and puts on his robe and slippers while Pearl is knocking on Ebony's door.

"Ebony, baby! Wake up in there! Is Lynn in there with y'all?" she yells through the door.

Ebony jumps up looking around. She dreamed Ajay was in bed with her. But only her girls are there.

"Ma'am!" Ebony yells.

"Ebony, open the door," Pearl says as she continues to knock, "Jo's looking for Lynn. She didn't come home, last night."

All of the commotion wakes the other 3 girls.

"What's going on?" T-baby asks.

"They're looking for Lynn," Ebony says, slipping on her slippers.

"What!?!" Nina asks as she jumps up and goes to the door too.

They unlock the door and open it together, as Nina nervously asks, "Mama P, what's wrong? Where's my sis?"
Rebbie has already started to tear up, just hearing something *may be* wrong with her crew.

"We don't know yet, sweetie. I thought she might be in here with y'all," Pearl says.

Big John had gone downstairs to check the living room. He returns shortly and says, "There's nobody sleeping down there. See if Jb is in his room. Maybe he knows where she is."
Pearl goes to the boys room door and knocks.

Jo had grown impatient on the phone. She hung it up and is now knocking at their side door.

"Did y'all call over Jan or Bre house?" Nina asks.
Her, T-baby and Rebbie are sobbing lightly and thinking the worst.

"Pearlie, it's Jo!" Jo yells from outside of the side door.

"I'll get it, ma," Ebony says as she runs down the stairs, unlocks and then opens the door for Jo.
She hugs her and they both come back up together. Ebony goes back to console Nina, who cries harder when she sees her mother upset.
Pearl is knocking very hard on the boy's bedroom door. Her knocking has awakened lil man. He gets up and opens the door, giving Pearl a full view of the boys room.

"John Junior! What the hell do y'all think this is!?" Pearl yells as she storms into the room.
She sees Jb and Lynn in bed together. Lynn and Jb sit up, abruptly. At the same time, Jo comes into the room. Jb and Lynn are still out of it.

"Lynora Shontay Jackson! Get your ass up, right now! What the hell is wrong with you?!" Jo screams, "You had me worried to death that something had happened to you and I find your *fast ass* laying up?!"
Jo screams louder. Pearl is screaming at Jb, just as loud. Jb and Lynn are both stunned but they won't remove the covers because they're not dressed.

"John Junior. Get up and come downstairs," big John says calmly. He's standing just inside of the door. His voice is firm but calm, as usual. "Pearl. Jo. Let's let them get dressed. Then we'll handle it," he says.
Pearl leaves the room and goes back to her room to get dressed. Jo goes down to the living room. Pearl hangs up her phone and puts her clothes on.

"Ebony, y'all go wait at Jo's house, honey," John says as he starts back downstairs, "And take lil man with you."
As the girls and lil man go out of the side door, Al is coming in.

"Is she here, Joanna?" he asks.

"Yes she is!"

"Thank God," Al says.

"Don't thank him yet, Allen," Jo says, obviously more upset now, "She was in bed with John Junior. Both of them was as naked as the day they was born!"

"Damn. What's wrong with that girl?" Al asks, showing agitation.

"Man, it wasn't just her," big John says, "John Junior is just as much to blame as she is."
He's trying to play to the ladies heads and Al knows this already. They knew Jb was sexually active and that he has females in the house, all the time. They had no idea Lynn was having sex. John has brought in 2 cups of coffee. He gives them to Jo and Al. Pearl comes in with 2 more for her and John. Jb and Lynn are dressed, as they come slowly down the stairs.

"Come on in here and sit down," John says, his voice is still firm.
Before he can say anything else, Jo and Pearl start in on Jb and Lynn again. They're fussing loudly. Jb and Lynn sit there, knowing not to utter a word besides, *"No ma'am"* or *"Yes ma'am."* Pearl and Jo are so loud they can be heard outside. They're yelling over each other. Firing words and logic at their offspring, in record time. John and Al sip their coffee while they stare at Jb and Lynn.

Ebony and the girls have awakened the crew, at Jo's house and filled them in on what's happening next door.

"Oh shit, man! Mama is going off over there," Tank says.

"They was to fucked up to get up, on time," Bre offers.

"Damn, man," Jan says, "This is fucked!"
Ajay doesn't say anything. He's thinking of how this could've been him and Ebony, 2 mornings ago.
Then Ebony says, "Y'all that could've been any one of us, over there."

"Not me," Rebbie says, "I ain't doing nothing."

"Me either," T-baby says.

"Not yet," Bre and Jan say simultaneously.

TIME TO LEARN-RELOADED-Time Will Reveal-part 1

"It could've been me and Tank or Ebony and Ajay," Nina offers.

"Ebony?!" Jan asks in surprise.

"What the hell did you say?!" Bre adds as she giggles and Ebony looks to Ajay for assistance.

"Yea, it could've been either one of us in that hot box, right about now," Ajay says while smiling at Ebony.

He doesn't mind that she'd told her girls. He told his boys before breakfast, the same morning it happened.

"Man, what are we gonna do?" Rich asks.

"What the fuck *can* we do?" June answers.

"Not shit, right now, man," Ajay says, "But wait and see what our folks do."

"This is gonna fuck *all* our shit up," Tank says.

"We're gonna have to freeze up on that fucking at our house, for awhile. Because you know they'll be watching now," Ajay adds.

"You're right. I wonder what they're saying now?" Tank ponders.

"Daddy must be talking because everything is quiet," Ebony says.

"Or my pops," Ajay says, "Don't neither one of them scream. They just look your ass, *straight* in your eyes and tell you what they *gotta* say."

"Yea and leave you feeling like you're about six years old," Tank adds with a laugh.

****

It has been almost 2 hours and the crew are still sitting around waiting on *the verdict*. Nina and the girls have made breakfast and fed the youngest ones too. Erica, Pam and Lil man are asking to go out and play.

"Not right now," Ajay says to his 2 youngest sisters.

"Hold on, lil man until daddy says it's alright," Tank adds.

Suddenly, Nina comes running back into the living room, whispering, "Here comes daddy."

Al walks in and grabs his keys off the kitchen counter. On his way back out the side door, he says to Ajay, "Ant, y'all stay here until we get back."

"Damn, man. Now what?" June whispers as he looks puzzled, "I wonder what he needs the keys for?"

"It ain't no telling," Jan says.

"I know they're not taking them off somewhere," Tank adds.

"Hell nah," Ajay says as they both go to the window to look out at their parents and siblings activity on the driveways.

"Mama Jo and ma, got Lynn in our car. Daddy, Jb and big Al are getting in y'all van," Ebony says as her and Nina look out the window too.

"I wonder where they're going?" Nina asks.

No one knows yet but Ajay offers a guess, when he says, "It's time for that heart-to-heart talk, probably. You know. Man-to-boy. Woman-to-girl."

"Boy, look here. I don't wanna get caught up like that," Tank says, "But y'all know I got my crew back, all the time. Right?"

"Hell yea, dog. We know," Ajay says.

"We know," the others add.

"We may as well let these brats outside before they run us crazy in here," Ajay says, "Let's let them play in the yard for awhile."

"Cool," Tank says as they all go outside to their front yards.

They all head outside, so the youngest kids can play in the front yards.

Ebony goes inside her house to get the cordless phone, in case their parents call. At the same moment, Uncle Greg pulls into their driveways.

"What up, uncle G?!!" Tank yells.

"It ain't nothing to it, man. Where's John?" Greg Sr asks.

"He went somewhere with big Al," Tank answers, "I don't know what time he'll be back."

"Oh, alright," he says. Then he turns to T-baby and asks, "Are you ready to go home, Trisha? Your mama sent me to pick you up."

"Not really, daddy," T-baby says, "I wanted to spend the day with Ebony. You know she leaves tomorrow."

"Well come home for awhile. We'll see what Sandy says about it," Greg Sr says, "If she says it's okay, I'll bring you back later. Alright? Ree Ree, Archie man asks me to bring you home too."

"Yes sir. But I wanna come back with T-baby," she adds, "We wanna be here until Ebony leaves."

"We'll see," Greg Sr says as they load into the car.

T-baby and Rebbie wave bye to everyone. They smile at Rich and June, who return smiles. Ebony and Nina look at their 2 best friends and grin. T-baby and Rebbie grin back, then they all giggle.

"Ebony, we're gonna call you," Both girls yell as Greg drives away.

"Okay!" she yells back to them, "Tell aunt Rena and aunt Sandy, I want y'all to spend the night with me!"

The phone rings

"Big June! Telephone!" Ebony yells across to mama Jo's yard from her front porch.
June runs over to get phone.
Ebony passes him the phone and says, "It's auntie Brenda."
"What up, ma?" June asks.
"Don't *what up* me. Did you forget the way home?" Brenda asks.
"No ma'am. I'm on my way now," June says.
"Is Jan with you?" Brenda asks.
"Yes ma'am," June says.
"Tell her Belinda said she needs to make her way home," Brenda says, "And Deb called her house looking for Bre."
"Okay, mama. We're all gonna walk home together," June says.
They hang up and he gives the phone back to Ebony. No doubt all of their parents know what happened at Pearl and John's house by now.
"Crew, y'all let us know what's up on Jb and Lynn," Bre says.
"Yea, homies. We out o' here like last year," Jan says and smiles.
"In a minute, y'all," June adds.
"Alright," Tank says, "See ya."
"I'm gonna get at y'all on that there thang, later," Rich says as he talks in code about his stash.
"Word, cuz," Ajay says.
He knows Rich stashed his product in the hiding spot near his house.
"Cool," Tank says.
As they stroll off, down the street, walking home, Ebony and Nina yell out, "Peace out, niggaz!"
Ajay and Tank turn, look at them and shake their heads. Then they all laugh. It's already passed the midway point of 1989 and things for this crew are just really starting to heat up.

CHAPTER 3

THE VERDICT

After this morning's scare, neither Ajay nor Tank will even try to get cozy with Ebony or Nina. Even with knowing their parents are away, they're still not willing to risk it at either house.

"It just ain't the time, man," Tank says to Ajay with a smile.

"No shit, Sherlock," Ajay says, "But I sure as hell wanna get with my baby, though. *Still.*"

"You and me, *both*," Tank agrees, "We'll get to that after this shit cools down."

"Word," Ajay says.

They laugh about it but quickly separate the boys from the girls. They fear their parents will return and squash their whole crew. And not even allow them in each others presence, ever again. They decide to play it cool and wait out the verdict in separate homes. Tank and Ajay take lil man with them to John and Pearl's house. While Nina and Ebony keep Erica and Pam with them at Al and Jo's house.

****

Jb, Lynn and their parents return before 2pm. Ajay and Tank are still at Pearl and John's house. Ebony, Nina, Erica and Pam are still at Jo and Al's. The girls have made lunch for everyone. Their parents return and go into Pearl and John's home. Jo sends Lynn home, as she heads inside with Al, Pearl and John. Lynn was told to put away the things she'd gotten, eat lunch and stay put. Tank, Ajay and lil man are in the living room when their parents enter, with Jb behind them.

"Where are the girls?" John asks.

"They're still at mama Jo's house," Tank answers, "Uncle Greg came by to get T-baby and Ree Ree. He asked for you."

"Alright. I'll give him a call and see what's up," John says as he picks up the phone to call his brother. He tells Jb, "Son, go put that stuff

away and stay up in your room until I call you down here. But only if I need too."

"Yes sir," Jb says and he heads upstairs to the boys room.

Within minutes, Tank and Ajay ease up the stairs to checkout *Jb's things*.

"Let lil man go up there with you guys," Pearl says.

"Yes ma'am," Tank says, "Come on, man."

The 3 of them join Jb in the room. They close the door behind them and lock it.

Over at Jo's house, Nina, Ebony and Lynn are talking in the big girl's room. Nina and Ebony want to know all the details of this morning and where they went on that infamous ride.

"It's cool," Lynn tells them, "First, they just fussed at us for two hours. Then we had to tell them how long we've been doing it. *Man*! They freaked out when Jb said *our first time was his 11th birthday*. *Boy*! Mama was crying and mama P was too."

Lynn's face holds a sympathetic expression, as she continues, "I started crying and saying I'm sorry. But daddy and big John just looked at each other and shook their heads. They didn't seem mad at Jb, *at all*. They only seemed like they was mad at me. We *already know* how easy the boys get it, when they have sex with other girls. That's the exact opposite of what we want them to do. But it seems to be cool with our fathers if they fuck over us. So long as they don't *fuck us*. That part wasn't a surprise."

"Was you scared?" Ebony asks.

"*Hell yea,* girl! Especially when we woke up and both mama's was standing over us! I tripped out! That was like a nightmare, *you know*? Like a bad ass dream," she says as she flashes back to this morning's awakening.

"Where did y'all go?" Nina asks.

"Check this out. This is the good part," Lynn says, "When daddy and big John took the floor, I thought we was dead, for sure. Finally, daddy asked me was I using birth control. I said, *no sir*. Big John asked Jb and he said, "*Sometimes*." Then they said, "*Well we're gonna take y'all to see somebody.*" Mama and mama P preached all the way downtown. They took us to family planning. We talked to some counselors, when we first got there. They gave us physicals and I had to take a pregnancy test. They

tested us for everything. Of course, everything was negative. So then, they gave Jb a bag full of rubbers and K-Y Jelly," she continues as she giggles, "And I got *these*."

She whips out her prescription and shows them her birth control pills.

"Ah man, Lynn! You're straight now!" Nina says, "I wish I could get some."

"Me too." Ebony says.

"Listen to y'all asses. We just got busted and all y'all can think about, is how y'all can get y'all fuck on, *safely*?" Lynn asks as she laughs.

They all giggle while Erica and Pam watch them.

"For some reason, big mama has been saying I need to be on the pill," Ebony offers, "It's like she has ESP or something."

"Or *ESPN*!" Lynn jokes, "But seriously, our grandparents are the hook up. Y'all are gonna see what I mean, now that this happened. They'll want us all to be strong, ready and wise. They'll make our folks get wit it and get us up on the *prophylactics and* the reproduction info. Which will eventually get all of us on some birth control."

"Yes because they want all of us to go to college," Nina adds, "And not have babies while we're still in school."

"And get married *before* we have sex and families," Ebony says.

"Like they did? *Not*," Lynn says, "But our parents are gonna fight it because they wanna have the final say so, over us. It's a battle between them and the grandparents. It always has been. I've been noticed that. Our grandparents was already married with kids, at our ages."

"It's just like Renee always says, '*They don't want the girls in this family to have sex,'* Ebony recalls.

"But the boys can fuck whenever they want too," Nina adds.

"As long as they're not fucking us, until marriage," Lynn finishes.

"The opposite of what we want," Ebony says.

They laugh as they discuss how unfair the double standard's are but they know it's the foundation of their families. It's *been* this way for the crew. In the world, for that matter. There's a double standard when it comes to males, females and sex. Males are given praise for having many partners and lots of sex. While females are frowned upon for the same thing. A logical question would be, *Who the fuck are the males suppose to be sexing?*

TIME TO LEARN-RELOADED-Time Will Reveal-part 1

Meanwhile, at Pearl's house, Jb, Tank and Ajay are still in the boys room. They're discussing the incident and giving their take on it.

"Man, that's a trip," Tank says, "You ain't even on lock down or nothing?"

"Hell nah, man," Jb says, "They just said we know they didn't want *us* having sex. But that didn't stop us from having it, so if we're gonna sneak and see each other, we had better use protection."

"Damn. If I told them I was fucking, they would probably lock my ass in this room," Tank says with a disgusted look.

"They know already," Jb says as he smiles, "They know about all the guys. The men in this family encourage that part. Sew your wild oats. Papa and all the men say that to us. You need to listen to daddy, bro. They already know. They did the same shit."

"No shit but Tank is right, though. I'd probably get sent to juvenile or somewhere," Ajay says as he laughs.

"Or worse. If some of those ho's we done fucked wit, get caught with us, their grown asses would be going to county," Tank says and they laugh harder.

"Sshh! I ain't suppose to be feeling good about this," Jb whispers, trying to look serious, "I probably lost out on getting the basement too. Mama's gonna block that shit, for sure."

"But you feel good then a muthafucka, don't you bro?" Tank asks as he laughs more, "You got your girl back."

"Hell yea, I do. *Shit*. What you don't *know*?" Jb asks as he lays back on his bed. Then while still chuckling, he spills the real deal.
"On the real, the fathers expect us males to fuck. Just not the females in our crew. Not before commitment," he says, "Daddy don't even wanna think about baby girl having sex. And big *Al,* they can't accept that the girls in the crew are fucking. That's really the only problem our dad's had with this morning. *Plain as day.* But for us guys, they want us to get our fuck on and I'm not gonna disappoint 'em."
They all laugh again.

"I notice that with *my* pops, especially," Ajay admits, "He knows I've been bussing since before I could even bust."
They laugh as Ajay continues, "He knows I've been getting up on older women, for years. I was eight and got my first hit on a girl who was twelve.

Y'all remember miss Lou niece, Marsha, from Milwaukee? She gave me my first piece. A gee been off and running every since," Ajay says and smiles.

"I know daddy *been knew* I was fucking too," Tank adds, "But I didn't think he knew about the older broads."

"That ain't no *thang*, to them, like I said," Jb adds, "They know because they did the *same* shit. Ask papa and poppa. All the grandfathers will put you up on the real shit. They don't want us dumb to *anything*. They'd rather us know it before we get out there, then to learn it, *out there.* Y'all two are gonna get the talk, I got today too. Only y'all talk will be worse." Jb warns.

"What do you mean?" Tank asks as Ajay sits up and pays close attention.

"Because of *who* y'all fucking, in this crew," Jb offers.

He looks at Tank and says, "Nina."

Then he looks at Ajay, "And you're fuckin, baby girl. Even *your* dad *and Chill* don't want nobody fuckin over her. Or none of the foursome, as a matter of fact. Y'all know that already or you will."

"I know how my pops feel about Ebony," Ajay says, "But it's too late because I already want her and I got her. I'm not letting that go, so it might be a problem, real soon."

"Point is, we can get all the pussy we want, outside of our crew. Our fathers don't give a damn. But our mothers, that's a different issue," Tank asserts.

"The women don't want nobody fucking, regardless. You have to let the grandfathers put you up on that too," Jb says, "And then keep it moving. The men are the muscle in this family. They let the women feel like they are because that keeps their moods in check," he says and laughs.

"Yea. Damn, Jb," Ajay says, "That must've been one hell of a trip downtown. You came back, *philosophisizing* and everything."

All 3 guys are laughing hysterically at that comment. But they're still trying to keep from being heard outside of the room. Lil man continues to play his video games. To the 3 of them, he seems almost oblivious to their conversation. But he's listening and learning, the entire time.

****

TIME TO LEARN-RELOADED-Time Will Reveal-part 1

By 3:30pm everyone has gone home and the mothers have started dinner. By now, everybody knows about Jb and Lynn. The grandparents are upset with the parents, for 1 reason or another. But ultimately, the grandparents are still feeling that their grandchildren are innocent in it all, as grandparents tend to do.

With the commotion of Jb and Lynn, Ebony had a brief respite from thinking about leaving tomorrow. That is until Pearl comes into her room to help her pack. They begin 1 of their mother/daughter talks.

"Well, baby girl. How do you feel now?" Pearl asks.

"Like it's the last day of my life," Ebony says.

"Oh, Ebony. It won't be so bad," Pearl says, "You'll see. We'll see each other on holidays and we'll always be, just a phone call away."

"Ma, that sounds like jail," she says through pouting lips.

"Baby girl, it's not gonna be so bad. The time will fly by and before you know it, you'll have friends to hang out with-"

"All of my friends are here, ma," she says quickly.

"I know you've got your crew here but you'll meet some friends while you're there. Okay?" Pearl tries.

"Okay," she says but Pearl can see that she isn't.

"Listen. Mama really needs some help, right now. If I could go, I would go, in a *heartbeat* because that's *my* mama. I wanna be there. But as a mother and a wife, I have responsibilities here. Please do this for me. One day when you're all grown up with your own family and responsibilities, you'll understand why I have to stay here and work. Okay?"

"Yes ma'am," she says, "But I can't have a family, if I never start seeing anybody."

"Remember how you felt yesterday?" Pearl asks, ignoring that last comment.

Ebony had forgotten the lie she'd told her mother, almost as quickly as it had fallen out of her mouth.

"Yes ma'am. I know but today I feel different. I mean, I don't know what to do," she says, looking very depressed as she continues, "Ma, I wish we had time to do some mother, daughter things."

"Like what honey?" Pearl asks, pleased that Ebony is still interested in spending quality time with her or so she thinks.

"It's like. Okay, who's gonna be there to take me to the clinic and

stuff like that?" Ebony asks as she tries to figure out how to ask for birth control pills.
She asks, "Who's gonna understand my *female* needs?"

"Baby, if you get sick, mama and daddy will take you to a doctor, immediately. That won't be a problem and mama knows female needs too. Better than either one of us do," Pearl says with a smile.

"What if I'm not sick?"

"You're not making sense," Pearl says.

"I mean, what if I start to feel like Jb and Lynn and I'm not here?"

"Ebony, we don't have to worry about that, do we? You're going to Houston to take care of your grandmother. Not to get involved with some boy, right?" she asks, looking into Ebony's eyes for confirmation.
Ebony wants to talk about her and Ajay. She wants to let her mother know that she has done more than just *think* about having sex. She can't figure out how to say it. Especially not after Jb and Lynn's ordeal. But she knows for sure there isn't going to be another boy in her life. Not in Houston or anywhere else, so she answers her mother's question.

"You're right, ma," she says, "I just want to feel like I can come to you with anything and you'll be there and understand."

"You can count on it, sweetheart," Pearl says as she gives her a kiss on the forehead.
The packing is done. Ebony leaves 2 outfits on her bed. One, for the cookout tonight. The other one is for the trip to Houston. Chill is having a cookout party for her last night in town. Her curfew has been extended to 2am, since this is her last night with her friends, for awhile.

****

The foursome are dressed by 4:30pm. They meet up at Nina's house. Lil man is staying at uncle Greg and aunt Sandy's with Greg Jr. This will allow Pearl and John some time alone too. Jb is allowed to go to the party, at the last minute, only because John and Pearl *need* their time alone. Or at least, that's the excuse *Pearl* gave. John didn't give any excuse for allowing his son to go. He simply told Pearl that Jb could go. She didn't like the double standard. She never has but she knows, from history, that her husband isn't going to change his mind.

TIME TO LEARN-RELOADED-Time Will Reveal-part 1

"Can we, *at least,* make sure he knows he did something wrong?" Pearl had said to John.

They grilled Jb, one last time, about this morning's incident. He vowed to behave. John gave him another chance, which is typical behavior for a male child in this family.

Lynn is allowed to go, as well. Only her curfew is still 11:00pm. Jb gets to stay out until 2:00am. He's even suppose to chaperone Ebony. Although he did the same thing as Lynn. He was *caught with Lynn*. It's unfair but that's how the crew has and still operates. Youngest to middle age and older. The males aren't chastised for being sexually active, unless an unwed crew female is involved. There is even a crew code which actually permit's the male's infidelity.

For the good of the crew.

The females have fought it for years. *Time Will Reveal,* if that change ever happens.

By 5:30pm, all of Chill's crew are at he and Renee's house. Chill talks to Jb and Lynn, first thing. He tells them if they was going do something like that, he could've hook them up with a motel room.

During the party, Chill watches Ebony, almost the entire time. She's not in the party spirit, at all. He tells Ajay to go ask her to dance. He does but not before telling Rob to play 3 slow songs in a row. He's not the dancing type. He likes to grind with Ebony. It's the closest he can get to fucking her without actually doing it.

He takes her onto the dance floor where he holds her very tight and close to him. She feels so good in his arms. He's an excellent slow dancer. She knows that already. They've danced in his room to his *Isleys* tape, many times. Back when he first started taking his time with her, romancing her and sealing the deal. He would hold her tight and make her feel like she was the only female, in the world for him. But that was in the privacy of his room. Tonight, they're dancing where everybody can see them and he still holding her the same way. The feelings are the same to her. He even kisses her on her face and neck, occasionally. Just as he had done in his room.

This feels so damn good.

She feels like a princess at the ball. Ajay is definitely her prince. She notices

several of the females from their 4th of July event are in attendance. They're gawking at them, like they want to be where she is. Amongst them is none other then; Anita Davis. She's sporting dark sunglasses. Ebony laughs to herself. She knows that bitch is also sporting 2 black eyes behind those sunglasses too. She's certain of that. One other thing she's certain of is, this is her last night in town, she's with Ajay and she's going to feel him just once more before she leaves. She has too. Even if it means getting into trouble. She has too. She doesn't have a plan yet but her mind is working overtime. He must've been thinking the same thing, at that moment. He lifts her chin and kisses her with plenty of tongue. She can feel her insides melting. The crew hiss and cheer while they're kissing. Chill is the ringleader. The ho's on the sideline who was hoping to get with Ajay, aren't thrilled in the least. But at this point, Ebony doesn't give a fuck. She's where they want to be and where *she* belongs. In Ajay's arms. Where she's always going to come back to, for as long as she lives.

As the last song ends, they hold each other for a few seconds longer than the song.

"Uh. It feels so good to hold you, baby girl," he says.

This must be love!

She can't speak. She can only stare into his eyes. Ajay is showing her public displays of affection. At this moment, she knows what she had been hoping for all along has come true. He does loves her and he doesn't want her to leave. They hold hands and walk off the dance floor.

"What's up, Eb-bone nay?!?" Chill asks in a silly tone.

He's always happy to see them together.

"Hey, big Chill. What's up?" she asks while giggling.

Ebony is still glowing from her episode on the dance floor. Ajay still has his arms around her too. He's sticking very close to her. Perhaps he's feeling the same way she is about her last night in town. Chill passes him a fat sack of herb.

"That's for you and baby girl," he says, "For tonight, homie."

"Alright, dog," Ajay says with a smile.

He knows the weed is mainly for him. But he'll let Ebony smoke some, to help her relax.

"Hey, baby girl," Chill says, "Let me holla at my homie, for a

second. Alright? I need to run something by him, real quick. Its *all* good."
She looks at him with that, *just-one-second* type of expression. Chill takes heed with a smile, as he says, "Just one minute, baby girl. And I'm bringing him right back *here*."
He's pointing to the spot next to her.
"I'm bringing him back here, *personally*. That's my word. Just about five minutes, is all I need."
She laughs and says, "Okay."
He signals for Nina, T-baby and Rebbie to come stand with her, before taking Ajay into the kitchen. Ebony figures they have some street business to discuss and Chill needs to talk to him about it in private.

After seeing the foursome standing together, DJ lil Rob takes this opportunity to change the party flow. He plays *All Night Long* by *The Mary Jane Girls*. They are the foursome's favorite group to imitate. It's a group of 4 ladies who was introduced to the world by; *Rick James*. The foursome go to the dance floor, immediately. They sing the song, revamp the video plus add their own spice to it. Everybody gets into it too.

"*My instant party starters*!" lil Rob screams into the microphone.
The foursome laugh and continue to dance. The party's groove has gone to another level.

Chill and Ajay return to the living room after they finish talking. Chill grabs Renee and starts to dance, along with the foursome while Renee tries to scream over the music.

"I remember when me and my girls use to do this same thing!" she says to Ebony, "Big Kenny use to love seeing us do this song too."
Ebony looks at Chill. He's partying his ass off. As they dance out the musical ending, she looks over at Ajay. He's smiling. Obviously, he likes to see her and her girls dance to this song, as well.
Or is that really the reason he's smiling?

When the song is finished, Rob goes right into *Musical Love*. That's when all of the couples meet on the dance floor. Ebony wants to dance again. Ajay has other plans.

"Come here, for a minute," he says with a big smile, "I need to tell you something."

"I wanna dance," she whines.

"We'll dance, later. Just come in here, for a sec," he says as he pulls her into the kitchen.

Once in there, she wants an answer, right away, as she asks, "What's so important that you couldn't dance with me, Anthony?"

"Chill got us a room," he says.

"A what!?!"

"A room. *A motel room?* You know? A room."

"For real!" she says, obviously intrigued.

"Yea. He said it's already hooked up for us, if we want it and baby girl, I want it," he says, "What about you, baby girl? Do you wanna go? Do you want it?"

Ebony thinks for a second, then she smiles.

This is it! This is the hook up! Big Chill always comes through!

"Well, what are you gonna do?" Ajay presses.

"You know I got curfew, right?" she asks.

"Yea but Tank already told me you have until two o'clock. It's only six forty five. So what now?"

He steps closer to her and grabs her around her thin waist. He puts his arms around her and looks straight into her eyes. She places her arms over his shoulders and locks her fingers together. *Anita Baker's, Sweet Love* is playing in the living room and echoing throughout the house. She looks back into his eyes as they sway to the music.

"I'm wit it," she finally says as she blushes.

"Then it's on," he says as they finish their dance in the kitchen.

As the song plays on, they kiss again and again.

"So what are y'all gonna do?" Chill asks as he walks into the kitchen, "Since y'all doing all of this making out and carrying on."

He smiles.

"We're going," Ajay says and smiles.

"How are we gonna get there?" Ebony asks.

"Baby girl, I got all of that worked out, already," Chill says as he explains it to her.

Chill and Renee had already planned to move the party to *Gordon park,* after sunset. On the way there, they'll drop Ebony and Ajay off at the motel and then pick them up on the way back to Shaker Heights. The park access closes at midnight. They'll have time to get her home before 2am. This sounds like a brilliant plan to Ebony but there's only 1 problem. She has to get permission to go to the park and so does her girls. Because if her girls can't go. Neither can she. She leaves the kitchen and gathers her girls, quickly. She tells them about the party moving to the park.

Nina says, "Okay. Y'all come go with me. I'll ask my mama, first. If she says yes, then y'all know it's on for all four of us."

"Nina! Let mama know me, Lynn, Junior…, you know, all of us are going too!" Ajay yells from the kitchen, trying to help their case.

He's trying to help his case too. He wants to go to the motel with his girl.

"Alright," Nina yells back. Then to her girls, she says, "Y'all come on," as they head out the door, going to ask mama Jo for permission.

Jo says it's okay for Nina to go, without hesitation. Then they call Rena from Jo's house. She says okay for Rebbie and so does Sandy, as T-baby smiles. Then Nina asks her mother to call Pearl. They all know her and John are having private time. Jo calls and tells her the girls request.

"I gave Nina, my okay. Sandy and Rena are letting Trisha and Ree Ree go too. So, what do you say?" Jo asks Pearl.

"Let me talk to Ebony," Pearl says and Jo gives Ebony the phone.

"Hello," Ebony answers with her fingers crossed.

"You know you have a curfew, right?" Pearl asks.

"Yes ma'am. Two O'clock."

"Okay and it's for two o'clock, no later. Don't forget that."

"I won't, ma," she says.

"Also, Jb comes home when you come home. He's already been told, so you just remind him for me. Alright?"

"Yes ma'am."

"Have fun, sweetie. Bye-bye."

"Bye, mama."

Ebony hangs up. She looks sad, just to give her girls a scare. Then she breaks into a smile.

"I can go!" she yells as they all burst into laughter.

"Alright! Alright! Alright, alright, alright!" they chant together, as they collapse into a huddle and dance around in circles.

"Alright, already!" mama Jo yells, "Go on. Have fun and get your asses back here at two. And not, two oh one! Y'all got that?!"

"Yes ma'am. We got it," They say as they rush out of the side door.

"Y'all, this is gonna be the bomb," T-baby says, after they're outside.

"We're gonna be balling at the park," Nina says as they break into another song.

"Doing it in the park! Doing it after dark! Oh yea! Must be crew! Oh yea! Must be crew!"

Then Ebony stops them just before they get to Chill's front door.

"I have to tell y'all something," she says.

"What's up, Eb?" Rebbie asks.

"Me and Anthony. We're not going to the park," she says.

"What? What are you talking about now?" they asks.

"Chill got us a room at the motel. He's gonna drop us off and scoop us up, on his way back," she boasts.

"Oh shit! He should've got all of us a room," Nina says, as she's always down to have private time with Tank.

"I'm saying, girl," T-baby adds.

"What are you saying, T-baby? Remember you're not even doing it yet?" Ebony asks in a joking manner as she laughs.

"Oh please! Kid, if I had Rich in a motel room, I'll bet I would," she says in a matter-of-fact tone.

Though it isn't going to be tonight, they figure it won't be much longer. Because T-baby and Rich are getting tighter by the day. So are Rebbie and June, for that matter.

The foursome head back inside Chill's house. They're happy and content knowing they can go to the park with their crew.

"So what's up with the *awesome* foursome?" Jr asks.

"We're going too, cousin! What's up?" Nina asks boastfully.

"Well, alright then," Chill says, "Let's put this *muthafucking* party on wheels!"

Everybody grabs the gear and loads it into their cars. Ebony, Ajay, Nina and Tank ride with Chill and Renee, in their 1989 Blazer. Everyone pulls away together. They're in waxed rides with nice rims and their stereos

bumping. They parade down the street, slowly. Some of the crew members hang their heads and hands out and wave at neighbors as they pass.

Chill is bumping, *N.W.A.* when *Parental Discretion Iz Advized* comes on. He comes right in on *The D.O.C.*'s verse. Tank raps *Dr Dre's* verse to a tee. Ajay follows Tank with *MC Ren's* verse. Jb would usually do *Ice Cube* and June would do *The D.O.C.*, while Rich would do *Easy-E*. Since Jb isn't in the ride, Ebony jumps in, right on cue and does *Ice Cube's* verse.

"I be what is known as a bandit! You gotta hand it to me when you truly understand it! Cause you fail to see, read it in Braille. It'll still be funky!"

She continues as everyone bobs their heads. When Easy E's verse comes up, everybody chimes in. Everybody is jamming and bobbing their heads. Renee, Ebony and Nina are dancing in their seats and snapping their fingers, just having a great time. They arrive at the motel.

Chill pulls into the parking lot and up to the front of the room. All the other cars pull into the lot behind him.

This crew rolls thick when inside or outside of their area. This is a must. A rule Chill strictly enforces and for a good reason.

"Alright, crew. Here y'all go. I gave you the key, right?" Chill asks as he looks back at Ajay before looking at Ebony and smiling.

"Yea, dog. I got it," Ajay says as he opens the door, hops out and Ebony slides out behind him.

"Don't forget to pick us up at one thirty, Chill. *Please*," Ebony says as she grabs Ajay's hand, "And oh yea, remind Jb that he has to come home *with me* at two. Mama told me to remind him."

"Alright. They got it, baby girl. Let's go in," Ajay says as his face darns a slight smile.

"Yo, Ajay. Keep your beeper on, bro. If anything go down, we'll hit you up," Tank says.

Ajay nods as him and Ebony turn and walks toward room 111. All the vehicles remain exactly where they are, as they head to the door. Ebony looks back and waves to Nina, who waves back as Chill and the rest laugh.

"Get on in there, girl," Tank yells jokingly, "So we can go!"

"*Why* are they all still sitting there?" Ebony asks Ajay, "Nobody is leaving."

"They're waiting until we get inside," he says.

He puts his arm around her shoulders. When they reach the door, he puts the key in, turns the lock and pushes it open. He holds the door open, so she can walk in first. A few homeboys shout, *"alright"* and other forms of approval. Ajay walks in, closes the door and locks it. That's when the crew vehicles pull away.

Ajay turns on the light in Room 111. Chill had stocked the room with everything they'll need for a night of romance. Ajay turns on the boom box Chill had left in the room, immediately.

"Chill thought of everything, didn't he?" Ebony asks.

"Yea. He's always on point. That's why he's my dog, for life," Ajay says, "Check this out. I'm gonna roll this up, right quick. Just relax."

"Got to get our heads right, ha?" she asks with a smile.

"Uh huh," he says smiling back with that stare that always makes her insides tingle.

"Why don't you get comfortable, while I roll this up," he suggests as he glares at her and his eyes have a definite sparkle to them.

He's already in the mood. She can see it in his eyes. She knows that look now. Its the stare that took her the longest to decipher because she hadn't learned to think in terms of sex and what it is to him. How he yearns for it. It became clearer, Sunday night when she let him raise her night shirt above her breast, which gave him the full view of her in her bra and panties. His eyes turned to what they are now. They're dancing while smiling at the same time. It's *oh so* sexy and she's still *fully* dressed. Sunday night, he didn't remove her panties. He just moved them from over his target. The look in his eyes tonight, says fumbling and sucking nipples around lacy garments, isn't going to quench his thirst. He wants to have, *real sex.* The full on nudity with the lights on, so he can see *what he's working with,* kind of sex. That's what these eyes are that he's giving her, at the moment. He's never said it nor has he ever pressured her, for sex. But she swears at this very minute, he can see her naked. He has a vision in his mind. His stare is double the intensity it was Sunday. He finishes rolling the weed and puts it on the nightstand. His eyes never leave her.

"Chill got you some Zen [*White Zinfandel*] over here, on ice. Do you want some?" he asks.

"Yes," she says as she stands to go get her wine.

"Sit on the bed, baby. I'll bring it to you," he says with a smile.

She sits back down and picks up the remote. She clicks on the TV and switches it to *B.E.T.* She takes off her *K-Swiss* and ankle socks. The shoes was a gift from Ajay. He's always buying her nice things and giving her money to buy what she wants. He's a hustler, who always keeps a fat pocket. He brings their wine over in the glasses, Chill had provided. He sits down next to her and takes off his shoes and socks. Then he stretches over to the nightstand to get a blunt and his lighter. She's sipping her wine and watching video's. He's still watching her and how neat she's dressed. Her crop top which ties up just below her breast, makes her look even sexier to him. It reveals her six pack abs and her thin waistline. Her skin is cocoa brown and as smooth as a baby's bottom. She's wearing denim skorts, a skirt and short combo, which flatters her shape, nicely. She has her hair pulled up in a big bushy pony tail. She accents it with spiral curls. The curls hang down along her forehead, the side of her face and down the back of her neck to her shoulders. Her hair is long and shiny, just like her mothers. Her gold-hoop earrings with matching chain and ID bracelet, a birthday gift from her grandparents in Houston, accent her brown skin, perfectly. She's beautiful. He smiles when he realizes that, at this moment and for the next few hours, she's all his. There's no one here to interrupt them. No other women here to heave mean eyes at her and she is definitely all the woman he needs.

I want to see her body without clothes on it. I've never seen her naked.

"Here. Fire this up," he says as he passes her the blunt and the lighter, "Give me your glass."

She does. He takes it back to the ice chest to refill it.

"Are you trying to get me messed up or what?" she asks with a smile.

"Yea. Just a Lil bit. You know, so you can relax for me," he says.

He's very familiar with this action. He removes his shirt. She watches him as he walks over to the ice chest to fill her glass. He's drop dead handsome. At 14 years old, he is already 6 feet, 2 inches tall. He has a medium build and weighs 180 pounds, easily. He lifts weights religiously, so he can *"get bigger and stronger,"* he often says. The daily weight lifting is very evident. He legs are all muscle. His defined biceps and washboard abdomen gives his physique the look of a grown man. His skin tone is very dark. His shiny

black hair which he keeps in braids, is almost the length of hers. He has narrow dark eyes which seem to pierce her whenever she tries to look directly into them. He's tall, dark, slender and handsome. He's athletic and solid. And he's all hers tonight.
Am I ready for this? Oh God. He's got a big one. I remember that much.

He comes back over to the bed, sits her glass on the nightstand, next to his, then sits down near the head of the bed. He fluffs the pillows against the headboard and leans back against them.

"Here you go," she say as she passes the blunt back to him.
She's still sitting at the end of the bed. He wants to change her positioning.

"Bring it up here," he whispers, still with that glare in his eyes.
She makes eye contact with him and her heart races. She blushes. She feels almost afraid as she slides up toward the head of the bed, where he leans, surveying her every move. She rests her head on the pillows he had fluffed for her. She passes him the blunt. She can feel his eyes on her. She feels like *prey*.

"Are you trying to get *me* high?" he teases as he takes the blunt and takes a long hit off of it.

"Maybe," she says smiling again as she dares to look into his eyes.
Oh my God!

She's nervous. There's no doubt in her mind what these eyes mean. He picks up the remote and turns off the TV. Then he turns up the boom box where that favorite slow jam tape of his is playing.

"You want a gun?" he asks.

"Not too strong," she says.

"Come here," he demands.
They lean in and he blows her a charge.

"Hold it in," he says through his clinched teeth.
He's coaching her. Something he's use to doing. She holds the smoke in for as long as she can, then she blows it out of her nose and mouth.

"Uh. You've been practicing?" he asks.

"I guess," she answers.
They smoke the whole blunt, although he smokes most of it, as they sip their wine. She feels very buzzed and relaxed by the time they finish it. She's

keeps squinting her eyes because it seems extremely bright in the room, all of a sudden.

"Let me turn off this big light," Ajay offers.

He clicks on the lamp above the nightstand before he gets up to turn off the ceiling light. He comes back to the bed and lays down, scooting his body onto the bed. This time, very close to hers. He rubs his fingers across her very flat stomach. She's feeling very nervous and she can still feel his eyes on her.

"You can lay all the way down, baby," he whispers. He continues, saying, "Lay next to me and get comfortable I don't bite. Not hard, anyway."

She smiles as she scoots her body down until her head rest, firmly on the pillows. He's still watching her.

"Let your hair down for me," he says.

She lifts herself up onto her elbows and pulls the ribbon and ponytail holder, that until now had been holding her hair up. When she removes it, her hair parts off on the right side and rests on her shoulders. Having her hair down, makes her look more grown up to him. He says, "You're sexy as a muafucka, baby. Do you hear me?" He takes a big sip of his wine.

"I'll bet they're having a ball at the park," she says.

"I'm not even thinking about the park, baby," he says as his eyes are still surveying her. He adds, "It's all about you and me, tonight."

He pulls her close to him as *The Isleys* play from the boom box. He begins to kiss her, gently. He's running his fingers though her hair and caressing her body with his other hand. She moans. His kisses grow more intense. She can't believe for the first time, they are completely alone. He starts kissing on her neck.

"Ssss," is all she can muster.

He likes that and she can tell.

It must've sound normal to him.

He unties her blouse and unbuttons it, as he looks for her eyes. She can't even look at him now. He knows he's in complete control. His eyes are almost taunting her, as he slides his fingers underneath her top, then under her bra. He touches her nipple and whispers, "I wanna taste these."

He unfastens her bra and opens it, exposing her firm breast and nipples, which are instinctively hard. He caresses them as his tongue explores her

mouth. She rolls her hips because that feels like the natural thing to do. "Oh yea," comes from him but it sounds more like a heavy exhale.
He's obviously turned on by her reactions to what he's doing. He adjust his body and begins sucking on her nipples as his hand slides down her body. He breathes even harder as he unfastens her skorts and unzips them. He switches nipples while his busy fingers finds her clitoris. She moans louder and breathes harder.
This feels good.

"Uh huh," he moans.
All of this is normal to him. She feels as if she's doing it right. He plays with her clitoris, masterfully. He's doing that right too. That's for sure. She feels as if she wants to explode. Suddenly, he raises up and straddles her. He raises her up, so he can remove her top and bra, completely. He glares at her, for a few seconds, as his eyes meet hers. Then he's back to his mission of getting her undressed. He kisses her nipples and plays with them with his tongue. She breathes heavier. He removes her *skorts* while kissing her breast and stomach. He uses his free hand to remove her panties.
"I really like these," he says as he smiles and admires her underwear, "You know I'm keeping 'em, right?" he adds some light humor to relax her.
He wants her to relax and not focus on the penetration which is sure to come, momentarily. He's still smiling. Only now he's staring into her eyes. She feels as if she'll melt right off of the bed.

"What?" she asks in a soft voice, "What do I wear home?"

"Just me," he says and kisses her, quickly. Then he says, "You know I *gotta* keep something to remind me of you. I'll be looking at these panties every day and night, until you come back to me."

"I need something too. Give me something to remind me of you."

"I plan too," he whispers, "I planned this night, years ago."
He stands up and quickly removes his pants. She can see the bulge of his penis, as it protrudes out under his boxers. He catches her staring at him. "What? You want this?" he asks, "Tell me you want it, baby girl."
He pulls the top of his boxers away from his stomach, reaches down inside of them and grabs hold of his penis. He pulls it up and over the top of his boxers, exposing its full view to her.
Oh dear God! It's bigger than I remembered. I can't do this.

TIME TO LEARN-RELOADED-Time Will Reveal-part 1

She blushes, then looks away. She's embarrassed he'd caught her looking at him and at being afraid of the size of it. All in all, she's still very shy. He isn't shy, at all.
"Why are you covering this body?" he asks as he grabs the covers.

"Turn off the lamp, first," she tries.

"Ah, baby girl. Let me see you," he whispers as he removes his boxers and climbs back into bed, next to her.

"Uh uh," she says.

"Why not? You're gonna let me fuck you but I can't look at you?" He's impatient now as he rips back the spread, she's hiding under. He flings it all the way off the bed. His face takes on a totally different expression. Officially, this is the first time he's ever seen her, completely naked. He takes it in.
"I like your body, baby girl," he says, "I've laid in my bed and tried to imagine what you looked like, naked," he says as he glares at her nakedness, "You're perfect, Ebony. I love your body. All of you. Yes Lord. I like it!"
I like it, a lot. This is gonna be my wife. I want this, forever.

He smiles as he climbs on top of her. Soon, they're kissing again, very hard and with a lot more fervor. He grinds his body on top of hers while kissing her gently on her face, chin and neck. Then more aggressively, as he puts his tongue in her ear. She jumps, then moans. He feels she's ready and he knows he is, as he whispers in her ear, "Open your legs, baby."
She's feeling so good, she's forgotten to be afraid of the penetration or it being painful. Ajay has the skills needed to make her want him, even if she can't handle his size. She wants him, so she naturally obeys his commands. He kisses her again as he positions himself for insertion. He looks deep into her eyes. He wants to see her expression when he enters her. He definitely wants her to see his too. She can feel the head of his penis, touch the lips of her vagina. Before she can completely brace herself, with 1 quick dip of his hips, he's inside of her.
"Ssss. Oooo," he moans.
He's inside of her now, as he looks at her again. He smiles slightly. She's loosening her brace and allowing herself to relax.
It didn't hurt going in, this time. But I fill like I'm stretched. Oh God! A lot!

TIME TO LEARN-RELOADED-Time Will Reveal-part 1

He begins to move slowly, back and forth, inside of her. He's being cautious. He doesn't want to give her *too much*, too fast. He doesn't want to hurt her or make her shy away from giving herself to him. The way she had done on Sunday night. He has to assure her and make her feel comfortable, so she'll want to do this again and again.

"Mmm, it's so good," he whispers as he stares down at her face.

She blushes. His motions switch. Now he's moving from side to side. She moans at this change in direction. Her insides feel invaded and filled to capacity. Her vagina feels as if it could tear apart, at any second, if he makes any sudden moves.

But it feels good. It's not hurting like it did in my room.

"Do you like this?" he whispers as if he can sense that she's trying to work it out in her mind.

The vibration of him talking while inside of her, sends tingles through her body. Instantly, she learns that she likes it when he talks while he's inside of her. She's in luck. He loves plenty of conversation with his sex.

"Mmm, yes I like this," she whispers as she closes her eyes.

He adjusts his body again. He clinches both of his fists, full of her hair. He wants to take the pressure off of his elbows. He rests his head on her shoulder and goes deep inside of her.

"Oh! Oh! Wait a minute," she yells first, then whispers as she tries to pull back because she's just a little bit afraid.

"Uh uh, baby. Let me feel you," he whispers softly into her ear.

"Don't hurt me, Anthony. Please," she whispers.

"Okay. I won't," he says as he kisses her cheek.

He strokes her, ever so gently. He's breathing faster and directly into her ear. This makes her insides tingle, a lot more.

"Mmm. Uh huh," she whispers in response to this new feeling.

Damn! That sounds sexy as hell!

He strokes her a little faster. It feels even better to her. Her pussy becomes moist, which eases that feeling of choked tightness, she'd felt earlier. She starts to move with him like he showed her on Sunday night. She hadn't been able to do it then, because it was her 1st time. It was too painful then. But that's not the case tonight. Tonight is great! Tonight is wonderful!

TIME TO LEARN-RELOADED-Time Will Reveal-part 1

"Yes, baby. Bring me these hips," he whispers.

She begins to grind against him. He lets out a deep moan. She can't help but flash back to the 4th of July incident, of him in his bed with Anita. How she was able to handle his thrust and throw them back at him. She starts to imitate what she'd saw Anita doing. As soon as she starts to mimic Anita, he pauses and looks at her. His facial expression changes to 1 of confusion.

"Where did you get that from?" he asks, of her gyrating movements.

"I'm just trying to do what you want me to do," she tries.

"Just do what I taught you, okay? That's exactly what I like. Do it like we've practiced it, for three years," he instructs.

She does as she's told. He responds with a slight gasp, as he whispers,

"Ah, Ebony. Your pussy is so good. I've waited my whole life for this."

"Oh! ssss oooo yes." she moans, almost non-stop from this point on.

"Do you like it like this, baby girl?" he asks, "I need to know what you like, so I'll know what to do to you from now on. Okay?"

"Mmm. Yes, Anthony."

She holds him tighter and he starts to stroke her in rhythms. She can feel a tingling in her body.

"Oh! Oooo, Anthony. Yes. Ssss."

"Come on wit it, baby," he says as if he's ordering her too.

She buries her face in his chest.

"I wanna get this pussy wet, baby girl."

"Mmm."

She moans and holds him tighter. They grind against each other. He's sweating and moving his ass like a professional.

"Mmm, baby yes," she whispers.

She can feel her body start to tighten up. This feeling is so tantalizing. Her body feels so good inside. She can't hold back her words, anymore. She's talking about every feeling that's coming over her, right now.

"Anthony! I like it!"

"Ssss, baby," is all he can muster because she feels good to him too. His motions switch again. Now they're going back, forth and side to side. Eventually, they move in a circular motion. She can feel her body tightening up, even more. She squeezes her eyes closed as she wonders what's happening to her, at this moment. He squeezes her tighter and jams his dick into her, in rhythms. He's talking, a lot. They're in a solitary motion as they

ride against each other in perfect harmony. He's still whispering in her ear and mixing the whispers with kisses, while sucking passion marks on her neck and chest. She feels a seizure coming on but it's not a painful one. The seizure feels good. But a seizure? She wonders why is she having a seizure?
What's happening to my body? He's gonna think I'm crazy!

There's a feeling creeping up on her. One that she can't control. She tries to breathe normal but she can't. She can hear him. He's still whispering in her ear and licking on her. Still kissing her, sucking on her body. He knows where she is, even though she doesn't. She's exactly where he wants her to be. He starts to whisper in a demanding tone,
"Come here, baby. I want you to cum for me."
What is he doing to me? I like it. I like it, a lot. God! I hope he knows I like it! Keep doing it like this, Anthony baby!

"Yea. You're about to get this pussy wet, baby," he whispers, which drives her farther into that realm known as satisfaction.
Her body is out of control. This is definitely not something she has felt before and this isn't even the best part. That's still to come. There's no holding back now, even if she wanted too.
Sex is so good! I see why he wanted to do this again.

She wonders why she had *ever* been afraid to do it. His 6 years of sexual experience is definitely paying off. He's making her feel, *so good*.

"Oooo, yes baby! Ssss. Mmm, baby. This is *so good*!" she barely manages to say, before her body suddenly explodes.
"Oh, Anthony!" she screams as her lips and her body start to quiver and shake uncontrollably. "Oh baby! Yes! Yes! Yes! Oooo, yes! It feels *so good*!"

"Uh huh, baby girl. Yea. Get it, baby! Get it! Get it!" he says, still in her ear and still in a demanding voice.
His voice sounds stern and yet, sexy at the same time. A voice much louder than the whispers, earlier. He's nearly yelling and almost out of breath. But he keeps at it. He keeps kissing her and sucking on her. On her breast and on her neck. He knows where they both are and he's got much more to give.
"This is what I wanted to give you," he says as he stares down at her face, "I want you to remember this about me. Do you like it, baby? Ha?!?"

He wants to know if she's enjoying it as much as he is. She nods her head, very quickly. She's unable to speak coherently but she's *totally* into it. She has flung her legs out to either side, giving him full access to her. He likes that she's comfortable with how he's making her feel, tonight.
"Mmm, yes baby. That's that juice, right there," he whispers, "Ebony, you look so sexy when you cum. Damn! I get to see this for the rest of my life."
He watches her climax and becomes even more aroused. She's way out of control, right now. She's kissing him all over his neck and face. The way he was doing to her, at the onset. He rams his tongue deep into her mouth. He's kissing her like he's thirsty and the only source of quenching his thirst, is deep within her throat. He pulls her legs up into the air and strokes her like a piston into the well oiled machine, which she is. She has just had the 1st orgasm of her lifetime. She's in ecstasy.
This has to be what Lynn and the older girls always talk about. The reason why they like sex.

She's loving this session. All of sudden, he goes for broke. He takes his dick straight to the bottom of her pussy. He goes for all of the pussy she has and for the 1st time tonight, she feels pain. She hadn't realized it. But until now, he hadn't submerged his entire penis inside of her.
"Ouch! Ouch!" she screams.
"Give me this pussy, baby girl," he demands.
"Wait! Anthony?!" she pleads, "It hurt me, baby. It hurt me."
He's gone deaf?!

Thinking he can't hear her, she says it louder and louder, still. She's feeling that with his heavy breathing, he hadn't heard her the first 4 times. But he *can* hear her. He can hear her, well. He's just at the point of no return. She'll learn that later too.
"Take it, baby. Take it, for me. Come on," he whispers, breathing very hard and pleading with her not to make him stop.
"Oooo, Anthony! Please, baby! Stop it, please! I can't take it!"
She pleads but he continues giving her more than she can handle.
"I want to fuck you good, baby. Before you take my pussy away."
His voice is so deep now, that it drags. It's rather odd but he sounds very sincere. She wants to please her man, so she tries to hold him and caress his

back. But each painful stroke, causes her to dig her nails into him, just as she had done on Sunday night. He feels the need to control her wrist.
"Baby, give me your hands," he says, still breathless.
He pulls her arms up above her head. Holding her hands down at the wrist, with 1 hand, he grabs her leg with the other hand and pushes her knee in an outward direction. This move spreads her completely open to him. He grinds harder, still. She pleads with him more. But he is passed the point of compromise. He wants his climax. He wants his first nut with her.
"I waited a long time for this, Ebony. Please let me have it, baby."
She can feel tears rolling down her face. She's not ready for all he has.
How will I ever be able to be his lady, if I can't please him in bed? Anita was able to handle him.

Anthony is a very sexual young man. She feels the woman who pleases him in bed, will be the one he'll spend his time with. He knows what he's doing. He's been training her to be that woman. It's what he had said each and every time, over the 3 years of first, that led up to Sunday night. Then after he had her virginity, he told her things would be different the next time. He said she would be able to handle it better. He promised her pleasure from then on.
Okay. I felt pleasure and it was great tonight. At first. Sunday night, I couldn't scream loud. Now it's taking all I have not to call for help.

"Oh stop! Please, Anthony!"
He pauses and whispers, "You said you was gonna let me finish, the next time, baby. You can't tell me to stop now. I gave you yours. You have to give me mine's too. Don't tell me to stop. You're mine, Ebony," he resumes, "Give me these guts, girl! Come on. Work it for me. Ssss. Mmm. Yes! Yes!"
I can't do this! I'm going to die in here. Oh God!

He's going for gold and maybe even Platinum too. He's loud enough to be heard outside of room 111. She doesn't know whether to hold on to him or to scream for help. He's getting louder. His demands, more fierce. He almost sounds angry as he talks to her.
"Oh baby! This is good! Mmm. Oooo shit! Oh! Shit! Shit! Uh!"
His body gets tight as he slings dick in her like she's been fucking for years.

Suddenly, he throws his head back. The expression on his face is so intense, it nearly frightens her. She realizes he's getting his. He's at his climax. It last for 20 seconds or more but seems longer. Eventually, he slows down the jabbing of his dick into her and catches up to his breath. He lays still on top of her with his back rising and falling with each breath. The quick jerks of her body settle down as they both become calmer. The only movements right now are involuntary.

I lived through it. He's kissing my face. It feels so good! He must still like me.

"Oh, damn. Baby girl, baby girl, baby girl," he says as he lays on top of her, "That was *so* good."

She's still crying from the post orgasmic pounding she'd taken from her man. He's kissing her wet face. He's still inside of her. His dick is a bit softer now but not completely. She can still tell that it's there. She can feel it pulsating.

"Don't cry, baby. Come here," he whispers as he's still barely able to breathe.

"You hurt me, baby," she says softly.

This makes the tears continue and become even heavier. She wants to be spoiled and *right now*.

"I'm sorry. I'm sorry, baby girl," he whispers as he wipes her tears away, "You felt so good to me. I couldn't stop ," he pauses a second as he looks down into her eyes, "I couldn't stop."

He's still trying to catch his breath. He says, "Don't cry. Please, baby. I don't want you to cry. I wasn't trying to hurt you. You was throwing this pussy so hard and good. Shit, I got carried away. I'm sorry. I mean that. Okay? I didn't wanna make you cry."

"I thought I was ready, for a minute. *Dang*," she says as she smiles slightly, though her fading tears.

"You was working it, girl."

"Yea *right*," she says in a doubtful tone as they both laugh.

"Trust me, baby. You're working wit something," he whispers, "Something I want all for myself and for the rest of my life too."

For the next 5 minutes, they lay staring into each other's eyes. He's looking at it like he's laying with and holding his future. She feels as if she's let him down. Like she didn't learn the skill she's been training for, for over

3 years. His eyes aren't saying this to her but she doesn't know this stare yet.

When they catch their breath, he kisses her. His kiss has so much passion in it that it brings a tear to her eye.

Then he says, "Damn! I'm starving in this muthafucka."

"Me too," she agrees.

"You want some pizza?"

"Oh yes. That'll work!" she says very enthused.

"Order it baby. Order whatever you want."

That phrase rolls off of his tongue, so effortlessly. He stretches across the bed, on his back. He grabs a blunt and lights it. While smoking, he watches her from his peripheral. She's still naked when she stands up.

"Ssss, sexy," he says and smiles.

She smiles as she puts on his white t-shirt and grabs the phone. She calls *dominos* and places an order for delivery. She already knows his favorite pizza. She orders a meat feast with a root beer for him and an Italian sausage with a coke for herself. He lays on the bed, in the nude, blowing smoke rings toward the ceiling. He's not shy with her. He feels absolutely comfortable.

Suddenly, his pager vibrates. He picks it up and checks the number. It's from their crew at the park. Ajay sits up, still naked and puts her panties on his head. She laughs as she hangs up the phone.

"It'll be here in thirty minutes or less," she says as she still laughs, "You call, *me* goofy. That's goofier than anything I've *ever* done, Anthony."

"Uh huh. Let me see the phone," he says and smiles.

She places the phone on the bed, next to him. He dials the number he was paged from. It's Chill's cell phone number but it could be either 1 of his crew brothers.

There are only 4 people *they know* who own a mobile phone. Dr. Gladys Weston, Attorney George Wheeler, Ebony's father John and big Chill.

"Yo! What up!" Tank yells, answering Chill's cell phone.

"What's happening, crew?" Ajay asks.

"Look here, man. Y'all cool and shit?" Tank asks.

"Yea. We *chilin'*. We just ordered some pizza. What's up?"

"Alright. Well check this out. We fixin to try to move something. You know what I'm saying?"

"Alright, alright. Hey y'all need to swing through and get me. You know I'm down with that shit. Y'all need to come through," Ajay says. He's always down to do some crew dirt.

"Hey, we got you this time, homie. I know my twin is in heaven, right now and shit. She's kicking it with, *her Anthony*. This is her last night. Go on and kick it wit her. She'll stop talking to me, if I pull a move like that. We'll handle it. For real," Tank says and chuckles.

"Alright. I feel you, man. We chilin then," he says.

He can hear his dogs in the background, still sending chants of approval.

"Guess what, man?" Tank says suddenly.

"What's up?" Ajay asks.

"Rich and T-baby done got lost, for a minute. You think he gone hit tonight or what?" Tank asks as he laughs.

"It's time too. Much as they be fuckin wit each other," Ajay says.

"Nina boo and Ree Ree bout to drive me *and June* crazy. They talking bout let's go look for them. They not trying to be found," Tank says while still laughing.

"No shit. I know that fool ain't, anyway. I don't know bout T-baby but Rich not trying to see y'all muthafuckaz," Ajay says and laughs.

That statement makes Tank laugh harder. Ebony is trying to figure out what Ajay is talking about, just from hearing his end of the conversation. She knows it's something about her girl and his 1st cousin.

"Look here, man. It's just ten o'clock. Y'all still got time to do whatever," Ajay says, "I'm gonna get back to my baby."

"Alright, homie. I'm gonna step for now. Cool?" Tank asks.

"See ya, man" Ajay says.

"In a minute, partner," Tanks says.

They hang up and Ajay turns his full attention back to Ebony.

"You okay, kid?" he asks as she sits on the bed, next to him.

"Yes."

He moves closer to her as she looks into his eyes.

"You was good, baby. That's real," he says, "I really enjoyed you."

He's kissing her face and rubbing up and down her body.

"Was I better than her?" Ebony asks.

"Who? *Anita*?"

"Yes."

"Oh *God*, yea. Baby, it's not even close. I hate I did that bitch, even more, cause you caught me. And you're never gonna let it go. If I could make it where it didn't even happen, I would."

"I think it hurts more because you did it with her, in your room. We've never done it in your room," she says as she looks down.

"We can but I don't wanna get caught like Jb and Lynn did," he says, smiling while lifting her chin up.

"I don't want too, now. She's been in there."

"Okay, we won't. One day, I'm gonna build a house for us. You know I'm already drawing it. Me and you will be the only ones who'll have sex in it. Until I have a son," he says as he laughs. Then he changes the subject and says, "You know we got some time left before the pizza comes."

"Oh please, man. Already? Jesus! You amaze me," she says.

"Jesus? No, baby. I don't need that kind of competition," he jokes, "But amazing you, *is* my job."

"Well you're doing a good job, then," she says.

"Oh yea?" he asks while smiling.

"Yes."

"Well let me get back to work. Uh huh. Give me my shirt."

He smiles as he pulls his t-shirt over her head. He pulls her down on the bed, next to him. He starts to rub her, passionately. His body heats up. He starts kissing her again, as he rolls her over and on top of him.

At the park, everyone is having a blast. T-Baby and Rich are down the drive having private time in Jr's Cutlass. It's a chilly night for July.

"I've been waiting a long time for us to be alone again," Rich says, "Our families always have the celebrations at Ajay and Tank houses. They be using their own rooms. We never have a chance to get ours on."

"For real. We don't have them by my house, either," T-baby says, "But I could've used Ebony's room when she would go to Ajay's house. She won't do that now. Not since he had Anita in there. I know Ebony. She won't go in there and have sex. Not behind her."

"Yea but we're here now," he says, "We need to get to it."

"You're always saying that," T-baby says with a smile.

"You told me if we could get to ourselves, you would be down to get to the real," he says.

"I know and I am," she says, "But here?"
Initially, she's hesitant. Not about the act but about doing anything sexual in Jr's car. Only she doesn't want to be a virgin, any longer than tonight. She doesn't want to be the last one to do it. These 2 have already discussed getting married, in the future. She's already promised herself to Rich.

T-baby is Ebony's 1st cousin. Their fathers are brothers. Rich and Ajay are 1st cousin's. Ajay's mother and Rich's father are siblings. But when it comes to Ajay and Rich, they couldn't be more opposite. Ajay is confident, dominant and self assured. Rich is like Ajay's follower. He'll dominant but only if he feels he already has an advantage. He lacks self confidence and he always has. He's not the out front type. He's more of a co-captain. He'll go along, to get along. Only if it earns him stripes and praise. T-baby is bold and very head strong. She's not as fragile as Ebony. She's the aggressor in this relationship. She's not afraid of what she doesn't know. She's a whiz with numbers too. Math is her best subject but she's never had sex. That's 1 of the 2 trumps, Rich has on her. The other is the street game. She knows nothing about that sort of distribution but she calculates his product and tells him how much he can yield from it. Other than being an A-plus math student, she's a ball player at heart. Her main dreams consist of playing professional basketball and marrying Richard Williams Jr. Her parents want her to be an accountant. She says she'll take it up in college when her and her girls go. She plans to go on a basketball scholarship. But as far as tonight, she'd like to get this virgin thing behind her. She wants to assure Rich that she's his and only his.

"I can get Chill to take us to the motel," Rich offers.

"But Lynn has to go home in an hour," she says, "All of the girls have to be together. In case all our parents say we have to come on in at eleven, with her."

"Then going to Mentor is out of the question, for sure," he says.

"Who's in Mentor?" she asks.

"I know a spot out there," he says, "Belongs to one of the Indians."

"Indians?" she asks.

"Cleveland Indians," he answers, "The baseball team?"

"Oh, okay. But we can't leave the park, baby," she says.

"What do you wanna do, then?" he asks, "We can do it right here. Nobody's around."

She says okay. She wants to be with him, just as much as he wants her. She climbs over and into the backseat. Then she summons him to come along. He follows her. She takes down her shorts and tells him to pull her panties down. He does. She undoes his pants. She kisses him to give him more courage. The fear of the unknown is on her mind but she lays back and receives him. He enters her and it hurts terribly. She's too much of a soldier to quit, so she lays there and lets it happen. Rich even asks her if she wants him to stop.

She says, "No."

He continues, as the warm air from his lungs mixes with the cool air inside of the car to form clouds. This makes T-baby think she's colder than what she actually is. She asks him to turn the heater on. He stops, reaches over to the front seat and starts the engine. He turns on the heat, then returns to her and back to the action. The car warms up. The warmth brings relief from the sting of his penetration. They continue.

While the rest of the crew are still kicking it, Chill, Tank and Rob are planning a take back. Earlier, on the phone, Tank had brought Ajay up-to-date on the business they have to handle. The crew have been planning a sweep. A roll down on some busters who are trying to set up shop at 1 of their spots. Tonight is the night to bring it all to a halt. These intruders will have to leave the crew's set, *this evening*, dead or alive. How they leave is of no consequence to the crew and it wasn't from the start. So long as they would've vacated but they didn't. They tried asking them to leave. The intruders stayed on and still failed to pay rent. That's never going to go over well, in the street game. One of the highest forms of disrespect is to sell from someone else's turf without paying the owners. Chill and his crew know this, too well. They figure if these intruders are in the street game, then they know it too and are choosing to be disrespectful.

"Ay, let's go, man," Chill says.

"Cool but I need to let my lady go by your crib until we go get twin and Ajay," Tank says.

"We're taking the ladies over by Stoney's, until we get everybody together. In case some of our folks are up, across the street," Chill says.

Chill tells Tank, "Tell them to come on and lets go."

Tank turns to tell Nina it's time to leave. But her, Rebbie and Renee have walked off to look for T-baby.

CHAPTER 4

MURPHY'S LAW IN EFFECT

"Man, I told them to wait here and we could drive down there. But y'all know how they are about each other," June says.

"It's alright," Chill says and smiles, "We'll go down there and catch up to them. It's not far."

Chill, Tank, Rob and June get into his Blazer. Bre, Jb, Lynn and Jan, Jr and Angie get into the van with Stoney. Everyone else loads up in their rides to move the party out of the park before 11pm and back to East Cleveland. They're going to meet up at Stoney's house. Then they'll go to Chill's house, only after everyone is together again.

Nina, Rebbie and Renee make it to Jr's car. They can't see anyone sitting in it, so Nina decides to walk up closer to get a better look. She opens the door on the passenger side. She spots Rich and T-baby, lying in the back seat. He's on top of her with his pants and underwear down to his knees. T-baby's shorts and panties are hanging on her right foot. Rich is lying between her legs and they're having sex!

"Ah man! My bad, y'all!" Nina screams as she closes the door back, quickly. She says, "Oh wow! I'm *so* sorry. Oh my God!"

She rejoins Rebbie and Renee. The 3 of them stand with their hands over their mouths, in disbelief. They don't want to laugh out loud and embarrass T-baby or Rich, anymore than they already have.

"Okay, y'all," Renee says, "Chill out, alright? Don't say anything to them."

She's trying to keep Rebbie and Nina calm. She doesn't want them to speak on it, just yet. They're in shock at what they have just witnessed. They thought surely T-baby would've told them before taking this huge step but she hadn't.

Within a few minutes, the door to the Cutlass flings open. T-baby and Rich start to get out.

"Dog, Nina! You didn't have to come bussing up in the car, like

that!" T-baby says, laughing to hide her obvious embarrassment, as she adjusts her clothes and crawls out of the backseat.

"I'm so sorry, T-baby. I didn't know. Please. I'm sorry," Nina says as she tries not to laugh.

T-baby smiles and looks at Rebbie, who's hiding her smile behind her hands. When Rich crawls out of the car, all 4 females burst out laughing.

"Damn. We was *too wrong*," Nina whispers to T-baby, "We was teasing you like you wasn't down. You proved all three of us wrong."

Her and Rebbie give T-baby a pound. Rich keeps his head bowed and takes a few steps away from the females, as he waits for the Blazer driven by Chill. The ladies continue snickering as they wait a few feet from him.

"My girl didn't even wait on the motel room *either*," Rebbie says, intentionally trying to sound like a small child and they continue to laugh. Renee puts her arm around T-baby's shoulders. They walk over and stand next to Rich.

"You alright, T-baby?" Renee asks.

"I guess so but I'm sore," T-baby says.

"That's natural," Renee says, "You know y'all could've went to the motel, just like Ajay and Ebony did. Y'all could've ask me or Kenny."

T-baby says, "We was gonna come back and ask but then we just got…, you know. So we just went on and did it."

"Just so you know," Renee reiterates, "Y'all can. Just ask us."

"Alright," T-baby says and smiles.

Chill's Blazer and Stoney's van pull up and stop next the 5 of them.

"Hey, we have to roll by eleven o'clock," Tank says.

Jr, Angie, Jb and Lynn get into Jr's cutlass. Renee, Nina and Tank ride with Chill. Rob and the rest, pile into the van with Stoney. They all pull away. The other cars follow them as they head to Stoney's house.

"Hey, Rich. Where did you go?" June asks with a partial grin on his face.

He acts clueless to what had just gone down but most likely, he knows. The guys tell their plans to the other guys, faster than the girls do.

"Ah, bro. I just went to chill for a minute, that's all," he answers as he looks at T-baby.

She smiles slightly, then looks over at Rebbie, who just stares at her.

"Y'all paranoid or something?" Jan asks as her and Bre laugh.

They have a clue about what has happened, just like the guys do. But they don't say anything. Not just yet.

"Nah," Rich says, "Let me hit the blunt."

Jan passes the weed to him, then she pinches T-baby on the cheek.

"What?! *Ouch*," T-baby squeals.

She has a rise in her voice, indicating she's agitated or perturbed, just a little. She's trying to pretend nothing has happened. She actually feels paranoid as she realizes the others may already know.

"You tell me, cousin!" Jan says in a loud voice as she smiles.

"Cousin, leave me alone," T-baby says and looks away, this time.

Everyone has already figured out what's happened. It's just a matter of getting the sorted details and they'll do that later. They have gone through *"deflowering"* as a crew and family before. Each girl has had her day to sit and feel shy about this step into womanhood, with more girls to come. The sexually active females are familiar with the mood, afterwards. Still, T-baby and Rich will fill them in because that's the norm. This crew keeps no secrets and they stand in total support of each other, always.

This act between Rich and T-baby was destined to happen. At least, it was in their hearts and minds. To them, everything in their lives is patterned after their parents and grandparents. They're just playing out their destiny, the same way the Williams, Wilson's, Logan's and Brown's did it before this generation started. *Together*. T-baby and Rich are 2 of their offspring who have found each other. The only question now is, will they have the staying power and strength that their predecessors have?

Time Will Reveal.

They're all sharing a laugh as they jam to the *Eric B and Rakim* tape, Stoney is playing. *Microphone Fiend* is a banger.

They arrive at Stoney's house and everyone goes inside. Stoney turns the music on and the party continues. But the guys have a mission to complete before they can hang out.

"Hey men. Let's do this," Chill says.

"I'm ready," Rob says.

Chill, Rob, Tank and June get into the Blazer. Jb and Rich ride with Jr, in the Cutlass. They all roll out. They have to go handle the fools who are trying to takeover, *The Grove*.

TIME TO LEARN-RELOADED-Time Will Reveal-part 1

The Grove is a section, about 8 blocks from their street. Everyone in the game knows that area belongs to Chill and his crew. And it has for more than a decade, when their fathers crew took control of it. Their grandparents had acquired a strip mall near the university, in a similar way. The 2 pieces of property was given up as repayment for debts owed to them, is what this generation of crew was told. Both properties was always intended to be something Chill's generation could take and build on. Something to keep the families entrepreneurial spirit going.

So far, they have a detail shop at the strip mall. It's run by Rich Sr and Brian Sr, on a daily basis. The other shops are being rented out with the full understanding that this crew can take possession whenever they get their bearings and degrees.

The small warehouses in the Grove had been rented, as well. Papa Jackson Brown had done the paperwork. A down payment and 3 months rent had been paid in advance. That was 6 months ago. It was 3 months ago when the crew learned that some wanna-be hustlers had run the renters off and set up shop for themselves. The renters had informed papa of the takeover and that they hadn't made anymore payments because they didn't still have physical possession. The Grove is in what is known as, the *high heels to the concrete or working girls* district. In the 3 months since learning of the squatters, Chill had discussed a payment option with them. The terms were said to be understood. Yet, the new tenants have made no payments. There will be no other notices given. Tonight, they're being evicted by any means necessary.

There are streetwalkers catcalling at the Blazer as they pass through. But the crew are on a mission and have no time to chat. They get 1 block away from their destination before both vehicles pull off into an alley which runs behind the warehouses.

Chill says, "Load your shit."

They all do, then they open the car doors and hop out.

"Let's straighten these muafuckaz," Jb replies.

Everyone gets out of the vehicles with their straps already locked and loaded. They conceal them under their clothes, then walk up the alley to the back of their warehouses.

Rob says, "Alright, crew. This is the spot where these niggaz have been hooking from and ain't paid crew, one damn dime."

TIME TO LEARN-RELOADED-Time Will Reveal-part 1

"Y'all know what to do," Jr says, "Split up."
Jb, Chill and Jr are the front men. They get low and ease around to the front of the building. There's 1 guy outside, standing guard. Jb steals on him, punching him hard in the temple and knocking him unconscious. They drag him around to the side of the building where June and Rich are waiting to grab him. They do, then continue dragging him to the rear of the building. Rob is waiting with a silencer on his 9mm. He puts a round between the trespassers eyes before he can regain consciousness.
Checking the victims pulse, June says, "One down."
Rich gives the signal to Jb, then Chill, Jb and Jr storm the front door. Tank, June, Rich and Rob enter through the back door, simultaneously. The busters try going for their weapons but the crew have caught them off guard. They blast on them, immediately.

Tank, June and Rich confiscate all of the cash, drugs and anything else of value, they can find. The others check the bodies to make certain none of them are still breathing.

"Alright, crew," Jb says, "No traces."

They clean up any possible links back to them, then make their way to the back door and head back up the alley to their vehicles. They stash the loot and weapons in the trunk of the Cutlass. Tank and Rob jump in the Blazer with Chill. Jb, Rich and June get into the Cutlass with Jr. Before they pull away, Chill confirms the rendezvous point and time. They'll know what move to make, if 1 vehicle doesn't arrive. Slowly, they drive away in opposite directions.

Jr heads west, past Lorain and to The Chamber. Chill heads toward Euclid. He's going out of the way, in case *five-oh* are near. This way he can head them off by getting their attention, if need be. Thus, giving Jr enough time to get to the stash spot and get rid of the weapons and loot, then wait for the lead vehicle to arrive.

Chill hits Euclid Avenue and turns on Highland road, just to double back. Suddenly, a cop car jumps behind him. The patrol car drops way behind the Blazer but Chill knows it's there. They already have the high beams on him. The patrol car pulls up even closer and puts the spotlight on the Blazer.

"Fuck you," Chill whispers, "I saw you from jump."

"Everybody knows what to do," Rob says with a chuckle, "Damn, man! I'm on paper and shit."

"Hell, me too," Tank adds as he snickers.

All 3 of them are calm. Random traffic stops is something they're very familiar with because it happens to them about once a week.

"We don't have *shit* in here," Chill says, "They don't have no win. Just stay cool, homies. We're straight and we're all going home, tonight."

It's at that moment when the cops turn on the flashing lights and siren.

"Uh huh, muthafucka," Chill says, "I been seen ya ass. Come on wit it."

He's looking at the squad car from his side view mirror, when he says, "Be cool crew. As long as these muafuckaz don't try no brutality shit, then we're cool. We don't have nothing on us, so it's all cooler than a fan."

"What difference do *not* having nothing make?" Tank asks as they all snicker quietly.

They are all relaxed. Anyone young, black and of the male gender, are programmed to have a certain anxiety when in the spotlight of the boys-in-blue. It's common knowledge that young black males in America have an automatic bull's-eye on their backs. Crew are always prepared for non-warranted searches and temporary interruptions of their routine. Just to be jacked up, then sent on their way but not without a threat or two. With most likely, a taunting from 1 or both officers. That's the way most officers tend to treat them in hopes that they can entice 1 of them to speak foul or act aggressively. Any reason to justify cuffing them and hauling them off to jail. But the crew was reared on injustice. No such actions will come from these 3 young men.

Finally, they hear 1 of officers on the P.A, as he says,

"Pull your vehicle to the side of the road."

Chill does as the officer request and the squad car pulls up and parks behind them with the lights still flashing.

"Driver! Open your door, with your right hand and leave your hand on the door."

Chill does.

"Okay, driver. Slowly step out of the vehicle with your back to me!"

"Why? So you can shoot me in that muthafucka?" Chill whispers to Rob and Tank.

They all snicker as Chill follows instructions. The officer orders him to lay face down on the pavement. He orders Tank and Rob to get out and do the same. They do so, slowly. The 3 of them lay as close to each other as possible, so they can still communicate when the officers aren't paying attention. Neither of them say anything to each other. They know how to handle these situations. On any given day, 1 of them gets *jacked up* by the police. Tonight, these cops say the same lines that all of the others have said in the past, when they were jacking them up.
"This vehicle looks suspicious. We have to run your tag. Blah, blah, blah!"

First, the cops run their plates. Then while they wait for word from the station on the license plates, they frisk each of them. Crew knows this is bullshit. These officers know Chill, well. They've run his plates before and they know the plates are clean, just like the 3 of them are. But they still ask all 3 of them to provide identification and run them through dispatch. They find out each of them have priors for misdemeanors. Two are on probation. Neither are in violation. Not until after midnight. These police seem determined to change that, as 1 officer walks over to the Blazer and claims he smells marijuana. They know he's fishing for probable cause and even without it, he's most likely going to fabricate it.

"You guys got any drugs on you?" 1 officer asks.

"No sir," all 3 say.

"Then you won't mind if I check out the vehicle then, right?"

"No sir," Chill replies in a chipper tone.

In the past, he would've told them to get a warrant. But tonight, he knows he has to pick up Ebony and Ajay, so he's trying to save time. One officer goes over to the Blazer to conduct the search while the other officer goes back to the car to answer dispatch. The Blazer comes back registered to Renee Stewart, as it always does. Even though these cops knew that, they still question Chill about who the owner is.

"That's my fiancée', man," he answers routinely.

The officer asks for a phone number where she can be reached. Chill gives him his home phone, knowing no one is there. But he knows his answering machine will give the officer all the proof he needs, if that were all the officer really wanted. But theses officers want more. Like something they can hold the crew on. The officer radios the station, so they can try the phone number. Chill, Rob and Tank are still lying on the pavement as they give each other the, *this is the same bullshit* look.

A few minutes later, the officer replies, "We got an answering machine and the female said, *'This is the home of Renee Stewart and Kenny Payne,'* so your story just might check out this time."

Both officers chuckle as the guys lay still and quiet. They're wondering if the other car made it to the rendezvous point, unobstructed.

All of a sudden, the officer in the Blazer jumps out as if he's run across a gold mind and he needs witnesses.

"Well *lookie* what we got over here, partner," he says in a voice which is as arrogant as ever.

He has a partially smoked blunt in his hand. *He says* he found it in the ashtray of the Blazer but he didn't. The crew knows this, right away. They never smoke weed while in the process of carrying out a mission. They never drink pass legally drunk, when they have a mission to do. This sort of harassment is the very reason they don't. Not even when they're just riding around, do they smoke and drink. Even if they do, they always smoked it to the end and threw the residual out of the car. But these cops was looking for a way to frame them, from the moment they spotted the Blazer. Still, the crew remain calm. The officers call backup, for transport. Chill figured they would try this as soon as they called in the tags. The same tags they call in every *fucking* week.

"This is some more bullshit," Rob whispers.

"Hell yea, it is," Tank agrees.

"You guys are in violation. We're just gonna have to take you downtown," 1 officer gloats.

The cops around Cleveland want Chill, badly. They've been trying to get him for 2 years and couldn't. They always run him in for 1 thing or another. But they can never make anything stick. This will turn out to be bogus, as well.

The crew remain calm as back up arrives. The officers put Rob and Tank in 1 car, together. They put Chill in the other car, alone. They're going to try, once more, to see if they can get Rob and Tank to talk. But they're shit out of luck, this time too. This crew is all the way down for each other and they'll never turn.

The 2 arresting officers was planning to take a detour with Chill and try to beat any confession out of him, they could. But a call comes over the radio which stalls their plans.

"Calling all units in the area....," The dispatcher says.

The dispatcher continues, saying, *"there's a possible multiple homicide,"* and gives the incidents location. Chill comments that while they're wasting time jacking them up, they have some real work they can and should be attending too. The officers don't like his comment and they want to beat Chill for his arrogance. Two things prevent this. 1, they have to hurry up and get them in for booking and assist on the other call. 2, the crew are represented my attorney George Wheeler and these officers aren't willing to risk their pensions. This turns out to be a lucky break for the crew. At least, it seems like it at the time.

After arriving at the station, they place all 3 guys in the holding cell, together. It's 1:00am and Tank knows they aren't going to be out in time to pick up Ebony and Ajay. Furthermore, since he's a minor, he can only be released to his parent or guardian.

"Shit, man. This is fucked," Tank says, "I hate these assholes."

"This is some old trumped up shit and you know it," Chill says.

"Hell yea, man. I know these muthafuckaz is always on our dicks with this same fuck shit," Rob comments, "But they fucking up our plans."

Tank tries to stall the desk officers out, on calling his parents but to no avail. They're going to call, momentarily.

Chill uses his 1 call to contact Renee at Stoney's house. She calls George Wheeler. Within minutes, they are both in route to the station to pick up Chill and Rob. Renee had left Nina on the phone with Chill, so they could come up with a plan B for Ebony and Ajay.

"Tank doesn't have a bond. But because he's a minor, they'll only release him to mama P or big John," Chill tells Nina.

"Who's suppose to get Ebony and Ajay?" she asks.

"I need you to handle that for me, Nina," he says, "Page Junior and Jb. Tell them what's up."

"They've already called here for y'all, two times," she says, "That's why Stoney and them went to try and find y'all."

"Just beep him and tell him to go by the *tellie* and scoop your girl before Tank calls home. Alright? Because once Tank wakes up big John,

they're gonna already be on a tear. If they find out baby girl has been in a motel room, all night, the shit's gonna hit the fan."

"Alright. Let me page Junior, now," she says.

They hang up. She dials Jr's pager number, immediately. Rob is going to use his 1 call to check back with her and see if plan B has worked, before Tank makes his call home.

In the meantime, Tank still stalls the desk clerk, saying he'll call last. Everything seems as though it's going to work out but they're running out of time. The 2:00am hour is fast approaching. It's 1:30am and Ebony has only 30 minutes to make her curfew.

****

Meanwhile, at the motel, Ebony is growing nervous. She's been worrying Ajay for the past 30 minutes, about why they can't reach Chill or Renee. He's working overtime to keep her calm while trying to remain calm and appear at ease, himself.

"Where is Tank and them at?" Ebony wonders aloud.

"They'll be here, in a minute. Just calm down," Ajay tells her.

"I can't calm down. My mama and daddy are gonna kill me if they find out about this!"

"They're not gonna find out. We're gonna make it back in time, baby girl. Okay? Don't get all bothered, for nothing. They're not gonna find out."

"I hope not," she says.

She's trying to be calm about it, after noticing he isn't worried. But he never worries or shows emotion. Even when he should.

****

In Shaker Heights, Pearl has gotten up to look for her children. She goes out on the front porch and looks across the street to Chill's house. She looks up and down the street. Everything is quiet.

At the same time, Jo walks out onto her front porch. She's obviously concerned too. She sees Pearl outside, looking around, as well.

"You're looking for your crew too, ha girl?" she asks Pearl.

"Girl, yes. They know they was suppose to be here at two o'clock. It's a quarter till, by my clocks."

"Allen is walking the floor, in there, already," Jo says, "Lynn had better get her ass here soon or he's gonna be all over her."

"Jb too," Pearl says, "Ebony is suppose to bring him with her. I'll bet you she's sitting somewhere, trying to wait for him, to keep him out of trouble."

Suddenly, John comes out of the house in a hurry and rushes to the car. He's dressed and obviously upset.

"John, where are you going?" Pearl asks.

"To the police station to get Jeremy."

"What!?!" she yells.

"They called and said they picked him up, about eleven," John says, "He was riding with Kenny. The police claim they had drugs on them or something but they always tell that same lie. Jeremy was refusing to call home. They looked up the number, in his file and called."

"Oh Lord," Pearl says, "Wait, John. I'm going with you."

"No, Pearlie. You stay here and wait for the other kids. They're not together. Jb and baby girl must be on their way home, already."

He gets into the car and starts it up.

"John, calm down and be careful," she says.

He backs out of the driveway and pulls away in a hurry.

"Lord! These kids are gonna be the death of me," Pearl says.

After watching John leave, Jo goes into the house to get the keys to her van. She's worried now. Her and Pearl can't just sit and do nothing. Jo tells Al what happened with Tank. Then she asks him to watch the homes. He agrees to do that, so her and Pearl can go out to look for their other children. Jo and Pearl get into the van and head straight for the park.

****

Jr finally gets the page. He calls Stoney's house. Nina tells him about Chill and the others and that now, he has to pick up Ebony and Ajay. He's been sitting at the chamber, waiting for Chill, Rob and Tank, knowing something wasn't right.

"Alright," he says, "We're on our way to get them. But we're still across town. It's gonna take us a minute."

"They haven't called here," Nina says, "I know Ebony is tripping, by now. The desk clerk is away from the desk, so I can't even call them."

"They probably don't know where y'all at," Jr says, "I'll bet they've been calling Chill's house. Anyway, we're out."

They hang up. Jr and the guys are heading toward the motel. Jb is telling them he knows Ebony has panicked because it's passed her curfew. It's already 2 o'clock. He is correct.

****

"It's two o'clock. Where can they be?" Ebony asks, nearly in tears. Ajay tries to be cool about it because he doesn't want to upset her, anymore than she already is. But he knows something's wrong too because no one is answering his pages. He tries Chill's house again and again. He gets no answer. Suddenly, he gets a page. He reads the number out loud,

"Five-five-five-one-four-four-one. That's Stoney's crib."

He dials the number.

"Hello," Nina answers.

"Where the fuck is Tank and them at?" Ajay asks and Nina tells him what happened.

He's angry, as he says, "Damn, girl. Why didn't you page me?"

"I don't know your new pager number, by heart. My purse is still at Chill's house with my address book in it. I've been trying to call y'all for the longest. But there's nobody answering at the front desk. Jan and them just came back and gave me the number. Stoney *and junior,* on the way. Junior should be closer because Stoney and Bre just left," she says.

"They need to hurry they asses up. Baby girl's gonna lose her mind, in a minute."

"Let me talk to her," Nina says.

Ajay gives the phone to Ebony. Nina tells her what has happened with Tank and that Jr is on his way to get them.

"Oh, girl. Daddy's up? Oh *God*," Ebony says.

"Just chill out, Ebony. We're all gonna go home late and we're all gonna be in trouble, together. Just like always."

Nina tries to keep her best friend calm. So far, it's working. Ebony manages to laugh a little.

****

Jo and Pearl check the park from end to end. Of course, no one is there at this hour. The park closed at midnight.

"Let's head back our way," Pearl says, "Maybe somebody's home, by now. Or we'll go by Stoney's next. That's the only other place I would expect for all of them to be, outside of our neighborhood."

"You're right, I hope. You'd better be," Jo says as they start back toward home.

When they're passing the motel, Jo spots her nephew Jr's car. She watches as he turns into the motel parking lot and pulls forward to the front of the rooms. He pauses for a few minutes, then continues.

"Hey. There's Brad junior's car," Jo says.

"Go over there," Pearl suggests, "Let's see if he knows where the rest of them are."

Jo pulls into the intersection to make a U-turn. Jr doesn't see her when she does. As a matter of fact, he hasn't seen her at all. If he had, surely he wouldn't have stopped at the motel. Jo makes a U-turn and comes back, just in time to see Jb walk up to room 111 and knock.

Pearl yells, "John junior!" as Jo pulls up and parks behind Jr's Cutlass.

"You were suppose to be at home, an hour ago," Pearl says to Jb.

He looks stunned. Jr, Rich and June are still in the car. Their eyes are like a deer in headlights. They see Pearl and Jo and they know some shit is about to go down. Some bad shit, at that. Jb has already knocked on the door. So of course, Ajay, not hearing the commotion outside, opens the door and looks right into his mother's face.

"Ant!? What the hell are you doing in a motel?" Jo asks as she gets out of her van and barges her way through the door.

She's thinking he's in there with that older woman she'd heard he was messing around with, awhile back. She's been wanting to catch *this bitch* with her son. She's had plans of whipping her ass, for months.

But when she gets inside of the room and sees Ebony, her whole

expression changes. Ebony sits down in the chair, near the window, in the front corner of the room. She's already crying and scared to come out. Pearl, who's still outside fussing at Jb, is unaware of Jo's discovery. Jo walks back to the door. But first, she looks at Ajay in awe and confusion. Ajay takes a seat on the dresser.

"Pearl, you'd better come in here," Jo says softly, "You're gonna wanna deal with this one. I don't even have the words to explain it. Just come on in here and see it for yourself."

Lord. What is it Jo?" Pearl asks as she approaches the door.

She spots Ajay and thinks something's wrong with him, just by his expression.

She asks, "Ajay, what are you doing in here?"

Ajay looks down at the floor because he knows Pearl is about to get angry.

"Ajay, do you hear me talking to you, son? Answer me," Pearl demands.

She's so concerned with Ajay that she goes directly to him. She hasn't seen Ebony, off to the side, in the chair.

"What's wrong with you?" she asks Ajay with concern in her voice.

He doesn't say a word. He just looks at her, then at his mother, who's still standing in the doorway. Finally, he looks at Ebony and shakes his head. Pearl follows his eyes. She turns around and sees Ebony sitting in the chair, crying. Her pride and joy. Her only daughter, whom she trusted to do the right thing.

Initially, Pearl can't even speak. She tries to figure things out in her head. She stares at Ebony, for what seems like 5 minutes. Actually, its only seconds. Nobody says anything. The other guys get out of the car, just as Pearl's knees become weak. She drops down on 1 of them.

"Please tell me this is *not* what I think it is," Pearl whispers to Ebony, "*Please*."

Pearl gets louder, as Jb comes into the room to pick her up and tries to keep the situation from escalating while Ebony cries, even harder.

The next 15 minutes are complete chaos. Pearl pulls away from Jb and goes after Ebony. She begins slapping her in her face, her head and anywhere else she can get her hands. Ajay jumps up and grabs Pearl. With Jb's help, he tries to get her off of Ebony. All Ebony can manage to say is, "Please, mama. I'm sorry," over and over.

TIME TO LEARN-RELOADED-Time Will Reveal-part 1

Jo grabs Ajay's shirt and yells, "Let her go, son! This didn't have to happen. Why did you have to mess with her, now?!"
Jb has Pearl. He's trying to get her out of the room. Angrily, Ajay pulls away from his mother and goes to help Ebony.

"Are you alright?" he asks her.

The other 3 guys come into the room to help while Pearl is screaming out of control.

"Why Ebony!? I trusted you, girl! I trusted you and you *betray me* like *this*?! Why do you wanna do this to me?!" Pearl screams more, "I trusted you! I really did! Of all my kids, I always thought I could trust you, *not* to defy me!"

She's crying too. Jo has tears in her eyes as she shakes her head.

"What the hell is wrong with y'all children?!" Pearl yells as she looks around at everybody.

Still no one else says anything. They're just waiting for her instructions.

"I can't take this shit. Do you hear me?" Pearl says, slightly calmer, "Ebony, it's good you're going to mama's."

Pearl isn't known to curse in regular conversation, like Jo would. But this morning is an unusual circumstance. She looks at Ebony, as Ajay is still trying to comfort her. He puts his arms around her. She leans her head against him. She's still crying. She won't even make eye contact with anyone else in the room. Especially, not her mother.

"Move Ajay!" Jo screams, "I think you've done enough!"

He doesn't answer her. Instead, he wipes Ebony's face and tries to smooth down her hair where Pearl had pulled it out the ponytail holder.

"Leave her alone!" Pearl screams at Ajay.

She tries to pull Ebony away from him. Ebony clings to him, for dear life. Pearl pulls away from Jb and grabs Ebony again. As she goes to slap her, Ajay grabs her hand and pushes her, nearly pushing her to the floor.

"Move out of my way, Ajay! This is between me and my daughter!" Pearl screams, "This is not the time or place for you to be challenging me!"

"Then don't hit her no damn more and I'll move!" Ajay yells back. Yelling is something he *rarely* does and he doesn't even flinch. Everyone else looks shocked.

"Ajay, get your ass out of the way, right now!" Jo yells.

"No ma'am! I'm not gonna do that! I don't care how mad y'all get with me. I'm not gonna just *stand here* and watch her get hit, *like this*. Hell no! I'm not about to let *nobody* beat on her. Fuck that!"

He stands his ground as Ebony cries uncontrollably. June, who comes over to get Ebony out of the room, starts to plead with his aunt.

"Come on, Auntie Pearl. Please don't hit her no more," he pleads.

"Get your ass out of here and get in that van. Right now," Pearl says to Ebony.

Her voice is shaky but not quite yelling.

She adds, "All of you. Get the hell out of here."

June takes Ebony past Pearl and Ajay. They pass Jo, by the door and go on out to the van. Ajay watches Pearl as Ebony passes her. Pearl is staring at him but not in an angry way. It's a stare of surprise, shock and revelation. Ajay concedes his respect for Pearl through his eyes. Then he speaks.

"I can't let you hurt her, mama P," he says, attempting to explain his actions. He continues, "I didn't mean any disrespect to you. But I'll never hurt Ebony and I won't let nobody else hurt her, either. No matter what you think about me. I promised her that."

"Get in the van!" Jo yells to him.

He leaves both mothers in the room and heads to the van to check on Ebony. Pearl tries to calm herself before going out. Jb gets into the van with Ebony and Ajay. He gives Ajay a pound.

"We're gonna follow y'all," Jr says after getting Chill's ice chest, glasses and boom box out of the room.

He doesn't even look at his aunt Jo. He knows she'll just start yelling directly at him, if he looks at her. She does, anyway.

"You're damn right, y'all are!" Jo says, "Where the hell is Nina and Lynora?"

"At Stoney's house," June says.

"Well, let's go!" Jo demands as they all get in and pull away.

In Jr's car, they're discussing the events in the motel room. But in the van, it's quiet. Still, Ajay comforts Ebony during the ride while their mother's protest. He doesn't care. He's more concerned for Ebony's well being, than he is with their mother's being angry with him. Pearl can't take her eyes off of him.

They arrive at Stoney's. Renee has made it back with Chill and

Rob. Everybody is outside. They see Jr's cutlass park, then Jo's van pulls up and parks right behind him.

"Oh shit. There's mama," Lynn whispers to Nina.

Nina stands still and silent, as she looks at the van. She knows Ebony and Ajay are in it without even seeing them. Jo gets out and heads straight toward her and Lynn. She grabs Nina and pushes her toward the van.

"Get your ass in the van, now!" Jo shouts, "Come here, Lynora!"

Jo grabs Lynn and nearly pulls her to the ground, trying to get her to the van. Jb and Ajay jump out to go help Lynn. Jr tries to help too.

"Come on, auntie. Please let her make it," Jr tries.

"You'd better get out my way, boy!" Jo yells and Jr does just that.

Lynn manages to get free, as she stammers to her feet. She runs to the van and jumps in.

"Breanna, you and Janice, Trisha, Rebbie! Let's go! Right now!" Jo screams, "For everybody involved! All of you had better get your asses to my house, in five minutes. Let's go and you'd better not let me beat you there!"

She's very angry and everyone knows it. Those who don't know why, don't dare ask. The look on Jr and June's faces are telling enough. With Ajay and Ebony being in the van already, they figure the rest out. When Nina gets into the van, she's surprised to see Ajay holding Ebony and her laying on his shoulder. Especially with their mothers present. Immediately, she knows something *really* bad happened.

Pearl didn't get out of the van at Stoney's house. She couldn't stop staring at Ajay. His actions at the motel had shaken something in her and actually, reminded her of her young life with big John. Meanwhile, Ajay still comforts Ebony. Ever so often, he stares back at Pearl. He isn't planning on deserting Ebony. No matter what or whom.

Chill loads everyone, he can fit, into his blazer. Jr packs his car with crew. Stoney brings the rest, as they burn rubber trying to beat Jo to her house. There's about to be a powwow. The 1 they thought would've happened after Jb and Lynn got caught. It didn't happen the morning prior. But the whole crew knows it's about to go down, this morning.

For the 2nd morning in a row, the crew parents are about to talk to them about sex. The reason isn't because it was just *any member of the crew.*

No! This time it's Ebony Eloise *"baby girl"* Brown who was caught in a motel room. She's big John and Pearl's pride and joy. The 1 teenage girl in the crew who still gets baby dolls for Christmas. She was caught with Anthony Devante' *"ever ready"* Jackson. The 1 teenage crew boy who's most likely to tear the heads off of her baby dolls and melt them in the fireplace. This isn't going to be a jury on whether or not 1 kid is good enough for the other one. These parents see *only* their friends children as good enough for theirs. This is something more. To the females in the crew, this is *that same* double standard, once again. Because the guys are always out all night, *every night,* doing God only knows what. They never have *these* types of meetings. They just have testosterone parties with their fathers for updates on who's killing the pussy and who's getting pussy whipped. There's never a session for them to check *themselves*. As long as they aren't running trains or wilding out with a female from this family, they have no repercussions to worry about. For instance, Chill and Renee are all but engaged and they have a young son. Still, Renee can't stay out all night without consequences. Chill stays out at least, 3 nights a week. And it use to be 7 nights. But since miss sweet Lil Ebony has given up her cherry, this calls for a family meeting. If it were all the same to Ebony, she'd rather her mother not broadcast it to everyone. But that isn't her call. There is no lie to get her out of this one. Face to face, the truth will be told. Her father, aunts, uncles and everyone else will know that she's sexually active.

It's 5:00am and Jo's house is full. Her and Pearl have called all of the parents over. John has brought Tank back from lock-up. Most mothers and fathers are present. They are all curious as to what the meeting is about. The parents who aren't here are either at home with small children or on their jobs. There is at least 1 parent here, for each of the crew involved. Except for Stoney and Rob's parents. Stoney and Rob are 19 and 18 years old, respectively. Their parents are working. Or in Stoney's case, they're unavailable or doesn't seem to care, all the time. His father's in prison, somewhere in California. His mother Jackie had gotten married and moved to Columbus, almost 2 years ago. She makes contact when she has time and she attends most holiday functions.

Everyone sits or stands quietly. There are a few questions from the

parents who aren't sure why they've all been gathered. Jo and Pearl come into the room and call everyone to order.

"We've made coffee for those who want some," Jo says to the parents.

She starts off the meeting by explaining the conditions on how last night started out. She talks about how they put their trust in their youth to do what they had given them permission to do.

"Amen," Anna says.

Rich has an uncomfortable expression on his face as he looks at his mother. Jo continues by telling them how she, like the rest of the parents, had given permission for her offspring to go to the barbeque, then on to the park. They had even extended curfew, in hopes that their children would party out and come on home, on time.

"That's right," Brenda says while June squirms in his seat.

Jo continues on into the events of the late evening. She talks of how they were all pacing the floors but stuck to their word, as long as they could, not to go look for them. And again, how they were trying to see if their teens could be responsible. Pearl stares at Ebony from across the room. She's still in shock. Ebony sits there, next to her father. He has his arm around her. Ebony thinks to herself.

If he knew what happened. He'd surely choke the life, right out of me.

Ajay watches her. She looks at him, then to Nina and back to her mother. She looks at Tank and everyone else. She knows everybody is about to find out what she's done. T-baby is biting her nails. Ebony knows her 1st cousin only does this when she's nervous.

What is she so nervous about?

Another hour later and all of the parents have made it to the meeting. After learning about Tank, Chill and Rob going to jail, then Ebony and Ajay getting caught in a motel, every parent comes by to show support. Even the ones with small kids. Uncle Greg has brought Ebony's baby brother, lil man, back home. He runs to his daddy and climbs onto his lap. He speaks to his big sister.

"Hey, Ebony," he says with a smile.

"Hey, man," she whispers, then gives him a peck on the cheek.

Pearl still stares at her but Ebony can't even look at her mother, at this point. She's too ashamed. For the first time in her life, she knows how it feels to loose someone's trust. It's a horrible feeling. One she wishes she could change. But not at the risk of not being with Ajay. She never wanted to disappoint her parents. She use to think she would do anything to change it back, if it had ever happened. Now, she's not so sure. She wanted last night with Ajay to happen and it did. Her mom found out and hit her. Ebony sits and thinks about her relationship with her mother. She's not sure if it will survive this. But she feels damn good about her relationship with Ajay. She looks at him again and smiles, slightly. He smiles back.
Is he thinking the same thing?

Jo is speaking on yesterday's events while Jb and Lynn squirm in their seats. She talks about Chill, Rob and Tank going to jail.

"I don't believe, for a minute, that Tank, Chill and Lil Rob is guilty of having marijuana in that Blazer," she says, "I don't believe it because they know better than that. All of you know better than that."
Chill has been like a 2nd son to her and Al. Every since his parents were killed, *they've* been his parents. His mother was killed in a car accident when Chill was only 9 years old. Jo, Al and their crew helped his father Paul to raise him. Naturally, when Paul was killed, they all took him under their wing.

Lil Rob is just as close. They know his mother, very well. She worked 2 jobs and raised him by herself, after his father was killed. Rob is an only child, same as Chill. His mother is the only Cleveland parent who's still living and absent today.

The meeting continues. Just before Jo brings up the motel scene, Pearl stops her. She wants to speak.
She asks, "Jo, may I have the floor, please?"

"Of course, you may," Jo says as she yields the floor.

"To all of our children," Pearl starts, "I need to ask a question. How many of you are sexually active?"
Everyone looks around. She repeats it, for good measure.
"Kids or should I say, *young men and women*. I asked you, how many of you are sexually active?"
All of the mothers sit up to look at their children, as Pearl continues,

"We know us parents are. You are *all* proof of that. What we don't know is how many of *you are.* But we have a situation here and we need to find this out, *this* morning."
Pearl is more impatient than the crew has ever seen her. They take notice. "Now, you can either do a show of hands, speak up or whatever. But don't think you're just gonna sit there. We need to get to the bottom of this situation! Right now!"
She's growing noticeably frustrated, so Jo steps back in to get the 3rd generation's attention, just a bit faster.

"Don't everybody move at once," she interrupts as her voice has a hint of sarcasm.

"Lynn. Jb," Al says, "We already know about y'all, so what are you two waiting for? Get up and stand *next to* each other."

"Uh huh. Get on up, son. Right now," big John says to Jb, "It's time to let your crew know who it is you've picked to settle down with."
Jb gets up, walks across the living room and stands next to Lynn, as she stands there. Bre, who's parents are already aware of her sexual activity, goes over and stands next to Stoney. Jan and Rob stand up together. Chill and Renee are already standing. Angie, who isn't a member of the crew, stands with Jr since they've been together. The rest of the crew, who are still seated, look around at the others. Then Tank, Rich and June stand up. Tank slowly crosses the room and stands next to Nina, who reluctantly stands. Jo looks disgusted. Rich stands up next to T-baby, who's even slower to stand than Nina had been. Ebony looks at T-baby but doesn't speak. Ajay finally stands up.

"I was wondering what was taking you so long to stand up, Ant," Al says, "We all know you've *been* out there."
Ajay was taking his time standing, because he knew once he stood up, Ebony's intimacies would be exposed and known by everyone in the room. Ebony isn't going to hold out any longer. She stands, walks across the living room floor and stops next to Ajay. All of the parents, who wasn't aware of the motel incident, have shocked expressions on their faces.

"What!?!" Some of the mothers say.
The parents start to talk in a frenzy, after noticing all of the kids are standing. All of their kids are standing except Rebbie.
Then suddenly, Rebbie stands up and moves over to stand next to June.

TIME TO LEARN-RELOADED-Time Will Reveal-part 1

"Hell no!" her father Archie Sr yells out, "You'd better sit your ass down, right now!"
Rebbie sits back down, quickly. But then, she stands right back up. Everyone in her crew looks at her with a puzzled expression. Even big June. The 2 of them haven't been together. Rebbie is still a virgin but she's determined to stick with her crew, regardless.

"She said active, Trisha. Sit down, honey," Greg Sr says.

"That's right, Nina. Sit down," Al says, "We need to get a handle on who's *sexually* active. We want to know how many of you are actually having sex, as of today."

"*Active*. Not just if you *like* each other," Richard Sr adds, "We wanna know how many of y'all are actually *having sex*."
He chuckles after his comment.

"Baby girl, sit down," big John says as Ebony looks confused.
She thought her mother had already told her father about the discovery at the motel but she hasn't. Pearl decides to let it be known, right now.

"No, John. She needs to stand *right* where she's standing," Pearl says, "The people who didn't know about it, are you and I."

"I know *damn well* you're kidding me," John says, "Already?"
He sits lil man on the couch and he stands up. He's usually calm about things but not this time. He walks over to Ebony and looks her directly in the eyes.
He says, "Tell me it ain't true, baby girl. That's all you have to do. Then explain to daddy *why* you felt like you had to stand up."
John knows Ajay has liked Ebony, for years. But he had no idea she like him, as well. Ebony looks at him, then to her mother. She looks at Ajay. She can't lie. Not this time. Ajay is looking at her. Then he grabs her hand.
Softly he says, "Tell him, Ebony. Now is the time to let our whole crew know about us."

"Okay," Ebony says.
She looks at her dad and tells him she has been with Ajay and that she loves him. Before John can even respond to Ebony, the other parents are up. They have questions for their own girls. The parents knew all of the boys was sexually active. And as usual, the fathers are okay with that part. But they had no idea about most of the girls and definitely, *not* the foursome.

There's so much confusion with everybody talking at once, that

John and Greg Sr walk outside. Al looks at Nina and Lynn, then at Ajay. He walks outside as well. Soon, all of the fathers walk out and leave the mothers inside to say their peace.

Not long after, the mothers become disgusted. They walk outside for a breath of fresh air and leave the crew standing. But before the mothers walk out, they dare any of the youth to sit down before they tell them too.

Once their parents leave, the crew start to whisper to each other. They're trying to see what brought forth this meeting.

"Ree Ree, why are you standing up?" Nina asks.

"Cause all y'all standing up," she says and giggles.

June looks at her and smiles. She moves and stands close to him again. As she does, her mother Rena, who's coming back into the side door to get Archie's cigarettes, says, "Girl, I'll bet you'd better go sit down. Since when have you been fooling around?"

"I haven't been," Rebbie answers.

"Then why are you standing over there like something crazy?"

"Cause all of my friends are standing up, ma," Rebbie says softly.

"If all your friends go jump off a cliff, are you gonna do it too?"

"They're not gonna jump off a cliff, ma," she answers, this time rolling her eyes to the ceiling.

"You'd better watch your tone with me, young lady. Or you'll get some help over a cliff of your own! You heard your father tell you to sit down. Didn't you?"

"Yes ma'am," Rebbie says softly, as she looks down at the floor.

Still, she doesn't sit. Rena goes back out the door, mumbling a few other sorted comments. The crew laugh as Rebbie shakes her head and says, "I *knew* she was gonna clown on me."

"That's because you're standing up with us guilty folks," Bre says.

"T-baby, you and Ree Ree didn't have to get in trouble. Neither one of y'all have done anything," Ebony whispers, "Y'all shouldn't even be standing up."

"Oh, Ree Ree hasn't but my girl *T-baby,* suppose to be standing up with us guilty folks," Lynn offers as she smiles at T-baby.

Ebony looks at T-baby in surprise but she doesn't comment. Only because their mothers are coming back inside for what the crew thinks will be round

2 of the *powwow*. But instead of telling all of them to sit down again and talk, the mothers have another option.

"All of the guys need to go outside," Pearl says, "Your fathers are waiting for you."

"Yes and you girls have a seat, so we can tell you how this shit is gonna be," Jo spits, as the disgust still lingers in her voice.

The guys exit and all of the young females take a seat, while the mothers stand. Jo excuses Angie from the room. She isn't crew and she won't be around once Jr's girlfriend and crew member, LaTonya returns. She's due back today, after visiting with her family in Detroit.

The mothers begin talking to their daughters while the fathers have taken the guys over to John's house to talk to them. A rap session is about to go down in both homes. Ebony looks at T-baby, in shock. She didn't know her and Rich had sex, last night.

By sun rise on the morning of the 6th, this crew knows there is no turning back. They all have to come clean. One by one, the girls have to tell their mothers every single detail about whom they're liking or trying to bed down with, for the future.

****

By 9am, everyone has gone to their own homes. Each mother gets her daughter or daughters and each father gets his son or sons, for individual talks. All of the parents figure this is the make or break time for them. They need to get a handle on who's seeing whom and who's sexing whom. And for how long. Instead of talking to Ebony, right away, Pearl tells her to go up to her room and wait for her to come up there.

John, Jb and Tank go into the boys room. Lil man has gone across the street to play with Lil Kenny, so everyone can talk openly.

Al and Ajay go up to Ajay's room to talk, while Jo, Nina and Lynn go into the big girls room, where Erica and Pam are allowed to stay in the room with them. As father and son go, Al and Ajay are closer than most. They're more like buddies, than father and son. Al knows Ajay is sexually active and has been since the very early age of 8 years old. He's always told him about protection and being careful about whom he lays with. And

though young Ajay didn't always take his dad's advice, he still tells Al about his conquests, from time to time. However, he hasn't said anything about him and Ebony moving toward sex. Partly because Ajay knew his father would react the way he's reacting today.

"Son, what's going on?" Al asks, "What went down, last night?"

"Pops, I went to the motel, that's all," he answers, rather antsy.

"And!?!"

"Well, you know. I got busy," he says with a slight smile.

"With baby girl?!?"

"Yes."

"Now I know you've been around the block, a few times and all. But how *in the hell* did you end up in a motel room with Ebony?"

"A partner of ours got us a room and we went."

Al knows Chill is the partner who got the room. He doesn't even have to ask that.

He says,"You're telling me y'all planned to do this, *all along*? Even after what happened with your sister, yesterday?"

"No, pops," Ajay says impatiently, "We didn't even know about the motel room until after we got to the party and before we left for the park."

"So you had a free room and you just decided you would get Ebony to go with you? That's too thin, son."

"No. Look here, pops. The room was *for* me and her," Ajay tries, "You know what I'm saying? It was for us to go too, together. That's how it was set up, from the start."

"How son?" Al asks, "Since when did you and baby girl become sexual? I can't figure out how you ended up in a motel room with Ebony. That's the part I'm trying to figure out."

Ajay takes a deep breath. Then he says, "Look here, pops. Me and Ebony are not *just now* hooking up," he says, "You know I've been liking her since I was in first grade. She started liking me about three years ago. She liked me before she was my date for my crew induction party. But I didn't even know how much she liked me, until the night of that party. Since I turned thirteen, we've been kissing and touching. But it didn't really get sexual until Sunday night, when I stayed at mama P's house. It was something *she* wanted to do too. She always told me she would tell me when she was ready and I let her tell me. I never asked her too."

TIME TO LEARN-RELOADED-Time Will Reveal-part 1

"For how long, son?" Al asks, "How long has this hooking up thing been going on?"

"We've been kissing and things like that," Ajay says, "But we didn't get serious until Sunday night. Pops, you always knew I liked her. And you knew I liked her, for real."

"Ant, this is so-"

"We've been liking each other, for like three years. But Sunday night, she wanted to go all the way, so we did. We've been messing around. She always wanted me and I wanted her too. You know that. So we did it and that's it. When she found out she was leaving for H-town, she said she didn't wanna leave here as a virgin and she's coming back to me."

"So you was just more than happy to do this for her, huh?" Al replies and he's acting disgusted.

"Yes."

"You're moving way faster than Ebony is, Ant," Al says, "She's still very innocent. I mean, she ain't ready for you and your ways, you know? I'm thinking about your experience and all of that. Think about it."

"I did, pops," Ajay says, "But see, that's why I didn't tell you about this part of it. I knew you would trip. But she's the one for me. I think you *and* big John know that."

"Wait a minute, Ant," Al says suddenly, "Baby girl has been through some things in her life. That girl is probably ready to fall in love. What are you gonna do about that?"

"Whatever it takes," he replies quickly.

"Are you gonna wait for her?" Al asks.

"What do you mean wait, pops? We're already doing it."

"Are you ready to be with, *just* her? That's what I mean."

"She's the girl who's gonna be my wife," Ajay says emphatically, "She's the only girl I kiss and look out for. Because I know she's the only one for me. I don't know how else to say it. What's all this for, anyway? See, this is why I didn't say nothing to you about this part. I knew you was gonna trip about it."

He's growing slightly impatient.

"What if she ends up pregnant, Ant? Ha?" Al asks, "What then? Did you ever think about that?"

"Yes, the first time, I did," Ajay says, "But the condom broke. And last night, I didn't. I counted her days, pops. Grandpa Al and you, told me how to do that and that's what I do. And still, I was gonna stop before I got off but I couldn't, so I just finished. I counted the days, pops. Shoot man, she ain't gonna get pregnant, *pops*."

"I sure *as hell* hope not," Al says, "Because both of y'all are to young to be strapped down with a baby. She might have a future in basketball, if she wants one. And I know you have the potential to go to the NBA, if you took it more serious and gave the streets up a little bit. Do you know what I mean?"

"Alright, pops," he says.

He's just ready to end this discussion, at any cost.

"Listen, son," Al starts slowly, "There are some things that you may not understand, right now. Maybe one day you'll know what I'm speaking on. And then, you'll be able to feel where I'm coming from. But for now, I'm gonna ask you, as a favor to me. Please just leave her alone, for right now. Alright? Let her grow up. You got other lady friends for that sort of thing, if you just gotta do it. But I don't think Ebony is the one for you. Not right now, I mean. You're *way* more experienced than she is. You've already been out there. She hasn't. I don't want you to hurt her. Our families are *too* close. I just don't feel like John and Pearl could handle that. You know they still treat her like a baby. Besides, she's been through a lot in her young life. Things you may not be sensitive too."

"Like what?" Ajay probes.

Al shrugs him off without any more details other than to say,

"If and when the times comes for you to know, you'll know. And *she'll* tell you. But not until she's ready. So you don't go pressuring her, alright?" Al pleads.

"Alright, pops. I said alright, a long time ago. Come on."

But now, Ajay is slightly curious as to what his father is talking about. He knows Ebony had been a virgin before him. So what can this secret be? And why does his father know something about her life and he doesn't know it? Al is still insisting he let it go and don't ask anymore questions.

"Give me your word, son," Al demands.

Ajay sits quietly, for a minute. He knows he isn't ready to be a 1 woman man but he likes Ebony, a lot. She's very special to him and he knows he'll never *intentionally* hurt her. She's the only pure female in his life. The only girl he's ever kissed and allowed to kiss him. He also knows she will always be faithful to him too. She's going to be his wife and the mother of his children, one day. But he knows he hasn't been faithful to her. He knows his father is right about that part. Eventually, he will hurt her again. Just like the Anita situation, 2 days ago. He doesn't ever want to hurt her like that again. But he knows Ebony isn't going to except them not being together. He tries to express that part to his father.

"She's not gonna go for that," he tries.

But Al isn't backing down. He says, "I need your word on this. Just for now."

"You got my word, pops," Ajay says reluctantly.

"Thank you, son," Al says.

They shake hands, hug each other and Al leaves Ajay's room.

After Al leaves, Ajay sits there and thinks about what he has just agreed too. The agreement his father wants him to make is for right now. Al didn't say he didn't want Ajay to see Ebony, *at all.* Just not now. Ajay thinks to himself.

Can I really stick to it? What has she been through and what does that have to do with us being together? What will Ebony think of me now?

She'll surely think he was only out for 1 thing because he's dumping her after they had sex. He wants to tell her, himself. He's going to have to do that somehow and soon. He reaches into his pocket and pulls out his *Isley Brothers* tape. Jr had gotten it out of the boom box and gave it to him at the infamous powwow, earlier. He reaches over, pops the tape into his boom box and turns it on. Then he lays across his bed as *Voyage to Atlantis* plays. He pictures Ebony's face when she hears this song. It's her favorite song on the whole tape. It's the same song that played softly on Sunday night, when she had given him her virginity. He thinks about last night in the motel and how nice it was for him. He remembers how he felt he had to protect her from her mother's rage. She's special to him, alright. So how could he hurt her? He knows he isn't ready to be faithful, though. Not this early.

"I'm sorry, baby girl," he whispers to himself, "You'll always be my baby. We just have to wait awhile, that's all."

He reaches into his other pocket and removes her panties. He looks at them and smiles.

"I don't wanna make you cry," he says as he puts the panties under his pillow. He closes his eyes and before long, he falls asleep.

****

Big John grounds Jb, Tank and Ebony. And as time always reveals for this family, only Ebony's grounding will stand. John had to postpone his trip to Houston for family court, on Tuesday the 11th. That's Ajay's 15th birthday and Tank's court date. John and Pearl was ordered to attend. John and Ebony's trip to Houston has been rescheduled for Thursday the 13th. John and Pearl sit and discuss today's events.

"So this is what it takes to get time off, ha?" John says to Pearl as they sit on the loveseat in their living room.

"I sure wish it was under better circumstances," Pearl says.

"Have you talked to baby girl?" he asks.

"No John, not yet," she says, "I don't even know how too, this time. She's becoming a woman, already."

"You know, honey. Deep down, we all knew our children was gonna like each other," John says suddenly.

"Yes, I know. Remember when they were babies? We always said *'We're keeping it all amongst our own crew'*," she says and smiles.

"Yes. We just didn't know how right we was about it, then," he says and smiles.

"John, you know they're doing the same things we all did at their ages," she says.

"Yes but baby, we were older," he tries.

"Not much. We was what, *John junior's age*? Fifteen and sixteen?" she says as she reminisces.

"You're right, baby," John says, "But it's harder when it's your own kids, isn't it?"

"It sure is," she agrees, "Mama and daddy keep reminding me of that part."

"When you talk to baby girl, you tell her I still love her but she's grounded until we leave for Houston," he says, "She's not allowed to talk to Ajay, at all. Not for a *long* while."

"I can't believe I beat my baby girl, like that. In her face and all. I

feel like a mad woman. When I saw her sitting in that motel room, I *lost* it."

"Pearl, go talk to her now. You have too," he insists.

"Okay. I know I do."

She gets up and goes up the stairs to Ebony's door.

When she walks in, Ebony sits up on her bed. She looks so innocent. Pearl finds it hard to believe she's about to have *this* conversation with *this* child. She sits on the bed, next to Ebony, who's holding the teddy bear she'd given her when lil man was born. On the bib it reads;

To mommy's Baby Girl. I give you the world.

She finally looks at Ebony. She notices how puffy her face has become from where she'd hit her.

"Ebony, I'm *so* sorry I hit you," Pearl says.

Ebony looks down. Pearl lifts her chin and continues talking to her.

"When I turned around and saw you, it took me back to when I was fifteen, all over again. I guess I'm kind of mad at myself."

She tells Ebony the same thing had happened with her and John. She tells her about how big mama and granny found them at Brad Sr and Deb's house. Pearl remembers how angry big mama Eloise and granny Pearline got with them. Pearl remembers how she had wished she could make them understand how much she loved John and how much they wanted to be together.

"Is that what you was trying to tell me, yesterday?" Pearl asks.

"Yes ma'am," Ebony answers and starts to cry, "I didn't know how to tell you something like this. I really wanted to and I've been trying to figure out *how* to tell you."

"I do understand now, baby. I understand what you *think* you're feeling. But you have to understand that this is hard for me to deal with," Pearl says softly.

"But mama, you and daddy stayed together," she says, "Y'all loved each other. He took you away and *married you* so you wouldn't have to go to Texas."

"Yes, I know. Mama and daddy was against it," Pearl remembers as she smiles, "Well, mama was against me staying behind but not daddy. He wasn't against it, not so much."

Pearl and John's relationship is more similar to Ebony and Ajay's, than it is different. Only back then, they had causes to fight for. Rallies and protest to plan and take part in. Ebony and Ajay aren't taking part in any causes. Only parties and now, adult situations. Pearl still can't even think *Ebony* and the word *sex*, in the same sentence. But Ebony tries to plead her case.

"Mama, I love Anthony the same way you love my daddy. Can't y'all see that?" she tries.

"Is he ready to love you the same way?" Pearl asks.

"I think so."

"Do you know this?" Pearl asks, "Ebony, you have to know for sure. Not just think so, honey. You are both the offspring from my crew. There's a lot at stake here."

Ebony waits for a second or 2 before she answers slowly,

"The way he holds me, ma," she says, "The way he touches and looks at me. I know it's real."

"Ebony, I have to make sure you understand one thing," Pearl says, "He has experience and he knows how to make you feel like he's the real thing. He's much more advanced than you are, in that area. He's been with older women too. You do know this, right?"

Ebony doesn't want to hear this part but Pearl continues,

"How are you, at thirteen, going to compete with women, twenty years old, for Ajay's time and affection? Ebony some of these women give him money and the use of their cars. Whatever they can do to get his *and your brothers* attention. Now, I'm not saying I agree with any of that. But that's the way it's been. How are you gonna compete with that type of thing?"

"I don't have to compete with anybody for his attention. He gives that to me, freely. And as far as me giving him money, mama he gives me money, all of the time. I keep his money and he tells me to use whatever I need and to let him know that I need to use it. Plus he's always buying me things."

"What kinds of things, Ebony?" Pearl asks with concern.

"Like tennis shoes or clothes, jewelry or whatever he thinks I might like. He bought these for me," she says, pointing to the *K-Swiss* she's still wearing.

"I thought your brother bought those for you," Pearl says looking at Ebony as if she feels she's been conspired against.

She adds, "He even told me he bought those shoes for you."

TIME TO LEARN-RELOADED-Time Will Reveal-part 1

"I asked Jb to say that because I wanted to tell you about it, myself," Ebony tells her, "I asked him to lie because I wasn't ready to explain my relationship to anybody. I'm sorry for that too, mama."

"Just how long has this been going on, Ebony?"

"About three years-"

"Three years! My Lord!"

"But not the sex part, ma. Please don't start screaming. *Please*," Ebony pleads, "I never wanted you to get mad. I didn't wanna hurt you."

"Well, what has it been?" Pearl digs.

"We use to just kiss and stuff like that until. Until Sunday night."

"Sunday night?" Pearl asks for clarity.

Ebony nods yes.

"In my house?" Pearl asks.

Ebony nods yes again.

"Ebony, this is too much, young lady. You and Ajay had sex under my roof? *What am I saying*? You shouldn't be having sex, *anywhere*. Ebony, you're only thirteen. You've got your whole life ahead of you. If you start this now, you're gonna get pregnant or worse than that. Are y'all even using protection? And don't tell me you're already on the pill because I know I haven't authorized *anything* like that."

"The first time we did but it broke," Ebony admits. Then she says, "But last night, well no. We didn't use one. It was our second time."

"Listen to me. You are not ready for this. I know y'all think this is the love of your lives," Pearl says, referring to Ebony and her girls, "But the guys aren't ready for the same. Not right now they aren't. Oh, they're gonna be respectful to you because they were raised to be and you're all crew. They're gonna give you they're attention. All of the attention you want, if they know they can have sex. It's just the way boys are, at this age. They know what to say to get you to do whatever it is they want you to do. Then when you're no longer brand new, it's time for the next girl."

"Was my daddy like that?" Ebony asks.

Pearl pauses for a minute and thinks about her early days with John Sr.

"Yes. Maybe he was, in the beginning. But he's always respected me. He never let me see him do anything. Even though I would hear the stories or catch him, from time to time. And of course, there was always some tramp who was trying to get with him. Me, Jo and the girls would have to get in their asses, often. Like Nina and your girls did the other day, right?" she asks as she laughs and says, "But Ebony, that was then and this is now. It was just different, back then."

"How?" Ebony digs.

"It just was. Anyway, I'm not gonna have my daughter trying to compete with some tramp for any boy and that's final," Pearl says.

"I know Anthony cares for me. I don't know how to prove that to you, right now. But if I have too, I will," Ebony offers.

"No way, baby," Pearl says while shaking her head, emphatically, "I'm not gonna just sit by and let you get hurt. No way."

"But how do you know he's gonna hurt me?" Ebony asks.

"Because they always do. When it comes to sex, males and females are looking for different things," Pearl says, "For you, you're planning your future. For him, he's seeing how long he can last before he gets off. Comparing one girl to the next."

"Ma."

"I'm serious, baby," Pearl says.

"I promise it's not like that," Ebony tries.

"Okay then tell me what really happened over at Jo's house on the fourth?" Pearl asks as Ebony looks at her with a surprised look.
Does mama know about Anita? She can't know.

"What happened with the girl, T-baby and them beat up, back there in Lou Ann's yard, on the fourth of July?" Pearl asks, "When Ajay tried to cover for you and him by saying he walked into the bathroom on you. Ha?"
She knows. Just like always. She knows. Mama always knows.

She tells her mother the whole story from the beginning until the present.
"Three years, ha? Ebony, you never even told me you felt this way. I never saw *this* one coming. At least with your brothers, I knew it or I suspected it. But I never even thought you was thinking about boys. I didn't pick up not *one* sign," Pearl says.
She smiles suddenly and adds, "You know that's the same thing my mama said to me, when she found out about me and John?"

"Ma, I wanted to tell you, all along. But I didn't know how too. Big mama knows how much he likes me. I think she does and poppa too.

Granny knows about him liking me. I wanted to tell you before we did it the first time and I wanted to tell you, myself. Not let you find out the way it happened. We didn't go all the way until Sunday. After I found out I had to leave for Houston and *I* wanted too, ma," she says, "He never tried to make me do it. He would only do what I let him do. He has always been that way with me. No matter what it is, he always told me to move on, my own time. I wanted my one and only to be, Anthony. He's the only one I've ever wanted in this way," she says.

Ebony is feeling now is the time to tell it all and get it out in the open.

They go into the master bathroom where Pearl keeps an in-home pregnancy test kit, just for times like this. She instructs Ebony on how to use it, then leaves her.

After a few minutes, Ebony meets her mother back in her bedroom and brings the pregnancy test stick with her.

Pearl looks at it and says, "Negative. What a relief. I don't want you to get pregnant, sweetheart."

"Will you put me on the pill?" Ebony asks, "Because I know I'm gonna be with Anthony. I love him."

Pearl doesn't answer, right away. They talk for 2 hours. They talk about boys, sex, her friends and even Pearl's younger days. Still, after they've opened up to each other, so well. Pearl still has to ground her.

"Well Ebony, this is gonna be hard for you to accept but we have to punish you. You will not be allowed to go to any parties or anything like that, for the remainder of the time you're home. Not without your daddy *and or* me, going along. You won't be allowed to see Ajay, either. Do you understand?"

"No, mama. I don't understand," she says, "Why not? I told you the truth about *everything*."

"I know you did and that's a good start, Ebony. But sweetheart. Look here, honey. I am your mother. I have to set some boundaries. If you're not able to see Ajay, then you won't be tempted to do anything else. I'm trying to protect you from getting into trouble, okay?"

"Ma, please don't say I can't see my friends. *Please*. I have to leave in a week, for God knows how long. I can't even spend time with my friends before I go?"

"Ebony, you did wrong," Pearl says, "You took advantage of our trust in you and you have to hold up for that. You and Ajay may very well become true love. But I can't allow you to pursue it now. You're not old enough to be thinking of settling down. *Take your time."*

"Please, mama," she begs as she starts to cry again, "Please don't do this. *Please*. I don't wanna go against your rules. I didn't mean to break the house rules. I love him and he loves me. Please don't ground me."

But Pearl's mind is made up. Ebony cries frantically but Pearl doesn't budge, an inch. Even though inside, Pearl knows her daughter is going to defy her. She'd done the same thing, herself. But she still has to tell her she can't. It's the same scenario that played out between her and Ebony's big mama, 18 years ago.

Pearl leaves Ebony's room with the test stick. She has to show it to John. She leaves without answering Ebony's question about birth control pills too. She knows she'll get them for her, when she's ready. Until then, Ebony and Ajay are just going to have to make due.

Ebony's other crew members haven't faired any better either. Almost all of the crew have been punished. Jb, Tank and Ebony. Lynn, Nina and Ajay. Trisha and Rebbie, Rich, June, Jan and Breanna too. No one is allowed to see anyone or talk on the phone or go to any parties.

Later Chill, Renee, Rob, Stoney and Jr hang out after picking up Tonya, from the airport. Though they're on their own, for the most part, they still don't feel it's right to have a get together when their whole crew can't be present. They hang out at Chill's and make plans for later.

The neighborhood is dead for the next 2 days. Ebony can't talk to her girls or Ajay. Her and Tank sit in her room, for hours. Playing cards, writing poems and doing a lot of talking about Nina, Ajay and the crew.

****

On Saturday morning, Ebony sees Ajay come outside to take out the garbage. She watches him from her bedroom window. On his way back to the side door, he glances up and sees her looking at him. He stares at her, for a few seconds. Then he waves. She smiles and waves back. He gestures

for her to wait there for a minute. He goes inside and closes the door.
What is he trying to say?

She stays in the window. A minute later, she looks across at his window and there he is. Their bedroom windows face each other.
This is perfect!

She had never thought of this before. They open their windows and talk.

"Hey," she says.

"What's up?" he asks.

"I miss you," she whispers.

"I know you do," he says arrogantly, then adds a smile.

"My parents said I can't see you anymore. But I can't even see that," she whispers as her eyes sting from the urge to cry.

"Yea. My folks are stressing the same thing," he says, "But that's gonna be hard for me to stick too. I've been in my room, just wondering when you was gonna think about our windows and look over here."

"I just thought of it after you told me to wait here," she says.

"*I've been* looking at your window," Ajay says, "I could see your shadow in there at night."
Suddenly, he looks back toward his door and says, "Hold up." as he closes the window quickly.
There is a knock at his door. It's Nina. She's coming to talk to him again. It appears they've been spending the last 2 days the same way as Ebony and Tank. He lets her in.

"What are you up too?" Nina asks.

"Talking to Ebony in the window," he says with a smile.

"For real? *Alright*," she whispers as she rushes to the window and raises it up again.
She sees Ebony is still there. She smiles and asks, "What's up sister? I miss you, girl."

"I know. I miss you too," Ebony says.

"Where's Jeremy at?" Nina asks.

"Hold up. I'll go get him," Ebony says and she does.

When she returns with Tank, Jb has come back with them. Nina goes to get

TIME TO LEARN-RELOADED-Time Will Reveal-part 1

Lynn and the 6 of them talk through the window, for hours. They agree to meet at the window later today and everyday, if they have too.

This crew is tight. They refuse to break from each other, no matter what anyone says. Because together, they feel stronger. Ebony remembers what big mama Eloise always said.

"In adversity, what doesn't break you or kill you, only makes you stronger."

They haven't been broken. They certainly aren't dead and through each other, they find strength. That's as true to their rearing as they can get.

Roll on crew!

CHAPTER 5

JEREMY'S TRIALS

****Sunday morning July 9, 1989****

This Sunday, like *Any Given Sunday,* all of the families are preparing to go to Sunday school and Church. Nina and Ebony usually ride in the same car but not today. Because of their punishment, they have to ride in their parents cars. Pearl and Jo talk briefly while John and Al start their vehicles. They call the youth out of the house to load into the cars. Then they go down the street and on to church. Ebony sees Jan and her family getting into their car. She waves to her. Jan waves back and they both smile.

Everyone is at church. On the 2nd Sunday, the adult choir sings. This is Pearl, Jo, Deb and Belinda, Rena, Anna, Sandy and Brenda's crew of ladies and some of the fathers, as well. Their choir sings beautifully, as they always do. Rena leads a song and so does Anna. During the service, the foursome pass notes to each other. Granny Pearline catches them and demand they stop immediately, which they do. She asks them to say a special prayer for all of their parents and ask God to give them the strength to get through the ordeal, they've put themselves in. They do that, as well.

After service, they try to huddle together and talk but their parents foil their attempts. Granny Pearline tells her sons about the note passing in church. Then she ask if her and papa Jackson Brown can take the girls to their house in The Point, for a few days. The parents don't want the girls to be able to get together, per the terms of their punishment. But they aren't willing to argue reasons with granny Pearline, so all of the parents agree.

Ebony is disappointed, initially. Tuesday is Ajay's birthday. He's turning 15 and she knows he's going to find a way to celebrate. That's just the way he is when it comes to getting his way. He'll play cool and let his parents think he's honoring the punishment rules. But on his big day, he's going to get out. Ebony wants to be a part of that celebration but she has no plans, as of yet.

TIME TO LEARN-RELOADED-Time Will Reveal-part 1

Tank has to go before a judge on Tuesday morning. The traffic stop, the other night, was his 3rd offense. Or rather his 3rd time getting caught. He could get some time, this time around. Ebony considers begging her parents not to make her go to granny's. But once she gets word that her girls are going, she decides it just might be okay. With the 4 of them together, they can coax granny into giving them a break. Even if she doesn't, they're going to put their heads together and work something out. Soon, she realizes going to granny's is the best move. The foursome head to The Point with granny and papa Brown. Their mothers agree to bring them enough clothes to last for a day or two.

After Sunday dinner, papa Brown decides to take granny and the girls to the movie to see *Batman*. Papa picked this movie for 3 reasons. It's rated pg. It's based on 1 of his favorite comic strips and it was the 1st thing him and granny Pearline found out they had in common. They both like *Batman* comics. The girls get a kick out of watching papa and granny on a date. They aren't particularly into Batman comics but they know papa feels it's age appropriate for them. Besides, they're just happy to be together and out of the house. Plus granny smiles the entire time, so it's worth it, all the more.

After the movie, papa buys them ice cream and they head back to the house. It's been awhile since the girls spent the night with grandpa Jackson Brown and granny Pearline. It's still a fun time, like usual. Granny always have them in the kitchen baking sweets. This stay is no different. Papa plays the piano while they sing. They love gathering around the piano for a session of familiar tunes. They cover the songs from papa Brown and poppa Jones band touring days too. Bedtime is always at 9pm, sharp. They kiss granny and papa goodnight, then head down the hall to get ready for bed.

After their baths, they settle into their beds until all is quiet. Then they flick on the lamp and sit up, so they can talk. First, they discuss the trivial events of the day. But everyone is eager to hear T-baby and Ebony's stories about that chaotic night which brought forth the punishment. T-baby begins first. She tells them how her and Rich did it at the park.

"It wasn't planned though y'all," she says, "We was kissing and touching and all of that. I just couldn't say no, this time. I wanted to, just as bad as he did."

She tells them how they had discussed coming to the motel but Jr wouldn't let them leave the park in his car.

"So Rich just parked down the way and we got busy," she says.

"Did it hurt?" Rebbie asks.

"Yes it did," T-baby says, "He asked me if I wanted him to stop but I didn't. I didn't want him to stop, *even* though it hurt bad. My dumb ass thought my hole would close back up," she says and laughs along with them. Then she adds, "So I just laid there and closed my eyes."

"Close back up?" Rebbie asks, "Even *I* know better than that."

"I do too," T-baby says, "Well mama told me all about of that stuff. But at the time, you really can't think straight."

"If it hurt, you should've let him stop or asked him to stop," Rebbie offers.

"He wouldn't have anyway," she says.

"He should have, if you would've told him too," Rebbie tries.

"Anthony didn't stop either" Ebony jumps in, "And I did ask him too. I *begged* him too."

"What?" Nina asks with a look of concern on her face.

"He didn't," Ebony continues, "First, he was gentle and it was *so good*. But after I came or at least I think that's what it was, he seemed like he lost control or something. He started pumping me like, I don't know, like he was angry or something."

"That's how Rich was too, girl," T-baby says, "It seems like the more I tried to move, the tighter he held me."

"You know a man can't stop when he feels his nut coming," Nina says as she laughs, "It's like Jeremy turns into a monster or something."

They all giggle. Everyone except Rebbie. She looks terrified.

"Hey y'all, we're scaring Ree Ree," Nina says.

"Sorry, sis," Ebony says and smiles, "It ain't that bad. You just have to try to hang. He'll get his,… eventually."

She has a puzzled look on her face.

"Well Rich didn't get to get his but that's probably because Nina, Ree and Renee came and burst our shit up," T-baby says and laughs.

"We told you we was sorry, T-baby. Okay?" Nina tries as she nudges T-baby on the shoulder with her elbow and continues giggling.

"Crew, that was embarrassing," T-baby says and they still laugh.

TIME TO LEARN-RELOADED-Time Will Reveal-part 1

"Did y'all hear about those six guys who got popped that same night?" Nina asks.

"Yes girl, I heard about that," Rebbie says.

"I heard my mama and them talking about it," T-baby says.

"I think our crew did it," Ebony whispers.

"Me too," Nina adds.

"Why do y'all feel that way?" T-baby asks.

Ebony and Nina explains how the timing was just right. Also, Ebony tells them about the conversation Ajay had with Tank.

"Yes and then all of a sudden, they dropped us off," Nina continues, "Right after that, is when it happened. So it fits."

"Then nobody could contact Jb and junior, for awhile," Ebony says, "And you know that's how they do when something goes down, like that. That's the only time our crew splits up, like they did *that* night. So one of them can head off them folks."

"And the cops are always around when it comes to our crew," Rebbie adds.

"For real, Ree Ree," Nina says, "And while the first car is a trap for them folks, the rest of the crew go stash the shit and lay low until they hook up again. Once everything cools down. Jeremy told me all about how they roll."

"If that's true, then we're not gonna ever mention this to anybody but each other," T-baby adds, "They're not gonna tell us about it anyway."

"I know that's right," Rebbie says, "Tank tells Nina but that's it."

Nina smiles and says, "He puts me up on crew stuff because he wants me to be able to trust him. But that block where them six fools got popped at, is the crew's block. I didn't know none of them niggaz. Did y'all?"

"Hell no," the 3 girls answer.

"Then *fuck 'em*," Nina says trying to sound like Ajay.

They all giggle. Then they take a vow of silence and close that discussion.

"Oh yea. What did you mean, *eventually*, Ebony. When you said he would get his?" Rebbie asks.

"Eventually, he will," Ebony explains, "Because the first time it took about ten minutes, maybe fifteen. But every time after that, took a longer and longer time."

"Every time? *Damn*. How many times did y'all do it?" T-baby asks.

"Four."

"Y'all was boning, girlfriend," Nina says as she smiles.

"One time he put me on top but that hurt the most," Ebony says.

"Oh no, girl. See *you* got control then. Control of how much you take in and all that," Nina says.

She has been sexually active with only Tank since May of last year.

"Not when he keeps pulling you down while he's pushing up in you," Ebony says.

"Ebony, you've gotta learn how to take control when you're on top," Nina says with confidence, "That's your turn to wear him out."

Ebony looks doubtful and says, "That's just it. With Anthony, I'll never be in control during sex. Because he *knows* what he's doing and he's so big." She lays back and looks at the ceiling.

"I'm never doing it," Rebbie says suddenly.

"Never say never," the others advise.

"The way y'all make it sound. Shoot, I don't know," Rebbie says.

"After the first time, it's all good," Nina says.

"Yea unless he's a mad man, like Anthony," Ebony says while smiling and still starring at the ceiling.

"My brother's got problems. You know what I'm saying?" Nina asks sarcastically.

"Yes and so does mine," Ebony responds, using the same tone Nina had just used, "Big problems. Tank needs counseling."

"Oh wait, baby. There's nothing wrong with *my* man. Understand me now, girl," Nina says as she giggles, "Its all good with him."

They're all laughing as Ebony and Nina go back and forth against their own brothers. T-baby and Rebbie are very use to *this* jousting by now.

Nina is smiling. She knows Ebony is going to respond in kind. Ebony does.

"Its all good with *my* baby too. Understand me?" Ebony asks, "He just gets carried away with this and who can blame him?"

She's pointing at herself, as they all laugh. Rebbie has a serious question.

"How will I know when to do it, though?" Rebbie asks.

"I don't know," Nina says, "You just do."

"I wanted to do it before I left for Houston," Ebony says, "That's why me and Anthony went all the way. But on that night, we all thought I would be gone by now."

TIME TO LEARN-RELOADED-Time Will Reveal-part 1

"If my baby wouldn't have gone to jail, you would be," Nina says.

"I know," she says, "That part of the night was really messed up. Plus my mama beating my ass, like that."

"Ajay told me *he* stopped her," Nina says.

"He did. He got between me and her. He pushed her off of me. She almost fell down. He stayed by me, the rest of the time until she chilled out, so she couldn't hit me anymore," she says with a glare in her eyes.

"He must care about you to do something *like that*?" Rebbie says, "Because we all know mama P don't *play*."

"He does care for Ebony," Nina says, "He just has a fucked up way of showing it, sometimes."

"I hope so because I know big Al told him not to see me. He thinks Anthony is gonna hurt me. My daddy told me it's mama who don't want me to see him. Daddy's just trying to keep the peace with her. I don't know if she means forever or what. But she can forget that. There will *never* be another man for me," Ebony says with conviction in her voice, as she lays back, twirling her hair around her fingers, "That's right. I said *never*!"
She smiles and they move on to discuss what may happen to Tank on Tuesday. This is his 3rd offense and he's only 14 years old. The foursome are praying he gets a break.

Tuesday is Ajay's birthday, as well. There is only 1 thing that will stop the crew from getting together. That would be if Tank gets locked up. But then, they will try to get together, even more so, as a tribute to Tank. One way or another, it's going down and the foursome are determined to be there, no matter what it takes. But they need a plan to get out of granny and papa's house.

"Ebony, go get the phone out of the hallway. Lets call somebody," Rebbie says.

"Who are we gonna call?" T-baby asks as she laughs and says "*Ghostbusters*? Everybody in our crew is on restriction, just like us."

"For real," Ebony says, "We can't even answer the phone at our house. I think we came out better by coming over here."

"We can't either," Nina agrees, "We *are* better off over here."

"I know who we *can* call," Ebony says with a smile.

"Who?" the others asks.

"Renee."

"Oh yea, kid. Brilliant," Nina says.

"We can get her and Chill to do our communicating," Ebony says, "I know they will. They're the ones who hooked me and Anthony up with that room and all of the fixings."

They call and talk to Renee. She tells them to give her some time to think of a plan. But to rest assured, her and Chill will come up with a way to get the crew together.

Renee is the big sister to this crew. She has been in the game with Chill for over 8 years. She'll be 20 in November. She definitely has her props in this crew. The foursome know her and Chill won't let them down.

After sneaking the phone back to the hallway, the girls talk awhile longer until everyone is sleepy. They turn out the lamp and go to sleep.

On Monday morning, they help with breakfast, then clean up the kitchen. Granny calls Houston to talk to big mama Eloise. Something they do every 2 days. The foursome talk to her too. Of course, she has some choice conversation for Ebony but Ebony knows big mama still loves her and she always will. No matter what she's done.

After they hang up, the girls help out in the yard. When the yard work is done, they watch TV and sit around acting bored. Finally, papa Brown gives them permission to call home and talk to their families. They had counted on him feeling sorry for them and giving them permission to talk on the phone.

Nina talks to Tank when Ebony calls home. She tells him to try to get in touch with Chill and find out the plan for tomorrow night. He reminds her that he may not even be around, tomorrow night. She tells him she knows in her heart that he will be.

After their conversation, she calls home. Lynn answers, though she isn't suppose too and Nina tells her about the plan.

"Okay, kid. That means we're gonna get out the house and get our crew together," Lynn says, "I know they'll come through with something."

"Mama and daddy must be at work?" Nina asks.

"Mama is," Lynn says, "Daddy's in the bathroom, right now. He's getting ready to go. That's why I answered the phone. He's in the shower."

Since big Al is still at home, Ajay won't even come to the phone. He isn't taking a chance on getting caught talking to Ebony. Not after giving his

father his word. Actually, what he's doing is stepping back to prove a point to his parents and hers. He feels like their parents blame him and they thinks he convinced Ebony to start having sex. His plan is to avoid Ebony and make her come after him. This way, hopefully their parents will see that and cut him some slack. As hard as it is for him, he doesn't take the phone. Ebony is disappointed. She wants to hear his voice, so badly. She knows she has to see him now. She knows if they're face to face, he can't refuse her. She has to believe that. Any other explanation hurts too bad.
Please don't let my mother be right with what she said about you, Anthony. Don't make me chase you.

She remembers what her mother said to her before this punishment was given. With Ajay making her chase him, it *could* look to Ebony like her mother was right about him.

Later in the afternoon, papa and granny take them to the mall. The girls aren't suppose to go but the grandparents can't bear to see them so depressed. They was sitting around like their hearts were broken. That's exactly what the foursome had counted on. Papa buys everyone an outfit. Then he takes them to *McDonalds* for lunch. After lunch, they go back to the house and help granny prepare dinner.

After dinner and they clean up the kitchen. It's the same routine as the night before, then they settle in for bed. T-baby goes to get the phone, this time. They call Renee. She isn't home but Chill is there. Ebony talks to him about Ajay not talking to her earlier and about tomorrow's plan.

"Baby girl, you know we're gonna hook all of that up if we can," Chill says, "Me, Rich and June was just talking about that."
When T-baby finds out Rich is there, she takes the phone and asks for him. He takes the phone from Chill.

"Hey. What up, boo?" he asks, sounding exuberant.

"Nothing. Just bored to death. What's up with you?" T-baby asks.

"Chilling with my crew. That's about it," he answers.
The other 3 girls talk about how the boys are able to break punishment but they can't. While Rich and T-baby continue their talk.

"I wish I could chill with you," T-baby says.

"I wish you could too," Rich says, "We're suppose to hook up tomorrow night, right?"

"We're trying too, if everything works out," she says.

"Y'all gonna sneak out?" he asks.

"Shit, yea. Y'all gonna come get us?"

He tells her, Renee is suppose to do that and she'll have to give them the details. Then, June takes the phone and asks for Rebbie, who takes the phone from T-baby.

After a few minutes into their conversation, June asks her if she's down for sneaking out too. She says yes, she's coming with her girls.

While they're on the phone, Ajay comes over. Rebbie lets Ebony know he's there. Ebony takes the phone and asks June to put Ajay on. Ajay takes the phone but doesn't say a word, so Ebony takes the initiative.

"Hello," she says.

"Uh huh," is Ajay's response.

"What's up? Why wouldn't you talk to me, earlier?"

"Cause my pops was there. You know what the deal is, right? I'm just chilling on all of this."

"So you're not gonna talk to me *anymore*, Anthony?"

"I don't know. You know what I'm saying? I'm not trying to fuck up nothing for nobody or myself," he says, making his voice sound very unconcerned, "Besides, you got something going on that don't include me. Don't you?"

He's referring to what his father told him during their talk. About her going through something in her life that she may not be comfortable with revealing to him, right now.

"What?!" she asks, with a rise in her voice.

"Who are you raising your voice at?" he asks, as calm as Al and John would but still having to be in control, "You need to calm it down."

"I didn't mean to raise my voice," she explains, "But I don't know what you're talking about."

"Yea well, really I don't either," he says and his voice is cold as ice. He's working extra hard to sound unconcerned. Even Chill and the guys notice how over the top he is but they don't say anything to him about it. They just stare at him and try not to laugh. Even though Ajay is excited just hearing Ebony's voice, he'd given his father his word. That's only for the meantime, though. Not forever. He's determined Ebony will be his wife, in the future. He's making sure she can handle his ways, his sternness and his

no-nonsense attitude. At the same time, he wants her to show him that their relationship is worth all the griping he has to hear from his mother and hers. Everyday since the room 111 incident. He knows she's going to think he's taking her for granted but he's not. As a female in this family, she has to follow rules, more than he does. They're on punishment. They can't see each other until both sets of their parents give them permission. And it's up to him, as the male, to make sure she adheres to it. It's hard for him to hear her voice and not speak his heart. But he's disciplined. He's thinking about the long haul and how he wants her to respond to his wishes and demands in the future. He's a Jackson, descended from Williams blood. Preparation is everything. It's a true sign of a quality leader. He'll be the head of his household and she'll have to learn to follow his lead. Naturally, he's still curious about what happened in her life that he isn't suppose to be able to understand. But he has given his word, on that part as well. He isn't going to bring it up. Not directly. His only refuge now, *is* to stall. Ebony doesn't know what to make of it. She has to say something to change the tone of their conversation.

"I wanna see you tomorrow, okay?" she asks suddenly.

"I don't even know what's up on tomorrow yet, alright? Just slow your role, baby girl. We'll see."

He's trying even *more* to be nonchalant about it. All of a sudden he says, "Look here, I have to go, alright?"

He hangs up. Not even giving her a chance to say goodbye.

For him, he couldn't fight the urge to give in to her. For her, it's like the end of the world. He holds his breath. She's crushed.

Why is he being so cold towards me? Is he really gonna stick to the word he gave to his father? How could he just hang up the phone without giving me a chance to speak? OH GOD! Is he through with me, just like that? And how can he think any part of my life doesn't include him? NO! It can't be over! I know it can't end like this.

She doesn't join her girls talk for the rest of the evening. She's preoccupied over her dilemma with Ajay. Her girls try talking about happier times but she can't shake her sadness. Not after the 2nd call. Something has to give.

What am I gonna do now? Can he refuse me? Will he? Why is he listening to his dad now? What does he think I have going on?

She has no answers for her own questions, at this point. But 1 thing is for sure. She's going to see Ajay, tomorrow. No doubt.

Her and her girls lay quiet, after Ebony turns off the lamp. Ebony cries herself to sleep. Her girls feel sad, even though their phone calls had gone well. They feel for Ebony. They fall asleep while Ebony lays there calling Chill's house over and over. And speaking to everyone except Ajay.

Tuesday after breakfast, the girls are told to get dressed for the courthouse and they do. They are all very nervous about the trial.

At Pearl's house, Tank is already dressed. He barely slept last night. He's certain the judge is going to send him to training school. He searches his dresser drawers, trying to find pictures of the whole crew to take to court with him. After finding them, he goes downstairs.

Jb is in the living room. He isn't going to the courthouse. Instead, he has to stay home and watch Jesse or lil man. Several of the crew's parents call to tell Pearl and John, they'll meet them there. Before leaving, Tank stands outside on the double driveways with Jb and Ajay. They're giving him words of encouragement. Ajay has been in this situation, more times than any other male in his crew.

"Man, this yo birthday and I'm fixin to get locked up," Tank says.

Ajay says, "Ah man, no you're not. Cause if you do, this is gonna be a fucked up day for me too. I'm not doing nothing for my birthday, if you get locked up."

They all hug and shake hands as Pearl and John comes out of the house.

"Let's go, son," John says.

"Jb, be sure to feed Jesse and keep a close eye on him," Pearl says.

"Yes ma'am," Jb replies.

Pearl and John speak to Ajay, as Al comes out the side door of his house.

"Y'all ready to go?" Al asks John and Pearl.

"Yea man," John says, "About as ready as we'll ever be."

Al gets into the car with them. Jb and Ajay watch as they back out and drive away.

"Man, if my little brother get sent off, I'm fucking something up, tonight," Jb says as his face holds a solemn look.

"I'll ride wit you on that one, homie," Ajay says, "All because of some buck oh fives and that frame up bullshit."

"Maybe I should catch one of them bitches off his pee's," Jb starts. While Ajay finishes with, "And pop goes the weasel."
They notice some of their crew walking up the street toward them. They sit on the porch and to wait for them. They figure Tank should be arriving downtown, soon. They're anxious to know how it's going to turn out.

****

At the courthouse, everyone is trying to be optimistic about the potential outcome. When Tank arrives, granny gives him a hug and kiss and wishes him well. Nina and the girls hug him and wish him luck too. Nina holds onto him for, at least 5 minutes. The parents are too concerned about the trial to even care that the crew are talking to each other today. After a little over an hours wait, the bailiff calls for Jeremy Brown to come into the judges chamber. This is where the hearing will take place. Only Tank, his parents, grandparents and Attorney Wheeler are allowed to go back. The 6 of them go in, while everyone else has to wait in the corridor.

Jan and Bre arrive at Jb's house to wait for the decision. They join Lynn, June and Rich, who are already there on the porch, with Ajay and Jb. Mama Jo comes out of her house, from time to time, to check on them and to see if there has been any word. The parents don't mind them talking today. They *expect* it. This is family going to trial. Their parents have been here, many times and so have their grandparents. All 3 generations have dabbled in and out of this same *injustice* system.

Renee has left for the courthouse. Chill, Rob and Stoney decide to come across the street and wait with the rest of the crew. When they get to Pearl's porch, it's obvious Jb is nervous for his lil brother. He's pacing back and forth, a lot. All they can do for Tank, right now, is wait and pray.

****

At the courthouse, while all Tank's supporters are sitting around waiting for the outcome, a group of girls walk up.

"Excuse me," says 1 of the girls, "Are y'all here for the Jeremy Brown case?"

"Yes, we are. I'm his aunt," Brenda says, "And you are?"

"I'm his girlfriend. My name is Alana. Alana Casey," she says. Nina and the foursome sit up to get a closer look.

"Who?" T-baby asks.

"Sshh" Nina demands, "I wanna hear this."

They try to listen as the girl continues, saying, "I went to Pittsburgh to visit my grandparents when we got out of school, last month," Alana says to aunt Brenda, "When I got back to Cleveland, on Sunday, my girlfriends told me what happened to Jeremy and that he had court today. I *had* to come down here."

"And you are?" Brenda asks again, as if she didn't hear Alana's introduction the 1st time.

"His girlfriend. My name is Alana Casey."

"Well honey, I don't know about all of that. But no one is allowed inside. Everyone has to wait out here," Brenda says.

Without an invitation to stay, Alana says, "Okay. We'll wait with y'all, if that's okay."

Brenda waves her off. She knows there is some trouble about to brew. She was hoping the new girls would've taken a hint from her smug attitude and left. But they didn't. Instead, they sit down to wait with everyone else. They sit dangerously close to the foursome, who go right in on Alana, instantly.

"Where do you know Tank from?" Ebony asks with a look of displeasure on her face.

"Yes. Where do you know him from?" Nina chimes in.

"Oh, we met at a junior high track meet, in April," Alana says.

"*And*?" Nina asks.

"Well, we hooked up from there," Alana says dryly.

"We've never heard of you," Rebbie says.

"I was a freshman, last year and we went to different schools."

"I went to the same school as Jeremy, so *what*?" Nina asks.

"My brother has never told me about you," Ebony says, obviously growing more upset.

"You must be Ebony?" Alana asks as she smiles, "He told me about you. Don't you play basketball, real good?"

"Yea, whatever," Ebony says, "He never mentioned you, to me and we talk about everything and everybody!"

Ebony's voice rises as she becomes angry and stands up. Uncle Greg motions for them to quiet down. He looks down to where the girls are and tells Ebony to sit down. He's unaware of the hostility that's brewing between the 2 groups of girls. Ebony sits but she continues to stare at this girl who claims to be her, closest brother's girlfriend. She's about to speak again when the doors to the courtroom open up. As the bailiff comes out to call in the next case, granny comes out.

"What did he say, mama?" Greg Sr asks as everyone holds their breath and waits for granny to answer.

"He's gonna be fine," granny answers.

She tells them the judge decided Tank *will* be sent away, just not to training school. She says the judge wants him off of the Cleveland streets, for a year. The only reason he didn't send him to state school is because Pearl and John agreed to take him to Houston, for the 1 year he has to be banished. The judge stated he was not to be on the streets of *any* Cleveland community for 365 days. If he gets another strike against him, during the next year, he would be sent to training school, immediately. And he would have to waive his rights to a trial.

"Pearl, John, Wheeler and Jackson are in there with him, finishing up the paperwork. Look's like he'll be going with you to Eloise's house, baby girl," granny says to Ebony.

Ebony runs up and hugs her granny when she learns Tank isn't getting locked up. She's happy he'll be with her in Houston too. Nina and the crew all hug granny and each other. But they still have to get to the bottom of this accusation from Alana Casey.

All the parents and the foursome, hug Tank when he comes out of the Judge's chamber. He's all smiles and very happy to be done.

"Alright now, son. This is your second chance," big Al says.

"I know it, sir," Tank says as he keeps a pleasant smile on his face. He hugs big Al. Nina catches his hand and he hugs her again.

"Was you scared for me?" he asks Nina.

"Yes I was," Nina answers as they start to walk out.

"Congratulations Jeremy!" Alana yells, refusing to be ignored.

"Thank you!" Tank says with a frown.

He's trying to place where he knows her from. Their parents have gone out the front door. They're relieved everything went so well. They don't even care that the crew are together, still. Tank and Nina, T-baby, Rebbie and Ebony lag behind. The foursome want to confront Alana without the grownups around. They're about to get their chance.

"Oh, I don't get a hug?" Alana asks.

"Hell no!" Nina screams as she turns around to face Alana.

"Who are you suppose to be?" Alana asks in a very agitated voice.

"Nina Shalon Jackson, bitch! That's who! Write it down!"

"Yea ho! This is Tank's girlfriend!" Ebony adds, pointing to Nina.

"So who the fuck are you!?!" T-baby yells.

"No damn body!" Rebbie adds as they are all ready to back Nina.

"Hey, look here," Tanks says, "Lets go. Y'all wanna get me into some more shit? Right here in the damn *courthouse,* before I can even get out the damn door?"

He's turning Nina back around. He tries to walk her towards the door. Alana won't give up and stop addressing him, which keeps Nina planted.

"So you're leaving with them?" Alana asks as her 2 girlfriends mumble odd comments of displeasure.

"Hell yea, he is!" Nina yells as Tank prohibits her from going back.

"Come on, baby. *Fuck* that," he says as he grabs her by the arm and this time, he puts his arm around her shoulders and escorts her off.

"Twin, y'all come on, *right now*," he insists while still trying to force Nina to walk toward the exit.

After seeing Nina isn't going to leave without them, Ebony, T-baby and Rebbie turn to walk toward Nina and Tank.

"Fuck you, Jeremy! Nigga, you ain't shit, anyway!" Alana yells.

Ebony whips around and is heading straight for her. She looks as if she's ready to rip her head off, as she says, "So what you wanna do, bitch? With your stupid ass! You're not gonna be *frontin* on my brother!"

Tank grabs her in the nick of time and stops her girls advancement too. Alana and her posse retreat in the other direction, slowly but surely.

"Come on, twin! You wanna get me locked up? Y'all don't fuck me up, like this. Ebony lets go!"

Ebony, now realizing people are starting to gather, decides to calm down and get her crew out of there. But before they get to the door, Alana and her girls shout some more obscenities. This time from the other end of the courthouse. Nina flips a middle over her shoulder, to Alana and posse. The

crew laugh at Alana and her girls. When they do get to the door, John, Al and Greg are coming back up the stairs looking for them.

"Y'all come on and let's get the hell away from down here," big John orders.

The foursome go out and get into the car with granny and papa. Renee had come up late and gotten the verdict from Pearl. She hugs Tank, then she comes over to papa's car and speaks to him and granny.

"How have y'all been?" she asks.

They say, "Fine, as can be."

"I see y'all got my lil sisters again tonight, ha?" she asks.

She's trying to be certain the girls are going to stay with them, this evening.

"Yes, we're spending another night," Ebony says, while smiling slyly at Renee because she knows why Renee is asking that question.

"Oh, alright. Granny, what are you cooking tonight?" Renee asks.

"Well baby, we all decided to cook over at Pearl and Jo's, this evening," granny says, "Sort of a celebration for Jeremy and for Ant 'knees birthday too. It'll be a lil bit of everything, I suppose. We made the cakes and pies, already. The girls helped me. We got chicken and dumplings, greens, turkey's and all of the fixings."

"Well, I know me and my two aren't gonna miss that, for *anything*," Renee says, "You know I never pass on an opportunity to, *not cook*. Kenny took all of the soda's to mama Jo, already. I'll see y'all there," Renee says.

She gives the foursome the eye and kisses granny on the cheek. Then, she walks over to the blazer, gets in and drives away.

She calls the crew, back at Pearl's house, from her cell phone and gives them the verdict. They're relieved to hear it. Now Renee is sure her plan will work but she has to let the girls know how it's laid out.

The crew at Pearl's house are already in party mode, after hearing the verdict. They're giving pounds, hugs, high fives and all.

"I was ready to give up everything to get him back," Jb says.

"Me too," Chill admits, "I would've went all the way legit."

"I don't know bout *all* that," Ajay says while laughing, "You're rich, bro. I'm gonna be rich too, one day."

"No joke, he is," June adds, "You got a cell phone, man."

"The shit cost a *hundred* dollars a minute," Chill says and laughs.

He's the only non-business person this crew knows who has a cell phone. Attorney Wheeler has one. Dr. Weston has one. Big John has 1 in his rig, which belongs to the trucking company. He only uses it if he can't find a pay phone while on 1 of his many trips. Chill and Renee use theirs on a daily basis and they allow their crew to use it, as well.

"Hey crew, we're all doing alright," Chill says, "What I have, we all have. Y'all my crew and that's my greatest worth."

They celebrate as they watch the cars arrive back from the courthouse. It's about to be some good eating, going on. All of the crew and their families are meeting at Pearl and Jo's houses. Ebony and the girls are wondering what the plan is to get them out of granny's house, while everybody gets together for dinner, birthday cake and lots of pictures.

Jeremy's trial had taken Ebony's attention off of the heartbreak she'd felt from her and Ajay's phone call, yesterday. But she hasn't forgotten. She's on a mission to find out why he was being so cold towards her. She seriously doubts if he's going to stick to the word he'd given to his father. It's just something about the way he touches her. She know it's the real thing. It has to be.

****

By 5:00pm, they're all full of food and drink. Some parents and their small children have to leave. The parents have to get babysitters, so they can go to work. Mama Jo, Pearl and Al have to go in too. Bre, Jan, Rich, June and Jr are allowed to stay. Renee tells Lynn to go with the foursome to granny's house for the night. Lynn's youngest sisters, Pam and Erica are going to help Brittany baby sit her twin siblings at Brian Sr and Brenda's home. Jo all but pushes Lynn into the car because she doesn't trust leaving her home alone, not with Jb next door. Initially, Lynn plays it off, like she doesn't want to go, just to throw her mother off. But she gets clothes together and leaves with granny, papa and the foursome.

When they get to granny's, Lynn takes her bath, early. Ebony and her girls hang out in the room, still trying to figure out the plan. When Lynn comes into the room, they're all over her. Lynn calms them down, then tells them they are to take their bathes and go to bed by 9:00pm, as usual. After granny and papa are asleep, they're going to get dressed. She

says whomever is last out of the bathroom is to get the phone and bring it into the room.

"And whoever *gotta* curl hair, better wait and do it at Chill's house," she whispers.

At 10:30pm, they have to call Renee and let her know they're ready. Lynn says they're going to climb out the window and meet Renee down the block. After the party, this is how they're coming back into the house.

She concludes by saying, "So don't y'all get fucked up."

The girls follow Lynn's instructions. At 9pm, they all talk. The foursome tells Lynn what happened at the courthouse with Alana. Lynn tells them she's seen her once, at Stoney's house party. That was prom night, this past spring. Alana and some other girls had gotten dropped off there, after midnight. She says Nina and the foursome was long gone because they were still not allowed out after 9pm.

"Alana and her girls was hanging around with Stan and Patrick, from The Grove," Lynn says, "And I thought they was with them. But me and John junior left with Jan, Rob, junior and Tonya, going to Chill's house, around one in the morning."

"Was Tank still there?" Nina asks.

"Yea. Him, Ajay, Rich, June and Bre stayed at the party with Stoney," Lynn says, "But that's the only time I saw her and that was in May. I haven't seen her since."

Lynn tells them she also knows Alana from running track. Lynn is a sprinter. 1 of the best, *if not the best,* in the State. She's lettered in track since 7th grade. She's a sophomore now and a legend in her own time.

"Since y'all telling me that bitch is trying to move in on crew, I can't wait to get her slow ass on the track, next year. When that bitch get to high school and we meet on that track, I'm gonna burn that ass up," she boasts.

"I might burn that ass *way* before then," Nina adds.

The others laugh but Nina doesn't. She's serious about Tank and she's down to let the world know it.

At Chill's house, around 9:45pm, everybody is getting loose. Ajay, Jb and Tank are just arriving. Jo, Al and Pearl have gone to work. John has turned in early and the guys are out of the house and at the party, soon after. As if big John would've stopped them. The judge had given Tank a

week to leave Cleveland. During that week, he's suppose to be confined to the block he resides on. That's cool with Tank. Everything and everybody he has to see, lives near. The crew have already discussed it. No matter what illegalities go down tonight, he will not be involved in any of them. Chill was adamant about that part.

While everyone dances and enjoys all the party flavors, Tank and the crew reminisce on old times. They talk about his trip to Houston and how they'll all stay in touch. About this time, Alana and her crew shows up.

"Oh shit, man! What that ho doing here?" Tank asks as he slouches down, trying not to be seen.

"I don't know player. But she brought all her ho's wit her," Jb adds as he laughs.

Alana has brought 5 girls with her, this time. It seems very obvious, she's anticipating a confrontation. Amongst the 5, is none other than Anita Davis.

"Oh fuck! All the ho's out tonight," Ajay says but he's obviously not interested in Anita's company anymore.

"That bitch must've healed up," Rich says.

They all laugh. All except Ajay. He's always the serious one. He just shakes his head. *Negatively.*

"What's up, fellows? Happy Birthday, Ajay," Anita says.

Her and the other 5 girls have made their way over to where the crew guys are standing. Jan, Bre and Renee peep the situation, instantly. They put their eagle eyes on these 6 outsiders. They have to confront them now too.

"Listen here, y'all," Renee states to the 6 outsiders, "It's not gonna be any bullshit up in my crib. I wanna make damn sure you muthafuckaz understand me. Any drama tonight, had better be somewhere besides here." She's looking directly at Anita.

"We just came for the party, Renee," Gloria says, "We're not trying to start nothing.

Gloria is 1 of the 6 females. She's Renee's age and knows Renee, from the set. She also knows Renee is taking no shit from anyone.

"We're chilling. We're all chilling, for real," Gloria says as she looks around at her 5 friends.

"Word up, because if any shit get started tonight, I'm gonna be the one to finish it," Renee adds, "Do y'all understand me?"

"We're chilling," they all say and taking Renee's hint to heart, they start to mingle.

Tank goes into the kitchen. He eased away from the front. He doesn't want to be near Alana. He goes and gets brews for the crew. But Alana sees him go in there and she follows him.

"You're gonna act like you don't know me, Jeremy?" she asks.

"Nah, I know you. I just don't dig the way you play games."

"I know you do. *Know me*, that is and well, at that," she says walking up closer on him.

"Look here. I don't know what kind of shit you on. But I'm not wit it. I hit it, one time and shit. You know what I'm saying? We banged one damn time. You sucked the dick and lick the balls, like a pro. You offered me some asshole but I declined that. See, I remember you. But that still don't make us homies or no shit *like that*."

"What's wrong, Jeremy? I don't see your girlfriend around, so why are you being so cold?"

"Like I said, we fucked! That don't make us homies, crew and we damn sho not friends. I don't even get why you keep rushing up on me," he says, "You're a *real naggin* type of broad. I wouldn't have fucked you, if I knew that. And that still don't mean we're homies, so step off."

"No. But I tell you what it does make us," Alana says.

"What the fuck does it make us?" he asks.

He really isn't interested in her response. But she jumps right up in his face and shouts, "Parents!"

"What!?!" he yells and fumbles, then drops 1 of the 3 forties he had in his arms.

"That's right, Tank! I'm pregnant and you're the daddy!"

Jb and Ajay come into the kitchen to check out what the crash was.

"Bitch, you tripping now!" Tank yells, growing angry instantly.

"Call it what you want but I'm not gonna deal with this by myself. Both of us played a part in this child being made."

"I used a jimmy when I fucked you! Some other nigga done played yo bitch ass! You got me fucked up wit this dumb shit!"

"No. It's yours, Jeremy. I know that. So don't even come with that shit," Alana counters.

"Nobody is trying to hear this shit you talking about, bitch! You're

gonna have to ease up out of my muafuckin' face, right *the fuck* now!"
He sits the other 2 forties on the counter. Ajay has cleaned up the glass and beer from the floor. Him and Jb are listening to the conversation. They notice Tank is about to rush her, so they step in and grab him.

"Chill out, man," Ajay says "You don't need this shit on you."

"Come on, bro! Get your *brewski* and come in here wit us," Jb says.

"This bitch on this fuck shit, crew," Tank argues still.

The guys look at Alana, in disgust. Ajay grabs another forty out of the fridge. The 3 of them walk out of the kitchen, leaving Alana standing alone.

The phone rings.

"Yo! What up?" Renee asks as she answers the cordless phone.

"Yo, homie. We're ready," Lynn whispers on the other end.

"Alright, peep this. I'm gonna scoop y'all up on the corner by North street. Y'all stay out of sight until I pass the house, turn around and come back," Renee instructs.

"I got it," Lynn whispers, "When are you leaving?"

"Now," Renee says.

"Word," Lynn whispers again, "See ya."

"In a minute."

They hang up.

Lynn and the foursome climb outside of the bedroom window and climb the chain link fence too. As soon as they see Renee pass, they go to the corner. She doubles back, picks them up and they head to the party.

CHAPTER 6

"HELL AVA" PARTY

Their street is lined up with cars and there are people standing along the street, when Renee arrives with Lynn and the foursome.

"I want y'all to come in through the back, with me," Renee says, "That's in case big John is still up and looking out."

"Cool," they all say.

Renee drives around to the back of the house. They finish off the rest of the blunt they was smoking on the way. Then they all get out, go in through the back door and into the kitchen.

"That weed got me thirsty as shit," Lynn says.

"Me too, kid," Renee agrees as they each grab a 40 from the fridge. They pass Ebony 1 for her and Nina to share. They give Rebbie 1 for her and T-baby to share.

Then Renee says, "You're on your own until three. Then I have to get y'all asses back out to The Point."

"That's good time, Renee" Nina says, "Hey! Where my man at?"

She walks into the front room. Ebony and the rest go in behind her. Nina spots Tank, immediately.

She says, "What's up baby!?!"

"Hey, Nina boo. What's happening?" Tank says with a huge grin on his face as he gives her a kiss.

T-baby goes to Rich, for a hug as Rebbie does the same with June. Tonya, who's here with Jr, comes over to speak to the foursome and Lynn. She had seen the foursome, only briefly, since returning from her visit to Detroit.

Ajay seems to be in a mellow mood, from Ebony's observation. He's standing quietly while swaying and he looks to be a million miles away.

"Happy birthday," Ebony says to him.

"Thank you, baby girl," he says with a half smile, "So you and your girls broke out of jail, ha?"

Nina breaks in after overhearing her brother.

She says, "Uh huh, bro. We had too."

"Y'all some bad girls," Rich adds as he kisses T-baby on her cheek. T-baby smiles at Ebony and says, "We're not bad but we wasn't missing this party for the world, man!"

"And everything in it," Ebony adds and looks directly at Ajay.

Alana and her crew had been out in their cars. They come back inside, just as the foursome are settling in with their guys. The foursome see Alana and her 5 friends for the first time.

"I know she's not up in here!" Nina yells.

"Oh hell no!" Rebbie adds.

Tank and June hold their hands and hope they'll stay calm. T-baby and Ebony have their say next.

"She fuck up and that's her ass!" T-baby says, "I dare her to come this way. I'm just itching for a scratch. I need to buss on them, anyway."

"She fucked up by showing up here," Ebony says and she's quickly taken to task by Ajay.

"Watch your mouth, baby girl," he says, immediately, "My girl don't curse like that."

Jan and Bre peeps the situation with their younger crew and immediately come to their side.

"We already got them ho's in check," Bre says.

"Don't even sweat it," Jan adds.

"Oh we ain't *sweatin'* shit," Nina says, "They better be."

"Chill out, baby. It won't be nothing," Tank says, "Unless it's me whipping that ho's ass. Don't even worry about that lil bit."

"Bro, you not getting into shit, tonight, man," Ajay says, "I'm not having it."

"Hell no, cuz," June agrees, "He's right about that shit. There will be no stress for you. None at all."

"None of it, gee," Rich adds in a matter-of-fact tone.

"Hey, crew. Them bitches know what's up, already," Bre says to Nina, "That shit was handled from jump."

"Cool. As long as that ho stay in her place," Nina says as she pulls Tank onto the dance floor.

Ebony notices Anita is with them. She looks at Ajay. He has his eyes closed while bobbing his head to the music. Ebony drinks from her forty as she notices Anita watching Ajay, like she wants to come over.

"If she comes over here, I'm breaking this bottle across her head," Ebony says.

Ajay opens his eyes to see who she's referring too.

He asks, "She who?"

Ebony says, "Her," as she gestures toward Anita, then looks at him.

"Ah that bitch don't want *nuttin*," he says.

"That's good," Ebony says, "Because that's exactly what she's gonna get. *Nothing*."

"Come on, baby," he says, "Dance with me, alright? Let's calm your ass down."

He looks at her very seriously, "Are you gonna dance or not?"

He's backing onto the dance floor and swaying his body to *Sade's, Smooth Operator*. Ebony smiles as she follows him onto the dance floor.

This is the perfect song for him.

She's watching him, as they dance.

It's definitely smooth the way he handles me.

He holds her close to him, as he continues to sway while bringing her along for the ride. She likes this. But it gives her mixed signals, at the same time. He wouldn't even talk to her on the phone. But the minute he sees her, he has to touch her. She isn't going to complain. She's going to take advantage of it. She feels whatever his problem was yesterday, it must be over.

"Do you feel older, man?" Tank asks Ajay as Nina laughs.

"Hell no. I feel better," he answers and smiles.

Ajay is a good dancer, though he doesn't do it often. Not at parties and such, unless it's to a slow jam. To Ebony's knowledge, she's the only girl he has danced with. She has never seen him on the floor with any other girl, unless it was a girl from the crew, 1 of their grandmothers or mothers. Or him and the guys, clowning around. They jam to *Smooth Operator*. Then Rob goes right into *Never as good as the first time.* This song brings all of the crew couples to the floor, including Rob and Jan. The party has started to heat up. With Tonya back and the complete crew together again, it's on and popping. The guys whoop and holler, as usual. While the girls chant along with them. This is the way they kick it together, all the time. There is so much love shared between the crew, that anyone on the outside can't help but feel left out during times like this.

Anita and Alana continue to watch Ajay and Tank. On occasion, they make strange eyes at Ebony and Nina. They don't say anything. They just make taunting eyes, just not enough to get disturb Ebony or Nina. Ebony and Nina are on the floor with *their crew* guys. Anita and Alana wishes it were them.

After the song ends, they all leave the floor. They are thirsty and ready for another cool drink. Those that need a brew, go get 1 or send for one. Nina and Ebony finish their 40 ounce.

"We want another one," Nina says.

"Y'all trying to get drunk or something?" Ajay asks as he looks at Ebony.

"No. We just wanna party with y'all," she answers.

"Give them one of those singles, man," Ajay says to Tank, who's going in the kitchen for beers.

"Together!?!" Nina yells as she frowns and Ajay laughs.

"Nah. Both of y'all can have one," he says while smiling at Ebony.

"Get us one too!" T-baby yells.

Her and Rebbie have finished their forty ounce, as well.

"Alright, y'all know y'all gotta go back to lock down, while y'all trying to get fucked up," Ajay says, continuing to smile.

Everybody laughs. Tank gives each of the foursome a 12 ounce beer.

"Oooo we. It's hot as a muafucka up in here," Chill yells and laughs, "But y'all know where the party at, *right*!"

He has been on the dance floor most of the time with Renee.

"Sho nuff!" Renee agrees with him.

"Hey crew, let's step to the backyard for some air," Chill suggests and as the crew head to the back door, everyone else follows them.

"We should move the party back here, anyway," Ajay suggests.

Everyone agrees and while the guys roll the equipment to the backyard, Renee goes to get the camera.

She keeps plenty of film. They always get fucked up and take pictures of everybody. Then tease each other about their fucked up pictures, at their next event. Soon the music is going again and more people show up. It's close to midnight. First, Renee gets a picture of all the guys

in the crew. Chill, Rob, Stoney, Jr and Jb. Ajay, Tank, June and Rich. Then Chill takes 1 of the female crew. Renee, Jan, Bre, Tonya and Lynn. Ebony, Nina, Rebbie and T-baby. They take 18 snapshots of each pose. This way each member will have a copy. All 18 of them get together and the females stand in front of their guy. They take 18 of this pose, as they all yell, *"Crew For Life!"*, instead of saying cheese. They have to reload the camera several times but they get photos of everyone. The couples get individual shots together, as well. Then each member by his or herself. All of this takes about 30 minutes before they start snapping party shots of everyone else.

Alana and Anita are more determined to ease up into the group shots. They pretend they're just trying to get included in the picture taking. But it's much more than that. They're trying to get to Tank and Ajay. To avoid them, Ajay and Tank decide they want to leave.

When the picture taking is done, Tank asks Nina to go to her house. She says okay. Before they can leave, Alana approaches Tank again. Only because she notices he's about to leave with Nina.

She says, "Jeremy, we really need to talk."

"Bitch, don't call him Jeremy," Nina yells.

She's had enough of Alana's interfering, as she adds, "And what is your problem!?!"

"I don't have a problem. Except the way you're trying to act about this situation," Alana says to Tank, while trying to ignore Nina, who had asked the question and who is directly in front of her.

"What situation, you dumb ass ho!?" Nina asks, refusing to be ignored, "You and Jeremy don't have a situation! And he's *Tank* to you!"

She's all up in Alana's face, for real, by now. Alana pushes her back. She shouldn't have even done that. Because before she can get her arms adjusted, Ebony punches her in her face. T-baby and Rebbie pull her to the ground while Ebony and Nina commence to stomping her.

"Oh shit, man! Here we go!" Chill yells.

Alana's posse tries to counter but Jan, Bre, Lynn, Tonya and Renee swarm on them like bees from a hive, which has just been disturbed. They attack before they can even get close to the foursome.

This is learned behavior. This crew was taught to stand and fight together. For years, their parents and grandparents had told them of the many times they had fought together and how they used assault tactics.

Everyone is to be aware of where their crew are, at all times. This came from the days when people of color, marched for civil rights. When folks would come up missing, daily. Never to be seen *alive* again. Sometimes, they were never seen, at all. Those days they had attempted to makes peaceful strides, when they was sure to be attacked. In those days, they weren't able to fight back publicly, without certain death. But they'd had some days when they did get some reciprocity. A little payback. The type of payback where, if it had been discovered that they'd done it, it would've meant certain death too. They had to have damn near military tactics and evasive maneuvers, back then. All evasions was a means for setting a trap for their perceived enemies.

But Chill's crew took it and ran with it. They learned any time there is a perceived threat to 1 of their crew, they are to respond with action. While some of their crew wait to react. Tonight, the foursome was really the evasion. Renee and the older girls had wanted Gloria, Angie and Anita, from way back. There are fights and piles of girls, all over Chill's yard. The guys have seen enough. Satisfied that their girls have had their revenge, they decide to restore order. Eventually, Tank grabs Nina. Him, Rich, June and Ajay try to break the fights up. They finally manage to get most of the girls to stop. But then, Ebony spins away from Ajay, turns around and starts punching Anita. This is who she had wanted a piece of since the 4th of July. As she beats Anita, no one else moves. Anita tries to back up and swing. But Ebony punches her hard in her face and she falls on her ass. Ebony jumps on top of her and continues to beat her, about the face and head. The guys have broken up the other fights but Ebony is still going.

"No. Leave her alone," Chill demands, "Let her get in her ass. That ho been fucking with her, all night! I peeped it. Let her beat her ass good."
The crew adheres to Chill's command and Ebony fights until she's too tired to swing anymore. She starts to scratch and claw at Anita's eyes. Anita's ass is thoroughly whipped. Ajay has been standing directly over them, the entire time, to make certain Anita didn't get the best of Ebony. Finally, he grabs Ebony. He has to struggle just to pull her off because Ebony isn't letting go of Anita.

"Come on, baby girl," Ajay tries, "You whooped her ass. She ain't got nothing left," he tries but Ebony wants to end this, once and for all.

"Stop Anthony! Let go!" she yells as he continues pulling her away.

She screams to her 1st cousin, "T-baby, reach that bottle to me!"
She grips Anita's throat while stretching her body, trying to reach an empty beer bottle, that's near. Rich holds T-baby, once she does manage to get to the bottle. He's not allowing her to reach Ebony. Nina and Rebbie are both trying to get away from Tank and June, so they can help. Jb can't allow his only sister to commit murder in sight of all of these witnesses.
He yells, "Y'all chill out! Come on now! Y'all not gonna help my lil sister kill nobody, out here, *are you*? Don't give her no *fuckin* bottle! Baby girl is gonna use that shit!"
He's barely managing to keep Lynn at bay. At last, Ajay gets Ebony to free her hands from Anita's throat. He has to wrap her up tight, in his arms, in order to keep her from getting any part of her body on Anita's. Still, Ebony doesn't give up. She keeps trying to kick her. Finally, Ajay pins her against 1 of the cars and holds her there.
He's whispering, "Come on, baby. It's over, alright? Cool out before them folks be out here," he says, still trying to calm her down.
Angry tears roll down Ebony's cheeks. She makes no sound.
Chill and Renee come over to her and assist Ajay with getting her calm.

"Baby girl, you've kicked the living shit out of her, so calm down. It's alright, now," Chill says as he smiles.
Renee chuckles and says, "But if them po-po's come out here, Tank is going to jail. All of us are going to jail, so cool out. I know she's feeling you."

"Everybody should be feeling you, by now," Chill adds, looking directly at Ajay who nods.

"*And I got it all on tape*!" A Q-dog named Arthur Owens yells.

"Alright, *money shot*!" Stoney says to Arthur as everyone laughs, "We'll check the playback, later."
Arthur has been videotaping the whole party. Ebony looks at him and gives him a half smile, as she straightens her clothes. Ajay brushes the dirt from her legs, as she looks around at everyone.

"I look a mess, y'all?" she asks as she comes around and laughs.

"No. You're straight," her girls say as they chuckle, "That ho look a mess!"
Alana and her crew have been escorted to their rides by some of the other partygoers, at Chill's request. Truth be told. The only reason Chill had allowed them to stay at the party was for their girls to get their revenge, if

they wanted it. Chill had no doubt the foursome wanted to get in Anita and Alana's asses. Now that they have, it's past time for the ho's to leave. For once they leave, everyone can feel at ease.

"Come on, y'all. Let's go chill for a minute," Tank says to Ajay, Rich and June, "Come on, twin. Y'all come on wit us."

T-baby, Rich, Rebbie and June plus Ebony and Ajay, follow Tank and Nina across the street to Jo's house. Ajay smoothes Ebony's clothes and hugs her, while they walk to his house. Alana and her crew can only watch them walk to Nina's house, as their cars are driving away.

"Daddy can't be up because he would've been out here by now," Tank says as they head inside of mama Jo's side door.

It's already 12:30am. The girls have 2½ hours before they're suppose to go back to granny's. Nina and Tank go directly to her parents room. She tells Rebbie, her and June can go into the big girls room and they go in, right away. She was going to send T-baby and Rich into Erica and Pam's room, since they're spending the night at Brenda's with Brittany, where they're getting paid to watch the twins. But Rich and T-baby are already making out on the couch. The very same couch they all sat on during the rap session, less than a week ago.

Ebony walks upstairs behind Nina and Tank. Ajay stands at the bottom and watches her. She walks into his room and gets undressed.

I'm not gonna be denied! I won't be!

She undresses completely and sits on his bed, in the dark. *Butt ass naked*!

He walks into his room, turns on the lamp and asks, "You wanna get me broke down, don't you?"

"No."

"Why do you continue to overlook the program?" he asks as he tries to appear unaffected by her being naked.

But he's very affected and she can see as much. There's a bulge in his pants.

"Because it's a shitty program," she offers.

"Who are you cursing at?" he asks, very seriously.

She notices his expression and adjusts her language, saying,

"I just don't like the program, that's all."

"Apologize," he demands as he still stands next to the lamp table.

"Why?" she asks, looking puzzled, "What am I apologizing for?"

"For *cursing* at your daddy," he says with a slight rise in his voice.

"Are you serious?"

"Uh huh," he answers.

"*Man*. Just forget it. You don't have to be like this, Ajay!"

"You don't call me Ajay," he says and becomes really agitated. She gets up to reach for her clothes. He steps over her, snatches the clothes from her hands and throws them back on the chair.

"Apologize to me," he demands again and this time he's standing right over her, as she sits on the edge of his bed.

"Anthony, you're wrong for this," she says as she stands up again to go get her clothes.

"Sit down!" he yells, this time startling her, "You got naked. Now you don't *wanna be naked*? What are you reaching for your clothes for? Make up your mind."

This time, he pushes her back down on the bed as his face grows very intense. She tries to move away from him but he puts his knees up on the bed, on either side of her.

"Move, Anthony. This ain't even right," she tries.

She can feel the tears welling up in her eyes, as she tries to slide back from him. He pushes her down on the bed. She starts to struggle with him but he holds her down, effortlessly.

"What is wrong with you?" she asks as she starts to feel frightened.

"Nothing's wrong with me," he says arrogantly.

He starts to undo his pants. Again, she tries to get up. He grabs her hair and this time, he slams her down on his bed. She struggles hard as the tears come. He has his pants and boxers down. He's kissing her very aggressively.

"Uh uh," she tries as his lips muffle her cries.

He continues to kiss her while rubbing her breast. Within seconds, he's inside of her.

"No!" she screams, because this isn't anything like the lovemaking sessions she's use too.

Ajay is obviously not himself, tonight.

He asks, "Is this what you want? Ha? Is this *all* you want from me?!"

This aggression is frightening to her and nothing like a week ago, in room 111. His thrust are hard from the onset, as if he's angry with her for even being here. His thrust grow harder and harder still. She remembers telling

Him, she never wanted to have sex in his bed since Anita was in here.
Is that the reason he's being so mean to me?

She's trying to sort it out in her head while he pounds into her flesh like a madman. She doesn't recognize anything about the boy who's fucking her, right now. This isn't familiar to her, at all. She just wants to get out of this room.

"No Ajay, no! Please stop! I'm sorry! Please don't do this. Don't do this to me!" she pleads.

"Don't call me, Ajay. Do you hear me?" he whispers.

He puts his hand over her mouth. He's stroking her like she's being punished for something. She figures it's something she did tonight, that he didn't like. She cries harder as she tries to get her hands free. He's holding her wrist together with 1 hand, while he has his other hand over her mouth and his body weight pins her to his bed. She realizes no matter how much she tries, she can't break free. She tries to bite his fingers but he manages to keep his hand cupped over her mouth. Through muffled screams, he continues for more then 5 minutes. She stops struggling. All she can do is cry. He's looking into her eyes, the entire time. She cries more. She hopes he'll snap out of whatever zone he's in and realize that, not only is he hurting her. But he's scaring the hell out of her too. She cries, many tears. She isn't sure what hurts more. The way he's treating her body or the way he's treating her.

Then, all of a sudden, he stops. He doesn't even climax. But as suddenly as he had started this encounter, he stops and gets up off of her. He pulls his clothes up, grabs her clothes and throws them to her. He walks out of his room and closes the door. He leaves her in there. Alone, naked and confused. She rolls over on her side. Her private hurts her, very bad. She gets up slowly and puts on her clothes, as she continues to cry. This encounter has hurt her deep in her heart. Not only was he mean to her. But instead of giving her the pleasure she'd sought, it felt like he had sexually assaulted her.

Dressed now, she walks slowly down the stairs and out of the side door. She wants to go to her room to be by herself. But she can't go home. She isn't even suppose to be in Shaker Heights. She stands outside of the side door, for a few minutes. She can hear the crew, still partying in the

backyard at Chill's house. She walks slowly toward the front of the house. When she gets next to the porch, she sees Ajay. He's sitting on his porch alone, staring into space. She turns to face him.

"Anthony," she calls out.

He props his forehead on his fist, as he turns his head toward her. His face is so sad and shiny. He's crying. She's stunned.

Anthony cries!?

This is something she had never even envisioned. Not to mention, expected to witness. He's always in control. Even when his grandfather Allen Sr died, she didn't see him cry. But tonight, he's crying. She walks closer to him.

"I'm sorry," she whispers, "for whatever I did to you. I don't even know what I did but I'm sorry. I'll write to you from big mama's. I love you."

She turns and walks away.

"Ebony, come here," he says softly but she keeps walking as tears roll down her cheeks again.

"Ebony, will *you please,* come here?" he tries again but she continues on into the street.

"Ebony, I love -," he pauses.

She walks faster, then she starts to run until she gets to Chill's front door. Without looking back, she opens it and goes inside.

Everyone is still out back. She can hear them mixing party cuts from *Michael Jackson's Thriller* album. She sits down on the couch alone, as she thinks about the episode in Ajay's room. The girls they had fought are long gone. There's only the crew left. This use to be the best time for her, when back, not so long ago, she was able to sneak over here. It use to be the best of times at the crew parties. But tonight, for her had been a *Hellava Party*! She puts her hands over her face and cries.

****

At 2:30am, Lynn and Jb come downstairs. They're laughing and enjoying each others company when they notice Ebony asleep on the couch.

"Baby girl, wake up," Jb says as he shakes her.

Ebony is startled as she jumps up and looks around at her older crew.

"What are y'all doing back over here, of all people?" Renee asks.

She had come inside with Chill when most of the crew had gotten fucked up and left to go, do their own thing.

"Sis, I thought I was gonna have to come and drag your ass back over here," Renee adds and laughs.

"For real, cause y'all two are usually the main ones who go over the time limit," Lynn adds as she puts on her sandals.

Ebony says nothing. She just stands there. She notices Ajay is there also. He must've come in and sat in the recliner, next to the couch, after she had fallen asleep. He had watched her while she slept.

Did the incident at his house really happen or did I dream it all?

One look at his face and she knows it was real. The crew are always aware of a problem with 1 another, even without 1 word being uttered. They know something's wrong with Ebony and Ajay. For them to have a chance to be off to themselves and not be, was the surest sign.

"Man, what's up wit y'all?" Jb asks.

"Trouble in paradise?" Lynn asks as she smiles at Ebony.

Ebony still doesn't say anything and neither does Ajay. Chill, who's sitting on the loveseat, doesn't say anything, just yet. But he's watching Ajay. He has an idea that something happened over at mama Jo's house. They can hear the other 3 couples coming toward Chill's house. They are very loud.

First Nina, with T-baby and Rebbie hot on her heels, runs in and blows up the stairs to Chill's bathroom. T-baby and Rebbie run in the bathroom behind her and slam the door. Ebony still stands downstairs, motionless and frozen in her tracks.

A few seconds later, Tank, Rich and June blow through the door with Tank asking, "Where did Nina go?!?"

He's out of breathe and obviously nervous.

"Just chill out, man," Rich says, "Give her time to calm down and think about that lying bitch, for who she is."

"She's gonna be cool," June says.

"What the fuck is wrong with everybody, tonight?" Lynn asks as she stands up to adjust her clothes.

Her, Jb, and Renee are trying to calm Tank so he can tell them what went on. They're all talking at the same time. Ebony, Ajay and big Chill remain quiet. Chill watches Ajay's expressions, then Ebony's. Then he speaks.

TIME TO LEARN-RELOADED-Time Will Reveal-part 1

"Hold up, everybody!" he yells as he stands up slowly and says, "Everybody needs to calm the fuck down. First things first. Ajay what's up with you and Ebony?"

Ajay shakes his head, as if to say nothing is wrong or he doesn't know. Chill isn't sure which. Ebony still looks dazed and she doesn't even offer an answer. Chill presses her.

"Well, baby girl. Maybe you can tell me."

"I'm alright," she finally whispers.

"Oh yea?"

"Uh huh," she says.

"Then why haven't you gone to check on your girls, like you usually would?" he asks with his raised brow. He says, "Something is wrong in here, tonight. I mean, *really* fucked up. Tank you told Nina what that bitch said, didn't you?"

"Yea, man but that shit ain't true. I told her that bitch is lying."

"Look here, Renee," Chill says, "You need to go get those girls down here and take them to the point."

As Renee runs up the stairs to get Nina, Rebbie and T-baby, Chill says to the rest, "Tomorrow, we'll get together and straighten all of this shit out."

He looks at Ajay and Tank and repeats, "*All* of this shit."

Everyone shakes their head, affirmative. Ebony and Ajay look off into the distance.

Renee comes back down with Nina, T-baby and Rebbie and tell them to go get into the Blazer. She ask Lynn to take Ebony out. Then she gets the keys, her purse and joins them.

Chill is outside talking to Ebony and Nina when Renee makes it out there. Before he lets them get into the blazer, he tells them not to stress over whatever happened. He promises them he'll get to the bottom of it, *this morning and* not wait until tomorrow. Then they get into the Blazer.

As Renee starts up and backs out, Ebony looks at her watch. It's 3:00am. They back out into the street. Her and Nina look toward Chill's house. Tank and Ajay have come outside and are standing on the porch. They're watching the Blazer as they drive away. They both look stressed out. As if there's still something each of them want to say.

The girls climb back into the window and lock it. Nobody says

anything. They all get undressed, put on their nightshirts and climb into bed. Ebony turns off the lamp and they all lay quiet in the dark. There are no more tears for Ebony to cry. She wanted to see Ajay and she did. She wanted to kick Anita's ass. She did that too. She wanted to be alone with Ajay, just 1 last time, before she left for Houston. She had been in his room alone, with someone, tonight. But that was not her man.
Not my Anthony.

Rich, June and Jb are laid out in the living room asleep, when Renee returns. Chill, Ajay and Tank are having, what seems to be a very serious conversation at the kitchen table. Renee goes on upstairs to check on Lil Kenny, then she goes on to bed.

Downstairs in the kitchen, the very informative and much needed conversation continues. Ajay has just finished confessing his experiments.

"Man, I don't want you doing no more of that shit," Chill says to Ajay, "None of y'all don't need to fuck with that powder. The shit will ruin your life. Ajay, you got camps to attend in a week. If they drug test you, you're *through*, brother."

"This ain't my first time trying it," Ajay admits.

"Make it your last," Chill states, "I'll take you out myself, before I let you ruin your *fuckin* future. Daddy Al and all of the fathers in this family will kick both of our asses, Ajay. You're going to the NBA, bro. Fuck with the shit again and I find out, that's yo ass. I'm bringing it to the heads. Do you understand me?" he says before starting in on Tank.
"And you best get your shit straight too," he says to Tank, "You can't fuck with ho's, like the one who done started showing up around here. That's a fatal attraction bitch. She'll *make* you kill her, to get rid of her. You make Nina understand that bitch is nobody and a one night stand. I don't care how you have to get that point across. But you had better get it across to her and do that, tomorrow."
Both Ajay and Tank say they understand. Ajay promises not to experiment with his supply anymore. Tank swears off of Alana, for life and the issue is closed.

Tank and Ajay go home and Chill goes up to his bedroom to get some sleep. Jb, June and Rich are still asleep downstairs in the living room.

In his room, before falling asleep and now down off of his high,

TIME TO LEARN-RELOADED-Time Will Reveal-part 1

Ajay thinks about the terrible way he had treated his girl. He knows he loves her but he has been forbidden to see her. Only she wants him to ignore that and not accept the consequences. All he wanted to do for his birthday, was to numb the pain of losing her to Houston by blowing a little powder cocaine. He hadn't even been able to take her out or spend their last few nights together. He has been so torn over what he's going to do in her absence. And even more, how is she going to handle herself, out of his presence. He knows how much everyone wants him to be successful at basketball. If he gets hooked on cocaine, that will definitely end his career. His forefathers had experimented with 1 substance or another. His father had always told him the dangers of alcohol and drugs. What these grown folks in this clan expect of Ajay, has been made crystal clear by his father Al. He's expected to be successful at life. He has no other options. He comes from a long line of leaders. Strong minded and strong willed men, who accept nothing short of achieving their goals. Whatever fruitful goals those are.

"I've got to make it right with baby girl," he says aloud, "Before she leaves here. Or she's gonna go off and find somebody else to take my place. I'll kill that muthafucka before I let him have my girl."

He has to make it right with her, some kind of way. He decides he isn't going to accept that he isn't the man for her. And it doesn't matter to him what his or her parents think. Or anyone else, for that matter. There's no doubt in his mind, after tonight, that he wants her. That's for certain. But he know she's just as strong willed as he is, when it comes to disrespect. She demands a high level of respect and compassion. He's prepared to be the man she needs. But now, he wonders if he has lost her for good, after how his cocaine high saw fit to treat her tonight. He thinks about how he can approach her the next time. He tires out and goes to sleep, without figuring out his formula.

Meanwhile at granny's, Ebony and the girls are still awake. All except Lynn. The foursome still haven't said anything. Ebony can hear sniffles throughout the room, from her girls. But it seems to be overclouded by the agony of what she's now dealing with, just as it was at Chill's house. She's trying to grasp her own situation. After trying to no avail, to make sense of it, she falls asleep. The birds had started to sing. Alerting her of the coming morning and the fact that she has, just 1 full day left in Cleveland.

TIME TO LEARN-RELOADED-Time Will Reveal-part 1

The next morning after breakfast, Lynn, Nina, T-baby and Rebbie are going home. Ebony's parents said she has to stay another night.

After her girls leave, she lays around all morning until 11:00am. Then she calls Tank. He's packing his bags for their trip, tomorrow.

"What happened to Nina?" she asks him.

"I'll tell you later," he says.

He can't go into details with Pearl in the room. She's helping him pack his things.

"Mama said your stuff is already packed from last week. And granny is suppose to wash up the stuff you have over there," he tells her.

"Okay. I'm gonna call you at two thirty, at Chill's house, so you can tell me. Alright?"

"Yea, alright," he says and they hang up.

She can't imagine what has Nina, so upset, that she wouldn't even talk about it earlier, with all of them. She knows it has to be something dreadful.

At exactly 2:30pm, Ebony calls Chill's house and Chill answers the phone. After saying hello, he immediately ask how she's doing. He tells her, he already knows what happened. With that, she forgets the interrogation she has for Tank. She wants to know how Ajay had responded to Chill. Chill tells her, he had a long talk with Ajay and Tank. Then he asks her to give Ajay a chance to explain himself.

"I don't know, Chill," she says, "He was acting real strange, last night. He's never been mean to me before and I didn't like it, at all."

She feels the urge to cry, as she thinks back to the episode in Ajay's room.

"He was wrong, baby girl. *Dead* wrong. I have no doubt about that. But just give him a chance to talk to you. *Please*? If you don't like what he tells you, then you do what you have to do. Alright?"

"I'm scared to see him alone," she says, "I know that sounds weird but-"

"No it doesn't, Ebony. It really doesn't," Chill says, "Look, we're gonna work something out, alright? I know he don't want you to leave, as it is. But definitely, not like this."

He tries to reassure her while Ajay is sitting right there during the entire conversation. And this time, he's asking for the phone. Chill lets Ebony know he wants to speak to her.

"You can put him on, if he wants to talk," she says with her voice sounding very unsure, still.

"Oh yea. He wants to talk today, baby girl. That's for sho," Chill says, "He's right here. Hang on a sec."

He gives Ajay the phone.

"Hello," Ajay says.

"Hello."

Immediately, there is an awkward silence. After about 10 seconds, Ajay says, "I need to talk to you about something."

"Talk."

"Face to face," he says, "You know that's the rule."

"I don't know about that."

"Please let me talk to you, Ebony. I need to tell you some things about what went down last night and how I was feeling," he says and his voice is it's usual calm and rather chilling.

"How?" she asks, "I have to stay here until daddy picks me up, in the morning, so we can leave."

"If I can come up with a way for us to talk, will you see me?" he asks, almost begging.

She thinks about it, then she answers with, "I'm not sneaking out, anymore. Not after what happened last night."

"I'm not asking you too. I just need to talk to you, baby girl. You're not even gonna give me a chance to make it up to you?" he asks, fearing now that he's messed up with her, forever.

"Ebony, please do. Just give me a chance to tell you what's up."

She listens. His voice is sincere. She can hear the desperation in his every word. She doesn't want to leave. But certainly not with a rift between her and her man. Today, he sounds like his usual self. Forceful and stern but in a caring way. Not in a violent or aggressive way, like he was last night.

Does he have two personalities?

Maybe he does but this is the man she plans to marry. This is her future husband and the future father of her children. The *Time To Learn* him is right now, if it's ever going to happen. She can hear the advice from poppa, in her head. It has become her blueprint and guide. It's what she uses as a gauge for their relationship.

"The best way you can tell if a young man cares about you, is when he knows he's in trouble with you. If he lets it linger and don't bother to handle it with you, right away? Keep moving. But if he doesn't let the sun set on it. Meaning, if he comes to straighten it out, as soon as possible. Then he's a keeper. But you still have to let him sweat, even if he does come to you, right away. That's so he'll remember, if he gets another chance, not to hurt you again."

The last few lines are ringing in her head and her ears, as loud as a damn bell. She can't pass on this man.
"But you still have to let him sweat, even if he does come to you, right away. **So** ***he'll remember, if he gets another chance, not to hurt you again."***

For her Poppa to have even said the next part;
"Is when he knows he's in trouble with you."

Meant, the women she admire, knows and she has to expect, that a man is going to make mistakes. Because he's human. A man is going to be a man and making mistakes doesn't mean, he isn't a good man or a real man. Just a, ***human*** **man.**

"I'll talk to you but you have to come over here. That way I know you won't get out of hand."

"I'll come wherever you want me too. So long as you say you'll see me. I don't care where it is," he says, wasting no time conceding to her stipulations.
But if he doesn't let the sun set on it. Meaning, if he comes to straighten it out, as soon as possible. Then he's a keeper.

"Well, you need to come over here," she says.

"When?"

"Come for dinner."

"*What*? Is that cool?"

"My granny will let you come. Especially since this is my last day. They'll figure as long as they're right here, we can't do nothing wrong," she says.

"Alright. I'm coming too. So let them know whatever you have to tell them. I'll be there, about four forty five, straight up. Alright?"

"Alright. But first let me talk to them and be sure. I don't wanna assume anything. I'll call you back."

"I'll be waiting for that call," he says.

They agree to talk in 30 minutes. After she's had a chance to talk to her grandparents.

In no time, her grandparents agree to allow Ajay to have dinner with them. It didn't even take 5 minutes, let alone thirty. And in her opinion, they were surprisingly understanding.

Granny seems almost happy and honored that Ajay wants to come over and have dinner. She moves about the kitchen singing and with an extra pep in her step. She sings upbeat songs while she prepares dinner.

"You will certainly wanna help me cook this dinner too, my dear," granny says to Ebony with a huge smile.

"Okay," Ebony says as she returns the huge smile.

"You have Eloise' smile and my eyes," granny says.

"I know and big mama is always saying *'I have to give it back to her'*," she says and they laugh hard.

Throughout the preparation of dinner, granny flashes her bright smiles. Ebony returns larger smiles. She's happier now as she goes to make the phone call to her man. She can't help but feel blessed. This is the start of things to come, as she sees it. She has 2 grandmothers who look forward to her having a good husband, as much as she does. Now, if only they can convince her parents to look forward to it, things could be *so* much easier.

She calls Ajay back with the news. He isn't shocked at how soon she had called back. He can hear granny singing in the background. He laughs. Then he tells her, he'll be there as planned. He asks if she minds holding the line for a minute because he still has to get permission from Chill to use his Blazer. She says she'll hold on.

Chill says it will be okay but he has to be careful. This isn't because of his driving. Ajay is an excellent driver. Chill said this because of the police and their tendency to harass them. Besides, Ajay hasn't gotten a license yet. Suddenly, Stoney who's also present, comes up with a surefire solution. He says Ajay can roll with him to The Point, if he wants too. Stoney is going to be out there at a friends house during the same time.

"Cool, man. But you know Breanna is gonna kick your ass about that bitch, out there," Chill says and he isn't laughing.

Neither is Stoney. Bre doesn't play that, player type shit. She's younger than he is but she's a serious ball of fire. She kicks ass and takes no names. She's a gangster girl without a doubt and many folks, who know her outside the crew, say that too. She loves herself some, Cheston *Stoney* Coleman.

"Ah man, you know I'm not ever fixin to fuck with her, like that. I'm gonna get in and get out, in a hurry," Stoney says and laughs.

Ajay relays the plan to Ebony. They agree to see each other at 4:45, then they hang up.

Ebony goes into the bathroom to prepare herself for his arrival. She's nervous about seeing him. Plus over dinner with her grandparents. But she still wants to look nice for him and she can't wait to see him.

Ajay goes home to take a shower and change his clothes.

At 4:15pm, Ajay and Stoney leave for *The Point*. He feels nervous, for the 1st time. But he's excited, more so. He loves her grandparents. Both sets. They treat him like he's their own. Probably because they've known him since before his birth. They know his history, his pedigree and his potential. They had helped to form this family's crew with the help of his grandparents, so he's all good for their oldest granddaughter.

Ebony and her girls hook up a 4-way conversation, after she's done helping granny with dinner. Since this is her last evening, all 4 girls are given permission to talk on the phone. For the 1st time since last night, they have a chance to talk. Nina lets them know that Alana claims to be pregnant for Tank. This makes Ebony, both angry and sad. But she understands why Nina didn't want to talk last night and why Tank couldn't today.

"That's why he couldn't tell me," Ebony says.

Nina also says they broke up. Ebony can tell this makes Nina, very sad.

"That can't be true," Ebony says, "You're the one who's gonna have my nieces and nephews. Not a *tramp* like that. She'll never be a part of this family. No way will that ever happen. None of our mothers, fathers or our grandparents will except her or her ways and y'all know it."

Nina tells them how much it hurts her, as she starts to cry again. They all tear up.

"If he says it ain't his, then I believe him," T-baby says, "But he shouldn't have been messing with a ho like that, anyway."

They all agree, as the 3 girls try to get Nina to cheer up.

TIME TO LEARN-RELOADED-Time Will Reveal-part 1

Rebbie has some news to share. Her and June had gone, all the way. She's no longer a virgin, after last night. They discuss all the intimate details. Rebbie is happy to have that behind her but feels like she's always the last 1, of the foursome, to do everything.

Ebony reminds her, "You had your boyfriend before me. June asked you out before Anthony asked me."

Rebbie giggles and says, "Okay. Well that's one time I wasn't last."

T-baby tells them that her and Rich was intimate again.

"And this time, it was nice," T-baby says and laughs.

Rebbie and T-baby have made strides in their relationships. When Ebony tells them Ajay had been disrespectful and mean to her, they get upset all over again.

"But he's coming over here, in a little while, to eat dinner with us," she says, "He said he wants to explain something to me."

Her girls insist that his explanation had better be a good one. The 3 girls promise to write her a letter tonight. They're going to put them in the mail and she'll get them all, as soon as she gets to Houston. Then comes the time for their tearful goodbyes. Before they can hang up, granny comes to the door to tell Ebony, Ajay has arrived.

"I have to go. He's here. I love y'all, so much," Ebony says.

"We love you too, Ebony," they all say.

Then they all say, "See ya."

"In a minute," she says and they hang up.

When she walks into the living room, Ajay is sitting on the couch talking to her grandfather. They speak to each other. He looks handsome. The look in his eyes assures her, he likes the way she looks also. She goes to help granny set the table while Ajay and papa talk. She tries to eavesdrop but can't hear a thing. Granny can't stop telling her how special it is to have him over, knowing that he's sweet on her grandbaby. Ebony's thinking maybe her granny doesn't want her to hear what the men are saying. Their conversation did seem really deep when she peeped in there. They are definitely chopping it up nicely, about something, from the way it looked.

During dinner, her grandfather talks to both of them about their lives. Ajay listens intensely, as papa tells them about how all of their parents came together. And why, no matter what or whom, this clan has to stick together and always be there for 1 another. That's when he gives his approval of their relationship, which surprises Ebony. Ajay doesn't seem shocked at all. Papa has an interesting opinion on the motel fiasco. One that puts both of them on the spot.

"If I hear about the two of you sneaking around again, like a couple of dogs in heat," he says, "I'll have you married and working jobs the next week. Do you understand me?"

They both say, "Yes sir."

"Those types of actions are good, alright. I'm not saying it's wrong for a man and a woman who care for each other-" He stops mid-sentence and questions them.

"Do you love my granddaughter?" he asks Ajay.

"Yes sir."

Ebony snaps her neck and looks at Ajay. She has never heard him say it and didn't know when he would or if he would. Her papa observes her shocked expression.

"Baby girl, you seem surprised that he says he loves you," papa says, "I know you was raised to only have sex with the man you're going to marry. Period. He was raised by a woman and a man, from this family. So he surely knows what sex with a girl from this family means."

He looks at Ajay.

Ajay says, "Yes sir, I do. I definitely know."

Then papa looks at Ebony and asks, "Do you love Ajay?"

"Yes sir," she says softly.

Her and Ajay's eyes meet and he smiles. Now she knows what they were talking about while her and granny was in the kitchen. *Marriage*! Papa had gotten to the good part. That question from papa and that answer from Ebony, also assures Ajay that he's in the right place and doing the right thing. She returns a smile to him. She feels all tingly inside. Then papa says they are only following their parents examples. Granny cosigns him on that.

"When you truly love somebody, you just love them," granny says, "You really don't worry about the consequences. Like Eloise and me. Pearl and Joanna too. Lord knows, John wasn't gonna leave your mama."

"No he wouldn't let go, for the world," papa adds, "Percy and Eloise was moving back to the south. To that land they're on, right now, in

Texas. Lil Pearline was determined she wasn't leaving. She asked us to vouch for her to stay here."

"And we did," granny says, "They knew we wouldn't allow harm to come to any child from our family. John was planning to marry her. She loved my son and he loved her. She was the best lady for my son. She was my best friend's daughter. It was what we had always planned."

"So how was we gonna go back on something, we had just as much to do with putting together as they did?" papa asks.

Ajay looks at Ebony. She looks back at him. That was a revelation. As her grandparents talk, she begins to think about all of the couples in the crew. From the 1st generation until now and how they are all connected.

Could this be what our parents and grandparents intended to happen? Me and Anthony being husband and wife?

Surely, they had to have known, if their children only mingled with each other, then eventually they would form relationships. Now listening to her grandparents version of it all, it seems like her and Ajay's relationship was inevitable. He smiles at her again. He must be feeling the same way.

"Ajay's daddy Al, met Jo, fell in love with her and refused to go back home to Boston," papa says, "His parents didn't worry."

"And big Joanna didn't either," granny says to Ebony, "He had her husbands name and passion. I see that look in Ajay's eyes when he looks at you. Eloise said the same thing."

"You already know she's your future," papa says to Ajay, "The only thing you're worried about is not messing it up before you can get a future together and take her off of John's hands. Ain't that right?"

"Yes sir," Ajay answers with a big smile, "That's it, exactly. I have to be able to spoil her and give her what she needs and wants."

They all laugh. Ebony is so happy about this dinner. She knows now, without a doubt, her grandparents, both sets of them, love Ajay and they accept him with her.

By the end of dinner, Ajay is glad he came over and so is Ebony. This has been an enlightening evening for both of them. While she helps granny clear the table and do the dishes, Ajay ask papa if he can have a few minutes to talk to Ebony alone. Papa tells him it will be okay and they can talk out on the back porch, in private.

"It's good to know this next crew is not going against the grain," papa says to Ajay as he lights his pipe.

"Do you remember me telling you, when I took lessons from you, that all of my life I've seen myself with Ebony?" Ajay asks.

"I do," papa answers.

"I feel like my pops and big John see it too. But it's hard to gauge our mothers," Ajay says.

"Steady your road, son," papa advises, "Follow your destiny. Never forget the crew she's from and what's expected. The rest is laid out in front of you. Only when you start to stray from it, will a man in the family pull your coat. Steady your road."

With that said, they shake hands and Ajay is excused. Papa takes his lit pipe and goes to his piano. He's satisfied that his 1st granddaughter is well on her way to keeping his tradition alive. For all intents and purposes, granny and papa have set the example for their crew to follow.

Once the dishes are done, Ajay and Ebony go out back and sit in the swing. They're both quiet, in the beginning. They can hear papa playing the piano inside.

"He's good," Ajay says, "You know I took lessons from him until I was eight. Before I started going to basketball camp, every summer."

"Yea, I remember that," she says softly, "He taught me the lil bit that I know too."

Her papa has been a music teacher for decades. They talk out back while inside, granny calls John and Greg on 3-way. She tells John they had dinner with Ajay and how nice it was. John doesn't like the idea of his parents letting Ebony see Ajay. But he knows not to say so. Granny can hear the lackluster in her oldest son's voice, so she tells both of them, Ajay had been wonderful. She also tells them to remember that any young man who will come over and have dinner with a young lady's grandparents, even after being forbidden to see that young lady, can't be all bad. He had to care for that young lady, somewhat.

"Do you want me to stop baby girl from seeing Ajay, when he loves her? It's the same way you loved her mother and didn't want me to allow her to leave you, John. Do you remember that?"

"Yes ma'am, mama. I sure do," he says.

TIME TO LEARN-RELOADED-Time Will Reveal-part 1

"You don't want your mama to be a hypocrite, do you?" she asks with a chuckle.

"No mama. I don't want you to be a hypocrite. Not at all," big John says.

"Then let them see each other before she goes away. At least, she ain't refusing to go, like her mama did," granny reminds John, "They both just want us to give them a little room to find their own way, okay?"
After some considerable time on the phone, she convinces them to talk to their wives and the other parents about letting the crew come together, for a few hours, before her 2 grand babies have to leave. John and Greg agree to call their crew and make it happen.

Ajay and Ebony, who are unaware of the phone call, are still out back and still rather silent, until he opens up and starts to talk.

"I'm sorry for what I did last night," he says suddenly.

"I'm sorry for cursing at you," she says.

"That's still was no reason for me to do what I did."
She sits quietly as he tries to explain the things that was going on with him and what was going though his mind, at the time.
"First of all, I wish you didn't have to leave. I thought I was ready to let you go, last week. Then after y'all had to stay longer, I felt like maybe it was a sign and maybe you wouldn't have to go, at all. All this week, I've been thinking about what my daddy said to me. Plus how we got busted at the motel. I felt like it was my fault mama P jumped on you, like that. You know? I was so mad when I saw her slap you. My whole body got hot. I started sweating. Just all of that, together," he says, "It wasn't working."

"That wasn't just on you, Anthony. I wanted to be there too."
He goes on to explain how he felt, thinking Tank would get locked up and she would be gone. That was bothering him more than he was willing to let show. He tells her that, for the first time, he hadn't really looked forward to his own birthday because he thought he would be loosing 2 of his closest friends. That's why he didn't want to talk about his birthday, on the phone, the other day. At the time, he thought Tank would be going away to state school. As if that wasn't enough, Alana came into the picture claiming to be pregnant for the guy that his sister loves, with all of her heart. He knew that would hurt her and the family, if it were true.

"I didn't like the way Anita kept trying to pick with you, the whole night, either. She know I never liked her, like that. That was our first and last time, solo."
He says the best part about the whole night, was when she beat Anita's ass. "I wanted to do it myself," he says, "But you know we don't hit girls. My pops would beat me like I stole something, if I did that."
He talks about when they went to his house and how he wanted to be with her. And he was going to be with her but he wanted to take his time.
"I didn't want you to just get naked, like that. I never thought you would've done that. Ebony, I wanted to hold you for awhile and try to tell you what I was thinking about. I wasn't sure how to say it. I'm just use to you always being shy with me. That's the one thing I figured would keep you mine. But you went to my room without me even asking you too. And when I came up there, you was already naked. Even after you told me you never wanted to have sex on my bed. I was gonna go in Nina's room and send June and Rebbie in my room. But you took off all of your *own* clothes. I didn't like that. I felt like you was getting too loose."

"I thought that's what you wanted me to do."

"I didn't like that. I wanted to undress you, myself, when the time was right. When you started talking all flip to me, I just snapped. I never wanted to hurt you, baby girl. I mean that. On everything I love, I never wanted to hurt you. I wanted that to be a special night. Special for you, you know? Before you had to leave me. But instead, I fucked it up because for the first time in our relationship, I didn't have complete control over the situation," he says softly, "As a man and as *your* man, I must have control. That's just me. I have to be in control of the situation, at all times. The one thing I didn't want to do, was to make you cry or run away. But that's exactly what I did," he says, "I just wanted my *innocent* Ebony, last night. But you was acting like one of them ho's you had just beat down."
She sighs. He's opened up to her about his feelings, for the 1st time in their relationship. She takes it all in. She has no desire to immolate Anita or Alana nor Darlene or anyone who acts like them. Not ever, in her life.
"Girls like her, act like that," he says, "They be already naked before you can get them in the room and shit. They'll do that with anybody or for anybody. I hope you don't."

"Oh *please*," she says quickly, "I'll never be like neither one of

them stank ho's. Never! And you can put that on everything *I love*." He laughs at hearing her speak like him. But he treasures what she has just said.

"That's what I wanted to know," he says softly.

"What?"

"Will you stay true to me?" he asks, looking into her eyes.

"Will you?" she asks, knowing the males in her crew, from top to bottom.

"I'll try too," he says and smiles.

"No you won't," she says smiling too.

"Now that's what I really wanted to see from you, last night," he says quickly.

"What?!?"

"Your smile," he says softly, "I like to see you smile, baby girl. It's like daylight for me. It makes my day. I just always like to see you smiling." She blushes openly. "Either way, I'm not ever gonna stop seeing you, no matter what nobody says. Because I can't. I don't want too and I'm not going too. I know what my pops said. But I'm gonna talk to him, some more. Bring him around. I will never stop seeing you, okay?"

"Yes," she says as she smiles big.

"I hope that answers whatever questions you might have," he says as he kisses her on her cheek, "Because I wanna be with you, just like you wanna be with me. I always have. Even before you liked me."

"When my papa asked you, did you love-"

"I said yes *I love you* because I do love you. Why do you think I can't stand to share you?" he asks, "I was gonna tell you, last night. But I had already fucked that up. It hurts me to know I treated you like that." She can tell this is a big step for him, so she doesn't push. But it makes her heart flutter to hear him say that he loves her. At this moment, she knows she will never leave this man.

"Will you forgive me for fucking up?" he asks.

"I already did, Anthony. When you came for dinner," she says as she smiles.

"Can I kiss you?" he asks.

"That would really make my day," she says, looking innocently into his eyes.

She learns it's her innocence which attracts him to her. He never cared that she had no experience. She doesn't have to feel like less of a woman than Darlene or Anita, just because they had fucked a lot of men and could handle his size. He doesn't want a whore. He doesn't want his wife to teach him about sex. He wants to teach her and in time, he *will* teach her everything she needs to know. He gives her a passionate kiss, lays her head against his chest and starts to swing. She can hear his heart beating rapidly.

"Anthony, I love you!" she says effortlessly.

"I know you do," he says as he gives her a kiss on her forehead. "You already know how to love. You've always been like that. You can see the good in people and you always try too. One day, you can teach me that."

"Me *teach* you?" she asks looking up at him.

"Yea. That's the one thing you're gonna have to show me," he says, "Because I'm keeping you, no matter what. You've been mine from the start and as far as I'm concerned, you're gonna always be mine. But I know I have to learn how to treat you, in order to keep you true to me. I'm gonna do that too. I'm gonna learn how to treat you, so you will always smile."

She's in awe of his maturity. Listening to him now, she knows she didn't understand the caliber of man she fell in love with. When it comes to him and her, he's focused. She knows now that she can trust him with her life and she will, from this day forward.

"Teaching you how to love. Now that's a job," she says and laughs.

"Yea but you already got all of the qualifications. Now all you have to do, is go to work on me," he says as he leans over and kisses her again.

"Mmm, my first job. I *like* working," she says as they laugh.

"You are *so* goofy," he says and laughs.

"Anthony, there will never be another man for me. I promise you that," she says as she looks up into his eyes, "Do you believe me?"

"Yes, baby. I believe you," he says, "Because I wouldn't be able to live with that. I would kill you, if you fucked over me."

He laughs before kissing her again. This time they kiss long and hard. Still, she believes he meant what he'd said about killing her if she cheated.

"Look baby, your first raise," he says as he looks down at the bulge in his pants and they both laugh and kiss again.

Ebony knows her grandparents are probably spying on them. Papa is no longer playing the piano.

"There's no part of my life that doesn't include you," Ebony says suddenly, "You're my heart, Anthony. I can't live without my heart. If you didn't love me back, I don't know what I would do. Because all I know is you and all I *wanna* know, in that way, is you."

He smiles and kisses her again. He decides not to tell her about the cocaine use. At least, not right now. That's 1 less thing she'll have to stress about while she's away. He's going to tell her, though, when the time is right. Perhaps when she reveals her secret to him. He decides not to pressure her for an explanation of what she's been through in her life, before they got together. This moment is all that matters to him. She's in his arms and she's smiling. That's more than he feels he deserves, after his actions last night. He had worried she would leave and move on with her life, after his altered stated mind saw fit to abuse her. But now, he knows she wants to love him for life. Not only that, but she's willing to help him learn how to love her better. They kiss again and again. Then she realizes it's getting closer to 9:00pm. She tells him she wants to be with him, once more before she leaves for Houston. She doesn't want last night to be her last memory of them. He assures her, he wants to make it right too.

"But how?" he asks.

"That's how," she says as she points to the window of her bedroom. He looks puzzled as he asks, "What does that mean?"

"That's the room where I sleep, right there," she says and smiles.

"Uh huh and what about it?" he asks as he's smiling now.

"Well now, I know you know how to get into a window, right?"

"Oh baby, you're bad. You know that?"

He's obviously interested in hearing her plan. He listens as she tells him how this plan can work. She tells him at 9:00pm, she has to go to bed. Her grandparents will be asleep by 9:30. Then she can let him in through the window and they can spend the night together, before her daddy comes in the morning.

"You're bad. I told you," he says and smiles.

"Only for you, though," she says in a matter-of-fact tone.

He agrees to come back around 10:30pm. They kiss, once more, then go inside. It's 8:15pm and she has to prepare for bed. He says goodnight to granny and papa, after thanking them for dinner. Ebony walks him to the door. They hug each other, quickly. Making certain not to disrespect her

grandparents. They say goodnight. He walks off down the street to Stoney's friend's house, looking back at her, every few steps. Once he's out of sight, she closes the door and goes to take her bath.

Once she's in her night clothes, she comes back into the living room to kiss her grandparents goodnight. She thanks them for the dinner with Ajay, then she goes into her bedroom.

She locks the door and lays across the bed. She's happy she's made up with Ajay. She knows he wants her and he wants to love her too. She feels good, as she gets out her pen and notebook and begins to write him a long letter.

Meanwhile at Pearl's house, John has talked to all of the parents about letting the kids get together, the next morning. He has decided he'll leave at noon, to give them a couple of hours to say their goodbyes. All of the parents have agreed to bring their kids by or to make certain they know they're allowed to come.

Tank is at Chill's house when he gets the news. He has already been trying to persuade Lynn to go to her house and get Nina. Nina was reluctant, at first. But she wants to see him before he leaves. She has already written a letter to him and Ebony. She decides to go with Lynn to Chill's house.

As soon as she walks in the door, Tank comes to her. They look at each other with longing eyes.

Without hesitation, he puts his arms around her waist and says, "I'm sorry, baby. I'm sorry that I fucked around. But I promise you that's not my kid."

She feels the urge to cry as she hugs him back.

"That's not my baby and I know it's not," he says.

"I pray it's not because you know that's suppose to be me," she says, "I'm the woman that's suppose to have your children."

"It's gonna be you," he says smiling, "You're the one who's gonna be my wife and the mother of my kids. These Brown genes *are not* for just anybody."

There are other crew in the living room, who cosign him, before going into the kitchen or the backyard to give them privacy.

"You know I wasn't leaving here without getting back with you, right Nina?"

"That would've been bad," she says.

"Real fucked up, baby. You know I can't leave here without seeing you," he reiterates.

Ajay and Stoney come walking in the door. Ajay sees them embracing and he smiles, as he approaches them with his hands out.

"Oh yea, its good. It's all good, partner," Ajay says.

He's in a jubilant mood as he walks in with his fist out to Tank, for a pound. They shake hands and do that half embrace that the crew guys do.

"So man, how was dinner with my folks?" Tank asks as he laughs.

"It was *real* dope. No bullshit. It was straight," Ajay says.

"Did you talk to Ebony?" Nina asks.

"Oh yea. We're gonna be alright," he says as he smiles.

"That's all good, homeboy," Tanks says, "We're gonna be alright too. Or at least I hope so. What you say, baby?" Tank ask, looking at Nina.

"Yes we're gonna make it, baby," she says and smiles.

"Where's Chill at?" Ajay asks.

"He's out in the backyard," Tank answers.

"I need to get the Blazer, tonight. For real. I need to be somewhere for ten o'clock," Ajay says, "I have a very important date with a lady, who's gonna be my future. You know what I'm saying?"

He heads out the back door while he's still talking. Nina smiles. She knows what's up with that time frame.

Ajay tells Chill about his evening and that him and Ebony have made up. He also tells him he has to go back at 10:30 to see her but he needs a ride. Chill says it'll be okay for him to use the Blazer. The same conditions apply, as earlier.

"Alright. I squared it away with Stoney's friend, to park in her driveway while I'm out there. Just in case you would've said yes."

"Well, alright man. Handle your business, homie. Tell baby girl I said hello and to have a good night. I'll see her later."

He gives him the keys and Ajay says, "Cool. I'm out."

He goes home to freshen up.

After he's dressed, he goes back to Chill's house and informs him he's about to leave.

Chill says, "Cool, bro."

He walks with as Ajay to the door, then stops as Ajay walks on out.

TIME TO LEARN-RELOADED-Time Will Reveal-part 1

Ajay is only thinking about spending time with Ebony. He walks over to the Blazer, gets in, backs out and drives away.

Chill goes back into the kitchen to get another drink. Just that fast, his living room is empty. He smiles to himself. He knows Tank and Nina have made up and gone upstairs.

"I guess everybody is on, again," he says to himself, "I did a good job."

He smiles to himself, as he grabs a beer from the fridge and joins the others in his backyard. His crew are still rolling thick.

During his drive back to granny and papa's, Ajay plays a tape by *Prince*. It's a favorite of Renee's and it's always in the tape deck, if Renee is the last one who drove the Blazer. A song comes on titled: *With You*.

He likes the musical start, so he turns it up. He listens as the first verse starts.

"I've held, your hand, so many times. But I still get the feeling I felt, the very first time. I kissed, your lips and laid with you. And I cherish every moment we spend, in each others arms. I guess my eyes can only see, as far as you,~~~~~~~~ I only want to be, with you."

He smiles to himself and lets it play on. He loves the words in this song and it's very fitting for the way he feels, right now.

"I need to listen to *Prince*, a lot more," he says to himself as he continues to smile.

He finishes by saying, "I'm gonna miss you, so much, baby girl. But I ain't ever gonna live without you. Just like *Prince* is saying it. I only wanna be with you. And I'm gonna learn how to show you that, if it's the last thing I do."

CHAPTER 7

TIME TO GO!

It's 10:15pm and Ebony is laying across the bed in her pajama's. She's watching TV and waiting for Ajay. Minutes later, she hears him tap on the window. First, she turns the lamp off, then she opens the window. She can smell his cologne as soon as she catches a breeze from under the window seal. He smells great. He has a huge smile when their eyes meet. It's obvious he's only thought about this moment since leaving dinner, the same as her. Together, they take the screen off. He slides through, so quickly, one would have to know he's done it a few times. He's done it to get to a girl, most likely. Because he has never been about burglarizing anyone. Burglary isn't 1 of the crew's many street trades. That's not to say they've never taken anything, for they have. They will strong arm, to get what's owed to them. And only when something is *owed* to them. The person or people whom the crew have taken from, knew exactly why it was happening to them too. Most of the folks outside of their circle are indebted to them. Then and only then, will the crew take from their own. And only when it's a debt being collected and never for greed.

Once Ajay is inside, they attach the screen back in place. He closes the window, locks it, then turns to her and whispers,
"Well, I'm here baby. In the flesh."

"I see and you're early too," she smiles.

"I couldn't wait," he says as he smiles big, "That's alright, ha?"

"Yes. You know it's alright with me."

He kisses her, quickly. He's curious about how she'd spent the moments waiting for him to arrive.
He asks, "What was you doing when I came?"

"Lying across the bed, watching TV," she answers.

"That sounds good."

He takes off his basketball sneakers and lays down across her bed, on his stomach. She climbs onto his back.

"I'm glad we made up," she says as she kisses him on the back of his neck and adds, "And dinner was the *bomb*."

TIME TO LEARN-RELOADED-Time Will Reveal-part 1

"Yea I am too and yes it was," he says, slightly perturbed.
She continues kissing him on the back of his neck, then she nibbles on his ear and smiles. He watches TV as if he's unaffected by what she's doing. Once she realizes she isn't getting a positive response out of him, she slides off of his back and lays on the bed, on her stomach, right next to him.
He cuts his eyes at her and says, "*Take your time.* What's your rush?"
He smiles and so does she.

"No rush," she says trying to be sarcastic as she adds, "You smell so good. You always smell good."
She's about to learn an important lesson from his actions, all this week. When it comes to sexual encounters, he isn't turned on by a female who puts out quickly. His impression of that type of female is that she's easy. He will still fuck her but she'll have to serve him, totally. And with the sex acts he's never even wanted to try with Ebony. For instance, at this early stage in their relationship, he has no desire to have her do oral sex. But any other girl, would have to start there because she's not the 1 he's into. He sees that type as loose and willing to be with any man that will have them. He doesn't view Ebony in that way. She's a good girl, raised with morals. Plus she's loyal. She's going to be his wife, so they'll have plenty of time to experience any and all those other things, later. What he loves the most about Ebony is her innocence. He wants her to hold onto it for as long as she can and keep it for him and him only. Her innocence is what attracted him from the start. He's been with older, more experienced women, enough to know that he likes innocence more. Ebony is a girl he can grow with *and* grow old with. She had to be conquered each and every time. Just to be in her presence, from the beginning, he had to come at her, correctly. He had to constantly pursue her, coax and reassure her and pretty much, give her, her way. Then let her find her way to him and his desires. The other girls he's been with chased after him. In his opinion, a reserved girl, like Ebony, is a true sign of a girl he can build with. Besides, he wants to teach Ebony and turn *her* on. That's what turns him on, so much about her. He's a predator type and like all predatory animals, he doesn't want to be fed. He wants to hunt. In other words, he wants to learn what it takes to get her in the mood, each time. He feels that's what will keep her coming back for more. Her actions this week will teach her what keeps him attracted to her, It's her reluctance to dive in when it comes to sex. He likes that she's shy about sex. He knows he's more

than qualified when it comes to bringing her to the point of submitting to him. She doesn't need to press that issue. Ever. Because for her, he's a sure thing.

As they both lay quiet, he reaches over and touches her chin. She looks at him. He rolls over on his side, so he can watch her and play with her hair.

"Where's your brush?" he asks suddenly.

She looks at him in surprise, then says, "On the dresser."

He gets up and goes to get it. He can barely see, in the room, dimly lit by the TV. But he finds the brush and makes his way back to the bed. He sits down next to her and begins to brush her hair. It feels so relaxing to her. She steady's her chin, with both hands, as she rest on her elbows and closes her eyes.

"Leave your eyes closed," he whispers as he brushes her hair and talks to her, "You've got soft hair. I like it."

"Thank you," she says, "I like this."

"You do?" he asks.

"Uh huh."

"I'll remember that," he says, "I watch my pops brush my mama's hair. It looks like a pretty smooth move," he chuckles and says "Sit up. I wasn't gonna play with baby dolls with you. But I'll brush your hair."

She smiles as she spins around and sits with her back to him. He brushes her hair down to her shoulders and along the side of her face. Then he takes the brush back to the dresser. He comes back and sits down in front of her. He kisses her lips while unbuttoning her top and removing it completely, along with her bra. He tells her to stand and she does. He slides her pajama bottoms off, then her panties.

"Are you keeping those too?" she asks with a goofy giggle.

He doesn't respond. He's in the zone. He's focused on his mission. He kisses her belly button before he stands up. While rubbing her breast, he pulls her close to him and kisses her gently. He sucks on her tongue as he lets his hands roam up and down her back. He grinds hard against her. He's already aroused and he wants her to know that he is. This way, she'll remember what got him to this point. His seduction of her and not the other way around. She places her arms around his neck and he starts to kiss on her neck.

TIME TO LEARN-RELOADED-Time Will Reveal-part 1

This feels so good. This is my Anthony. This is my man, right here.

The man who gives her the most pleasant feelings when they're all alone. He takes her fingers and places them on the top button of his shirt.
He says, "Take it off for me."
He instructs her, as he grabs her ass with both hands again. This time he kisses her wildly on her face and neck until she has gotten all of the buttons undone. She slides the shirt off of his shoulders. He lets it drop to the floor. He's *so* ready.

"The t-shirt too?" she asks.

"Yea," he whispers as his eyes search for hers, in the dark room.
She pulls the t-shirt over his head. He takes it and tosses it on the chair, across the room.
"The pants too," he demands with a sexy smile.
He stays busy pleasuring her, while she undresses him. He takes her head in both hands and sticks his tongue, deep into her mouth, sending chills down her body. She unbuttons his pants, unzips them and lets them drop to his ankles. He removes them from his feet and kicks them aside. She slides his boxers down before he can request it. He smiles at her boldness as he kicks his ankles free. Alas, they stand completely nude. He pulls her closer to him, holds her tight in his arms and kisses her, aggressively. Then he leads her over to the wall, where he lifts her up and leans her against it.
"Wrap your legs around me," he instructs and she does.
He uses his body to hold her up, as he rubs her breast, aggressively. He places 1 nipple in his mouth and suckles it, ever so gently. She moans softly. One of his hands supports her, while the other finds her throbbing clitoris.

"Oh yessss," she whispers involuntary, as she kisses his face.
He positions his penis, just outside of her already moist pussy, then pulls her down on it. His penis seems to know it's own way. This is a welcomed familiar to her, as his large penis invades her very tight shaft. She's filled to capacity, instantly. His breathing pattern changes. He's obviously liking this invasion too.

"Ssss mmm," he moans which sends waves though her body, once again.
This is a different position but it's very good. Oh God! Anthony's so good!

TIME TO LEARN-RELOADED-Time Will Reveal-part 1

She lets her thoughts dance randomly, as they make love standing against the wall. He pulls and rotates her hips to his liking. He kisses her hard. It's obvious he's feeling good too. His pace is on point. Ajay has the stamina of a Clydesdale. They continue in this position, for several minutes.

Suddenly, he spins around while still inside of her and carries her to the bed. He lays her down, gently. While still standing, he pulls her bottom towards him, for maximum penetration. He starts to grind again.

"Oh, Anthony. Ssss," she whispers as his full penetration stings her.

"Uh uh, baby. I like this," he whispers, "I need to get it wet."

He lets her know this action pleases him and as he goes deeper, her moans get louder.

"Sshh. They're gonna hear you," he whispers as he smiles.

"Okay, okay, okay," she whispers, trying to control her tone and get her *bearings,* at the same time.

Before she can adjust to this new position, he's ready to show her something else.

"Turn over for me and get up on your knees," he whispers.

She does as she's told.

In an instant, he's back inside of her. This time it's *doggy style*. He seems to enjoy this position, the most. Considering the amount of talking he has started to do.

"Oh yes, baby," he whispers.

She can hear him gasping for air with each stoke. She can also feel his body trembling. Then out of the blue, he smacks her on her ass.

Caught off guard, she asks, "What did you do that for?"

He strokes her more aggressively and says, "Because it feels good, baby."

To whom?

It's beginning to hurt her. He's stroking her in rhythms and humming as he works her over. She buries her face in the pillows, so he doesn't notice her grimacing. He's enjoying her and she wants, more than anything, to please him. She has learned that the pain is part of it. She accepts that tonight. He has a huge dick and it's the only 1 he has and will have. She's going to have to get use to it and hang on for the ride. Because it's the only 1 she's going to get for the rest of her entire life.

"Ebony, you got some good pussy. I'm not sharing this with nobody. You

know that, don't you?" he whispers while pulling her up towards him and kissing her wildly, down her back and on the back of her neck.
She can hear his body slapping against hers. He's breathing so hard, right now. She can feel the sweat from his face dripping onto her bottom. He's *all* in.
"Mmm yea, yea, yes," he moans.
She buries her face into 1 of her pillows again. She bites down on a pillow to keep from screaming out. He's in the zone, as she thinks.
How can something that can hurt so bad. Feel so good at the same time?

"I want it all, baby," he whispers and he isn't near done.
"Anthony, ssss oh," she manages.
He slows a bit, realizing now that he's hurting her.
"Oooo baby," he whispers, giving her a slight smile as he pulls out.
"Turn over on your back," he whispers.
Again, she does as she's told. He climbs on top, looking down into her eyes. He has sweat beads on his brow. He plays with her breast and clitoris as he continues looking into her eyes. This makes her tingle inside. He smiles.
"I want all of this tonight," he says as he enters her again.
He wraps her legs around him and whispers, "Wrap these pretty legs around me, Ebony. Let em hold me tight too."
She feels wet but she knows she hasn't been to ecstasy yet. She remembers that part is still to come and she surely wants it. She kisses him on his neck and chest. She wants to go there, so badly. He knows she's anticipating her orgasm too. He likes this a lot because he wants her to expect and demand it. He knows it's his job to give it to her. That will make her come back to him for it, again and again. This is exactly where he wants her to be.
"Mmm baby. It feels so good to me," she says in a whisper which sounds more like a long moan.
She can feel something which seems like a feather brushing against her clitoris, almost playfully. It feels so good. It's causing her back to lift up off of the bed towards him. Her hips have a mind of their own, right now. He sucks on 1 of her nipples as if that's the only place he can find to hold onto her. She explodes.
Ecstasy is that you? Are you there? Oh yes! Yes! Yes! Oh that's you!

TIME TO LEARN-RELOADED-Time Will Reveal-part 1

"Yea you like that, don't you, baby girl?" he asks in a whisper. Then he says, "I need to know what you like. I *wanna* know what you like, the most."

"Mmmm yes. I like it, Anthony."

"Show me how much you like it. Let me feel you work this pussy," he demands and she begins to grind and roll with all that she has.

"Uh huh. Uh huh," he whispers, "Is this my pussy, baby?"

"Yes! You know it's yours, Anthony."

"It's gonna stay mine. I'm gonna make sure it does," he whispers in her ear as he strokes her very well.

She feels pain but ecstasy is right there lingering. Her body tightens more and as she begins to tremble. She can hear him whispering and sounding, so sexy in her ear.

"Come here, baby. Come on," he whispers in her ear while kissing it and sucking on it and running his tongue in and out of it.

Her body explodes again and at that same instant, his body tightens against hers. He's in ecstasy too. They're climaxing together and this shit is *damn good* to the both of them. This is their 1st *dual climax*.

"Oh baby. Give it to me," he says as he holds her tight.

She squeezes her legs around him. Their bodies are wet with sweat, as they slide and pound against each other until neither of them can move anymore.

"Oh yes, ssss," he whispers as he lays down on top of her.

They're both breathing heavily, as she rubs her fingers through his braids and holds him close to her. She can't help but think about the fact that, 1 day from now, she won't be able to hold him. She feels the sting of tears forming in her eyes. She tries to fight them back but she isn't successful. He kisses her softly and wipes her tears as they fall. They lay in silence, for the next few minutes, just marinating and wondering how they can stall time.

Meanwhile at Chill's house, Nina and Tank are into their 2nd round. Nina is on top of him. He's holding her in place while she rocks back and forth on his dick. In Nina's opinion, when she's on top, this is her time to give it to him.

"Mmmm. Ride it baby," Tank whispers, "You know this pussy is good to me, don't you?"

"Uh huh," she moans softly, "I have to be good to my baby."

Tank is raising his pelvis up, to give her all that he has. She clinches her knees to his sides. She's about to get hers again.

"Come on, baby. *Gimme* that juice," he whispers.

No sooner than the words are out of his mouth, Nina starts to moan.

"Oh Jeremy baby! I'm coming, baby! Oh yes! Yes baby! Oh! You feel so good!" she screams.

Tank flips her over onto her back and begins to grind hard, inside of her.

"Damn! I'm gonna miss my pussy, baby. *Shit*," he says.

He's rather loud as he feels another orgasm coming.

"Ssss. Oh yea, baby. Ugh. Ah shit," he moans as he cums.

They slow to a steady pace and eventually, dead still. All they can do afterwards is lay motionless, in each others arms.

"I love you baby. I really do," Nina whispers, "And I always will."

"I love you too," he says, "I'm coming back to you. Do you hear me?"

He's looking into her eyes, "Always," he adds as they kiss.

It's getting late. They both know she has to get home, even though her parents are at work. They know they'll be calling soon.

After they cool off, she gets up and gets dressed and so does he. Then he asks her to sit on the bed next to him. She does. He talks.

"Baby listen. I want you to believe in me. I'm gonna show you that you can trust me. I mean this," he says.

"I know," she smiles.

"Will you wait for me to come home?"

"Hell yes, I'm gonna wait for you. You didn't even have to ask me that. No matter what happens. You are *my* man. *Forever,* baby."

They kiss again, then go downstairs. Some of the crew are relaxing in the living room. Most of them are at home, waiting until tomorrow to come over, so they can see Tank and Ebony off. Their parents have told them to stay home tonight and this time, some of them actually listened. Jb and Lynn have gone home. Rich, T-baby, Rebbie and June are at home too. But Bre, Stoney, Jan and Rob have gone out on the set to check on the business. They have to get all monies collected, so Tank can have his cash for the trip to Houston. Only Chill, Renee, Jr and Tonya remain. Nina and Tank say goodnight to them, then leave.

It's 1:00am. Tank walks her home and they talk on the front porch.

"I guess Ajay is still at granny's house," she says.

"Yea, they have to have some time together too," he says.

"My brother loves her, Jeremy. I know he does."

"I know. But Ajay just has a different way, then the rest of us have, of showing it. But I know he does and he has for a long time. He's liked twin longer then she's liked him. He loves her, just like I love you. Me and Ajay been through a lot of shit in our lives," he says. Then he changes the subject and says, "I'm gonna miss the hell out of you."

She smiles as tears come to her eyes. He holds her in his arms and let's her cry on his shoulder.

At granny's, Ebony and Ajay are at it again. This time it's long, sweaty and very passionate. He had to feel her just once more before he could let her go away. They kiss so much, her tongue has become numb on the tip. Afterwards, he holds her in his arms. She's been crying since the end of the 1st session.

"I don't want you to go," she says, "I don't wanna leave you, Anthony."

"I know you don't," he whispers, "I don't want that either. But you know I can't stay here, all night. I wish I could but I can't. Chill and Renee would kick both of our asses, if we get in trouble like that again. And *especially* in papa and granny's house. Plus I have to get his Blazer back to him by three. They got runs to make."

"I promise I'll stay true to you. I don't even know how I'm gonna make it without you, my girls *and* the crew," she says, continuing to cry.

"I know you're the real deal, Ebony. But don't cry, please?" he pleads, "I need you. I have no doubts about that. You are my girl for life. And I can't stand to see you cry. I wanna remember you with a smile on your face. If you leave me with the expression of you crying, that's gonna make it ten times harder for me to deal with you leaving. I'll be stressed out and all of that. I'll be hell to deal with for my first year of high school, is what I'll be."

"I know but I can't help it," she cries, "This is the hardest thing I've ever had to do, in my whole life. I wish I could run away with you, Anthony. I wish my big mama wasn't sick. I wouldn't go, if she didn't need me to come."

He needs to change the subject, so he does. He says, "When you look at me for the last time tomorrow and I'll be outside too. I want you to look at me and smile. Okay? No matter how hard it might be."

"I'll try," she says.

"Do it for me, baby. I need you too."

They kiss again. Then he has to get up and get dressed. He does.

After another long kiss and a hug, he climbs out of the window. He reaches back through the window, grabs her face with both hands and kisses her again.

"Keep it tight, baby," he says and winks his eye.

"I love you, Anthony," she says and tries to smile, "I'm gonna miss you, so much, baby. I don't wanna leave."

He smiles at her, though it's hard for him too. Then he says, "I know you love me, baby. I love you too. I'm gonna talk to Chill and Renee and see if we can't come up with a solution. Just hold on to tonight, baby girl. Until I see you and can hold you again."

Then he walks over to the fence, where she can no longer see him. She can hear him when he climbs up and jumps over it. That's when she locks the screen and the window. She's missing him, already. She prepares to put her pajama's back on when she notices her panties are missing. She smiles, lays down on the bed and turns the TV off. She decides to sleep without any clothes on and pretend Ajay is still there with her. She thinks of him, all night, until she finally falls asleep.

Tank has gone home. Nina is in her room when she hears Ajay come in and go into his room. She lays there thinking about Tank and how much she's going to miss him. She thinks about how it's going to be for her and Ajay, without him and Ebony around. She can't help but feel sad, as the tears come back. Then she remembers they're all suppose to hook-up in the morning. She gets up, runs across the hall to Ajay's door and knocks. When he answers, she can see it in his eyes. He's upset. She understands why. She tells him about tomorrow's plan. The news seems to make him feel a little better, as he says, "*Alright*" and closes his door back, quickly. He wants to be alone. She goes back to her room, where Lynn is already asleep. She thinks about how lucky Lynn is that Jb isn't leaving. She gets into her bed, covers herself under her comforter and sobs herself to sleep.

TIME TO LEARN-RELOADED-Time Will Reveal-part 1

The next morning, granny wakes Ebony up for breakfast at 6am. She tells her, her father will be there to pick her up at 7:30am. Ebony takes her time bathing and getting dressed. She drags herself into the kitchen and sits down. She doesn't have much of an appetite. Granny insists she eat something, so she tries. She picks over her breakfast until granny tells her to help clear the table.

She does the dishes, then goes back to her room and lays across her bed. She wants to call Ajay but she knows the punishment is still on. She's longing to see the crew again before she leaves. Today feels *so* final. She's still unaware of the little get together her granny has arranged.

John arrives at 7:30am, sharp. Ebony gets her bags and puts them in the car. Then she kisses and hugs her grandparents. They give her money for her and Tank. They also give her some gifts for big mama and Percy or Poppa, as he is called. They say their goodbyes to her and their oldest son, then watch from the front porch as John and Ebony drive away.

On the way home, John tries to cheer her up but it's no use. He decides to drive on quietly and save the meeting with her friends as a surprise. When they turn onto their street, she looks around at everybody's house. No one is outside.

Where is Jan and Bre? Where's June? I'll bet they all stayed up late, last night.

She feels a sudden sadness, knowing she's about to leave town and her crew are at home sleeping it off. When they get closer to her house, her face lights up. She begins to smile. Everyone is out there waiting. She realizes they are there for her. She looks at her daddy, expecting him to disapprove of her crew being out there to greet her. But he's smiling at her.

"Surprise, baby girl. They all wanted to see y'all off," John says.

"Thank you, daddy!" she says as she leans over and kisses him on his cheek.

She can barely wait for him to pull into the driveway and park before she bails from the car. She runs to her girls, immediately.

"Man! You would think y'all haven't seen each other in years," Archie Sr says as he smiles and follows John into the house.

The crew of 18 gather on and around mama P's porch. They start

their talk about the old times, they've already shared and try to be cheerful.

"We're not leaving until twelve," Tank says to Ebony.

"That's a lil better," she says, "But not at all, would be the best."

"True that," Jb agrees.

They're all quiet, for a minute. Chill breaks the silence by telling them, him and Renee have been discussing trying to come to Houston for the Labor day weekend.

"Yes, crew," Renee adds, "We're gonna come down there before y'all go back to school."

"I wanna go," Nina says as Rebbie and T-baby agrees.

"We want everybody to be able to go, so we're gonna take the van. Then with the Blazer and Jr's car, everybody will have a seat," Renee says, "We'll work it out."

That makes Ebony smile. At least, she'll see them before Christmas, which is when she's suppose to return home. Ajay had told her he would talk to them about something. She knows this is *that something* and she's happy about it. She remembers when she use to love going to visit big mama, for the summer. But that was before 2 years ago and before her and Ajay became serious. Now, she never wants to be away from him.

They all decide to walk up the street, then back down the other side, for old times sake. They stop at each crew members house to reminisce about some memory they had there. They have a story for each house, at 1 time or another. They smoke a few blunts during their stroll too. That was the reason they went on the stroll, in the first place.

By the time they make it back down the street, Chill suggests they stop on his porch. They all gather around for his talk. He reminds them of the loyalty they all have for each other. He says, no matter what happens, he's always down for the crew and he knows they're down for him too. They all agree. Ebony and Ajay look at each other. He makes his way over to her and sits down. She feels complete now. Before long, all of the couples are either sitting or standing, together. When Chill finishes his talk, Renee brings out the pictures from Jb and Ajay's parties. She passes them around for everyone to see and share. They all have a good laugh. Nina and Tank exchange photo's of each other. Renee gives Ebony and Tank their pictures of the whole crew. Chill gives Tank his money, they had collected from the set. Ajay gives him some money for Ebony, so he can give to her later.

TIME TO LEARN-RELOADED-Time Will Reveal-part 1

"Oh yes! This is what I needed," Ebony says, as she waves the photo's, "I can show the folks down in Houston what my crew looks like." She's smiling while everyone else laughs. Ajay notices their parents coming out of Ebony's house. They're helping Pearl and John put suitcases in the truck. Ebony notices them and looks at him. He's looking at her but he has no expression. As if he's looking right through her. Then he calls Tank and asks him to go inside Chill's house. This leaves Ebony sitting next to Nina, who then notices the activity across the street.

"Its eleven already, girl? *Damn*," Nina says after looking at Ebony's watch.

"Yes it is and I guess its really going down, this time, ha?" Ebony says sadly.

"I guess so," Nina says, just as sad.

"I need to talk to Anthony. Come on, Nina. Lets go in," she says. They both get up and go inside Chill's house, where they find Tank and Ajay seated at the kitchen table.

"Anthony, I wanna talk to you before..," Ebony starts.

Nina pulls up a chair next to Tank and sits down. Ajay looks at Ebony. He wants her to come sit by him.

"Come over here and sit down," he says to her, as he pats his hand on the chair, next to him. "What's up?" he asks.

He's smiling. She looks at Nina and Tank. They're already kissing.

"I wanna give you this," she says and hands him the letter she'd written before he came to granny's house, last night.

She gives him the solo picture of her, from his party and 1 of them together.

"I really wanted this picture, baby girl. I want you to have mine too," he says as he smiles, "I gave it to Tank. I made him promise me, *not to give it to you* until after y'all are on the road. If he sees you starting to look sad or something like that."

He's still smiling, so she smiles too. And even though she wants the picture right now, she knows he isn't going to change his mind about the way she is to receive it. She knows she'll get it from Tank before the day ends.

T-baby and Rebbie come in with Rich and June. They join the 4 of them at the table. They double check addresses and phone numbers. Ajay watches and appears unaffected. But Ebony knows he is.

Jb comes in and says "Daddy said he's ready to go."

He looks at Ebony and Tank. His expression says he's going to miss his younger siblings, a lot. They hug all of their crew. Nina and Tank kiss once more, before they walk outside. Before Ebony can kiss Ajay, he has already stepped out onto the front porch, in plain view of their parents. She walks out with her girls. She looks puzzled as they walk toward big John's truck. Tank and the guys follow close behind. Ebony hugs all of her crew and the parents. She thanks Renee and Chill for the $300, which she still has. She looks at Ajay as she climbs into the truck. Tank gives hugs to everyone. Chill had given Ajay a special package for Tank. Ajay had given it to him while they were in the kitchen. Tank climbs into the truck with Ebony. John kisses Pearl and lil man, then he hugs Jb. He says goodbye to everyone else and climbs into the driver's seat. He starts his rig, as Ebony still looks at Ajay. Before John can pull away, she throws open the door. While still looking at Ajay, she climbs down out of the truck.

"Where are you going now, baby girl?" her father asks.

She doesn't answer. She simply walks, straight up to Ajay, while everyone is watching. She grabs his face with both hands and gives him a big kiss. He puts his arms around her waist and kisses her back. Everyone looks. Some smile while their crew cheers. No one else says anything. Afterwards, Ebony turns around, walks back to the truck, climbs in and closes the door.

"Now we can go, daddy," she says.

John says nothing. He just smiles, shakes his head and looks at Pearl, who's shocked beyond speech. But she is able to say,

"I guess some things just have to be taken with a grain of salt."

"What are we going to do with our brats?" Jo asks Pearl as she shakes her head and smiles.

Tank starts laughing which makes Ebony laugh too. When John pulls away from the curb, she's still laughing as she looks at Ajay. He's still smiling at her. He likes what she'd done. She notices everyone laughing at what she'd done. She shrugs it off and waves goodbye to everybody. She mouths the words, *I love you* to Ajay. He nods yes, in return. They pull away from the curb and begin to roll down the street. Her and Tank watch out the window until they turn the corner and head for the highway. Ebony knows the *time to go* is here. John hits I-90, then heads down 71 toward Cincinnati. Ebony and Tank settle into the bunks in back of the cab, to catch up on some sleep. They know it's going to be a long ride and they're asleep, early into the trip.

TIME TO LEARN-RELOADED-Time Will Reveal-part 1

When big John hits his highway stride, he turns on his CB radio and talks to his usual good buddies, all afternoon. He's use to keeping himself company on the road.

John keeps up his radio talk, for over 5 hours, until Ebony and Tank wake up. They had slept until dusk. Pearl had packed food for the 3 of them to eat, along the highway. John tells Ebony and Tank, he won't stop for sleep until he gets to southern Tennessee.

****

Back in Cleveland, Chill and the crew are preparing to hit the streets. Nina and T-baby are staying at Rebbie's tonight. The 3 of them had mailed their letters to Ebony, earlier. They decide to stay in tonight. They're all sitting around talking about the usual things and already missing Ebony and Tank.

Ajay and the rest of the crew leave for an all-night-in-the-park event. It's the 1st night of the park staying open, all night, for the rest of the summer. Chill has been expecting to hear from a guy named Eddie. Eddie is a worker, who owes him money. The crew was counting on running into him and they do. Ajay spots him. He gets out and approaches him.

"Hey, man. Chill needs to holla at you," Ajay says.

Eddie knows it's time to pay up and he doesn't have the money. Chill has extended his deadline, twice. The crew won't allow a third time. Rich, June and Jb get out of the Blazer and join Ajay. The 4 of them surround Eddie. He's visibly nervous and tries to stall.

"Tell big Chill I'll be over there, in a minute," Eddie says.

"Nah, he don't have a minute," Ajay snaps.

"You needs to bring yo ass on," Jb adds, "Right now, nigga."

Knowing he won't get away, if he tries to run, Eddie reluctantly walks over to the Blazer.

"Get in, nigga," Rich orders.

He's directly behind Eddie. As Eddie gets in, Rich pushes him to the 2nd seat and tells him to slide to the middle. Ajay, Rich, Jb and June look around for witnesses and see none. June climbs into the back while Ajay and Rich sit, to either side of Eddie. Jb sits in the front passenger seat.

TIME TO LEARN-RELOADED-Time Will Reveal-part 1

"You got my paper?" Chill asks from the drivers seat, not so much as even turning around to look at Eddie.

"No, Chill man. I need a few more days," Eddie tries.

In a few more days, they'll be planning your funeral.

Ajay thinks to himself. He's going to see to it that it happens too. Chill puts the Blazer in drive and pulls away. Jr, Stoney and Rob stay at the park to handle new business. The crew keep the eastside, rock steady. There's never a drought in *CrewLand*.

Chill drives Eddie to *The Chamber*. The same place Jr and the others had gone to stash the loot, when they rode down on those squatters in *The Grove*, last week.

The Chamber is an empty warehouse near Lorain, on a mostly deserted cul-de-sac. It's where the crew take merchandise which is too large or too hot to take home. It's also where they take any ne'er-do-well, who has gotten out of hand and has to be taken out of the game. They named it the chamber to represent that final walk, house of death or a prison chamber. But unlike prison chambers where poisonous gases or the electric chairs are used, the crew beat their victims. Torturing them before they kill them. More like a concentration camp without the overnight stay. No one goes to the chamber and lives to talk about it. The Chamber is final. The crew doesn't believe in 2nd chances for anyone who tries to fuck over them. They believe it sends the wrong message to other workers, who might be thinking of taking the disrespectful route.

They arrive at the chamber and take Eddie inside. Chill does what little talking that's done. He assures Eddie he's going to die tonight. There isn't anything else to discuss. The guys start to hit him with chains, bats and brass knuckles. Some stomp him while others hit him with their bare fist. Anything to inflict as much pain as possible before he leaves the world. He begs in vain. They continue to hit him and scold him, at the same time. If he was going to live another day, he would know the crew law, verbatim. The beating takes several minutes, until Chill calls it to a halt. That's when Ajay pulls his strap.

"This one's mine," he states and no one else pulls.

Ajay walks over to Eddie who's lying on the floor, curled up in a ball and very bloody about the face and head. He has several broken bones and he's still begging for his life. With no words, no expression and no hesitation, Ajay cocks the hammer back on his .44 caliber pistol and fires 2 rounds into the side of Eddie's head. He dies instantly. They strip his body of anything and everything of value. Even his clothes and shoes. They tie him up in plastic, put him in the back of the Blazer and drive him to a site outside of East Cleveland. They dispose of his body, then drive back to the park and proceed to get their buzz on.

Stoney, Rob and Jr are still at the park when they return. Jan, Bre, Tonya, Renee and Lynn have arrived, in Tonya's Sentra and joined them.

Tonya is Jr's girlfriend. They graduated high school in June. Both of them are starting their freshman year of college, just off the shore way at Cleveland State, this fall.

Angie, the girl from across town, is at the park tonight as well. She's riding with a girl named Nicole, who's looking for Eddie. They drive around, then park right next to Jr's Cutlass and get out.

Initially, they walk around the park, as they are still looking for Eddie. Needless to say, *he isn't around*. They come back and ask Renee if they've seen him.

"No we haven't seen him but we need too," she says, "So when you do find him. Tell him he needs to roll through here and holla at my man." Renee is playing the game. Ajay gets in on it too.

"You ought to be looking for me, baby. Wit yo *fine* ass," he's says while checking out her frame and playing the role.

"Oh yea and why is that?" Nicole asks, smiling and obviously interested in hooking up with him.

"I'm the *muafuckin'* man. You haven't heard about me?" he asks as he goes right into *Mack* mode.

That's something he's known to do. For Ajay, this is the way to play the game. If a guy fucks over the crew, they take everything he has. Even his woman. What better thrill could Ajay have, then to kill an enemy and fuck his girl, afterwards? There's only 1 thing that could've made it better. That would've been, if he could've fucked her in front of Eddie. But she would've had to die too. Eddie's gone and Nicole isn't on to them. However, she is very interested in fucking Ajay. She's all over him, within minutes.

"I've been wanting to meet you," Nicole admits, "I know you're a superstar and all. I've been wanting to *holla* at you."

"Oh really? Well why didn't you say something, a long time ago?" Ajay asks, "Cause I've *been* the man."

" I thought you was on lock down with your girl next door." Renee and Lynn give each other the eye.

"Oh, I am," he says quickly, "Ebony is her name and she's my one and only girl, *for life*. But she's not here at the moment."

He's checking for Nicole's reaction. He wants to fuck her and that's it. He doesn't want her hanging around him or his crew, like these types are known to do. Her merely mentioning Ebony has gotten under his skin. He doesn't like her comment nor the way she chose to say it. She notice he didn't like her being salty about Ebony, so she plays it cool and doesn't go any farther. She doesn't mention Eddie's name anymore, either. Ajay tells her to come sit on the car, next to him and she does. He smokes a blunt with her and treats her like it's all about her.

By the time the crew are ready to leave, she's ready to follow them to Shaker Heights. Ajay even drives her car, while Rich rides in the back seat with Angie. Angie knew not to say anything to Jr, if he didn't speak to her first. Which he didn't. She's about to make the most fucked up move a female can make, with the crew. Hooking up with another member.

During the ride to Chill's house, Rich who is Jr's 1st cousin, starts kicking it to Angie. She goes for him. Hook, line and sinker. When they pull up in front of Chill's house, she's ready to go down on him. He doesn't stop her, either. She's known for giving it up quickly, anyway. She could never be Jr's girl or any other man from the crew.

Chill and the rest of the crew get out of their cars to go into the house. Ajay and Rich stay in the car with Nicole and Angie. They know it's against the rules to bring any other females in front of the ladies, in their crew. Jr is still getting evil eyes from the girls, for bringing Angie to Chill's house, the first time. Tonya had been told about it, less then 24 hours after she returned from Detroit. Ajay and Rich aren't willing to chance that because that's totally going against the G-code of the crew. Ajay tells Jr they'll be back in a while.

"Cool, man. Y'all do what you do and get back, players," Jr says as he notices Angie is all over Rich and he laughs.

He tosses Rich and Ajay a couple of condoms as Ajay restarts the car.

"Hey, Cuz. We got jimmy's already," Rich says, laughing more.

"Extra tight too," Ajay adds, though his expression is a serious one.

"Well, keep those too," Jr says.

He's still laughing as him and Tonya walk toward the house.

Ajay drives to a spot, a few blocks away. It's where the crew usually take females whom they want to keep on the down low. It's a baseball park which no one really uses anymore. Except the crew, for this type of venture. Other than them, there are base heads, drunks and homeless people hanging around and sleeping in it.

****

After a late dinner at the *Waffle House*, John decides to stay at *The Peabody hotel* in Memphis. It's already 1am. Ebony asks Tank to give her the letter from Ajay, after their father is asleep. Tank does. She opens it and begins to read. One picture falls out. Then the other. The 1st one is of Ajay, the night of his party. He looks so smooth and handsome, she thinks to herself. And sexy too. She looks at the other photo. It's them, together. On the back, Ajay had written;

Anthony-n-Ebony. A&E=Always<>Eternal. July 11, 1989. 2 years down on Forever.

This gives her good feelings inside, as she stares at the 2 of them together. She reminisces on the times when they had been one. The letter is very sweet, as well. The part that really grabs her attention, are the lines where he had written:

Remember whenever you want to feel me. Just go someplace quiet, lay back, close those sexy brown eyes of yours and I'm there. You know where, right? [smile]

She smiles as she kisses his pictures, then puts them both in her bag.

"It must be good?" Tank ask as he smiles.

"Uh huh, it is," she says and blushes.

"I wonder what they're doing, right now?" Tank asks as they both lay on their beds.

"There is no telling what they're up too," she whispers, with no idea of just how right she is, at this moment.

Her and Tank turn out the light and watch TV until sleep takes over.

TIME TO LEARN-RELOADED-Time Will Reveal-part 1

Before Ajay can even park the car, Rich is getting out with Angie. She's hot, horny and can't wait to fuck. They go into 1 of the dugouts, which the vagrants have closed in to make shelter. Rich gives the tenant a $20 rock to use the shelter for 20 minutes.

Back in the car, Nicole is already hot too. She's taking off her clothes and trying to kiss Ajay. He won't allow her to kiss him on the mouth. She unbuttons his shirt and starts kissing on his chest, as she unbuttons his pants. He pulls her by the arm.

"Let's get out," he says.

She gets out with him, although she's half-naked and meets him at the back of her car. She tries kissing him again. He tells her it isn't going to happen.

"I'm not about to let you kiss me, alright? So you can cancel that," he says sternly.

She pushes him against the trunk and goes down on her knees. This isn't a new experience for Ajay. He likes oral sex, as long as it's performed on him. But he isn't about eating pussy. Every brother in the crew thinks likewise, to hear them tell it. He holds Nicole's head in place while he gets his. She's asking for the contents to flow into her mouth, as she tells him she wants to taste him. He's wearing a condom and she wants him to allow her to break it. He says no, she can't break it. Nor can she have the condom with his deposits in it. This is 1 female who will never be the object of his affection.

"And if you want me to fuck you, you have to get it hard again. Or we can go on and roll out," he says.

Nicole is more than willing to oblige him. She does her duty, once he straps on another condom. Then he puts her face down on the trunk of her car and fucks her, doggy style. She's loving it.

Before they can finish, Rich and Angie are coming back to the car. Ajay doesn't stop. Angie is interested in fucking him now. She watches with glazed over eyes, as he goes in and out of her friend. Nicole is turned on by Rich watching her fuck Ajay. Rich tells Angie to serve Ajay, just to see if she will. She starts kissing him on his back. Rich sits on the trunk, next to Nicole and starts playing with her mouth. She immediately gives Rich, the mouth and lip service. Ajay pulls out of her, sits Angie on the car, next to Rich and goes in her. Rich straps on another condom, puts Nicole on her knees, on the ground and takes a turn with her. All of this is going on while several vagrants and crackheads are going in and out of the park. They're

waiting for their chance to score some rock. Them seeing the crew in this spot, isn't unusual. The guys are always approached by some female who wants to be down with them, in any way she can. The crew men have reputations for being equipped to handle any job; business or pleasure. They just have it like that.

When they're done, Ajay drives back to Chill's house. They tell the girls goodbye, then go inside to chill with their crew. They play spades, smoke and drink, while the crew rag on them about their adventure with *used up* Angie and *soon-to-be, used up* Nicole. Chill suggests using them to break in the next generation of crew guys. It's most likely going to happen, in the near future, for Jr and Bre's younger brother, Bruce. He's the next family member who will be turning 13, after Rebbie. His coming out night will come later. It's nearing daylight and the crew really need sleep.

****

By 7:00am, John has been back on the road for a little over an hour. Ebony has Ajay, her crew and Cleveland on her mind. Her and Tank are growing tired of the highway, by the time they reach Arkansas.

After 11 hours more of highway, state-to-state, they arrive at big mama Eloise's house in Houston, at 6:15pm CST. The 1st thing they do is have a nice dinner, while they call Pearl to let her know they've arrived safely. During the call, she's pleased to hear her mother in such good spirits. After they hang up with Pearl, they sit around conversing. Later, they're ready to turn in for the night.

On Monday the 17th, John pulls out for his trip to Arizona. Ebony and Tank know, without a doubt, they're in Houston to stay.

The next few days are uneventful, with the exception of a letter Tank receives from Nina. Ebony receives letters from all of her girls. She answers them immediately and sends T-baby a card for her 13th birthday. It's coming up on the 24th. In her letter to Nina, she includes Tank's response letter. She hasn't received a letter from Ajay yet, even though she has written to him every night since she arrived. He hasn't returned a letter to her and the month of July is nearly over. Rebbie's birthday is coming up on August 2nd. Ebony sends her a card. Still, no letter from Ajay.

TIME TO LEARN-RELOADED-Time Will Reveal-part 1

On August 25th, Ebony receives a letter from Renee. She has written to inform her that the crew are still coming to Houston for *Labor day* weekend. She tells her, Nina, Rebbie and T-baby can't get permission to come. Not with Tank, June and Rich coming. Her girls had already revealed that to her, in a previous letter. However, Renee's letter states that everyone else is going to make the trip, including Ajay.

Poppa registered Ebony and Tank for school, the week they arrived. On August 28th, they start their 1st day of 9th and 8th grade, respectively. Poppa had also been teaching Ebony how to drive, every afternoon during the summer. She's become quite good. He promised her, if her and Tank get their driver's license, he'll get them a car. In Houston, you can get your license at 15 years old. Unlike Cleveland, where you have to be sixteen.

Ebony makes the 8th grade basketball team with ease. Tank makes the 9th grade team too. Though his best sport is track. The 1st week of school is boring for Ebony. She's use to having her girls by her side. She's met a few friends but all she can really think of to ease her mind, is Friday the 1st of September. That's when the crew are due to arrive. Her and Tank are looking forward to it.

Big mama has reserved 7 rooms at the local motel, under the name; Renee Stewart. With that many rooms, Ebony and Tank know a large portion of their crew are coming.

After finally talking to Nina on the phone, Thursday night, the same evening the crew had left for Houston, she knows whom to expect. Ajay has decided to make the trip. They're traveling in the Blazer and Stoney's van. Nina tells Ebony and Tank, the crew are planning to drive straight through the night.

The next day at school is Friday. Ebony has a hard time concentrating on anything else, except her Cleveland crew's arrival. She has made 2 friends on her basketball team who are very genuine. April Bradley and Yolanda Hall. She tells April and Yolanda all about her crew and shows them pictures, as she explains who everyone is. Both girls want to meet them when they arrive. After school, they have practice. After that, poppa lets Ebony drive home. Her 2 new friends are going to meet her at the motel later, when her crew gets settled and after she has seen, *her Ajay*.

TIME TO LEARN-RELOADED-Time Will Reveal-part 1

Tank is already home when Ebony and poppa arrive. He's on the front porch with 6 people, he'd met at school. He's more outgoing than Ebony, so he's adjusted well in Houston. On the porch, standing next to him are 3 guys. One named; Charles Washington. One named; David Jones. They're on the 9th grade team with him. There are 3 girls there also. Tina Evans and Shuntay Carter are sophomores. They play basketball at Smiley high school. The other girl is Sonya Watkins, a 16 year old junior, also from the high school team. Raymond White is the 3rd guy. He's 16 and a junior all-American at Smiley high school. Tank and the 9th graders attend school at Smiley high, while Ebony goes to Broadus Middle school. It's on the same property. Ebony sees Tank's new friends as rather superficial. They're obsessing over what they have or drive and who's names they wear. Ebony knows she won't blend well with them. Right away, she notice that Raymond White thinks he's got it going on, more than the others. He's very arrogant and conceited. From his 1st sight of Ebony, he tries to push up on her. She walks past, after speaking to everyone and goes inside to take a bath. She has to get ready for the crew's arrival and her man, Ajay. She has no intentions of being friends with Tank's new acquaintances.

Tank's friends know of a few parties going on, over the weekend. They have asked Tank to bring the crew and he agrees too.

"Hey man, is your sister coming too?" Raymond asks.

"Don't even try it, fool," Tank says quickly, "My sister ain't about to fuck with nobody, around here."

"Ah man, my bad, dog," he says, "I think she's cute though, you know. No disrespect though man, alright?"

"I ain't ya dog, nigga. And it can be whatever. *Try* me," Tank says. He isn't smiling and he's very sincere about what he has just said.
Raymond doesn't say anything. Even though, he thinks he's the shit, he can tell that Tank is street, for real. And if he disrespects Tank's wishes, he would have to hold up or get folded up. So he stays in the cut and relatively quiet, for the remainder of the afternoon.

After her bath, Ebony joins Tank on the porch. Raymond watches her the whole time, which makes her very uncomfortable. The 3 girls try to make friends with her quickly but she isn't particularly comfortable with them either. They remind her of Anita and her posse. She doesn't know it yet but she'll find out later. They are far worse than that Cleveland posse of tramps. These girls game is to pretend to be your friend, in order to get with your man or any man that fancies you. *Backstabbers,* that's what these whores are. Tina likes Tank and isn't shy about telling it. Ebony is definitely going to make her aware of Nina, the 1st chance she gets. But she finds out Tank has already told her. According to Tina, Tank had said, as long as she understands that rule, he *will* fuck her. Ebony doesn't like it but knowing Tank, as well as she does, she knows it's most likely true. Eventually, Raymond makes his way into her and Tina's conversation. Tank watches him with wicked eyes because he knows he's up to no good.

"So your name is Ebony, right?" Raymond asks.

"Uh huh," she mumbles but doesn't make eye contact with him.

"My name is Raymond. Raymond White. But everybody calls me, sweet Ray, around these parts."

"That's nice," Ebony retorts and she still isn't looking at him and she doesn't shake his hand when he extends it.

She has a bad feeling with him around. Ebony has always been able to sense bad luck. But Raymond's conceit won't allow him to concede easily.

"*Man*, you're mean, ha?" he asks as he smiles.

"No I'm not mean," she says and she isn't smiling as she looks over at Tank for assistance and he gets right on it.

"It seems like that to me," Ray says.

He's still smiling and trying to get some conversation from her. He's also trying to mask his embarrassment of being rejected, at the same time. He cracks an oddball joke and Tank comes to the rescue.

"Look here, fool. I done told you, she's not down like that, nigga. Why don't you recognize?" Tank says as he approaches Raymond.

"I'm cool. No problem," he says and steps away from Ebony.

But he continues to stare at her which makes her even more uncomfortable. She decides to go inside to her room and leave the 7 of them on big mama's front porch.

At 8pm, the phone rings. Big mama answers it. Tank and his friends are still outside. Ebony is still in her room.

"Jeremy! Ebony! This is Renee on the phone! They're here! Jb and June are trying to see if they can remember how to get here. But I'm sending Percy after them. I don't want them to get lost, somewhere!" big mama yells.

TIME TO LEARN-RELOADED-Time Will Reveal-part 1

Ebony comes into the living room, where she can hear Tank on the front porch. He's already hyped with anticipation.

"Oh yea!" He yells from the porch, "Its on now!"

Ebony feels large butterflies in her stomach. Big mama tells poppa to take Tank, David, Charles and Raymond with him and go meet the Cleveland crew. While the girls stay and help her put the food on the table. Ebony wants to go with poppa but big mama has already spoken. The guys leave and the girls set the table, while big mama gives instructions.

At 8:45pm, the guys return. The Blazer pulls in behind poppa, then the van pulls in. Ebony watches from the window while big mama, Sonya, Shuntay and Tina stand on the porch. Big mama is excited. Two more of her grandbabies are here, in Jb and June. But she claims them all and they all claim her too.

First, Tank, poppa, Ray, David and Charles hop out of poppa's car, then June gets out. He had hopped in with them at the rendezvous point. Second, the van unloads. Jr is the driver and he has Tonya, Rich, Bre, Stoney, Rob and Jan. Ebony's heart freezes, for a moment. Chill hops out of his Blazer and so does Renee, Jb and Lynn. Finally, Ajay slides out and Ebony's heart starts pumping again. She smiles from the window, while big mama gets hugs and kisses from everyone.

"Oh big mama's babies, made it!" big mama exclaims.

She's known this whole crew since before they knew themselves. Her and poppa are surrogate grandparents to each 1 of them, who aren't already blood related.

"We missed you this fourth of July, big mama. We had to come see you," Renee says and the rest agree, "And you too, poppa. Where the *Bud Light* at?"

They all laugh. He's the grandpa who's known to give them a drink.

"How have you been doing, big mama?" Chill asks.

"We heard you was sick," Jr adds, "How is that going? I know poppa got you *extra* spoiled by now."

"Oh I'm doing pretty good," big mama answers, "Y'all come on in. Have some supper and relax awhile. And yes, he's spoiling me."

"Oh yes, ma'am," Rob says, "We're ready to eat."

"We can do that!" Jan agrees.

"That'll work," Bre adds.

TIME TO LEARN-RELOADED-Time Will Reveal-part 1

"Big mama, I know you got some of that famous macaroni and cheese in there, ha?" Stoney asks.

"Big mama, they've been talking about your cooking since we left Cleveland," Jb tells her.

"Yes, babies. Big mama's got all the foods y'all like," she says.

They make their way into the house. They're all familiar with her southern cooking. She grabs Ajay by the hand and walks him in, with her. She knows he's sweet on Ebony. To big mama, Ebony is her daughter and she wants a close relationship with Ajay. She also wants to know what his plans are for her namesake. Ebony knows how fond of Ajay, her big mama is too. And she loves it because she knows Ajay loves big mama, the same way. She'll learn later, that isn't the only reason they're close. Big mama knows what she doesn't know.

When Ajay comes in, Ebony is frozen in her tracks. He looks so handsome and she can't believe he's here. He finally sees her and smiles. She smiles back.

"Ebony, come give him a hug," big mama insists.

That's when the rest of the crew see her. They had asks, several times, where she was.

Of course, Ajay gets the 1st hug and he hugs her tight. She scans the room looking for Chill and notice Raymond, *still* watching her. She jumps before holding Ajay tighter. She refuses to let go.

"What's wrong, baby girl?" Ajay asks.

They release their embrace. Already, he can sense that she's uneasy. He doesn't know it, just yet. But she *has* been, since she met Raymond White.

"I'll tell you later, okay?" she says, looking into his eyes.

"Alright, you be sure and do that," he insists.

He's very interested in knowing what has his girl, so shook. He stays by her side as she hugs the rest of her crew. Raymond mixes in with the crew and tries to get a hug from her. When she sees him, she backs away and looks uneasy. Ajay is right there and notices her nervousness of Raymond. He doesn't like it and he's definitely planning to take Raymond to task.

"I see what the deal is," he says to her, while looking at Raymond, "We're gonna talk later. I'm gonna handle *that* lil bit too, if I need too."

He never takes his eyes off of Raymond, who wisely backs away.

"Okay," she says as they all crowd around the table.

TIME TO LEARN-RELOADED-Time Will Reveal-part 1

Big Mama has cooked;
Ham, turkey, fried chicken, greens, macaroni and cheese [Bre and Stoney's favorite], green beans with potatoes, corn on the cob, potato salad, yams [Renee's favorite], corn bread, sweet potato pie [Jr's favorite], chocolate cake [Ajay's favorite], coconut cake [Chill's favorite], peach cobbler [all the girls favorite] and bread pudding [Jb and June's favorite]. There is sweet ice tea, kool-aid and soda's to drink.

She makes each of their favorites because they all call her their big mama. She has been preparing and cooking for the last 5 days.

"Everybody for they self!" Jb yells.

Poppa makes the guys step back until the ladies get their plates.

"See now, *that's* a gentleman," Bre says and laughs.

Her and the other females taunt the guys, by taking their time, fixing plates. Ajay keeps his eyes on Raymond, while they wait to eat. He notices him watching Ebony. Lynn laughs as she gets the plate from Jb's hand.

"Well, y'all need to move it along then. We're hungry too," Jb says as he jokes with the ladies.

After everyone has their fill of food, Renee tells big mama to have a seat and the ladies are going to clean up everything. Big mama protest but Renee isn't taking no, for an answer.

"Oh thank y'all, so much, baby," big mama says, "Big mama can sure use the rest."

Renee and the ladies clear the table. Then they go into the kitchen to do the dishes and put things away. Poppa and the guys go out on the back deck. He has beer, wine and Hennessy, on hand. Poppa is cool, like that. He has always let them have a drink, since as far back as they can remember. As a matter of fact, all of the grandfathers are cool. Poppa sends June inside with a glass of wine for big mama.

"You're not trying to get big mama drunk, are you?" Chill ask as him and poppa joke with each other.

This is a usual thing for them.

Poppa smiles and says, "Well, of course I am," and they all laugh.

The ladies finish in the kitchen and along with big mama, they join the guys on the deck. Ebony sits next to Ajay, who takes this opportunity to speak his peace. He turns to Raymond to introduce himself.

"Ajay Jackson. What's your name, dude?" he asks.

"Raymond White."

Raymond recognizes Ajay's name and face, from the list of the top players in the high school national basketball polls and he tells him so.

"I don't read that stuff, so I wouldn't know," Ajay says.

He's very cold about it, intentionally.

He continues, "I don't make friends with rivals, anyway. I think you should know that too."

Raymond thinks he means on the basketball court but Ajay means, *period.*

"Why we gotta be rivals?" Raymond asks, "I respect your game, man. You got game, *for real.*"

"I got Ebony too but that hasn't stopped you from trying to get at her," Ajay says, pulling no punches. Big mama smiles and Ajay continues, "I can tell she don't like how you keep watching her. Tank already told you to back off but you can't respect that. *Why* is that?"

"I don't mean to stare at her. It's a habit. I have a habit of looking at beautiful girls," Raymond tries.

"Well this beautiful girl," Ajay says as he looks at Ebony, "Is not *feeling* you. And she don't like you staring at her. So now, I don't either. She's *my* girl. You feel me?"

"Yea, okay," Raymond says quickly, not wanting a confrontation.

"Leave her alone because she comes with an army," Ajay says, not wanting to stop at just words.

He says, "She's it for me and I'm it for her. You're gonna have to find somebody else to stare at. I don't like her being uncomfortable and that's what you're causing her to be."

Chill, Jb, big mama and poppa take notice of the conversation, as Ajay continues to confront Raymond. He's trying to get him to understand that his actions aren't going to be tolerated.

"I'll check that at the door, man. I really didn't mean no harm," Raymond says, "I'm sorry for that."

"You need to tell her that and show her too," Ajay insists.

Big mama smiles at him. She likes his actions and she encourages poppa and Chill to back him up.

"Apologize to Ebony," Tank says suddenly, "I told you my lil sis is spoken for. She ain't getting down wit you. You're gonna have to *step off.*"

TIME TO LEARN-RELOADED-Time Will Reveal-part 1

Chill and poppa agree with Tank and Ajay. They tell Raymond that the women in this family, choose whom they like, not the other way around.

"I'm sorry," Raymond says to Ebony.

She says okay but never looks at him. She looks at Ajay, instead. He see that she's okay, so he lets up for now. But he's not done by a long shot.

"You're good but I don't think we'll ever be more than rivals," Ajay says, "I don't take names on the hardwood and nowhere else."

Raymond isn't sure if Ajay is saying they're enemies now, in person. Or just on the court or both. But however he's thinking Ajay meant it, he doesn't try to converse any farther. Ajay's posture now, almost dares him too. Big mama smiles, proudly. Poppa likes it too.

You can't fool elders. Ever!

Even Sonya, Tina and Shuntay seem to be smitten with Ajay. Even though, each of them have been known to sleep with Raymond, he isn't looking to tempting tonight, all of a sudden.

At 11:30pm, the crew leave for the motel. Ebony, Tank and his 6 friends go with them. Renee and Tonya gets them all checked in, gets their keys and everyone puts their bags in their room.

Chill and Renee's room adjoins with Jr and Tonya's. Stoney and Bre are joined with Rob and Jan, who are in the 4th room. Jb and Lynn have the 5th king-size bedroom which connects with Ajay, who has the 6th room. June and Rich are in the 7th room which has 2 Queen beds. They're already plotting on getting with the 3 girls that had come with Tank. The 3 girls are already interested and willing to get with them too. The crew are set and ready to see what Houston has to offer. They all gather in Chill and Jr's suite, to get a buzz. Charles calls his cousin Ron and a few of his homies down, to bring more party flavors. Chill, Ajay and the crew have some as well, so they match weed with each other and it's on.

April comes to the motel with her cousin Cassandra, who's in town visiting from Gulfport Mississippi, for *Labor Day*. Cassandra is Chill and Renee's age. She's as cool as ever. She has much game and reminds Ebony of T-baby. Cassandra says she wants them all to visit Gulfport, in the future, to meet her crew. The Diablo's are her guy crew and she's a member of her very own *Awesome Foursome*. The latter consists of 3 girls named: Cookie, C.C. and Ms Bren plus her. She tells them her street name is Black. Everyone from the crew decides they're going to call her Black too. She likes that, a lot.

"Well, we're gonna call you Black too," Rich repeats.

She says that's cooler than a fan. The whole crew are cool with Black, instantly. She's real and definitely down for whatever. They make a pact that 1 day, they'll all get together in Gulfport. Black says she'll visit them in Cleveland too because she wants to party with their entire crew.

Around 1:00am, they load up in the vehicles. They're going to a party thrown by some G's from Charles' set. Ebony is going too. This will be her 1st Houston party. Tank has been to many. She gets into the Blazer and slides up on Ajay's lap. This is the way she always rolls, whenever the car is crowded. Raymond can't help but notice how comfortable she is with Ajay, since he still hasn't stopped watching her. Ajay hasn't stopped watching his ass, either. Raymond finally goes on and gets into the vehicle that he's going to ride in, since no one is willing to make room for him in the Blazer. They know Ebony doesn't want him in there. They also know, Ajay does want him in there but that ride wasn't going to go smooth, at all.

"Time to go!" Ebony yells as Chill pulls away behind Charles, Raymond and their homies.

Ajay declares war on Raymond, from this day forward.

"He's one of those half slick types," he says, "The type that'll try to beat my girl up, just because I punked him out."

Some of the crew laugh but Ajay doesn't. He has no idea of just how right on, he is with his assessment of Raymond White.

They head out to a huge party in Houston's 5th ward, one of the roughest sections in the city. The crew feel right at home on the drive. Ajay and Ebony share an intimate conversation, in the back of the Blazer, on their way and before they arrive at the party.

"Hey baby, do you think I can get my sugar now?" Ajay asks.

He pulls her chin to his and they begin to kiss. He plays with her nipples, throughout the entire drive. They aren't alone but no one else seems to notice. If they do notice, then they're just use to it because no one says anything. Ajay can never seem to help himself around Ebony. He loves to touch her. As for Ebony, she doesn't mind it, at all. This is her man and he's in Houston. He's here to see her and to protect her from Raymond White and whomever else. She feels very secure.

CHAPTER 8

THE SOUTHERN WAY

The party is on and everybody shows the crew a nice time. Several fights break out but the crew aren't involved in any of them. After the party, they go back to their motel rooms for private time.

It's very late when Ebony gets to Ajay's room. She isn't planning to go back to big mama's house. Poppa and big mama was thinking ahead when they put her on birth control pills, the day after her father left for Arizona. Neither of her parents know about it yet. Poppa and big mama are not *condoning* her or Tank being sexually active. But they know about the motel incident, Jb and Lynn's incident and they also know about Ajay's serious affection for Ebony. Even Ebony was surprised when they took her to the clinic. Poppa had talked to papa about it and they decided to put her on the pill. They wasn't willing to wait for Pearl or John to approve it. Ajay knows she's on the pill and he wants to know *all* the details behind them taking her to get them and why they did.

"I guess they realize that I'm growing up," Ebony tells him, "Even if mama and daddy don't want too."

"Uh huh. I can see that you're growing up. Just by how fine you're getting," he says.

He's smiling and staring at her, as she lays across his king-sized bed. He asks, "But do you need pills in *H-town*?"

"Yes. For whenever you come to visit and they need to be in my system for when I come home in December," she says, "Big mama and poppa know about the motel, Anthony. They talked on the phone with papa and granny. Then they took me to the clinic. I've been taking them since July. I have enough to last until I'm eighteen too and they're in my system."

"I know they knew about the motel," he says, "And I got something for your system too, alright?" he adds, smiling at her.

She blushes openly as he lays down next to her. He ask how she's spent her days and nights without him. She tells him every detail.

"I've thought about that night at granny's, every night and every

day since I've been here," she says, "That was a great time. I loved it."
But he wants to talk more about Raymond. He doesn't trust him, *at all.*

"Why was you so tense when I hugged you, earlier? What was that about? Raymond?"
She tells him today was her 1st time seeing him, when he came home with Tank. She tells him how he stared at her and how uncomfortable that made her feel. He tells her he had noticed it too and he didn't like it either. He doesn't trust Raymond or any type like him. He's more concerned than he lets on. But he thinks Raymond will bother Ebony more, now that he's put him on front street.
"That's why I took it to him at big mama's house," he says, "I wanted to shank that nigga."
He tells that he has told Tank to watch and handle things with Raymond.
He says, "I told him to make sure that nigga understands that you are *my girl* and I'll do his ass, if he gets outta line."

After their talk, they make love. His kisses are so sensual, intense and very passionate. She knows, without a doubt, he has missed her. But she still has to hear him say it.

"Did you miss me, Anthony?"

"Yea. You can't tell?" he asks, as he looks into her eyes, "If you don't know, then we're going again. You're gonna have to give me some more pussy, right now, if you say you can't tell that I missed you."
She smiles. He kisses her until he becomes aroused, all over again. This time they make love, then cuddle until the daylight. They fall asleep in each others arms. Waking up together is something they've never done.

The rest of the weekend is spent, pretty much the same way. With lots of food, drinks, parties and back to the motel for private time.

"It's a good thing you're on the pill, baby girl," he says, "We've been fucking, a lot. I know I've sent about three or four seeds by now. I was full, baby," Ajay says and laughs as they cuddle in bed.

"*See*. Big mama was looking out for us," she says, smiling brightly.

"I *love* big mama," he says as if he's joking.
But he really does love her like his own grandmother. Ajay and big mama talk just as much, if not more, than her and Ebony do. They always have. Ajay and big mama have had a very special bond for all of his life.

They talk, all of the time, about Ebony and they have for over 8 years. Ebony isn't even aware of that part yet. She'll learn it later. Ajay had started confiding in big mama at age 6. It was when she had told him, she was going to be their grandmother since both of their grandmothers, her good friends, had died. What big mama saw in him, back then, was a young man who was mature beyond his years. He was already planning to spend forever with her namesake and Ebony couldn't even stand or understand him. Or so they all thought. This courtship is just Ajay's way of grooming her to be his ideal wife. Big mama is all for it. Only *Time Will Reveal* if it happens.

On Tuesday morning, the crew return home. Ebony and Tank return to their schools, reluctantly. Everyone who didn't meet the crew personally, have heard about the good times from Charles, Shuntay and the rest of the Houston posse. Ebony finds out, from some kids at her school, that Shuntay, Sonya and Tina had sex with June, Rich and Tank. She's planning to ask Tank about it later.

The next 2 months are long, boring and rather routine. Ebony has settled in, a little more. She's excited about her season opener. She keeps close contact with her girls, back home. She knows T-baby is looking forward to her 1st game also. This is their 1st year, not playing together. Nina and Rebbie are cheering for 8th grade. They all agree, it feels weird for them not to be in school together.

The James twins celebrate their 3rd birthday on November 4th. Brian Sr has already bought them a football and a basketball. Everyone at home are getting along fine and planning for Thanksgiving.

Ebony is having a great season, so far. She leads in scoring, rebounding and blocked shots. She's 2nd in assists. Her new teammates, April and Yolanda, are 2nd in the other categories. April leads in assist. She's a point guard, like Bre and her game is tight too. Tank is starting at small forward for the 9th grade team. Charles and David are on the team with him.

By Christmas break, Ebony is excited about going home. Tank is only going home to visit. He has to come back and stay until July. On the evening of December 15, him and Ebony pack the remainder of their clothes. They're looking forward to going back to Cleveland. But something awful, untimely and terribly unexpected happens, which changes their plan.

Big mama takes a turn for the worse and has to be hospitalized. Pearl and Brenda fly to Houston, immediately. They anticipate having to stay long past the start of the 2nd semester of school. Tank and Ebony are disappointed for 2 reasons. Big mama isn't doing well and they won't get to go back to Cleveland for a white Christmas. They have to send and receive their family gifts by mail. Ebony cries through most of her Christmas break. She cries all day on her 14th birthday, Christmas day.

On January 12th, granny flies to Houston to be with her best friend. This must have been the medicine big mama needed, because she starts to turn it around and get stronger. After 6 weeks in the hospital, she's finally allowed to go home. Granny, Pearl and Brenda stay another 2 weeks before they return to Cleveland on February 12th. By then, Ebony has already realized she has to complete the 8th grade in Houston.

Tank has turned fifteen. He's just looking forward to July. Ebony's 14th birthday had been uneventful, as far as she's concerned. She has decided to try and put the thought of going home out of her mind because big mama definitely needs her now.

During big mama's sickness and recuperation, she instructs Ebony on what and how, to cook for them. She teaches her how to cook all of those great southern dishes, they all love. Tank has his driver's license, by early February too and Ebony has her permit. She's driving, well enough, to drive her mother, aunt and grandmother to the airport, when they leave. With a licensed driver, of course. Poppa still promises to get them a car.

On *Valentine's Day,* Nina calls Tank and Ebony to tell them about the birth of Alana's little girl. The news now is that the baby's father is a football player from Smith High.

"I told you that wasn't my baby," Tank says in a confident tone.

"But she's still telling folks it's yours," Nina says as she is still very irritated with the whole ordeal.

"We'll get it straight when I get home," Tank assures her, "I can't wait to come home and get that shit over with. I might kill that ho for lying on me, like that."

The month of March marks the end of basketball season and the start of track. Ebony and her 8th grade team won the District Tournament.

Poppa had made every game. She played so well that, instead of her playing for the 9th grade team next year, Smiley High's varsity coach Hightower wants her to play with them. She's honored but tells Hightower she won't be in Houston for 9th grade.

Tank is tearing up the track for his 9th grade track team. He'll definitely letter by season's end.

In Cleveland, the crew enjoy similar success. T-baby's 8th grade team won their District. Jb and Ajay's team won the State title again. This season, Ajay was leading scorer as a sophomore which brings on an influx of division 1 college scholarship offers. But his tendency for getting into trouble had affected his eligibility to play during this season. Some say had he not been suspended for 8 of their 40 games, he would've been leading scorer in the state of Ohio. He only missed the top state scorers title by 22 points. He averages 24 points per game. Jb had been suspended for 4 games and he's 2nd leading scorer.

Lynn is All-State in track and Jan is All-State in softball. Bre leads her 9th grade team to 2nd place in District while June and Rich's 9th grade football team finished 2nd in District competition. All of them have scholarship offers. Their parents are very proud of each of them.

It's the end of the school year. Tank and Ebony are surely going to Cleveland, in June. The 1st day of June is their date to leave and all looks promising, so far. Up until this point, 1990 has been a bust. Things can only get better from here on out. Or so they think.

May 30th is the last day of school in Houston. They rush home to pack their clothes, once again. They have to wait for John to roll in town, tomorrow. Poppa allows them to call Cleveland. They call mama Jo's house and talk to Nina, Lynn and Ajay. They're excited about having only 2 days left in Cleveland schools. Their last day will be Monday, June 3rd. They're planning a big party at Chill's house. Ebony and Ajay talk for a long while. He ask her if everything is okay with the Raymond situation or is he still bothering her. She assures him, Tank had handled that situation, several months ago.

"That's all good then." Ajay says, "Have you been taking care of that smooth beautiful, fine and front cover of a magazine, body for me?" He's almost whispering. Still it sends chills through her body as she giggles.

"You know I have," she says as she smiles.
He can almost hear her smiling.

"I'll see, when you get here," he says.

"Yes, you will."

"I hope you're still taking those pills too," he says, "Because you're gonna need 'em."

"Yes, I'm still taking them," she says with a smile.
She's happy to hear that he's looking forward to seeing and holding her, just as she can't wait to be with him. After several more minutes of conversation, they all have to get off of the phone.

The next day, John pulls in, right on schedule. Ebony and Tank are beside themselves with excitement and can't wait to leave. All of their Houston friends come by, this afternoon. Including Raymond. He has gotten a *Benz 190*. He's always showing off. He doesn't say anything to Ebony. He hardly looks at her. She's pleased about that part. They all chill on the sidewalk, instead of the porch. Big John is resting up for the drive to Cleveland, the next morning. Everything in Houston is looking grand.

In Cleveland, things have taken a turn for the worse. Ajay has violated his parole. He gets busted with an ounce of marijuana and this isn't his 1st offense. He's being sent to training school for 60 days. No questions asked.

The next morning, John calls Pearl at 4:00am to tell her that him and the kids are about to leave out for home. She tells him about Ajay.

"Oh shit, baby. Wasn't there anything y'all could do to keep them folks from throwing him away?" he asks, very frustrated.

"No, John. We all went down there and tried to reason with the Judge but they treated us like crap. They said they want him off the streets. We even tried to send him to mama's, like Jeremy. But the judge said *'absolutely not'* and he wouldn't even give him a bond. He has to go before another judge on Monday morning, for official sentencing. But he has to stay. Wheeler said he's looking at two months for his parole violation. Even Parkwood couldn't get him better than that."

"I'm not telling the kids and surely not, baby girl," John says, after

a few minutes, "Because that'll break her spirits, for sure."
He gives the phone to big mama. They all agree, not to tell Tank or Ebony about Ajay's arrest. After Pearl talks with her parents, they hang up. John and the kids say their goodbyes to poppa and big mama. They pull out for Cleveland at 5:00amcst.

John is quiet. He listens to Ebony and Tank's plans for home and their crew. He doesn't want to make them sad. He says nothing about Ajay.

Later, at *The Peabody*, John overhears them talking about Alana. After getting all of the details, he tells Tank he wants him to take a paternity test, to be certain. Then do the right thing. Tank isn't suppose to be back in Cleveland for another month. He figures he can use this to his advantage. He's thinking of going to see the Judge and telling him, the child is the reason he returned early.

"Hmm, that just might work," Ebony says.

"It's got too," Tank says, "I can't stay inside for a whole month."
They continue talking at a whisper until they fall asleep. The total trip takes 55 hours.

When they arrive in Cleveland, they're so excited, they kiss the ground. Everyone is at Church except Chill. He's home alone. After taking their bags in, they walk across the street.

They hug Chill, then talk for awhile. Ebony goes back home to unpack and get dolled up for Ajay. It isn't until after she leaves, that Chill tells Tank about Ajay being locked up. Tank is upset and wants to see his friend. Chill reminds him that he needs to lay low until after July 12th. Tank tells Chill about his plans to go see the Judge about Alana's baby. Chill convinces him to do otherwise.

"You'll end up getting stuck, even if it's not yours, bro," he says.
Tank takes his advice. He's still going to take a paternity test to prove, once and for all, that he isn't the father. Chill agrees with him, on that part.

At 1:30pm, Pearl, lil man and Jb come home from Church. T-baby rides home with them, so she can see Ebony and Tank. Jo and Pearl's family pull up, at the same time. Ebony is standing in their side door, waiting. Rebbie has come with them, so she can see Ebony and Tank also.

As soon as T-baby, Nina and Rebbie get out of the vehicles, Ebony

runs outside. They all hug and kiss each other. Then Ebony hugs everyone else. She looks for Ajay but doesn't see him. Her and her girls go up to her room to catch up on the past 11 months, face to face. No sooner than they get into the room Nina asks, "Where's Jeremy?"

"He's over at Chill's house," Ebony says, "Where's Anthony?"

"Ebony, you haven't heard what happened?" Nina asks sadly.

"No. What happened?" she asks.

Nina tells her the details of Ajay's arrest, the day before. And that he has no bond. He only has a court date for tomorrow morning at 9:00am. Ebony's heart sinks to her stomach. She feels like she'll be sick.
How can this be happening?

She hasn't seen him in 9 months. Now that she's finally back at home, he's gone. Her girls talk, while she sits there, dazed and confused. It will be 2 more months before she can hold her man. She starts to think things just can't get any worse.

Later, they all gather at Chill's house. Ebony can't manage to have a good time, no matter how hard she tries. Her crew understands and can feel her pain. Chill has a long conversation with her. That still doesn't lift her spirits. She's devastated and wants to see Ajay, so bad, her whole body aches. She goes home and writes him a long letter.

The next morning everyone who doesn't have school, gathers at Jo's house to wait for news on Ajay. Only Jo, Al, Pearl and John attend the hearing with Ajay and Wheeler. No one else can come. Not even to wait outside. When the parents call back home with the verdict, the crew are saddened to hear what they'd already expected. Ajay has to go to training school until August 2nd. Ebony burst into tears. Renee tries to console her but she pulls away and goes home. The crew decide to leave her alone, so she can digest it all. She's feeling lost and alone without Ajay around and right now, 2 months seems like an eternity.

When the others finish their last day of school, they come by to get the news. Nina, T-baby and Rebbie come straight to Ebony's room. Her and Tank are sitting on her bed, talking. Pearl is leaving to take lil man and lil Kenny to Alicia or Ally's, 7th birthday party at Rebbie's house. All of the

kids in her age group are going. Before leaving with Erica and Pam, Jo tells Nina and Lynn to get some things together for Ajay. They know exactly what to get. He had been through this before, when he was younger, just not for this long. Ebony goes to Jo's house with them. She has to see his room, at least. Even though he isn't in it.

When she walks into his room, she can see that he had missed her. He has pictures of her and her letters to him, all over his walls. She missed him too. She's missing him, still.

Later, she ask mama Jo if she can go with her when she visits him. Jo says it will be fine if she comes. That gives her something to look forward too and a lot sooner than 60 days.

They take him some personal items, the next day but only his parents can make contact with him.

This is a pointless visit.

For Ebony, the next few weeks are boring. Everyone has their mate except her. Big June is about to turn 15 and Chill is turning 21. They're planning a party, as usual. Ebony doesn't have anything to celebrate.

On the day of the party, all the guys go visit Ajay for the 3rd time. Pearl doesn't allow Ebony to go with the guys. She can only go when Jo and Al visit. Ebony sent 3 letters and 3 pictures with Tank, each of the 3 times he's gone. She talks to Ajay, each time he calls home. He's doing fine. He could always adapt to any new surroundings. Sad part is, he's missing the All-American's camp. He was invited, specifically. They was on the phone when he told her, he hated to miss that particular camp. During the call, he tells her not to worry about him and that he's going to be alright. But still, she worries and misses him, so much.

"I'll see you before you know it," he says.

He has said that every time, before they hang up.

On the 4th of July, all of the families get together. In the early morning, the crew go visit Ajay. Ebony goes too, even though Pearl is against it. First, the crew visit. Then Ebony goes back alone. Ajay is happy to see her but he seems more distant than ever. His only concern is getting out. He tries to convince her of that. Even though, in his mind, he's thinking of sexing her, holding her and making sweet love to her, at this very

moment. His mannerisms doesn't say he isn't thinking about of being sexual with her and she can sense as much.

"We can talk about all of that other shit when I come home. I can't even be thinking like that, up in here," he says bluntly. Though he's thought about it often, "Get that off your mind until I come home. Okay?"

"Alright," she concedes.

She was the last 1 to go back. When the guard comes to get him, she feels sad. She knows he has to leave. She hugs and kiss him and holds on tight. "I love you, Anthony," she says fighting back tears.

"You're suppose too," he responds with a smile, "See ya."

"In a minute," she says and he's gone.

As she walks back up the hallway, the tears flow, very heavy.

This is the worst thing that could've happened. I need you baby. I need you, so much.

When they get back home, everybody eats. Then her crew goes to Chill's house for Jb's 17th birthday party. Ebony stays home. She doesn't feel like partying tonight or any other night, without Ajay. She goes to Jo's house to wait for his call and to find out when his parents are going back to visit him.

"Ebony, are you alright, baby girl?" mama Jo asks.

"No ma'am. I miss Anthony," she says trying to fight back tears but it doesn't work.

"I do too," Jo says.

Her and Ebony say a prayer and cry together. When Ajay calls, Ebony gets to talk to him for the entire 15 minutes. She tells him, his parents are coming back to see him for his 16th birthday, 1 week from today. She's coming too and she can't wait. Until then, she'll write too him everyday.

It's the morning of the July eleventh. It's Ajay's 16th birthday and they go visit him. Jo, Al, Lynn and Nina, Erica, Pam, Ebony and Tank make this trip. Chill and the crew have collected all of his money from the set. Tank is going to put it on the books for him.

Today, they all get to visit with Ajay on the grounds. He had earned it for good behavior. He behaved well because he wanted to be able to have contact with Ebony. He knew she needed it too.

TIME TO LEARN-RELOADED-Time Will Reveal-part 1

In Houston, things aren't on the pro side for Ebony and Ajay's reunion. Big mama has relapsed and is taken back to the hospital. She isn't given much of a chance for survival. Poppa calls Pearl and Brenda. He tells them to come, right away. The doctor has said big mama may not make it through the week. He doesn't think she's strong enough to survive the night and he's strongly suggesting she have surgery to prevent the further spread of the cancer in her breast.

In Cleveland, Pearl, granny and Brenda get 4 airline tickets. The 4th one is for Ebony. As she visits Ajay, she has no idea, she's about to return to Houston, the next day. Pearl and Brenda talk as they repack Ebony's things.

"Bren, I know Ebony's gonna react badly when she finds out she's going back. If mama pulls through, she's gonna have to stay again," Pearl says.

"I know Pearl but she won't have to stay so long, this time," Brenda offers, "Since Brittany's getting older, she can stay with mama some too."

"Brittany is *nine*," Pearl says, "She's not old enough to take care of mama, right now."

"Maybe if she goes with Ebony, this time and learns what to do. Then baby girl can come back home before too long and just let Brittany stay," Brenda tries.

"It's not the stay that she's gonna flip out about," Pearl says, "It's the going back, *period*. Especially with Ajay being locked up. You and I both know *why* she's planning to be here when he comes home."

"Yes and she should be here, Pearl. We would've done the same thing."

"We both know *why* she wants to be here," Pearl continues, as if her sister hadn't spoken or like she hadn't heard her comment, the 1st time. She's shaking her head and ignoring what Brenda says.

"Well maybe it's for the best," Brenda says, "She *is* growing up. She's not a baby, anymore."

"I don't want her to get pregnant, Brenda," Pearl says, "While she's running around after Ajay. I know they have plans of sleeping together again. There's no way they don't. Look at how she's running up and down that *highway*. She's better off in Houston, where she can cool her hot ass down!"

"Pearl, she's in love," Brenda tries, "You remember those days? We *can* remember those days, can't we? I know I can."

"Ebony doesn't know what love is!" Pearl snaps.

Brenda decides to remain quiet while Pearl rants. They finish packing with only Pearl talking. Brenda knows Pearl will have the last word on the subject of Ebony. It has always been that way when it comes to her baby girl. Pearl rambles on.

Meanwhile, Ebony and Ajay sit on the grass and talk. She tells him over and over, how she feels about him. Though he has asked her not too.

"I love your letters, Ebony. They're helping me to get through this. Just stay cool until I get out there. We'll work on our moms letting us see each other. Instead of sneaking around. Alright?"

She agrees and smiles. Before they leave, everyone kisses and hugs Ajay. He wants to be more passionate with Ebony but he can't. Not with his mother there. Al has let up off of him about Ebony. He lets Ajay know, him and John are okay with them dating. But they have to work on their mothers. Ebony doesn't know about that part yet.

After kissing Ebony, Ajay whispers in her ear, "I'll take care of all of that, later. Keep it tight."

The entire time he's whispering, Jo keeps a watchful eye on them both.

"I'll be back to see you, next week, okay?" Ebony says, "Anthony, I promise you, I'll always wait for you. It doesn't matter where you are or where I am."

"I know you will," he says with a smile, "I don't worry about you being true to me. I never have. I'm just happy you're my girl."

After the visit is done, they leave the facility. Ebony has no idea of how needed her last statement was. She's about to get the news that will ultimately change her life and her close relationship with her mother, for a long time to come.

When Pearl tells Ebony the news, Ebony is devastated. She's worried about big mama. But she doesn't want to move back to Houston.

She yells, "I'm not going back!"

This shocks and angers Pearl, to hear Ebony being so defiant.

"It's already set," Pearl yells back, "I'm not in the mood to argue with you about it, Ebony!"

They yell for over 20 minutes. Pearl isn't backing down and neither is Ebony. Ebony thinks about running away. But where could she go where Pearl couldn't find her?

I hate her! She's coming between me and Anthony. She knows he loves me. She knows he needs me here, right now!

"Please! Just leave me alone!" Ebony yells.

Pearl leaves her room and closes the door. Ebony writes Ajay a letter to explain this latest disaster. She cries so much, her eyes are nearly swollen shut.

Sure enough, the next morning, Ebony, Pearl, Brenda and granny take their flight to Houston. Poppa picks them up at *Hobby airport.* He drives them directly to the hospital, where the doctors inform them that big mama will have to have her right breast removed. Or the cancer will continue to spread. Big mama is against it, totally. Granny Pearline pulls poppa to the side for a brief talk.

"Percy, take the girls and go on home. Let me talk to her, for awhile," she says.

Poppa obliges her. He leaves her there with big mama, while him, Ebony, Pearl and Brenda head to his house.

By the time they make it there, big mama is calling. After a few minutes of granny Pearline in her ear, she had decided to sign the consent forms. The surgery has been scheduled for Thursday, July 18th. Big mama also asks Ebony to please keep Ajay informed of her progress. And though Ebony wonders why she only specifies Ajay, she writes him a letter, right then and there. She tells him the latest news. He hasn't written her back, not even once, since she first came to Houston. In her letter tonight, she tells him the surgery will be in a week. While she wonders why he never writes her back. She asks him that, in this letter, as well.

The surgery was a success and big mama regains her strength. She stays in the hospital for a week. On T-baby's 14th birthday, she comes home.

TIME TO LEARN-RELOADED-Time Will Reveal-part 1

Ebony calls T-baby to wish her a happy birthday and T-baby gives her the scoop on the crew. She also tells her that Ajay is still getting out on Rebbie's 14th birthday.

"I hope I can be there, by then," Ebony says, "So I can see my baby and hold him."

"I know you do, cousin," T-baby says, "I hope you be back too. Because he's loosing focus or something, while he's in there. I don't know what to call it."

"Why do you say that?"

"Do you remember Darlene?"

"Yes. I remember that old bitch's name. What about her?"

"She's been visiting him, since you left. She's taking him money and shit, trying to get with him."

"Why is he accepting visits from her, in the first place?" Ebony ask, on the verge of tears.

"I don't know. But Nina is pissed off with him about it too. Because Darlene is Alana's aunt. You knew that, right?"

"Yea. Tank told me that."

"Anyway, that bitch is too old to be fucking around with Ajay in the first place!" T-baby snaps.

"Isn't she twenty something years old or something like that?" Ebony asks, remembering what Pearl had said about a 20 year old.

"She's twenty six, cousin," T-baby says, "She was twenty two when she first started messing with Ajay and he was like twelve or thirteen. Mama Jo said, if she ever get her hands on her, she's gonna beat her ass."
Ebony doesn't respond. The rest of their conversation is about Darlene and Ajay. While they're talking, Nina and Rebbie come over to T-baby's house. They're suppose to go to a dance at the community center. Ebony talks to Rebbie, first and then to Nina.

"Of course, girl. You know I'm pissed off with his ass, over this shit," Nina says.

"Have you talk to him about it?" Ebony asks.

"Yes I did and he told me to stay out of his business!"

"He said that to *you*?"

"Yes, Ebony. He's changed, so much up in there, this time. It's like he thinks he don't need nobody!"

"He hasn't answered any of my letters, either. But he never does," Ebony says sadly, "He usually would send messages by you or Tank. But this time, I haven't heard anything from him."

They go on to talk about the crew, then how big mama is doing.

"She's getting stronger, everyday," Ebony says, "She's home now and I have to get in there. Nina, I have to go but listen. When you talk to Anthony. Please tell him, *I love him*. I will always love him and stay true to him. Tell him just like that, okay?"

"You know I will," Nina says.

Ebony has to hang up.

"I love y'all and I miss y'all," she says as she starts to cry.

"We miss you too," they say, "Don't cry, Ebony. We'll be together again, sooner than you know."

They hang up.

On Monday, Ebony is hit with news, she hadn't anticipated. She has to stay in Houston when the others return home on Friday. Friday is Rebbie's 14th birthday. It's also Ajay's release date. Her mother, grandmother and aunt are going home. But her mother is making her stay. Ebony goes into a fit of aggression against Pearl. Aunt Brenda, poppa and granny are trying to keep the peace. Ebony argues with Pearl, initially. Then she tries begging her to let her go back to Cleveland with them. Pearl won't bulged. Ebony swears at her and vows never to speak to her again.

The rest of the night, she stays locked in her room, crying and cursing. She feels as if she hates her mother for what she's doing to her. And how selfish she is to keep her away from her man, her crew and her home. Ebony hasn't considered how selfish she's being. Nor how this attitude *must* be affecting big mama. Brenda tries to talk to Pearl, out on the back deck. Again, Pearl closes her mind.

"Pearl, I need to know *one* thing," Brenda says, "Is Ebony staying in Houston for mama's benefit or yours?"

Pearl goes into a tantrum. Brenda eases out of the conversation, when their father takes over. He calms Pearl down. Brenda knows she struck a nerve, so she leaves well enough alone.

They leave for Cleveland, on an early morning flight. Ebony watches from the airport window and cries.

TIME TO LEARN-RELOADED-Time Will Reveal-part 1

In flight, Pearl is crying too. She feels guilty about what her younger sister Brenda, had said to her as well.

Later that afternoon, Ebony answers the phone and it's Pearl. She's calling to say they've arrived safely. Ebony gives the phone to poppa without saying another word. She doesn't even want to hear her mother's voice, let alone talk to her. Pearl asks her father to give Ebony her love and try to help her to understand, this is the best thing for big mama and not something personal towards her. Which is how Ebony feels. And she isn't far from the truth.

After hanging up, poppa ask Ebony to help him make dinner, for the 3 of them. While in the kitchen, he talks to her about everything that has transpired over the past year. She tells him her side of the story and he really shows understanding.

"I know you love that young man, baby girl. That's why Eloise and I, we let you visit with him when he was here. We tried to stop your mama from seeing your daddy, back when they was around your age. I feel like we lost her for a few years," poppa explains, "Listen, Ebony. Sometimes loving somebody means giving them the freedom to find their own way. In your mama's own way, I think that's what she's trying to do. I told you a long time ago how you could determine if you got a good man or not. But me, I already know that answer. You'll have to grow into it."

He smiles and so does she. She reluctantly agrees, as though she has much of a choice. She's over 1000 miles away from the man she loves and he's free to walk the streets. The only thing she can do now, is hope that somehow, those streets will lead him back to her heart and back in her arms. In his arms is still the only place for her. She ask poppa if she can call Rebbie to wish her a happy birthday. He says she can. She knows everybody will be at Chill's house and that's where she calls.

Sure enough, the crew are there. She talks to Tank, after speaking with Rebbie, Renee and Chill. Tank tells her, their father had taken him, Alana and her baby for a paternity test and he isn't the father. She's glad to hear this news. She knows that tormented Nina, for more than a year.

"I know Nina's happy *that's* over."

"Yea, she is. Here she go, right here. She wants to talk to you."

He gives Nina the phone. They talk briefly about Alana, before she reveals that Darlene had shown up at the party, looking for Ajay. She tells her Ajay tried to pretend he didn't know why she was there. But her girls knew what was up.

"Is he there now?" Ebony asks nervously.

"No. He went to take her home. He's suppose to drive her car back over here"

Ebony is hurt by that answer. But she wanted to know, none-the-less.

"I wanna talk to him," Ebony says.

"You need too. Because I'm about to-" Nina pauses as Ajay walks through the door. She says, "Hold up. He's coming in."

She hands Ajay the phone and rolls her eyes at him.

"Who's this?" Ajay asks Nina, who walks away without a response. She's still not speaking to him over this whole ordeal.

"Hello," Ajay says as he takes the phone into the kitchen.

"Hello, Anthony. How are you?" Ebony says cautiously.

"Oh, I'm good! Real good, now!" he says, smiling after realizing it's her on the other end. He says, "How are you doing in H-town?"

"Not good. Not good at all."

"What's wrong? That nigga fuckin with you again?"

"No. I just wanna be there and not here. That's what's wrong."

"You're suppose to be use to it, by now, ha?"

He isn't intending to sound so unconcerned but he does to her.

"I'll never get use to being away from you. You should know that, by now."

"I thought maybe you had settled in and was doing things *the Southern way,* since you stopped writing to me."

"Why are you doing this?" she asks.

"Doing what?" he asks, knowing all the time that she's referring to the unconcerned tone in his voice.

"You're acting like you don't care anymore," she says, "I wrote to you, everyday. Everyday since I've been here. I *think about you* every single day. I have trouble sleeping when I'm upset and I get upset when I don't hear from you. Since the first time I came here, I wrote to you, everyday. You never wrote me back once and-"

"You know I don't write letters, baby girl. I thought we had that understanding," he says.

She gets to the matter that's really got her bothered.

"Am I suppose to understand you seeing Darlene too?" she asks boldly.

"What's to understand?"

"Are you seeing her again?" she asks with baited breath.

"I see her. But hell, I was locked up and she started coming to visit me."

"Is that all?"

"What do you mean, *is that all*? What else could it be? I was locked up. *Damn*!"

He's getting frustrated and caught up. She knows it's because he's guilty.

"Well now that you're out, are you gonna be with her?" she asks.

"You mean am I gonna hit it? Is that what you wanna know?"

"Yes."

"Probably."

"Why?"

"Something to do," he says coldly.

"I thought that's what I was here for," she says desperately.

"Baby, you're way down there. I'm here. I've been locked up. I wanna fuck, *tonight*. Can you be here?"

She says nothing.

"That's what I thought. You don't have an answer for that, do you? Look here, baby. Keep it real, alright? You know your man better than anybody else, knows me. I'm not trying to replace you. I will *never* do that. It never will be that. But I'm gonna get my fuck on, with some ho, *tonight*. And that's all it is. Do you feel me?"

Ebony is upset. She can't say anything else. Feeling as if she will burst into tears while their on the phone, she hangs up. She feels like her life just keeps getting worse. She has to realize, 1 thing. She wanted to grow up but she hadn't ever imagined it would be so tough.

Is this the pain mama tried to tell me about? Or that she was trying to save me from? How am I suppose to compete with Darlene, for Ajay's affection, from way down here? Darlene is twenty six years old, with her on apartment, car and job. She's definitely more experienced than me. She has two kids, already. Both of them are over half my age. Eight and nine years old. Even more, Darlene is there in Cleveland and I'm not.

TIME TO LEARN-RELOADED-Time Will Reveal-part 1

Love hurts. It hurts down to the core of your heart, when it goes bad. Love heals. It heals from head, heart to toe, when it's good.

Right now, for Ebony Eloise Brown, it's bad meaning bad! This hurts a lot worse than seeing him in the act with Anita Davis. At least then, she was in Cleveland and could confront him. All she can do now is wonder.
Can it ever be good again? Like when we slow danced in his room? Where is the love I felt at the motel? Or at granny's house, on the back porch? Or when he came in the window? All the days in the park or at Chill's, after dark?

She's only 14 years old and feeling as though she has lived a lifetime. At this moment, she knows she has to pull herself up. She doesn't know how she'll do it. But she's going to find a way. No matter what happens with Ajay, she will always love him. But tonight, she realizes he has to love her too and all the time. Always and unconditionally! Because until he does, she will always find herself in tears, heartache and misery. Once again, she cries herself to sleep.

****

In Cleveland, the crew are grilling Ajay. They want to know what happened during his phone conversation with Ebony. He tries to convince them that nothing is wrong, saying, "She just had to get off the phone."
Chill knows there's more to the story and he's determined to get it out of Ajay. Chill tells him to come and drive him on a beer run. Ajay does.

Once they're in the car and on the drive to the store, Chill has a serious talk with him.

"You got your license yet, bro?" Chill asks, knowing he hasn't.

"No," Ajay says, "I still got the permit. But next week, pops is going with me to get them. You know I turned sixteen in lock up."
As they drive, Chill talks about life and how he sees it. He tells him he understands how he feels about Ebony. But he has to realize that Ebony may not fully understand yet.

"All she can see for herself is *you*," he says, "She's down for you until the end. Even if a nigga threaten her life, I know she'll die before she turns on you or lets you down," he adds as Ajay drives in silence.

"Ajay, you know if somebody fuck with baby girl, the wrong way, you'll kill a muafucka. Won't you?"

"You already know that," he replies, "But she ought to know that too. I try to put it down for her. But I ain't no punk ass that's gonna sit here and wait on the pussy, like that. It's good, don't get me wrong but-"

"I'm not saying you should. Not until you're married. I'm just saying, keep that shit low key, bro. Don't be flaunting no bitch in front of the crew, like *that.* And don't let them ho's show up at crew events like they're family. *Crew* is your family and Ebony *is a part* of that family."

"Hide them bitches," Ajay says and laughs. Then more seriously, he says, "I told her not to look for me but that ho showed up anyway."

"Whatever, man," Chill says, not willing to make light of this topic. He says, "Never put it out there, like today. Because you know you're not down with them muthafuckin ho's, so don't give em props. You feel me?"

"Yea, bro. I feel you," he says.

"Then when you're ready to chill with your lady, like I do with Renee. It's not a problem with them outside ho's. Because they know their position."

They laugh as they pull into the parking lot of the store, park and head inside.

Chill always put them up on game. Not that they don't have game, already. But somehow, after they hear it from him, someone who's just slightly older but still able to relate to their times and generation. It resonates with them better. For Instance, Chill had said;

"It's okay to have one lady that you treat special. Because that's all a part of being a man. Anyone putting down on your choice to be open about that one lady, is probably envious of you."

After they hear it like that, the guys feel more comfortable about it and it also jives with the way they were all raised. Hearing positives from someone they respect and kick it with, drives the point home, better. Chill knows, the very reason they feel more comfortable chilling at his house with their ladies, is because they see him putting it down for Renee. He knows, 1 day when they're all a bit older, they'll do the same thing. All of their parents and grandparents, did it the same way. Their forefathers had laid the ground work in 1 statement. Which goes:

TIME TO LEARN-RELOADED-Time Will Reveal-part 1

"Expect and accept real love from only one woman and do your damn best to return it. Thus, life will be simpler."

"As for Ebony," Chill says, once they're back in the car, "She's finding her strength while she's in Houston. You can quote me on that, bro. She'll be stronger, one day. Then the true test of your manhood will be before you. I had to learn that with Renee. Right now is when you need to make haste and not waste time, trying to game on her love for you. You know it gets no better than baby girl. Not where you're concerned. And how you handle a woman's strength, is what determines whether you are a real man or a mouse," he says as they drive, "Only a strong man can handle a strong woman and vice versa. Big Paul told me that and grandpa Paul did too."

"I hear you, man," Ajay says as he glances over at Chill to let him know that he's truly listening.

"How to be *good* to my woman," Chill adds, "That's something I can say I learned from my pops, other then this muthafuckin' street game." They pull back into his driveway and park. Chill gets out and grabs 3 cases of beer. He asks, "Can you bring the rest when you come in?"

"Yea, I got it," Ajay says as he sits quietly, in the car, as if it's something else he wants to say to Chill.

Chill goes on in the house. He knows Ajay, well enough to know that whenever he has to ponder something, he needs time alone. Besides, this is one situation Chill really wants him to think through, thoroughly.

After thinking things, over for several minutes, Ajay decides to bring the rest of the beer into the house. Then he needs to talk to Nina. He goes straight to her. Nina still has her aggression toward Ajay because Darlene had shown up. Coldly, she asks, "What do you want with me?"

"I wanna write Ebony a letter. I need you to give me the address," he tries.

"It's about time you come in out of the rain," Nina says dryly, "And anyway, where are all the letters she sent to you? Didn't you hang them on your wall?"

"Yea, I kept them but...., I want you to write it for me, alright? Look, Nina. Just write it for me and I'll tell you what to say," he says and she can tell that he's genuine, so she agrees to write the letter for him.

It isn't that he can't read and write. He can. But it's known fact that Nina

and Ebony can put words down on paper, better then anyone he knows. And he wants to be sure this letter gets his point across, the right way. He also misses the closeness him and his sister shared before this whole rift with Alana and Darlene came about. He knew Nina would agree. She would agree to do anything to make Ebony happy. That's what he had counted on. They leave the party with Tank, who wants to add some lines, as well. They go across the street to mama Jo's house.

They go straight to Ajay's room. Nina gets out the legal pad and pen and begins to write. Ajay dictates what he wants her to write and so does Tank. Between the 3 of them, putting their thoughts together, they end up with 18 pages, front and back.

"We're gonna need a big ass envelope to send this thing off in," Nina says with a huge smile.

"Will you mail it for me, in the morning?" Ajay asks.

"Yes. Just give me the money," she says with her hand extended to him.

"Here. Take fifty and send it for the next day or two days," he says.

"*Priority*," she corrects him.

"Yea, it's a priority for me," he laughs as Tank gives him a pound, "That's for my baby. It's very important."

"She's gonna be so happy when she gets this," Nina says as she smiles at her brother.

Ajay signs the huge letter and adds his cologne to it.

"If you send it tomorrow, then she should get it Monday or Tuesday, right?" Tank asks.

"Yes but the post office ain't open on Saturdays," Nina says, "I can give it to the mailman. He'll mail it for me. That's the only way to get priority mail out, on a Saturday. Aunt Jessica told Lynn that, back when her and Terrell use to write each other, all the time."

Aunt Jessica is Al's sister. Terrell is her only child. He's a little older than Lynn and they live in Boston, which is Al's childhood home.

Soon, Nina, Ajay and Tank are back at the party. Chill is pleased to know Ajay had taken the time to go write to Ebony, tonight.

"Bro, that means you was listening to me, ha?" Chill asks as they stand in the kitchen.

"Yea, bro. I always listen to you, Chill. I know you be coming real with the speeches and all, man."
They laugh.
Chill says, "Cool. See that's why I be talking to y'all. One day, I'm not gonna be around this muafucka and y'all will have to carry this shit on. There's no way you'll be able to keep your business right, if your personal ain't tight. You know?"

"I know that's right, man," Ajay answers.

"Good then, dog. Lets party and shit. *Class dismissed*," Chill says as they laugh again, "Party in this muthafucka!" he yells as they go back to the front room.

Near the end of the party, as all of the crew pair up to leave, Nicole and Angie show up. They've already gone and gotten a motel room and are hoping to get with Ajay and Rich. Rich is already gone with T-baby. The 2 of them, along with June and Rebbie, have already gone to the motel. Chill had set it out for them, for T-baby and Rebbie's birthdays. Ajay tells Chill, he's going with Nicole and Angie to the motel and leaving Darlene's car in his driveway.

"*Now* man, *that's* how you do that shit. You've been locked up *too*! Go on. Get your freak on, with both them ho's, dog," Chill says as they laugh and give dap.

"I told them to park down the street. I didn't want my mother-in-law to see me getting in the car with them," Ajay says.
He laughs, after realizing he'd referred to Pearl as his mother-in-law. He leaves the house and starts down the street. Nicole and Angie are more than willing to do a threesome with him. The 2 of them sit smiling, as he approaches their car. Nina and Tank are already gone to Ajay's room. Jb and Lynn have gone to Stoney's house with Bre, Jan and Rob. Jr and Tonya are upstairs at Chill's, in the spare room. Renee is on the loveseat, waiting for Chill. No one from the crew witnesses Ajay's rendezvous except for Chill. That is exactly what Chill was speaking on, earlier. Being discreet and sparing Ebony's feelings. Because she's a *good* girl, she's *his girl* and she's *due respect*.

After Ajay leaves, lil Chill wakes up and comes downstairs. His parents are alone, slow dancing in their living room.

"Where is uncle Ajay at?" lil Kenny asks.

"Kenny, what are you doing up, this late?" Renee asks as she goes to him.

"I wanna see uncle Ajay."

"Come here, man," Chill says as he sends Renee on up the stairs to wait for him in their bedroom.

He wants to talk, father-to-son. Kenny comes over to his father, who has sat down on the couch. Lil Kenny sits next to him.

"What's on your mind, man?" Chill asks.

"I didn't get to see uncle Ajay yet. I just wanna see him."

He calls Ajay, uncle, since Chill and Ajay consider themselves brothers. Lil Kenny had been taught to call Ajay his uncle and all of his sisters, he call aunts. He calls Ebony his sister, because she use to baby sit him before she became a member of the crew. They share the same birthday. This year when she turns 15, he'll be seven.

"He already left, son," Chill says, "He came up and looked in on you but you was sleeping. But he said y'all are gonna kick it tomorrow, alright?"

"Is he gone over Ebony's house?"

"Nah, man. You know Ebony went back to Houston, right?"

"I don't like her to be in Houston. I want her to come back and keep me."

"I know, man. But you know she has to take care of big mama, right now. She'll be back, as soon as big mama is feeling better, okay?"

"Okay. I want her to call me tomorrow, so I can tell her I'm gonna be in the first grade," he says with a grin.

Chill laughs as he stands up. He picks his son up, to take him back to his room.

"I'll tell you what. How about if I let you call her tomorrow, when you wake up, ha? Would that be cool with you?" Chill says as he goes upstairs to tuck him back into bed.

"Yes sir. That'll be cool. Yes," Lil Kenny says, very excitedly.

He's laughing as Chill tickles his ribs. Chill puts him to bed and stays until he falls asleep. Then he goes downstairs to check the locks again. He makes sure everything is secure, then joins Renee in their bedroom.

TIME TO LEARN-RELOADED-Time Will Reveal-part 1

Late the next morning, Ajay returns. Instead of taking Darlene's car home, he goes home and gets in bed.

Shortly after he's in his room, Darlene comes knocking on their front door. Nina and Lynn hear the knock from their room. Nina answers the door.

"*What*?!" she snaps, after seeing that it's Darlene at the door.

"Is Ajay here? I need my car," Darlene says smugly.

"I don't know," Nina says, "I know you don't think I'm about to go do *shit* for you. Be clear. I don't like your ass."

Nina really doesn't care if Ajay is at home or not. Not for Darlene, she doesn't.

"Can you see if he's here, so I can get my car, please?" Darlene ask, trying to sound a little friendlier.

"Just a minute."

Nina slams the door and goes upstairs. Ajay is in his room. He had just laid down. He tells her to get the keys from his pants pocket and give them to Darlene. She gets the keys and takes them downstairs. Darlene, who has taken it upon herself to come in, is standing in their living room.

"What are you doing in my *fucking* house, bitch?!" Nina yells, "Your ass is not welcome in here. So get out, now! You'd better get the fuck *outta* here, bitch!"

Lynn can hear Nina arguing and comes downstairs, quickly.

Lynn says, "Don't you say shit to my sister, alright? If she told you to get your ass outside, then get to stepping or get dealt with!"

She's ready to fight for her sister, if necessary. Ajay hears them and comes downstairs. He quickly calms the situation.

Their parents, who have worked the night shift, are pulling into the driveway.

"You have to go, Dee. Right now," Ajay says calmly.

"Not without you," she says.

"Look, I can't leave home, right now. Not with my folks coming in," he says as he laughs.

All he really wants is sleep. He figures he isn't going to get any, if he leaves with Darlene. And he feels, he want get to sleep at all, if Jo sees her. She's been longing for the chance to run up on this grown bitch, who has been fucking around with her young son. Jo and Al come in their side door.

"I know y'all know better than to have anybody up in my house, that I don't know, when I'm not here. Don't you?" Jo asks as she walks in to check things out.

"Hi. I'm Darlene Casey," Darlene says, extending her hand to Jo.

"So you're that grown ass woman who's been messing around with my son?" Jo asks as she removes her earrings and goes for her purse. "Is that who you are?"

"Y'all go on to your rooms," big Al says, "This is not something y'all need to be down here for."

Nina, Lynn and Ajay walk up the stairs. But they remain at a point where they can observe their mother's actions. Al grabs Jo and won't allow her to get to her purse. Darlene tries to reason with her but Jo manages to break away from Al. She starts toward Darlene. She swings but misses, only because Al is pulling her backwards. Darlene swings back and misses too. That's when Nina, Lynn and Ajay clear the stairs. They saw her swing on their mother. When Darlene sees them coming, she runs out the door and tries to make it to her car, which is still on Chill's driveway.

Before she can get across the street and get it unlocked, Ajay grabs her, around her throat. Nina and Lynn begin punching at her, connecting on a few. Jo has made it to them and she's punching Darlene, along with her daughters. Pearl sees the fight and runs across the street. She tries to stop Jo and her children, along with Al. Tank had gotten up to go to the bathroom, saw them through the window and ran out there as well. Still, it took the help of another neighbor, for them to get Jo to calm down. They calm Lynn and Nina down too. Ajay never *seems* upset and he doesn't now either. But he has something to say to Darlene before he can leave.

"If you ever swing at my mama again. Bitch, I'll *kill* you. Do you understand me?" he says calmly.

After that statement, he gets his family and they all go back home and go inside. Ajay heads up to his room. Soon after, he lays down and gets some, much needed sleep.

****

It's Monday afternoon. Ebony receives the large *Express* envelope from Cleveland. She's so excited when she see that it's from Ajay. Though

it's in Nina's handwriting, she knows it's from him, because she can smell him all over it. She opens it carefully and begins to read.

The first 3 pages, explain and talk about the time before he went to Juvenile detention. She knows he's trying to make up for all of the letters he hadn't written. He talks about training school and how it was. He talks in detail about the visits they had. And how much he really wanted to touch her but he didn't want to get all excited like that, knowing he couldn't make love to her. She smiles. When he talks about making love to her, he's very graphic. She recognizes when Nina's had enough too. That's where she starts to write her portion of the letter. Ebony smiles. Tank adds a few pages, before Ajay starts talking again. It's amazing to her, how she can tell who's speaking. Even though, all of the writing is Nina's. Before the long letter ends, Ajay promises her, he won't have sex with Darlene. She smiles again. They conclude, in the last 6 pages, by telling her what the whole crew are up too. All of the families and the youngest kids too. Then Nina adds at the end;

"Ajay's yours, no matter who or what! Love, peace n C-town peeps, always!"

Ebony gets her smile back. She's determined to keep smiling until she sees her man and her family again.

"I need to listen to some love music," she says to herself.

Poppa and big mama had gotten her a stereo for her 14th birthday, while she was here, at Christmas. She pulls out the sample *mixtape* which Renee and the girls had sent to her. It has many great songs on it. Ebony loves *Mariah Carey* and she already has her tape. But on the mixtape, Renee had added some *Prince* songs. She remembers the song Ajay talked about on their last night together, at papa and granny's house. She winds it up until she finds: "*With You*." She has to hear it and see what Ajay found so special about it. She play it and likes it, immediately. She smiles the entire time it plays. Then she plays: "*Still Waiting*", another song by *Prince*.

"This is so sexy," she says to herself and smiles, "My girls hooked me *up*."

She plays a song by *Whitney Houston* titled; "*Good Love*." She loves it too.

"This tape is gonna get me through this stay," she says and smiles again.

She plays the entire tape. From *Mary J. Blige* and *Jodeci*. To *Keith Sweat* and *Guy*.

"This is love music. *Do Me Baby* by *Prince* is a song I wanna make love too," she says and smiles as she lets the tape relax her to sleep.

CHAPTER 9

CREW TO THE RESCUE

It's well into the 3rd week of August and Ebony's 9th grade school year has begun. Since she's in Houston, for 9th grade, head coach Renee Hightower is still determined to get her on the high school team. Big mama and poppa agree to let her play varsity and she, reluctantly moves up. She wants to stay on the 9th grade team with April and Yolanda. That isn't going to happen. But Coach Hightower makes a spot for April and Yolanda, to make Ebony more comfortable. She's happy with that move. She doesn't realize it yet. But this move to the high school team will turn out to be the best move of her athletic career. Playing for the varsity team, in 9th grade, will expose her to college coaches for 4 years. Instead of 3, like most players. With the exception of Ajay, who has played high school varsity since 7th grade.

"Ebony, by the time you graduate from high school, you'll be able to attend any university you choose," coach Hightower or Coach H, as they call her, says while poppa and big mama smile proudly.

"This might be okay, then," Ebony says with a smile, "Especially since I got my friends here. Okay, I'll do it."

Ebony had written to her girls and told them the news, as soon as he got to her first class of 9th grade. Her parents had already given poppa and big mama their permission. John stuck his chest out and bragged for 2 days straight. Nina shared her letter with their entire crew. They are so proud of Ebony for this advancement. They know her basketball skills had to have improved greatly, just as Ajay's had. They send her a letter and every member of her crew adds a page. On the final page of the letter, as they all sign off and they say, *"Do your thing and represent, C-town style."*

Ajay brags on her too. He has started to call her, *"Misses Anthony Jackson. The female version of me."*

After seeing that on his pages of the letter, she knows she has to stay on top of her game now. Of course, she does and she loves her new name too.

TIME TO LEARN-RELOADED-Time Will Reveal-part 1

For the next several weeks, she works out hard with the varsity team. By the 3rd week of October, she has hustled her way into the starting lineup. She has settled into her role, as the starting small forward, very well. Then 1 day, she stays after practice to work on her shots. Satisfied that she has gotten her 100 extra shots in, she heads toward the dressing room. That's when she runs into, *Raymond White*!

He's a senior now and an All-American shooting guard. The way the press tells it, he's being highly sought after by many major colleges. They portray him as a stand-up kid. Ebony only sees him as a 2 bit hustler, wanna-be pimp type, fake ass punk. After all the foul things she's heard about him since she moved up to the high school varsity team, that's all he can ever be, to her. Raymond is use to getting what he wants from the local girls. He walks around school with a different girl on his arm, daily. He can have any girl he wants at Smiley High. But he can't have, Ebony Brown. She has never given him the time of day. She has a real star athlete in her life. One who's 10 times better than *sweet Ray* and not just on the court. Ajay is better than Raymond, on his worst day. Her man has swagger and sex appeal with a wicked cross over and a *wet* jump shot. Raymond makes her gag. He can't even hold Ajay's jock strap. She's heard he doesn't have enough jewels to fill it, either. Ajay is a leader, who fears no man. He's her man because he has the right pedigree, style and gangster, which gets her attention and keeps it. Raymond had left her alone during the previous school year because Tank had built up quite a reputation for handling his business, while he was in Houston. And being the true punk that Raymond is, he was afraid to try Tank. But now that Tank is no longer around, Raymond sees Ebony as easy prey. He isn't going to be denied, this school year.

When she tries to go around him, to get into the girl's locker room, he blocks the doorway.

"What's up, Ebony? That's your name, right?" he asks, pretending not to remember.

"No way. Nothing is up. Excuse me, please," she says while trying to push past him.

"Hold on. I wanna talk to you," he says and grabs her arm.

"Don't you touch me!" she says loudly, "I have to go to class. I don't have a minute, for you."

TIME TO LEARN-RELOADED-Time Will Reveal-part 1

She steps away from him and tries to pull her arm free. He tightens his grip. "Let go of my arm now!" she shouts while snatching her arm away.

"Oh shit! You're a lil feisty one, ha?" Raymond says slyly.

"Would you please move out of my way?" she asks again.

She doesn't want to risk brushing up against him, by going around. She looks around to see if anyone else is there. No one is around.

"Who are you looking for? Tank?" Raymond asks in a pesky fashion. "He's not here now, baby. He asked me not to mess with you, last year. I guess he didn't wanna see you *wit* a real man. But now that he's not around, we can be free to do our own thing."

"We don't have a thing. We're not ever gonna have a thing. Now if you don't mind, I'd-"

"Don't be like that. Come on now. I'm gonna look out for you, around here. You know it's a lot of crazy cats around," Raymond says.

"Yes, I see that!" she says looking at him for the first time, ever.

"Hey, I'm not one of them fools, baby. I'm the real thing. I'm that nigga to get wit, at this muthafucka," he says, sounding more conceited.

"I don't care."

"Are you sure you don't?" he asks growing frustrated but becomes embarrassed by her rejection.

"No, I don't and if you're all that. Then there must be somebody, *somewhere*, that you can be talking too. Somebody that's interested in you. Because I'm not the one. I have a man."

"Oh yea. That *nigga* Ajay, from Cleveland? I heard you was fucking him at the motel, when your peeps came down here, last year. That nigga tried to front on me, about you. I had you all wrong, at first. I thought you was a lil nice girl and shit. Until I heard you was fucking him. Then I said, if you was giving it up like that. Then *sweet Ray* gonna have to come at you, all together different."

He tries to walk up closer to her.

"I asked you, one time, not to touch me!" she yells.

She still looks around for anyone to come to her assistance. Suddenly, Ray grabs both of her shoulders and tries to kiss her. She struggles until she gets free. Finally, coach H comes around the corner to go to her office.

"Ebony, I didn't know you were still in here. You'd better get to class, honey. Before you're late," coach H says.

"I'm trying too. But-"

"-I was just introducing myself to her, coach H. And we started talking. And well, you know how it is? We didn't realize what time it was," Raymond lies.

Ebony can see he's use to telling a lie, on point. Just by how easily that one fell out of his mouth.

"Raymond, you're not even suppose to be in the gym, at this hour," coach H says, "And you'd better not charm my new star, either."

"He won't," Ebony interjects quickly, in a matter-of-fact tone.

"No, it's not anything like that, coach. We was just talking, that's all," he says as he looks at Ebony.

"Well Ebony, you go on and get changed and come to my office. I'll give you a pass, so you can get into your next class," coach H says.

"Yes ma'am. But if I take to long to come in there, will you come and get me?" she asks, just in case Raymond tries to come into the locker room after coach is in her office.

"Sure, Ebony. But try not to be too long. Okay?"

"Yes ma'am."

Ebony pushes past Raymond and goes into the locker room. Coach H gives Ray a pass and sends him on his way. Ebony is relieved.

Later in coach's office, Ebony tries to tell her about Raymond's actions. But coach Hightower seems to think it's all innocent. She tells Ebony that Raymond is harmless. Ebony explains that she doesn't want him to ever talk to her. Coach doesn't grasp the urgency of her request. She writes Ebony a hall pass, then walks with her to the 9th grade building. She walks her all the way to class and makes sure she gets in, without incident.

For the rest of the day, Ebony can only think about the incident in the gym. She sensed it in Raymond's demeanor. He's going to take it too far.

She writes Tank a letter during her 6th hour class. She tells him about everything that happened in the gym. She tells Tank, she's afraid Raymond will try to bother her again. Just like he had done in the gym. She wants him to move back to Houston.

When she gets home, she tells big mama and poppa about it. She isn't going to take Raymond's annoyances lightly, which is very wise of her. Because the news which comes out on Raymond, later, will prove as much.

The next morning, when Poppa takes Ebony to school, he goes in and talks to coach H and the principal about Raymond. He ask them to be sure he doesn't bother Ebony again. They give poppa their word, that they'll keep an eye on her.

"Keep a closer eye on him," poppa Percy advises, "I *mean* it."
The faculty and staff agree to watch out for Ebony's safety. Still, poppa stays around campus, all day. When Ebony practices after school, poppa is there in the gym.

After practice, he tells her about his meeting with the coach and principal. She feels better knowing that everyone is aware of Raymond and they will be paying closer attention to her from now on. She smiles to herself as poppa lets her drive home.

****

On the evening of the 29th, Pearl calls Houston and talks with her parents about the Raymond situation. Tank received the letter from Ebony, this afternoon. He told their mother what Raymond had done in the gym. Poppa tells Pearl, he feels that everything is under control now. But Pearl still worries.

"John is scheduled to be in Houston again, this weekend," she says, "I told him about this letter that Tank got, just a little while ago. He's planning to speak with this boy, when he gets there."

"Oh Pearl, honey. That could be bad news," poppa says and laughs, "You know John has got that temper on him, just as bad as mine."

"Yes daddy, I know," she says, "But this boy has got to back off. Baby girl is afraid of him and probably for good reason."

"Well so far, he hasn't bothered her anymore," poppa says, "I think he got the message."

"Well if not," Pearl says, "He will this weekend."
Pearl informs her father that her and Brenda's families are coming down for Thanksgiving. She wants it to be a surprise for Ebony. Poppa vows to keep it a secret. She ask to speak to Ebony, who takes the phone, at poppa's insistence.

Ebony is reluctant about telling her mother the Raymond story. She feels if her mother hadn't insisted she move back to Houston, she

wouldn't be here, going through this ordeal. She tells Pearl, in her own words, what happened. And that since then, Raymond's coach had gotten involved too. Pearl is pleased to know that everyone is looking out on her baby girl. Ebony gives the phone to big mama without saying goodbye.

Big mama is doing better, each time they talk. But Pearl and Brenda are still making the trip, so they can see, firsthand. Tank comes in as Pearl is hanging up the phone. He ask how Ebony is today and if Raymond is still bothering her. After he gets the latest details, he heads over to Chill's house to tell him and Renee the latest news.

"Man, look here," Chill says, "We need to handle this bitch ass muafucka, before he really tries some serious shit. I just have a bad vibe about this whole thing."

"True that," Tank says, "You know we're going down there for Thanksgiving."

"I'm gonna make that trip again too," Chill says, "Those players down there was talking upon some real business. So hey, we can kill two birds with one stone."

"Hell yea, man. I definitely wanna put that fool in check, though," Tank says, "For fucking with twin, like he is. And after I told his bitch ass not to mess wit her!"

Ajay comes in just as Tank is making that last statement.

"What's up like that, homie?" Ajay asks.

Tank, Chill and Renee tell him the details. Without a comment, he gets up, grabs the cordless phone, hands it to Renee and says, "Call baby girl."

Renee calls immediately.

"Hello," Ebony says.

"Hey, lil sister. What's up?" Renee asks.

"Hey Renee! How are you doing, girl?!?" Ebony asks, very pleased to hear her voice.

"I'm holding. But I hear it's some foul shit going on, down there. What's up with that nigga-"

Before she can finish, Ajay takes the phone. In one breath, he asks,

"Hey baby, what's going on, down there?"

"Raymond tried to stop me from going to get dressed after practice the other day," she answers, also in one breath.

"Tell me what happened," Ajay presses.

She tells him the entire story, including the fear she has now, in her own words.

"I'll come get you, if you want me too," he says suddenly, "All you gotta do is say the words and I'm coming."

"I want you too. I wanna come home," she says as she starts to cry.

He gives the phone back to Renee and walks out the door. Chill and Tank run behind him. Renee finishes her conversation with Ebony while Chill and Tank catch up to Ajay.

"Hold on, man," Chill says to Ajay, "I know how you're feeling and shit. We're gonna get together, on something, for his ass."

"How do you know, man?" Ajay snaps, "Your lady's inside!"

"Ajay, chill out, bro," Chill says, "We're gonna handle this."

Chill makes a few calls on his cell phone.

Within 20 minutes, all of the guys from the crew are there. Ajay is quiet, as Tank tells the others about what's been going on.

"What the fuck is on that punk ass niggaz mind, yo?!" Jb yells.

This is the 1st time he's hearing of Raymond, even bothering Ebony. Tank tells him it started before Labor day, last year. The 1st day he saw her and the same day the crew had come to visit. He tells him he had straightened him and he didn't bother her anymore. At least, not while he was still down there.

"Oh, so now that she's there alone," Jb says, "Now all of a sudden, this bitch ass *nigga* got balls?"

He's furious but appears calm, like big John would.

"When the fuck are we leaving?!" Ajay interrupts, "I can't handle this feeling helpless shit."

"Look here, man," Chill says to Ajay, "We're gonna handle it *and him*. Believe that. But Ajay, you have to stay here man and you know this."

"Fuck that shit. I'm there," he oozes in his usual calm.

"No he's right, Ajay," Jr adds, "You're on paper for six months, dog," Jr says, "Plus you have to call your P O every day, so he don't violate you. You can't miss school either or they're gonna lock your ass back up, Cuz."

"For sho, Ajay," Tank adds, "You remember how you was with me, before I went down there? We're looking out on you, the same way."

"This is not the same thing, man," Ajay tries.

"There's no differences, as far as crew go," Rob says, "The case is different but it's still crew looking out for crew's best interest. We're not about to let you get violated, Ajay."

"If you blow it, this time. Then you've got time coming," Stoney says, "*A lot* of time, at that. The NBA is already looking at you, Ajay. That's too much to lose, crew. We're not having it, man. We got this one."

"Ajay, you know they're right, dog," Rich adds.

"Look here, man. We're going down there for Thanksgiving," June says, "We'll straighten his ass, *then*."

"Y'all know how far away that is?" Ajay asks.

"Three weeks," Rich says.

"Ain't no telling what that *nigga* will do, in three weeks," Ajay tries. He's very animated, as he says, "She's *scared, man*. Y'all didn't hear her voice, on that damn phone. *I did*. I know she fears this muafucka. I'm not fixing to let no *nigga* fuck with her. *Period*."

"Bro, do you think I am?" Chill asks, "Would I allow something to happen to baby girl? You ought to know, by now, man."

Chill stops talking, after seeing the anxiousness in Ajay's demeanor. He knows mere words aren't going to suffice. Some solid action is needed to get Ajay through this day. He tells Tank to call Charles, down in Houston and he does.

Chill speaks with Charles, on the situation. Charles is with his first cousin Ron Banks, at the time. Ron Banks is the boss, Chill had met on the last visit. He's a kingpin and an O.G. of the fifth ward. The neighborhood which Raymond is bussed from, to play basketball at Smiley High. Raymond also sells product for Ron Banks. Ron assures Chill that he'll assign some of his crew to look out on Ebony. Ajay takes the phone and strictly enforces the issue. Ron guarantees Ajay, he will keep an eye on her. They end the conversation.

Then Chill asks, "Now man, do you trust your crew to handle this *nigga*?"

"Whatever," Ajay answers.

"You have to say it," Chill says.

"Look here, y'all better make sure this muafucka feel y'all," Ajay says, "On everything, crew. I'm not *bullshittin*. But when that *nigga* die, I get that honor. Because his bitch ass is fuckin with *my* girl. And if he fuck with her again, in *any* way, I'm leaving *that* day, going to kill his ass.

No discussion," Ajay says calmly as he fires up a blunt and steps away from the crowd.

"You still haven't said it," Jr adds as they step back to Ajay.

"Y'all handle it, players. Handle the shit," Ajay says, "But Chill, I need to be in touch with her, until then. Just so I know she's okay. You know what I'm saying?"

"You can call her from here, everyday. No problem, alright?"

"Cool," Ajay says as he passes Chill the blunt.

"Bro, you're in love, just like the rest of yo crew," Stoney says before he burst out laughing and fires up another blunt.

Ajay glances at him as he rubs his hairless chin. He has no comment. His crew feels it's settled. But they underestimate Ajay, who is as defiant as ever. Especially when it comes to Ebony, her wishes and her safety. As far as he's concerned, he's her protector. Not them or anyone else. He's the 1 who has to take care of Raymond, for her. He's going to Houston for Thanksgiving, just as they are. He just has to get some flight reservations together and check with Wheeler. But 1 way or the other, he's going to be there with Ebony.

Ajay takes the cordless phone into the kitchen. The crew figure he's calling Ebony back. But he calls Nicole and Angie. He tells them what he needs. They're stash girls, in love with his dick and he knows he can get his airfare out of them. And he most certainly does. Nicole and Angie buy the airline ticket, before he hangs up the phone. Plus they volunteer to take him to the airport, with spending cash. They'll pick him up when he returns too, if necessary. They're instructed not to tell anyone else about the trip. They swear not to talk to the crew or anyone else.

Next, he calls Wheeler and promises him season tickets to whichever NBA team he gets drafted too. With that, he gets his leave request approved and it's settled. Chill, Renee and Kenny are flying to Houston for Thanksgiving break. Little do they know, Ajay will be on a later flight to Houston, the same day.

Pearl and Brenda's families are driving down on Sunday, the 24th. They'll return to Cleveland, Sunday the 3rd day of December.

****

TIME TO LEARN-RELOADED-Time Will Reveal-part 1

Tuesday, November 19th, is Ebony's first high school game. Poppa and big mama are there to cheer her on. April and Yolanda invited the freshman team, as well. Ebony plays a good game. She scores 14 points, pulls down 7 boards and gets 2 block shots. After the game, everyone congratulates her, Except Shuntay. She's the junior, who's spot Ebony had taken in the starting lineup. She's envious of Ebony's success. Plus she dates Raymond, when he has time for her. She knows Raymond wants Ebony but can't get her. She wanted to get with Ajay when he was in Houston. But couldn't get his attention, either. Of course, Ebony had that too. Shuntay ended up having sex with June, during that Labor Day weekend.

"Congratulations Ebony," Shuntay finally says, "Good game."

"Thank you, Tay," Ebony answers, although she knows its fake. *You're fake as hell. I don't want you to like me because I don't like you.*

After the game, poppa allows Ebony to call Cleveland. She calls Chill's house to tell everyone the news about her game. No one is there. Everyone is still at MLK's opening game.

Jb is 17 years old now. He's into his senior basketball season. Lynn is 17, as well. She's a senior also. Ajay and Jan are both 16 years old and high school juniors. Bre is sixteen and a point guard for MLK high school. Her, Tank, Rich and June are sophomores. The guys are still 15 years old. Nina, Rebbie and T-baby are all freshman and 14, like Ebony. But Ebony and Nina will turn 15 years old, next month.

The 4th generation of the crew will have Bruce, who is Jr and Bre's younger brother, at the head. Bruce is 12 now and in 7th grade. He's a star on Abe Lincoln middle school's football team. He'll turn 13 on New Year's Day. Jan's sister Kim is an 11 year old 6th grader, who's sweet on Bruce. Rebbie's brother Shannon is in 5th grade. He had turned 10 on September 24th. Ebony's baby brother Jesse, whom everyone calls lil man, is 9 years old. He no longer wants to be called little man. Erica, Brittany, Sam Jr and Greg Jr are all 9 years old too. They're all in 4th grade. Lil man or Jesse and Sam Jr will be 10 on January 7th and February 14th, respectively. Pam and Ruthie are 8 year old, 3rd graders. Ruthie is Rich Jr's little sister and they all call her, Roo. She'll be 9 on the 8th of next month. Steven and Ally already like each other and they are 7 year old, 2nd graders. Lil Kenny is 6 and in the 1st grade. Archie Jr will start kindergarten in the fall. He turned 5, on October 4th. The twins, Brandon and Brina James just had their 4th birthday, on November 4th. They all make up the 4th generation of this stellar crew. This is the crew which will follow Chill and his crew's lead.

Jr and Tonya are 19 year old sophomores at Cleveland State. This semester, Jr is pledging *Omega Psi Phi* and Tonya is pledging *Delta Sigma Theta*. Rob and Stoney are 20 and 21, respectively. Both are partners with big Chill and Renee, who are now 21 years old. Renee had turned 21, on the 21st of November. The over 20 year old crew members, work together daily. They're getting the crew's club ready for opening. It's located in the strip mall property, near the detail shop. Chill had run the detail shop as a front, with his father Paul, before Paul's death. Chill's grandfather, who's name was Paul Sr, had acquired the property through a business deal or debt repayment. How it was actually obtained, isn't clear at the moment. But the crew are ready to put it to use, now that some of them are over 21 years of age. They appropriately name the club, *The Chill Spot*, an idea which had come from Renee, nearly a decade ago. They plan to open it up in late spring. About the same time colleges take their spring breaks. Most of the crew won't be old enough to go to the club. But still, they go and work with Chill, every afternoon or whenever they can. They're getting it ready for the opening. It's an investment for the entire family.

Renee got her associate's degree in business management, 2 years ago. Now she's enrolled at CSU, with Jr and Tonya, seeking her 4 year degree. They plan to open many more businesses and lock this city up, so tight, the maps will read: *CrewLand!* That's an ongoing joke amongst the crew. As for now, they're paying dues and acquiring the knowledge which will be useful to them, 1 day soon. For this crew of 18, every situation they face has a lesson to learn. And the lessons just keep on coming.

Ebony gives up trying to reach the crew at Chill's house. She decides to call her mother's home. She talks to Jesse and Kenny. Kenny is spending the night and getting off to school with Jesse, in the morning. Pearl had told Renee to let him sleep over, rather than waking him up when they come in from partying or working. Or whatever they're calling it, this week. Ebony talks to the boys, for an hour. She hangs up before her mother can take the phone. She's still not ready to talk. Unless Pearl will agree to

let her come home, immediately. She only wants to talk to Ajay, right now, anyway. She figures out why the crew aren't at Chill or Stoney's houses. Renee had told her they would be christening the club, after the MLK game tonight. It's getting late, so Ebony turns in for bed. She knows Ajay will call her tomorrow.

Meanwhile in Cleveland, Jb, Ajay and Tank have won their season opener and it's time to celebrate. The crew Christian, *The Chill Spot* in honor of MLK winning it's opening games. This party is for crew only. But a select few are allowed to join them, like Kilo, Wayne and Arthur, who is already crew. Actually, Ebony is the only crew member who's not present.

Bre is on the girl's varsity team and they won tonight, just as Jb, Ajay and the MLK boys team did. She's very popular for her basketball abilities. Now that she's on varsity, more attention is coming her way. All of the guys in their hood and neighboring sets, respect Bre, Jan, Renee, Lynn and Tonya for being strong, *ride or die females*, who hold down the crew. That's the way they carry themselves. But tonight, for some reason, Stoney finds the extra attention Bre is getting, hard to handle. He seems to have a problem with every guy, outside of the crew, who congratulates her on her game. After more than 30 minutes of it, Bre can't take it anymore. She steps to Stoney and confronts him about his attitude.

"What's wrong with you?" Bre asks.

"There's nothing wrong with me," Stoney says, "I'm just not okay with you hugging all up on these different *niggaz* and shit."

"Oh man, please. These are my homies from the high school," Bre says, "Why are you tripping on that?"

She's surprised he's got attitude about something so trivial. This isn't even like Stoney. He usually brings attention to her.

"You need to make up your mind," he says suddenly, "Either you're gonna kick it with me or them *niggaz.* Because I'm not having this shit here. Not at all."

Some of the crew notice the intense conversation they're having, over in the corner. Jr and Rob, along with Tonya and Jan, decide to go over and check things out.

By the time they make it over to them, Bre is very upset.

"Hold on, home girl. What's going on?" Jan asks.

TIME TO LEARN-RELOADED-Time Will Reveal-part 1

"He's trying to run me. Telling me what I'm gonna do and what I'm not gonna do," Bre says.

Stoney is trying to tell his side of the story to Rob and Jr, at the same time. Chill notices the situation and comes over. Right then, is when Bre turns to Stoney and says,

"You gave me a choice, right? Well here it is. I don't need this kind of shit in my life! I am my *own* woman, Stoney!"

"Well, do what you gotta do, then. If that's how you feel!" he yells, which is also unlike him too.

"Cool. I will!" Bre says and she walks away.

The rest of the crew decide to let it work itself out, as they continue with the party. Bre and Stoney never make up.

The next day at school, all of the crew are hung over from last night's party. Most of them sleep through their morning classes. By the end of the school day, they are just ready to go home and go to sleep.

That afternoon when Ajay gets home, Jo and Al are waiting for him. Apparently, while doing laundry, Jo found drugs in his pocket. Her and Al are very upset that he'd brought crack into their home. His mother gets all over him about it. Ajay, being the stubborn young man that he is, doesn't want to deal with her yelling at him. He tells her he's going to his room. But Jo becomes more heated because he refuses to stand there and listen. Without a second thought, she tells him to get out of her house.

"If this is the way you want to live, ruining your life and all. Then get the hell out of my house, Ant!" she screams.

"Fine, then. I don't care about you kicking me out. I don't *have* to stay here. I got somewhere to stay!" he shouts back.

He goes to his room to grab a few things. Al tries to calm him and Jo down but they're both too stubborn to give in. That's 1 trait, Ajay gets directly from his mother.

After he gathers some clothes in a bag, he storms out of the house and goes over to Chill's house to use the phone. Chill, not knowing what has just transpired, thinks he's calling Ebony, like he's done every evening since the incident with Raymond. Instead, he calls his trusty doormat Darlene, at her job. He tells her to come by and pick him up when she gets off. She's more than willing too. She has been trying to convince him to move in with her since he was in training school. He didn't want to move in with her, then. He still doesn't want too. But after the argument he had with his mother, his stubbornness makes this, his only option. He knows it will anger his mother more. And right now, that's all he wants to do.

At Jo's house, things are very chaotic. She's still very upset. Al is upset also but he keeps his cool, as usual. Jo continues to rant and rave while Lynn is trying to console Nina. Nina is crying and begging her mother to give Ajay another chance. Jo won't bend. Not even a little and she says her mind is made up. Lynn and Nina figure they need to try to get Ajay to give in and apologize to their mother, so she'll calm down and he can come back home.

They go next door to tell Jb and Tank what happened. Then the 4 of them go to Chill's house to try and talk Ajay into giving in.

No matter what either of them say, Ajay isn't budging either. Neither Chill or Renee say much. They mostly listen as the others debate the issue. Chill knows Ajay isn't moving because he wants to be with Darlene. They all know that's not his reason. They understand that it's a business move and not a personal one. Still, neither of them want to see it happen.

"There's got to be another way, Ajay," Lynn says desperately.
Chill and Renee offer him the spare room, upstairs. He refuses it, saying, "It's too close. Mama will still get in my business, every chance she gets."

At 5:30pm, Darlene arrives. Ajay gets into the car with her and they drive away, without another word. Nina watches from Chills doorway and cries more. Tank puts his arm around her and tries to convince her Ajay will be right back and everything will be the same. Ajay doesn't come right back.

As a matter of fact, he goes on to Darlene's apartment and unpacks his things. Darlene wants him to do her, right away. He tells her to go relax and wait for him. He picks up her phone and calls Ebony, just as he's done, on days prior.

By Friday, Pearl and Brenda are preparing their families for the Thanksgiving trip to Houston. T-baby and Rebbie are spending the weekend with Nina. Ajay has been gone for 2 days and Jo is very worried.

She feels better after hearing that he hasn't missed school or checking in with his parole officer. Lynn tells her, he had been at school, both Thursday and Friday.

After school, Ajay comes to Chill's house, in Darlene's car, before going back to school for his game tonight. The crew are happy to see him. He calls Ebony, first. Then he tells his crew, he thinks they should meet at The Chill Spot, after the game, to work on it some more. They're planning a Christmas and a birthday party for Ebony, who will be home to visit at Christmas break. The crew still has to get the tables and chairs organized, before Chill and his family fly to Houston, on Wednesday. The same day as Ajay's flight. All that's left to do to finish the club, is painting the inside and arranging the tables and chairs. Then they can stock the 2 bars and handle minor details. Rob will be the main deejay and Stoney will assist him.

On Saturday, they hang out at Chill's house. Nina and Rebbie spend time with Tank and June. They're leaving the next morning. T-baby and Rich are there also. The 6 of them stay up, all night, talking in Jo's living room. It was Rich's idea to hang out at Jo's house. Ajay feels it's because his cousin knew he wouldn't come there. Ajay knows Rich's ways, better than those in their crew, who are in their age group. Ajay leaves it at that and doesn't bring it up to anyone. He knows he'll see Tank and June in Houston. He's going back to Darlene's apartment for the night. But he needs to get with Tank before he leaves.

He gets Tank to meet him at Chill's house. He gives Tank a letter for Ebony which he had written himself. Wheeler has worked out a deal, with his parole officer, for him to make the trip without consequence. Actually, his PO is on the crew's payroll from Paul Jr's days. He isn't trying to loose money. Ajay not only gives Tank the letter. He also gives him some gold earrings and $300 to give to Ebony, as well. Darlene had bought the earrings and gave them to Ajay. She thought the earrings was a peace offering for Jo, from Ajay and herself. *Damn Ajay*!

In his letter to Ebony, Ajay finally tells her about his present living arrangements. He wants to be the 1 to tell her about his move, before anyone else does. He knows T-baby is going to tell Ebony about it because he knows Rich is going to suggest that T-baby do it. Ajay only hopes Ebony will understand why he felt he had to do this and why he didn't tell her on the phone. He plans to assure Ebony of his intentions to be her man, when he sees her face to face, during the Thanksgiving holiday.

Until then, he tolerates Darlene. When all the while, he's longing for Ebony. He just hopes Ebony will understand why he felt he had to move away from his mother's home.

On Sunday morning, the Browns and James leave for Houston. After church, the guys in the crew get together at Chill's to watch *NFL* games. Ajay comes over and calls Ebony, first thing, as he has done every single day. Renee and her girls don't like the move Ajay made. They feel it's giving Darlene a false impression of what her stance is, in Ajay's life.

"We need to put that bitch up on game," Lynn says to Renee, as the other crew females agree.

"Oh, we're about too," Renee says, "Let's do it while Ajay is here with Kenny and the guys."

"Word," Tonya says.

While the guys watch football, Renee gets the females together and they decide to pay Darlene a visit.

They drive out to Maple Heights and to Darlene's apartment. They remind her that Ajay is part of their crew and their crew is forever. Darlene isn't a very gracious hostess. Neither is her niece, Alana, who lives with her now. The girls hadn't expected hospitality. Just for her to adhere to their warning. The crew females make the points and then leave. Darlene locks the door as soon as they leave and beeps Ajay.

By the time the females get back to Chill's house, the guys are all laughing about the conversation Ajay has just had with Darlene. No one is upset with Renee and the girls. The guys knew it would happen, eventually. Ebony *is* their family. The guys are surprised everything had gone, so smoothly. They thought surely the girls would have beat her down for acting snotty but they hadn't. At least, not yet. It won't be long before they'll have too.

****

TIME TO LEARN-RELOADED-Time Will Reveal-part 1

Tuesday morning, when Ebony gets to school, she's very excited. Her family had arrived at 5:00am. Tank, June and Jb had taken her to school and after school, they meet her outside. They guys are hoping for a chance to catch Raymond but he has already left. But Smiley high has their last game before Thanksgiving break, tonight. The guys are going to speak with Raymond White, after tonight's game.

Ebony plays another great game and scores her season high of the first 3 games. She scores 25 points, as her family cheers her on. Jb and Tank are missing their game tonight. But at home, MLK wins by 4 points. Ajay scores a season high 65 points. 1 point off of his career high, which is 66 points.

During the Smiley boys game, Sonya, Tina and Shuntay come over and sit with Ebony and her family. They know Tank and June are in town and they want to be down. Every since Labor day weekend, last year, the 3 girls have been writing to June, Tank and Rich. They got their addresses from big mama's address book, while visiting, one day. The guys never wrote back. The 3 girls tried to get closer with big mama and poppa, just to get more information on the guys. Ebony can see through their ways, although big mama and poppa don't seem too. They would come by the house, 3 times a week, to sit and talk with big mama. Ebony really doesn't like this, because she's picky about whom she shares her big mama with.

Tonight, Sonya, who was with Rich last year, has set her sites on Jb. These 3 girls are nothing but whores. Ebony doesn't like that her family seems to be accepting them. She hasn't accepted them and she never will. She doesn't care that they're her teammates, either. Because in Ebony's opinion, they are enemies, off the court. She is absolutely correct. Only her nor her crew know how much of an enemy they are. Not just yet.

After the game, Charles, who is on varsity now, takes the guys to a party in South Acres. Tank and Charles had kept in touch, as did Chill and Ron. Charles is a sophomore. At the party, they're sure to see Raymond White. He had made a quick exit, after the game. Ron is hosting the party. Ron is 25 years old, a baller and still the kingpin and OG of South Acres. From this set will come a rap trio known as; *The Geto Boys*. They're the hottest thing going, in these parts. *The Geto Boys* will go nationwide with their album, *We Can't Be Stopped*. They're also cool with Ron. At his party, the deejay plays all of their music. Tank, June and Jb like the tape, so much, they're picking 1 up, before they go back home.

As they'd hoped, Raymond White shows up. He's from this set but no one in South Acres really likes him. Ron has always told Raymond, he needs to keep a low profile and stop flaunting his grip. But Raymond is a wannabe, who never listens. Ron knows he'll have to cut him lose, very soon, to avoid heat. When Charles tells Ron about the crews business with Raymond, Ron tells them he'll see to it they talk. He has 5 sisters, himself. He has been in this position, many times, about 1 or more of them. He understands the crew's position. He makes the meeting happen and when the crew talk to Raymond, Ron sits in.

Raymond denies everything but Ron doesn't believe him. He warns him to leave Ebony alone. He also warns him about his ways. He tells him to learn to respect the game, as well as any female who isn't interested in him. Raymond gives his word that he won't bother Ebony again. But inside, he's pissed off that she's told all of these people. The crew aren't convinced. They want to kick his ass. But they decide to be cool, since Ron's involved.

"I'm in this shit now," Ron says, "It won't be any more static, around here, for her. At least, not from this *nigga*. Or he'll have to answer to *my* crew. And they are some *straight* up killers. That's all they do is travel and off stupid ass *niggaz*."

Sonya, Tina and Shuntay show up, looking for Jb, Tank and June. Sonya and Shuntay are suppose to be girlfriends of Raymond's. They are 2 of the girls he can sex, anytime or anyway he wants. Shuntay really has feelings for him but he totally ignores her. Until he wants something. When she found out he liked Ebony, it was just 1 more reason for her to be envious. Though Ebony has never liked Raymond and never will, it won't stop Shuntay's plot. Her plan is to beat Ebony at something. Since 1, Ebony took her starting spot. 2, Ebony has Raymond's unwanted attention and 3, Ebony has Ajay. Shuntay wants all 3. She has wanted to get with Ajay since she first laid eyes on him, last year. These girls tried to get Ebony to come to this party with them. But she refused to go, because she wouldn't ever hang out with girls like these. She'd told them, just that. She stays home and goes to bed early. She wants to be rested for her half day at school. She lays in bed, wondering why Ajay didn't call her today.

TIME TO LEARN-RELOADED-Time Will Reveal-part 1

Chill, Renee and Kenny arrive, the next afternoon at 4:30pm. They have reservations at the motel. Ron is meeting them there to discuss a deal. Ebony keeps Kenny at the house with her. She's still a bit sad because Ajay hasn't called today either. But his flight is in the air. Once he gets to the Airport, he'll call Chill. If all else fails, he'll call poppa.

Tank gives Ebony the money, the gift and the letter, before he leaves to go to the motel with the rest of the crew.

Ebony reads the letter, several times. It leaves her in a devastated state. Immediately, she calls Nina without even asking poppa for permission to call. She has to find out what's going on and why no one has told her about Ajay's living arrangements. Nina answers the phone and fills Ebony in on all of the latest facts. Ebony is still very upset about the news of Ajay living with Darlene. She decides to try a plan of her own. She tells Nina, she wants to make Ajay think she doesn't care about him moving in with Darlene. She wants Nina to tell him, she has decided to start dating. Instead of playing the fool, while he keeps playing the field. Nina tells her she doesn't want to do it.

"Because it isn't gonna work to your advantage," Nina says.

"Fine, then. If you don't tell him, then I will," Ebony says angrily.

"It's not true, Ebony and you shouldn't play it like that," Nina tries, "Just talk to him until he comes to his senses. You know he will. *Eventually*. You're the only one who can talk sense into him."

But Ebony is more determined to go through with her plan. Since Nina doesn't want to help, she hangs up with her. She decides to tell him herself, whenever he calls. But he hasn't called. This makes her even more anxious and angry. She's thinking Darlene is the reason he isn't calling her today, so she goes for broke. She writes him a long letter. Some of the pages are soaked with her tears. She seals it in an envelope and gets poppa to take her to put it in a blue box. She wants it to leave, today.

When she gets back home, she's drained of all of her energy. She takes a bath. Then she goes straight back to her room and puts her *Mariah Carey* tape in her stereo. The stereo was bought for her to keep in her room here in Houston, for when she comes to visit. It has gotten her through, may emotions, during this stay. She cues up Mariah, for this mood. As the song *Vanishing* plays, she cries. She's thinking of how fitting this song is to her and Ajay's situation and their relationship. She drifts off to sleep.

TIME TO LEARN-RELOADED-Time Will Reveal-part 1

******The phone rings.****

Later, poppa wakes her up. Standing directly behind Poppa, it looks like she can see Ajay. She thinks she's dreaming. She rubs her eyes, then looks again. Ajay is still there. She jumps up and before she can think straight, she throws her arms around him.
He hugs her tight and asks, "Are you okay, baby girl?"
She finds it hard to speak. She just cries and holds onto him. He asks her to get up, get dressed and go with him outside on the back deck. She does. She wants to go home and she knows if Ajay knows she's scared, he'll make it happen. Once they're outside and seated, he asks, "Are you alright?"

"No. I wanna come back home," she says, "I know he's gonna try to bother me again. I can tell by the way he looks at me, whenever he sees me. He's mad because he knows all these people are on him because of me."

"I'm here now," Ajay says, "I'm gonna try to handle this shit, one way or the other. I need to let Chill know I'm here. I know he's gonna be mad that I came."

"Anthony, you're on parole. How did you get to come?"

"I talked to Wheeler and my P O. They gave me clearance to come. But I still have to call everyday, just like I would if I was in Cleveland."

"How long will you be able to stay?"

"They told me I have until Monday," he says, "But Chill ain't gonna go back and leave me here. I know that, already."

"Maybe if I tell him I want you to stay, as long as you can, he'll say it's okay," she tries.

"He's not gonna leave me in Houston. Not with this shit going on with Raymond. He knows I'll finish him, if I see him. And I'm here, so I'll make *sure* I see him," he says in a matter-of-fact tone.

"Chill and Renee are at the same motel we stayed at for Labor Day. Do you wanna call them or just go down there?" she asks.

"How are we gonna, *just go* down there?" he asks with a smile.

"I have my permit and you have a license. Poppa let's me drive. He might let me drive us over there," she says with a smile.

"Nah, that's alright," he says while smiling and looking doubtful, "I'd rather call Chill and have him go off on me, all the way over there."
They both laugh.

While still laughing, she says, "I can drive."

"Yea. Drive somebody crazy," he says as they continue laughing. He call Chill's cell phone.

"Hello," Chill says.

"What's up, bro?" Ajay asks.

"Chilling, bro. Kicked back with this air blowing up my ass," Chill says and laughs, "Waiting on family to come through. What up with you? You holding it down, up there? Or you done tore up something?"

"Nah bro and I'm not in Cleveland," he confesses, "I'm at big mama's house."

"What the hell are you doing?"

"Taking care of my girl," Ajay says, "That's my job and what I was raised to do."

Chill tells Ajay to stay put. He's on his way to pick him up. Ajay talks to big mama, poppa and Brian Sr, while he waits for Chill to come. Pearl isn't there, at the moment. She has gone out with Brenda, getting last minute Thanksgiving preparations, along with John Sr.

Ajay and Ebony leave with Chill to go meet Ron at the motel. Renee gets Ajay a room, only after her and Chill are convinced he's cleared to be out of Cleveland.

"You're gonna stay in our sights, Ajay," Renee says, "We're not leaving you here until Monday, either. You're leaving with us, on Friday."

"Renee?!?" Ebony exclaims.

"Baby girl, she's right," Chill says, "I'm not leaving Ajay here."

"Why don't y'all stay until Monday?" Ebony tries.

"We'll see," Chill says.

At that moment, Ron and his wife Carolyn show up, with their crew. Charles, April, David and Yolanda are included. Them plus the traveling killers, come to hang out with the Cleveland crew. Ron and Chill discuss the particulars. They set everything for the day after Thanksgiving.

The next day, Thanksgiving dinner is great. Pearl acts as if she's upset by Ajay being there. But big mama, poppa, John Sr and Brenda keep her in line. She's surprised he has come down to protect Ebony, even though he's on parole. She knows he cares for Ebony but her pride won't allow her to admit it. John does thanks him for coming to check on Ebony.

But he tells him, he isn't going to be okay with Ebony staying at the motel, "Like she did the last time you was here."

"Okay. No problem," Ajay says.

He knows they'll get some alone time. He knows she'll be at the motel with them, at some point and time. They'll have to make the best of whatever time they get.

After dinner, Ajay, Ebony and Brittany take Jesse, Kenny and the twins down the block to the park. Ebony has forgotten about his letter to her. More importantly, her letter to him. She's just happy he's here. In the excitement of him showing up, all of sudden, she hasn't thought of either letter. Not even once. She wants Ajay to beat up Raymond. That's what her mind is on. And he's more then willing to beat his ass or worse.

By dusk, Chill, Renee and the crew meet with Ron and his crew to seal their deal. Everything is set and Chill and Ron are definitely going to make a lot of money together. Ron, Charles and the crew hang out for the rest of the evening, at Ron's house. Ron tells Ajay about the conversation he had with Raymond.

"If he don't get his shit together, he won't be around to fuck with your girl," Ron states as Ajay agrees with him.

Sonya, Tina and Shuntay come by the motel to have sex, if Jb, Tank and June want too. The 6 of them go to Jb's motel room while everyone else stays at Ron's house.

Later, Charles takes Ajay and Ebony to the motel. He'll come back to get them in 3 hours. Ebony and Ajay hang out in his motel room. He takes the time to explain the situation with Darlene. He tells her he's only staying there because he had the argument with his mother. Ebony wants him to move back home. He tells her he doesn't want to talk about Darlene for the rest of his stay. And whether she believes him or not,

"Darlene's not an issue," he says, "I'm here with you. Where I *wanna* be."

She's pissed off that he won't agree to change his living arrangements. And still, she has completely forgotten about the letter she'd sent to Cleveland.

On Friday evening, everyone visiting from Cleveland leaves, except Ajay and Chill. John and Pearl didn't know Ajay wasn't leaving with Renee and lil Kenny. They find out while they're on the road, far from Houston. Now John has to listen to Pearl's displeasure of knowing Ajay is in Houston with Ebony, while neither of them are there to chaperone them.

"Mama, Ajay really does love Ebony," Tank tries.

Pearl yells at him, for the next 20 minutes. Until he gives up trying to convince her. Jb doesn't even bother to give his opinion. He's aware that his mother knows Ajay is serious about Ebony and she can't stop it. He also knows, that's what has her the most bothered.

In Houston, Ebony hangs out with Ajay, Chill and Ron's crew, for the rest of the weekend.

On Saturday, Ron arranges for Ajay to see, Raymond White. Ajay isn't interested in talking to him, at all. Ron and Chill insists he not hit him, unless Raymond disrespects him. Raymond is visibly nervous about being near Ajay. Especially with Ebony there too. Ajay tells him how things are going to be. Raymond, being the punk that he is, doesn't get tough. Nor does he talk shit about Ajay, like he'd done with Ebony in the gym. Ajay hits him, anyway. Knocking him to the floor. Chill grabs Ajay, takes him into another room and away from Raymond. Ron warns Ray, if he doesn't get right with him, he'll allow Ajay to finish him. Raymond has most of Ron's money, so Ron lets him make it until Sunday.

"Tomorrow night, you need to have the rest of my money," Ron warns as his killers make vicious faces at Raymond.

Raymond says he'll have the money, so Ron allows him to leave.

Ebony stays at the motel with Ajay, tonight. She still doesn't think about the letter she'd written.

Poppa takes Ajay and Chill to catch their flight on Sunday evening. Ebony is sad about them leaving but she's excited to know she's going to Cleveland, in less than a month, for Christmas.

Shuntay, Sonya and Tina have come by big mama and poppa's house, everyday after school, since Thanksgiving. Ebony is looking forward to the Christmas break, so she can get away from them. But now, as if dealing with them in Houston isn't enough. They're planning to go to Cleveland to visit, along with Ebony and her grandparents. Tina's family wasn't able to get her a plane ticket but Sonya and Shuntay have already gotten theirs.

On the day they get their tickets, they come by to tell big mama,

poppa and Ebony. Ironically, it's the same day Ebony remembers the letter she'd sent to Ajay.
Oh my God! I've gotta call him!

She calls mama Jo's house and Nina answers. She says she hasn't seen or heard anything about the letter. Ebony is even more nervous because she feels Ajay has gotten it and he's angry. Thus, he hasn't discussed it and he isn't going to talk about it. He's going to save his wrath for her, face to face.

"Girl, he probably got that letter," Nina says, "Why didn't you tell me you sent it? I could've got it, before he saw it."

"I totally forgot about it, after he showed up here," she tries, "Nina, you have to tell him why I wrote it."

"I will. Whenever he brings it up to me," she says, "He's gonna say I knew about this, the whole time."
Ebony's mind starts thinking overtime. She's trying to figure out what Ajay is thinking, right now. She figures he's mad. She knows she'll have to make him believe her. She feels like he won't even call her now. He doesn't want to discuss it on the phone. He's waiting until she gets to Cleveland.

She hangs up with Nina and gets her pen and pad out. From today forward, she writes him letters trying to explain why she had sent the 1st one. Days go by, still he doesn't call nor does he write. She really feel he's upset because he thinks she's dating someone in Houston. Only because that's what she'd said in the 1st letter.

****

It's the 3rd week of December. Nina is looking forward to her birthday and Ebony's arrival, same as T-baby and Rebbie. On the 20th, after their half day of school, T-baby and Rebbie come to Nina's house to wait for Ebony's flight to land.

In Houston, Ebony has her bags. She brings her *Mariah* tape and plays it in her walkman, in flight, to avoid any real conversation with Sonya and Shuntay. *Vanishing* still brings tears to her eyes as she thinks about Ajay and how upset he must be with her.

In the evening, when they arrive, everyone is at Pearl's house.

All except Ajay. Granny and papa are going to host big mama and poppa while they're here. Grandparents Logan and Wilson are here and everyone is having a great time. Ebony and her girls want to get rid of Sonya and Shuntay. They ask Bre and Jan if they'll let the Houston duo kick it with them. The girls don't mind and say they want to keep an eye on them, anyway.

After ditching the duo, the foursome go to Nina's room to talk and catch up on old times. Nina has already filled T-baby and Rebbie in, about Ebony's letter. The 3 of them are trying to help Ebony figure out what to do. They all know Ajay's temper. They're afraid of what he might do, if he thinks she's messing around. Ebony's heart had been in pain when she heard about him living with Darlene. She thought she had lost him. She foolishly thought, by making him suspect she would cheat, she could win him back. What she didn't realize is, she had never lost him. He told her that, in his letter, before she ever wrote her 1st one. She chose not to believe him. The foursome decide to try and talk to him, all together. If he has attitude with Ebony, then they're not going to allow her to leave their sight.

Later, when they go back to Chill's house, they notice Sonya and Shuntay have settled in but they still stick out like a sore thumb. Though the crew try to make them feel comfortable, they just don't fit in. As if anyone like them could. About that time, Ajay, who hears of Ebony's arrival, comes blowing through the door. Though she's very nervous, Ebony tries to act unaffected by his entrance. He notices her reluctance to come to him, so he approaches her. She speaks first.

"What's up, baby?" she asks.

"I don't know. Maybe you can tell me," he replies.

"Not a whole lot but I'm happy to be home," she says while smiling.

"Oh, are you?"

"Yes," she says as she smiles, the effect he has on her, in person. "Are you glad to see me?" she asks, expecting him to go into a rage.

"Hell yea, I'm glad to see you. I hear your b-ball season is going good too," he says, "Pops saw you in a national poll and showed it to me."

"The female version of you," she says with a smile.

"No doubt."

"It's going pretty good, I guess," she says, "But I know I'm gonna have to improve a lot more to beat you. That's been my goal since you first taught me how to play."

They laugh for a whole minute. Then he has to know about that trouble.

"What about that other situation?" he asks, speaking of Raymond.

"It's been cool, lately."

"Ebony, I don't get a *hug*, baby?" he asks, stepping closer to her.

Shuntay is watching from across the room. Ebony's girls are watching her and Sonya, closely too.

"I guess you can have one," she says as she bites her lip.

"You'd better come here, sexy," he says as he hugs her and squeezes her tight, lifting her feet up off the floor.

"Can we talk in private?" she asks, after he puts her feet down.

"Uh huh," he answers, looking at her with that familiar glare that always makes her weak.

He doesn't seem upset at all. Maybe he knows she was lying in the letter, just to get his attention.

"Come go for a ride with me," he says.

She agrees and as they walk out the door, the crew taunt and tease them. Her girls asks her if she wants them to go along.

Ajay says, "No."

When they're out the door, Shuntay whispers to Sonya,

"I'm gonna get with that before we leave here. *Watch* me."

Nina, T-baby and Rebbie go to Jan, Bre, Lynn, Renee and Tonya. They fill them in on all of the dirt, on the Houston duo. Even the fact that they had slept with 4 of the guys from the crew. Tank, Jb, June and Rich. Lynn is ready to burst their asses, right away.

But Renee reminds her, saying, "It's a time and a place for everything."

Lynn decides to stay cool and let the game come to her. She knows it will have too, very soon.

Ebony and Ajay ride around in Darlene's car. That's when she begins to question him about his living arrangements.

"So Anthony, are you still living with Darlene?"

"Yea, for now."

"Do you know how much that hurts me? For the man I love, to be living with another woman?"

"It's not that crucial, Ebony. It's just a place to sleep. Really." He's restating what he had written in his letter.

"I know you told me that, before. But do you have sex with her?"

"Sometimes I do. But only if I have too," he says, before changing the subject. He says, "Ebony, look here. I don't wanna talk about Darlene or anybody else, *tonight*. All I wanna do is talk about you. That's it. Can you understand that?"

"Yes, I understand. I understand you just wanna pretend it's not happening! I can't just put it out of my mind, Anthony! You *hurt* me!" she screams as the tears roll down her face.

She lets them roll, freely. He doesn't say anything as he pulls into a shopping center parking lot and parks. He tries to wipe the tears from her face. She turns away.

"Wait a minute, Ebony. Baby, you know she don't mean shit to me. I told you that, a long time ago."

"What do I mean then, ha? Do I mean anything to you?"

"Yes. You mean everything to me."

"I've been here for you, all of this time and all you do is-"

She can't finish her statement before the tears come heavier.

"You mean everything to me, Ebony. You have to know that. Don't even trip."

"I can't help it, Anthony. This hurts me! This hurts, so bad!" she screams as she burst into tears.

"Come here, baby," he says as he tries to comfort her.

"No! Don't do this! I don't wanna cry, all the time, Anthony! Every time I give my heart to you, you just break it! I mean, it seems so easy for you to hurt me. *Why?!* I could never hurt you!"

"I didn't wanna hurt you. I hope you know that. I was put in a situation where I had to get out of my mama's house. You know what I do. They're not gonna have that, in their house."

"Yea, I know. Anthony, it's time for me. If I don't get it together now, I'm gonna end up loosing my mind. I wrote it all down in a letter. I was trying to explain to you how I felt about *all* of this. I wasn't completely honest, though. I just really wanted to make you mad, so you would call me. But you still didn't call me, after you read me letter. That's how I know you don't care about my feelings anymore. Or what I do."

He says, "I just got the letters, a few minutes ago. I apologize for not reading them yet or answering them. I've been on the grind. Getting this money for the holidays, so I can do it up for your birthday. You know I don't check for my mail, at mama's. But tonight, when I went in my room, these letters was in my dresser drawer."
She freezes and thinks to herself.
Oh my God! He hasn't even seen that first letter!

She asks him for all the letters. She's going to destroy them, *especially* the 1st one. He won't give them to her. He puts them in chronological order and opens the 1st one. She holds her breath as he turns on the interior light, then unfolds it and reads quietly.

After he reads it, he says nothing. He simply folds it back and gives it to her. He doesn't read *any* of the others. He stares at her, for several minutes. Then he starts the car and drives off.

They drive back to Chill's house in silence. Whenever she tries to speak, he cuts her off saying, "I don't wanna talk to you, right now."
She knows she made the wrong move. She knew it, then. But what now? She can't just tell him she lied about dating because he'll just say she's only changing her story because he's upset. She tries telling him the other letters, explains the first one. And the 1st letter was written before he arrived for Thanksgiving, after she'd found out he was living with Darlene. But he just keeps telling her to be quiet, so she doesn't say anything else.

When they get back to Chill's house, everyone is planning her and Nina's birthday party, until they notice the negative energy between the 2 of them. Ebony goes to her girls, who already have an idea of what has gone down. She tells them, she needs to talk.

"What happened?" Nina whispers as the 4 of them go into the kitchen.

"He just got the letters *today*. All four of them. Just before he came over here," she says, "He didn't read it until we was at the store. But he only read the *first one*. He gave it back to me and hasn't said anything to me since. Y'all was right. It back fired in my face."
Nina tells her, she's going to fix things. The foursome join the others in the front room. Nina tries to talk to Ajay but he isn't listening to her. He tells her to mind her *own* business. Chill and Ajay walk outside to talk. Ebony

and her girls go to Jo's house and into Nina's room, to try and come up with a plan.

While they're gone, Shuntay makes her move on Ajay. She's pretending to be concerned for Ebony. Ajay tells her he doesn't want to discuss it. They're standing outside on the porch and it's a very cold December night.

After Chill goes inside, Shuntay begins talking for herself. She's telling Ajay how she has been attracted to him since she first saw him, in Houston. He reminds her that she has already fucked 3 of his crew.
She responds by saying, "That was only to get to you."

"That's a fucked up way to get with me."

"When you was down there, you was always *so* into Ebony. I never had a chance to get wit you."

"Really? What makes you think you have a chance now?"

"Well, I was kind of hoping, since things don't seem to be as tight as before, that maybe you would check out the *rest* of the scenery for a change," she says as she exposes 1 of her breast to him.
It has stretch marks on it but he's to angry to laugh.

"*Really*," he says as he frowns.

"Uh huh," she purrs.

"Oh, so you're doing it like *that*?" Ajay asks in disgust.
He means she's double crossing a friend. Though, he knows Ebony would never hang out with this sort of girl. This has to be a side of her, Ebony doesn't know about. Shuntay takes it out of context.

"Hell, she is too!" she says, "She fucked my man, so what's fair is fair, right?"
Ajay says nothing. He knows Ebony hasn't had sex with anyone. But his anger won't reason that. He looks toward his mother's house. He wants to go over there, snatch Ebony's ass out of there and get to the bottom of these accusations by Shuntay and the letter he read, earlier. His mind says the accusations and the letter go, hand in hand. Had he not known Ebony better, he would've believed it. He doesn't ask Shuntay for a name. He knows the game and now, he knows why Raymond is determined to fuck Ebony. Because the Cleveland crew fucked his girls. Ebony had told him, on the phone, Raymond was suppose to be dating Shuntay and Sonya. And that was another reason she didn't understand why he was harassing her.

Ajay thinks, as Shuntay continues to make her move. He isn't listening to her. He's plotting on something else. Like how to stab Raymond from long distance. Therefore, if Raymond cares about his ho's, surely he'll come at him, the way Ajay has been wanting him too. Ready for war and not bitching up, like he's done at every meeting.

Instead of going after Ebony, he goes inside to get Rich, Tank and big June. He tells them, Shuntay wants to fuck him now. They decide they're all going to do her and Sonya too. Show them, once and for all, how the crew get down on scandalous whores like them. The plan is for Ajay to leave with Shuntay and get her to pay for a room. Then, in 10 minutes the other 3 are going to bring Sonya and meet them at the motel. Ajay is to page Tank and put the room number in his beeper. The plan is set.

After Ajay pulls off, Chill learns of the plan. He's totally against it. As he says, "That's not the move. *Hell no!* That ain't about shit! Don't y'all know the foursome is still up, over there at mama Jo's? They're coming back and you know its gonna be some shit."

Within minutes, the foursome return. Ebony is looking for Ajay so she can explain and apologize for the dumb move she'd made. She noticed Darlene's car was already gone. Inside, she notice that Ajay is gone and so is Shuntay. All along, she knew Shuntay was up to no good. But she never thought she would take it, *this far*, here in Cleveland.

"Twin, where is Anthony?" she asks Tank.

"I don't know. I think he went to the store."

He's lying and Ebony knows it. The rest of the crew notice who's missing, by now too. Everyone is trying to put the rest of it together. Suddenly, Tank's beeper goes off. He tries to check it without drawing attention to himself.

"Who is it?" Nina asks, knowing something is going on.

Tank shakes his head, as if to say nobody. Chill knows of the plan now and he wants it foiled. He ask Tank for the number. When Ebony hears the digits, *2-1-5*, she knows, from past experiences, that it's about the motel. She's pretty sure of what's going on. She slips into the kitchen, as the rest of them argue. She grabs Renee's keys off the counter and exits through the back door. She jumps into Chill's Blazer, backs out and heads for the motel. She has never driven in snow, so she knows she has to be careful and not drive too fast. Though her adrenaline wants her too.

TIME TO LEARN-RELOADED-Time Will Reveal-part 1

At the house, Chill is preparing to go to the motel to get Ajay, when he realizes the Blazer is gone. Renee notices her keys are missing and so is Ebony. They know she left in it. The crew, with Sonya, take Tonya's car, Jr's car and Stoney's van and they all head to the motel.

At the motel, Shuntay is already trying to serve Ajay. He's stalling her out and trying to wait for Tank, Rich and June to arrive. Ebony knocks on the door. He goes to open it, thinking it's his boys. He sees Ebony standing there. She barges in and comes straight at him. She's no match for Ajay, as he pins her against the wall.

"I'm gonna kill you, bitch!" she screams at Shuntay.

"Well come on wit it, then!" Shuntay replies.

"Let go of me, Anthony! *Hell*! Get the hell off me!" she screams and manages to get 1 of her arms free.

She lunges at Shuntay and hits her in the nose. Ajay pulls her back, just as Shuntay swings, narrowly missing Ebony's face.

"Hey Shuntay! You'd better sit your ass down, somewhere! I got Ebony!" he yells, not wanting anyone to hit her, no matter what the case.

When the crew arrives, Ebony's out of control. Ajay is struggling to keep her away from Shuntay, who has wisely backed off. Chill and Jb grab Ebony. They hold her down in a chair until she calms down. The older females make their way into the room.

"You're trying to fuck *my girl's* man!" Jan yells, "You scandalous ass bitch!"

"Ah bitch! You're low down!" Bre yells.

"Fuck talking to these ho's. Lets do this!" Lynn adds.

"Bring your ass, bitches!" Tonya yells, as she squares off.

"Nah crew. Check this out," Renee says before turning to Shuntay and saying, "Y'all *muthafuckaz* coming with us."

Nina, T-baby and Rebbie are beating Sonya, who is still on the balcony as Tank, Rich and June break that fight up.

"Let's take this back to Shaker! When everything's chilled, we'll move from there. Everybody, lets go!" Chill yells as they all leave the room. Tank gets the room key from Ajay while Chill takes Sonya and Shuntay in his Blazer, with him and Renee. They wouldn't be safe, anywhere else.

Still, Renee preaches to the duo, all the way back to Shaker Heights.

"Y'all will never come up here and disrespect my crew, like this! We're way to tight for that type shit, *bitches*. And you better recognize!" Renee yells to them.

"I thought y'all was suppose to be baby girl's friends," Chill says, "See, females like y'all will never get respect from my knuckleheads in this crew. They was about to run a train on y'all. Do y'all *hear me*?"

As Chill talks, they sit quietly in the back. Shuntay holds tissue to her nose. Ebony's punch, drew first blood but it isn't over and won't be, for awhile.

Ebony refuses to ride back with Ajay. She gets into the van with Stoney and Bre, who are back together now. Jan, Rob, Nina, T-baby and Rebbie ride in the van with them. Lynn rides with Tonya while Jb rides with Jr. Tank, June and Rich ride back with Ajay, in Darlene's car. They all get back to Chill's house and go inside. That's when Chill lays down the law.

"Everybody keep your coats and jackets on. We're gonna go to *The Chill Spot*. Everybody except y'all two," he says, pointing to Ajay and Ebony. He adds, "Y'all need to get y'all shit tight and y'all will need to do that, *tonight*! Like, right the fuck now! Everybody else. Load up!" he says as he heads back out of the door.

He warns the crew females to be cool, as he notice them plotting to take Shuntay and Sonya as they come out the door. The crew ladies cool out, at Chill's request. But that's only for the moment. It's not *nearly* over. Not that easy. Even Chill knows that.

After they all leave, Ajay watches Ebony. She watches him back. She has to speak because she can't hold her tongue, any longer.

"You just go on and on, don't you?"

"Whatever it takes," he says coldly.

"Why would you wanna go sleep with her, right under my nose?" she asks, "It seems like you want whores, Anthony. Not a good girl, like you told me at granny's. Why her, Anthony?"

With that question, he erupts, yelling, "Why the fuck do you care?! Ha?! You're down there fucking that *nigga*?!"

She has never seen him, so upset. His voice is like thunder, rolling through Chill's living room. It startles her and so does his accusation.

She asks, "What!?!"

"*What,* my muthafuckin' ass, girl! You heard what the fuck I said!" He's livid, as he continues, "You're telling me all that bullshit, like you're gonna keep my shit tight! When all the time, yo ass is hoeing. Just like the rest of the ho's you run wit, down there?!"

He's yelling as he stands directly over her. His eyes have even welled up with tears. His lips are quivering.

"I haven't been with nobody, Anthony! And I don't hang with them. You know I don't. You know that. You're wrong."

"Fuck you! Don't try to fix that shit up now! You sent me a damn letter. *Remember*?! Then yo ho ass partner told me you're fucking her *nigga*! We both know who her *nigga* is. Don't we!?"

"That bitch is lying on me. She's talking about Raymond. You know I don't even speak to Raymond! I haven't been with no damn body!"

He snatches her up off the couch as he continues to yell,

"Then why did you write the letter, Ebony!? What was that shit about?!" He's so close up in her face that his nose touches hers. Ajay never screams and definitely, not at her. But tonight, he's trembling with anger. It's quite scary to see, as she now tries to make her voice extra soft.

He still doesn't believe she's messed around. He knows her. But what has him angry, is her having the nerve and the gall to lie to him.

"I just wrote that to try to make you pay some attention to me," she says, trembling in fear, "I would never mess around on you. I would never cheat on you, Anthony. I *promise*."

"Fuck yo lying ass!" he says as he is so riled up, right now, that he will have to wind down, gradually.

"Its not a lie, Anthony. You can ask Nina, Ree Ree and T-baby. They knew about it. They tried to tell me not to write it but I was hurt. Because you was living with Darlene. I didn't know, no other way to get your attention," she manages to get that out as she cries.

He pins her against the wall and shouts, "Are you planning on giving my pussy away!?! Ha?! *Yes or no*!?"

"No, Anthony. You know I won't be with *anybody*. That's the one thing, I know *for sure,* that you *do* know, about me. Why would I be calling all over Cleveland for you, *every night.* If I was interested in somebody else? Even if you had already called me, earlier that day. I couldn't even go to sleep without hearing your voice. I was writing you, every night and waiting

to hear from you, everyday. And you go and move in with that *woman*. I just wrote that letter to get your attention from her and I'm sorry. I'm *so* sorry. I never wanted you to be mad at me. It was stupid, Anthony. I'm sorry. Please, don't be mad. I'm scared, baby. I wrote the wrong things because I was hurting. I wanted you to call me and make it okay. But you didn't and I got mad. Just don't fuss at me. *Please*. I don't like this, Anthony. I'm scared."

Without thinking, he grabs her face and pushes her head back, hard against the wall. He knows she hasn't cheated and that she's telling the truth. He's just pissed because she lied and played games with him. He wants her to remember this night. And how he reacted to her when she lied to him. He wants her to learn, not to ever play this stupid shit with him again. He holds her, firmly against the wall. He clinches his teeth, then whispers into her ear, "If you ever let another muthafucka touch mine, in any way, it'll make me mad enough to kill you. You hear me? Do you under*stand me*?"

"Yes. Yes, I understand."

"I'll kill your ass, I swear to God. I'll kill you and still fuck your dead ass body, before I get rid of you. Do you understand that too?" he asks again.

He's deliberately trying to sound as heartless as possible. Now he's gripping her between her legs.

"This is mine. Always has been. It always will be. You understand?"

"Yes I understand. I do. I got it," she says, still trembling in fear, "I'm sorry. I promise. I understand. Please. I'm sorry, Anthony. I'm sorry."

"You better understand me," he says as he looks into her eyes, "Don't you ever come at me with no lying shit like that. *Ever* again."

He loosens his grip.

"I won't. I'm sorry. I was just hurting. I didn't know what to do," she says, feeling terrified and relieved, "If you read the other letters that I sent, after you came down there. I tried to explain the first letter and let you know I was just trying to make you call me."

"You're just saying you're sorry now, because you think I'm gonna fuck you up, right?" he offers.

"I am sorry, Anthony. I promise, I won't ever say anything like that again. I promise," she says as he lets go of her chin.

She stays there against the wall, waiting to see what his next move will be.

He grabs her by her hair, with both hands and stares at her. For a minute or longer. He still has her pinned against the wall. She pleads with him, not to fuss at her. She never once felt like he would hit her but just having him *angry* at her is scary. He stares at her, as she tries to figure out what to say or do next.

Suddenly, he sticks his tongue in her mouth. Her entire body trembles as she kisses him back. Now that she realizes he isn't really mad at her anymore, she cries harder. She isn't sad. She's simply relieved.

Earlier, when he walked away and left her in the car, it wasn't because he didn't want her anymore. He left because she'd hurt him. She had gotten his attention and even though, it brought out the demon in him, it was for 1 reason. He was thinking she would gamble with her innocence. The 1 thing, he feels is priceless. Before she left for Houston, she wouldn't have lied to him. He needs her to go back to that program, immediately.

In a drawn out and twisted sort of way, her letter is about to get her the results she had hoped for, all along. After a kiss that seems to last forever, he comes up for air and looks into her eyes.

"Don't make me hurt you. *Seriously*. Because I *will* fuck you up. You fuck up and I'll fuck you up. You got that?"

"Okay," she says as she continues to cry.

"Listen to me, alright? All this letter and drama shit, came about because of my living situation, right?"

"Yes."

"I have to tell you something about this arrangement, I'm in."

He raises her chin and wipes her face with his thumbs. Then, as he looks into her sobbing brown eyes, he says,

"This spring, me and junior getting an apartment together. We already talked about it. Tonya is gonna live there too. It's out by C-S-U. We went to check it out, the other day. When it warms up, after basketball season and my probation's over, we're moving. The crew wants that too. So does pops."

"Do you promise?" she asks, looking into his eyes for assurance, "Please, promise me."

"I promise you, Ebony," he whispers, "*This* spring. Can you give me until then?"

"What choice do I have? Just don't lie to me, to try to make me feel better."

TIME TO LEARN-RELOADED-Time Will Reveal-part 1

"Have I ever lied to you about something I've done? Or that I'm gonna do?"

"No. I don't *think* so."

"Nah, that's your thing. This lying," he says, "I'm gonna break you from that shit."

He continues to look into her eyes. He really is perturbed by her lying to him. He knows he has to make this moment memorable, so she knows never to do it again.

"I'm sorry for lying to you," she whispers, "I'll never do it again."

"Uh huh. I'm gonna fuck you up," he jokes.

She looks down and he quickly lifts her chin up, as he whispers,

"Keep your head up. You're still *my* baby girl. Can't nobody move you. I wish you could understand that."

He smiles and winks his eye. This is his way of letting her know, she's off the hook. She exhales hard and smiles too.

"Now that's what I'm talking about, *right there*," he says, "Your lie had you where you didn't even smile for me, when I first saw you. You was trying to figure out how you was gonna explain that lying ass letter to me. Is that why you didn't smile at me, when I first walked in here?"

"Yes that's exactly why," she says as she smiles, "I thought you had read it, already."

He steps back to admire her beautiful smile, as she blushes openly.

"I missed this smile, so much," he says as he touches her lips, "I miss the good old days, baby. Before all of this grief started."

"Uh huh."

"I miss tasting these lips and this tongue too," he whispers as he places 1 finger inside of her mouth.

His face is intense as he asks, "Can I taste?"

He's looking at her mouth and then, into her eyes. He doesn't wait for a response from her as he pulls her body toward him and kisses her gently.

"Mmm. Sweet as ever," he whispers and they both smile.

"I really missed you, Anthony," she whispers as she puts her arms around him.

"Did you really?" he whispers as he holds her close to him.

"Yes. I had to get back home. I had to show you that I love you, so much and to tell you. The only thing that keeps me going, from day to day is knowing you love me and that you're always here for me. I need to have that because it's so hard just knowing I have to go back."

"Baby girl, it's hard to be mad at you," he says and smiles, "Rather you know it or not. Baby, you keep me going too. Just knowing you're staying faithful to me. That's what keeps me focused," he whispers, kissing her neck and face, as he adds, "You'd better behave yourself, baby girl."
He's kissing her now and getting in the mood.

"Ssss. Oooo, Anthony. I wanna feel you, so bad," she whispers as she holds him tight.

"Uh huh," he moans, "You're about too."
He kisses her again. Long, hard and passionate, as he grinds against her. He begins to remove her clothes, swiftly. He removes his, after he has her completely undressed. He leaves the pile of clothes on the floor and gazes at her naked body.
"*Damn,* girl. Big mama's cooking doing you right. You done filled out," he says, admiring her nice frame, "Ssss uh!"
She smiles shyly and tries to cover her private parts with her hands.
"Oh, hell no. Why you always doing that? I've been waiting to see this body," he says placing her arms around him. "Come on upstairs, so I can lay it down, next to me."
He's still kissing on her face and neck, as he leads her up the stairs and to the spare bedroom.

Once inside, he backs her up to the bed and tells her to lay down. He turns on the clock radio. Then he lays down next to her. He begins to caress her, all over her body. *Keith Sweat's, I'll Give All My Love To You* plays on the mellow moods late night radio show. It's 1 of her favorites from the mixtape her girls sent to her. And, soon after, they're making love. It's as passionate as it's *ever* been. Its like they've never been apart.

Their love had been in danger of falling off. But as always in this family, they can count on the crew to come to the rescue, in any situation. She's finally where she has longed to be, for months. In Ajay's arms. She knows, at this moment and for the rest of the night, she's all the woman he's going to need. She's going to make sure he knows it too.

CHAPTER 10

SPRING FEVER

On Saturday morning, Ebony wakes up in Ajay's arms. She had stayed, all night. When she sits up to look for her clothes, Ajay wakes up.

"Baby, I have to get home," she says, "Mama's gonna kill me for staying out all night."

She remembers they'd left their clothes downstairs. She asks him to go and get them.

"I'll get 'em, in a minute," he says as he pulls her back down on the bed. He adds, "But first things first."

"Baby, I'm already in enough trouble," she says as she smiles.

"So what's twenty more minutes, then?" he asks, "You wanted to know what makes me stay out all night? It's sex in the morning."

"You're so crazy," she says as he climbs on top of her.

"Yea. But I'm crazy about you," he says, "Sex is *so* good when you first wake up. Pussy and a blunt is the breakfast of champions."

They giggle as he enters her. She grabs his shoulders. They make love and forget they aren't alone in the house.

Chill can hear them as he passes through the hallway, going back to his bedroom. Renee is still in bed. He smiles as he tells her what he'd just heard. She smiles and says,

"They got the right idea. That's the way you *always* wake me up."

"Sho you right," he says as he mounts her for their 2nd session of the morning.

That is, until lil Kenny knocks on their door, demanding their attention.

"Ah man," Chill says as he slides back off of Renee, "Now that's the difference between us and them. *Parenthood*."

Renee slides out of bed, puts on her nightshirt and opens the door.

"I want some cereal," lil Kenny says.

"Alright baby," Renee says, "Come on. Go brush your teeth while I fix them for you."

She looks back at Chill and winks her eye, then smiles. He lays back on their bed with a sigh and smiles. Lil Kenny goes to brush his teeth. When Renee passes the door to the spare room, it's quiet again, so she knocks.

"Yea," Ajay answers.

"I put your clothes right here, by the door, whenever *y'all want* them," she says as she laughs and goes on downstairs to the kitchen.

Inside the room, Ebony tells Ajay to get their clothes. He gets up, opens the door and reaches for them. That's when Kenny, who's exiting the bathroom, spots him.

"Hey, uncle Ajay!" he yells and sprints to the door, "I been looking for you, all day! I wanna go for another ride in your car."

"Hey, partner. What's up?" Ajay says.

"I didn't know you stayed over my house," he says.

"Yea, dude. I was too tired to drive," Ajay says as he smiles.

Kenny rushes the door and spots Ebony. She pulls the covers over her face.

"Ebony!" he yells as he tries to come into the room.

"Hang on a minute, lil Chill," she says as Ajay closes the door and they scramble to get their clothes on.

Once they're dressed, she lets him in and Ajay goes to the bathroom.

Chill is up now and getting ready to start his day. Ebony takes Kenny down to the kitchen where Renee has his breakfast ready. She looks at Ebony and smiles.

Ebony smiles back, before saying, "Good morning, big sis."

"I guess all is well, in *paradise* again, ha kid?" Renee asks.

She's happy to see that her young partners have made up.

"Yes, it's cool now," Ebony says as she smiles shyly.

They're soon joined by Chill and Ajay.

"Hey, baby girl. Mama P came over here looking for you, this morning," Chill says and laughs.

Ebony looks worried as she asks, "What did she say?"

"She was looking for you and Tank. But I covered for y'all. Or at least, I tried too," Chill says as he continues to laugh.

"Tank and Nina stayed in that motel room, y'all had," Renee says to Ajay, "Mama Jo was looking for her too."

"Oh boy. We're all gonna get it," Ebony says as she shakes her head.

"I think you already did," Chill says as he laughs harder, this time and looks at Ajay, who smiles slightly as he looks at Ebony.

"Where is Sonya and Shuntay?" Ebony asks dryly as she spreads grape jelly on her toast.

"Oh girl, we took them ho's to granny's house when we left here," Renee says, "They wasn't gonna be safe, hanging with the crew. Not after what they tried to pull."

"I know that's right," Ebony says, "They should've stayed in Houston. We don't hang together, down there. The only reason they came, is to do what they was trying to do, last night. *Sluts*. I don't hang with sluts and y'all know that. Tay told Anthony that I slept with Raymond."
She looks at Ajay and he responds.

"Yea she did but I didn't believe her," Ajay says as he laughs.

"Oh you *didn't*? I couldn't tell by how mad you was," Ebony says.

"That was because you was playing games and lying to me. And really, I was just horny," he says and they all laugh.

"They was trying to get at homies, from the crew, is all that was about," Chill adds, "I know that's why they came up here. I saw how they was carrying on, *way* before Ajay even got here. They wanted to get with the homies. Ron dropped the dime on them, awhile back."

"Uh huh. Well the *homiette's,* from the crew, ain't *even* having that shit, player! Tell them that's right, baby girl," Renee says as she laughs and looks at Ajay.

"*Homiette's*? Okay, true *that*," Ebony says as she laughs and gives Renee a pound while Chill and Ajay smile at each other.

"Mama P and mama Jo ain't the only ones who came by here, this morning, Ajay," Renee says as Chill tries to signal for her not to mention the other inquisitor.
But Renee wants to say it, so Ebony can put pressure on Ajay to leave that living situation.

"Who else came by?" Ebony asks.

"Nobody," Chill tries.

"You know who, home girl," Renee says and looks at Ebony with the eye, as she motions toward her driveway where Darlene's car had sat the night before.
Darlene had come and taken it when she couldn't locate Ajay.

"Oh, nobody is *right*. Too bad for her," Ebony says and smirks.

"She got her car," Chill says to Ajay.

"That's alright. She can have it," he says and smiles.

He isn't affected by Darlene coming by. Nor the fact that she'd taken her car. He has another option and he's about to capitalize on it.

He asks Chill, "Look, bro. I wanna know if that offer still stands?"

"What's that, player?" Chill asks.

"If I can still stay here, for awhile, until we move-"

Renee interrupts, saying, "Ajay, you know you're always welcome to stay here!"

She's about to get, for her young home girl, just what she wants. She looks at Ebony and smiles.

"Hell yea, partner. You know it's no problem," Chill agrees, "We can go get your shit, *right now*, if you want too."

"Yes he wants too," Ebony chimes in and they all laugh again.

Then Ajay says, "Yea man, we can do that," and smiles.

"You sure are smiling, a lot today, Ajay," Renee observes.

"Cause I'm happy," he says as they all laugh again and he pinches Ebony's cheek.

"Ouch! Boy, that hurts!" she yells.

"Who you calling a boy?" Ajay asks, "I'm a man. *Say it.*"

He starts playfully wrestling with her. Kenny comes over to help Ebony. They tackle Ajay to the floor. After they tie him down, they stop. Then they all laugh.

Ajay gets up and says, "Ah, lil partner. You're suppose to be on *my* side, man,"

He's shaking lil Kenny's head with his hand.

"Uh uh. I'm suppose to help my *sister*!" lil Kenny yells and giggles.

"That's right, baby. You *know*," Renee says as she hugs her son.

Chill smiles and tells Ajay, "Come on. Lets go handle this."

Ajay kisses Ebony before leaving the kitchen. Chill gives Renee a kiss. He kisses his son on the cheek before catching up to Ajay.

In the living room, they roll a couple of blunts, before heading to Darlene's apartment.

After they leave, Nina and Tank pull up to the back door, in Tonya's car. They come into the kitchen and join Ebony, Kenny and Renee.

TIME TO LEARN-RELOADED-Time Will Reveal-part 1

Nina ask if either of their parents have been asking about them. When Ebony tells her both of their mothers had come over and she hasn't been home either, Nina feels more relaxed. She knows they'll be in trouble. But no matter what happens, they'll stick together on whatever story they come up with. They decide to say they had drinks and passed out at Chill and Renee's house. Renee can cover for them easily, by saying Chill lied for them because he didn't want their mother's to see them in that condition. Then they'll promise not to drink again, in their convincing way and maybe avoid being grounded. In exchange for 1 of those famous heart-to-heart talks, their mother's are known to give. Nina and Ebony hate sitting through those talks but neither of them want to be punished. Especially not with their 15th birthdays, so near. Nina's is tomorrow and Ebony's is on Christmas day, 4 days from now. Tank has stayed out, many nights. He'll just say he spent the night at Darlene's with Ajay or tell some other lie.

"That'll work," they all say.

It has too. They have no other explanation except for the truth. Neither of them are willing to try that. Besides, they all figure their parents know the real truth, anyway.

Ajay and Chill reach Darlene's apartment, in Maple Heights. Ajay notice her car isn't home. They decide to go in, grab all of his belongings and leave. Ajay figures it's better this way. Now he won't have to be drawn into a discussion with her about last night or his decision to move. Ajay and Chill go in, get all of his things and put them in the Blazer. Alana isn't inside, which is even better. Chill gets in the Blazer while Ajay does a last check for any items he might've missed. He leaves the spare key, Darlene had given him, on her coffee table.

On his way back to the Blazer, Darlene pulls into the parking lot. She parks in the space, next to them. Alana gets out, speaks to Ajay and Chill, then goes inside. Ajay gets into the Blazer and closes the door without a word to Darlene or Alana. Chill does speak. Darlene gets out of her car and walks over to the Blazer.

"Are you leaving again?" she asks.

"Yea," he says.

"We need to talk when you get back."

"Alright," he says as Chill backs out and they drive away.

TIME TO LEARN-RELOADED-Time Will Reveal-part 1

"You know she didn't see your shit in here," Chill says as he smiles.

"Fuck it, you know? When she do notice my shit's gone, that bitch will try to clown me," he says as he lights a blunt and breathes a sigh of relief.

"Probably so, man. And we'll handle it. But you know you should've never moved in with that muafucka, from jump," Chill says adjusting the volume on the stereo.

"True that!"

"So I'm glad you and Ebony got y'all shit back right. Y'all had me bugging, last night. I knew shit wasn't right."

"I know, man. I saw red when that ho said baby girl was fucking that *nigga*, Raymond. And I *knew* it was a lie. Still, just to hear somebody say Ebony and *fucking a nigga,* in the same sentence, I got pissed the fuck off. *Quick*."

"Love is like that, man," Chill says as he smiles.

Ajay says nothing. He just looks out the window as Chill drives on.

"Did baby girl ask you to move out of Darlene's spot?"

"Nah. She didn't ask me too. It's just the way she looks when she's hurt. When she cries," he pauses.

"That shit fucks with you, ha?" Chill asks.

"Hell yea, man. I can't take that. I know I'm gonna have to do shit right. Or she'll be crying, a lot. I never wanted to hurt her, man. Not in my whole life. I have to get this thing right, somehow."

"So this was a surprise to her? You getting your stuff, today? She didn't know you was gonna ask about staying with us?"

"No. I was thinking about it, all along. Even before last night. I miss my hood and my mama, wit her mean self. I couldn't be living out there, with Ebony in Cleveland. I have to stay close to her while she's here. It just made sense to move back to Shaker Heights. I hope Darlene just take her El and keep it moving," he confesses.

"Whatever go down, partner. I got your back," Chill says as he gets the blunt from Ajay.

"I know you got me, dog," Ajay says.

He lays his head back on the headrest and listens to *Das EFX*.

For a few minutes, he reflects on the things that transpired in the past 24 hours. He remembers how sweet Ebony looked when he saw her, for

the 1st time, last night. She looked so beautiful. So sweet. He smiles.

"Here you go man. Damn! Where *the hell* you at?" Chill asks as he laughs.

He passes the blunt to Ajay, who takes it and laughs. Chill laughs more.

"Well shit, you know. I'm just reminiscing on things and things," Ajay says as he smiles and takes a hit off the weed, "Renee was right. I can't stop smiling today."

"You're just in love, cousin. It's all good," Chill says, "Take my word."

Ajay gives him a positive nod.

"Its alright, man. It is. I'm in love too, so I feel you," Chill says, "I'm getting ready to ask Renee to marry me."

"Now that's off the *chain*," Ajay says as he smiles, "That's what time it is, Chill."

"It's time too," he says, "There'll never be another woman in my life, like miss Renee Stewart. It's time for me to give her my last name."

"I'm in it. That's all I gotta say," Ajay says.

They laugh as Chill pulls into his driveway, drives around back and parks.

****

It's late afternoon. Pearl has the evening off and is finishing the laundry with Ebony's help. Pearl and the other mothers are planning to go Christmas shopping while the fathers decorate the homes. John is in route to Cleveland for Christmas break. He very seldom has the chance to be home for Christmas.

Pearl and Jo had their talk with Ebony and Nina. This time they didn't restrict them. They told them they're becoming young ladies and it's time they start acting as such. And they'll treat them accordingly. Nina and Ebony apologized for their disrespectful behavior. They realized it was wrong to stay out all night, at their age, in any situation. And they was surprised they didn't get any punishment, at all.

"It must be the Christmas spirit," they both said.

"I'm glad I'm not on punishment for my birthday," Nina says.

After their mothers go shopping, the 2 of them get together with Rebbie and T-baby at Ebony's house, to make out their Christmas list. The foursome

always pool their monies together, so they can buy everyone gifts from the 4 of them and 2 gifts for each of their guys. They always include everyone's parents, grandparents, all of the smaller children, the crew and of course, each other. This is the way they've done it for the past 4 years. Even when Ebony was in Houston, last Christmas.

By the time their list are done, the rest of the female crew are at Renee's. It's time for them to go do their shopping. Granny, big mama, Annabelle and Sally are gone shopping with the mother's. And though big mama had suggested Sonya and Shuntay stay and go with the younger ladies, the 2 girls insisted on going with them and the mother's, instead.
Wonder Why?

They knew it wasn't a good idea to be left in the hands of the female crew. Not after the stunt they tried, last night. They manage to dodge the bullet, again today. But the crew aren't stressing it. They know the 2 hood rats will fall into their trap. It's only a matter of time before they slip up and the crew girls are going to be there to catch them.

"Hey, ladies. Y'all ready to roll?" Tonya asks the foursome, as they stroll in the door of Renee's house.

"Yea, babe! Lets do this!" Nina says.

"Oh y'all straight, ha?" Lynn ask as she laughs.
She's happy Nina and Ebony didn't get punishment for staying out all night. They all head out shopping.

Chill and Ajay had put his clothes in the spare room and are out riding in the van with Stoney and the male crew. Ebony told Ajay, she would put them away for him, later. The guys are still hustling up that last minute cash for the shopping they have to do. They're also getting, *The Chill Spot* set for the party on Christmas Eve. That will be Nina and Ebony's birthday party, together. They've always had their parties together, for as long as they can remember. With the exception of last year. The crew are planning to make up for that, this year.

The ladies have 3 vehicles to do their shopping with. The Blazer, Tonya's Sentra and Jr had left his Cutlass for Bre, who has her license now. They shop until late evening and get all the gifts they need. When they're ready to leave the mall, it's impossible to get everything home in 1 trip. It takes 3 trips to get everything home. When the shopping is done, they meet

up with the guys, at the club. Rob cranks up the music and they start a jam session. Only the 18 crew members are there. It feels like old times. All of the couples together, the way it use to be, before Ebony and Tank went to Houston. It's good for about 2 hours, until others discover the crew party. As usual, they want to hang. Chill has to monitor the door because he isn't licensed to open until spring. So many people show up, him and Renee decide to move the party back to their house. If they hadn't, it was only a matter of time before the cops would've shown up, wanting to see permits. They move back to Shaker Heights, around 10pm and continue the party. Big mama and granny send Jesse and Kenny across the street to get the foursome.

When the girls come in, the grandmothers insist they invite Sonya and Shuntay to the party or stay home, themselves. Pearl, Sandy, Rena and Jo are with them, wrapping gifts. They agree with the Matriarchs.

"Besides that, Ebony. Your father is home. You or your brothers have been here to see him," Pearl says as she gives Ebony a shameful look.

"Where's daddy at?" Ebony asks.

"He's gone with his crew. They're doing decorations. He was here when we came back from the stores."

"I'll see him tonight, if he don't be too late coming back," she says with that daddy's girl smile.

"Uh huh. Or if *you're* not," Pearl says sarcastically.

"I won't," Ebony says, looking at Nina and her girls.

They all agree with her, as they coax their mothers too. They'd rather not be bothered with Shuntay or Sonya. But they don't want to explain to their mothers why the 2 girls aren't mixing with them.

"Y'all come on, if you want too," Ebony tells Sonya and Shuntay.

The foursome dash out of the door. Sonya and Shuntay run to try and keep up with them. They follow close behind and they all go across the street to Chill's house.

From the moment the female crew spots the duo come in, things get tense. Lynn and Tonya put their drinks down, immediately. They're about to confront them but Jb and Jr pull them onto the dance floor. Jan, Bre and Renee are standing together, smoking a blunt and at the same time, ready for the brawl. The foursome join the 3 of them and leave Sonya and Shuntay, standing alone. Stoney and Chill decide to introduce the duo to

some of the other guys at the party. They hope to ease the tension between their females. Once they introduce them to Andre and Joe, who already seem interested, Stoney and Chill get Bre and Renee to loosen up. Rob keeps Jan busy, helping him deejay. As long as the older females are cool, they'll be able to keep the peace with the foursome. For now, everyone is cool on the fighting. As long as the 2 rats keep their eyes, hands and everything else, where they belong.

As if there isn't already enough tension, smug looks and long evil stares going through the house, in walks Darlene, Alana, Gloria, Anita, Nicole, Angie and Samantha.

"Oh God! Damn, man! What is it? A *blizzard*?!" Rob yells.
He was just about to take a short break from the wheels.

"It can be whatever these ho's wanna make it!" Jan says.
She's getting hyped, for the first time tonight. All the crew, except the foursome, notice when the 7 females come in. The crew guys are all showing allegiance to their girl. They feel this will keep everything kosher. The foursome are on the dance floor with their guys while the other 5 couples stand around it. Initially, nobody from the group of 7 say anything. They just mingle and talk to party goers. Three of the 7 are visibly pregnant. Gloria, Angie and a girl named Samantha. Samantha, who had been at the courthouse with Alana and at Ajay's 15th birthday party, had escaped the last fight by locking herself in their car. This time, none of the pregnant girls are claiming any of the crew as the possible father of their unborn baby. But Renee just can't rest on it. Between the 2 whores from Houston and now the 7 uninvited Cleveland whores, she has to speak her peace.

"What the fuck are these ho's doing up in here?" she yells, after trying unsuccessfully to remain cool.
This is the moment when the foursome notice the 7 and stop dancing.

"Y'all come on over here!" Lynn shouts to them.

"Yea. Its gonna be some shit up in here, tonight. I do believe!" Bre chimes in.

"It's time to make these bitches feel the crew, for real. So they can stop barging up in our spots," Tonya adds.

"For real though!" Lynn hollers.
After reaching over and turning the music off, Jan yells, "Hey? What the fuck do y'all want?"

"We got it for ya!" Bre adds.

"Oh what? Y'all muthafuckaz can't hear us talking to y'all?" Lynn shouts.

Gloria says, "Hold on. We didn't come here to start another fight with y'all. I thought we squashed that stuff."

She's trying to reason for her posse. The other 6 are quiet.

"Well *that's* what you get for thinking," Tonya says as she eases closer to Angie.

"Wait. Wait Tonya. I don't have beef with none of y'all. I just came to party. Y'all have the best parties in C-town," Samantha explains.

"Who invited y'all?" Ebony ask as she notices Anita and Alana. She doesn't know Darlene, by face yet.

Renee yells, "Nobody invited any of these ho's. That lie is played out. This is *my* muthafuckin house! I know, *damn well,* I didn't invite 'em!"

"Well then, fuck! Its time to hold up or roll up outta here, muthafuckaz!" Bre yells.

Her and Lynn grab for Angie and Alana. They just happen to be closest to them. The guys, who have tried to remain quiet, have to step in. They have to hold back their females. The 7 are obviously not willing to fight, so Chill finally speaks up.

"Now, ladies. Y'all don't need to fight these muafuckaz. Hell they *all* pregnant and shit," he says as he looks at each of the 3 pregnant females. He continues, "Y'all don't even have no business up in here, carrying *babies*. You know my girls don't like y'all asses, anyway. So when you fell off up in this muthafucka. You knew it as gonna be some static, didn't you? Hell yea, you did!" He answers himself before either of them can.

"Why the fuck y'all bitches come here, ha?" Jr asks.

The guys are truly irritated with these hangers on. They want their girls to have a good time and not be distracted by their mistakes of the past.

"Yea really, man. What the fuck y'all want? Nobody in here is bout to fuck with, *not one* of y'all tramps, so scram!" Tank yells as he laughs.

"You can say that shit again!" Nina adds, buzzed just Tank.

"I need to talk to Ajay. That's why I came. They came for the party," Darlene says as she observes Ajay holding Ebony's hand.

"*Who* do you need to talk too?" Ebony asks, still unaware that this is the female Ajay had lived with, for the last 4½ weeks.

TIME TO LEARN-RELOADED-Time Will Reveal-part 1

The crew starts shouting, at the same time and nobody can hear anything. Until Chill and Renee grab the microphone and bring the room back to order.

"Everybody needs to shut the fuck up, right now!" Chill yells into the microphone.

"Hell yea! Chill out, for a minute, crew. Lets hear this," Renee adds as Chill takes the floor.

"Ajay, do you have any talk for her?" Chill asks.

"Nah, man," he says with a somber look on his face.

"Then, there it is. Y'all are excused," Chill says to the seven.

"Why did you move your things, Ajay?" Darlene asks, very calmly.

"It was time too," he answers, matter-of-factly.

"You wasn't gonna tell me anything, ha? You just leave without *even telling* me *why* you're leaving?"

"Just like that, yea," he says, calmer than she had.

"Surely, not for that lil girl," Darlene says and grins sarcastically while pointing to Ebony.

"Oh you don't wanna fuck wit her!" Jb steps in.

He has been calm during all of the chaos. Until now.

"I'm gonna be right here, *with* my girl. Yea," Ajay says, still calm, "You see where *the fuck* I am. And it's exactly where I belong. *For life*. Maybe you can't see it but she's a girl and I'm a boy, you *bitch*. You trying to salt her, for her age. She's one year under me. I don't play that fuck shit. Don't say shit else negative about my girl. You heard me? Check yourself."

Ebony realizes this is the older woman, her man was living with and she says, "I ain't worried about you or nothing you say about me. Because you can't touch this, *lil girl*."

"Oh, please," Darlene says and laughs.

"I do, *bitch*! That's why he's here with me," Ebony says.

"She sure as hell, do," Ajay adds as the crew cosigns them.

Darlene continues laughing at Ebony until Ebony puts her up on the game.

"And anyway, while you're running up in here with your *so called* posse, you need to check the ho's you're hanging with. That ho, right there, ain't her for you! She's here for herself," Ebony says, pointing to Anita, "I boxed her down last year, at this same spot. Your ass can be next."

She's unaware that Angie and Nicole have been with Ajay, several times, as well. She continues, "So it seems to me, age has nothing to do with wisdom, in your case. All of y'all can get the fuck on. Because Anthony's here *with me* and he staying here *with me*!"

"Damn right," Ajay agrees.

Ebony's feeling as though he'll scold her about her foul language, at any moment. He hasn't said anything yet but she feels he will later. Or at least, that's what she's thinking. He never liked her to talk flip and she usually doesn't. But tonight, the source of her heartache is in the room and she feels it's time to have her say. She had to get some things off of her chest and she did. She stares at Darlene until Renee steps in front and blocks her view.

"Ajay, do you have anything else for these bitches?" Renee asks, pointing to Darlene and Anita.

"Hell, no," he says, "And them other ho's either! Didn't y'all already give them walking papers?"

"Hell yea, bitches! Be out of here! We're trying to get our party on!" June yells as he opens the front door for them to exit.

As Darlene is turning to leave, she says, "You'll get yours, Ajay."

Lynn punches her in the face and says, "And bitch, you got yours! Don't threaten my brother! You know my mama *want* your ass kicked and I'm just the one to do it!"

Once again, it's on! The females drag Darlene, Anita and Angie out the front door. Alana, Gloria and Samantha run to the cars. They was outside the door before Darlene made her last comment. They jump in the cars, quickly and lock the doors. Nicole hasn't been grabbed yet. She's trying to convince Ajay and Rich to help her get Angie, because she's pregnant. Instead of running for cover. The guys decline to help. She tries to pull Tonya off of Angie. *Big mistake*. Renee gives up on trying to get Gloria to come back and fight. She spots Nicole, pulling on her best friend, so she grabs her and slams her to the ground. Ebony, Lynn and Nina have Darlene covered. Nina and Lynn has wanted to kick Darlene's ass, for a long time. Because their mother wants too. Her threatening Ajay tonight, was just the last straw. Ebony wanted to fight her, for all of the reasons her girls did and then some. How dare Darlene have Ajay living in her apartment, when he isn't, *her* man. She's the only female Ajay is going to live with, outside of his mother or crew's homes. She punches Darlene for every night she cried herself to sleep, down in Houston. For the letter she felt she had to write to

get his attention from her. And for finding out, Darlene never even had his attention, in the 1st place.
Oh yes! And for calling me a little girl! Take that!

T-baby, Jan and Rebbie have Anita down. Tonya and Bre are working Angie. Renee is beating Nicole, by herself. That's when the guys notice John and the fathers running over. They finally break up the fights.

When the men make it over to Chill's yard, it's all over. Ebony's shirt is ripped from Darlene pulling on it. Ajay doesn't like her being outside, like that. Plus the fact that Darlene or anyone else had done it, bugs him. He'll get her for that, later. But when the girls see their dads, they calm down, almost instantly. The men have just finished a card game at Al's and are buzzed too. But they still try to handle the situation, as fathers would. They take their youth home. All of the crew have to take it in. The 7 females get in their cars and leave. Al tries to get Ajay to come to their house but he explains to his father, he's living with Chill now and no longer living with Darlene.

"As of when, son?" Al asks.

"This morning. I moved all my stuff here," he says pointing at Chill and Renee's house.

"I wish you would just come home, where you belong, Ant."

"It's not cool, though. Not right now, pops."

"Damn what's *cool*, son. I'm talking about, what's right."

Ajay looks at the ground. Al is still determined to let him grow as a man. Plus he knows Ajay is refusing to surrender. This is how he'd taught him to be. If he stays at Renee and Chill's house, then Al knows he can see him daily. He also knows Chill won't allow any harm to come to him, if he can prevent it. He hugs his son, then turns to walk Nina and Lynn home. Ajay watches them. He knows his father understands his position.

Ebony, Tank and Jb go home with John. Greg takes T-baby home. Archie takes Rebbie and Jan leaves with Sam Sr. They're walking home, along with June and Brian Sr. With them, is Rich and Rich Sr, Bre is with her dad, Brad Sr. Those who remain are Chill, Renee, Jr, Tonya, Rob, Stoney and Ajay. A few true crew partygoers are still hanging around. So are Andre, Joe, Sonya and Shuntay. John hadn't thought to bring the duo, along with his youth. By the time Pearl reminds him and sends him back,

TIME TO LEARN-RELOADED-Time Will Reveal-part 1

Sonya and Shuntay are already out, cruising in the van. *Stoney's van*!

The 2 of them, with Stoney, Rob and Ajay, are out riding. Sonya and Shuntay gave Andre and Joe the slip, just as quickly as they'd met them, for a chance to bang the crew. Chill and Renee went to their bedroom before anybody left. Jr and Tonya had gone to the dorms. That's where they're going to stay, so Ajay can have the spare room. Ajay, Stoney and Rob was suppose to roll out to a late night place to get breakfast. After arriving at the *Waffle House,* Sonya and Shuntay, who was suppose to meet up with Andre and Joe there, decide once again, to betray Ebony and her crew. They make their move on the crew guys and dump Andre and Joe. *Didn't these girls learn anything at the house, when the crew stomped the other 7 hood rats?*

Stoney, Rob and Ajay go through a few condoms each, as they trick with the 2 Houston hood rats, at the dilapidated baseball field, around the way. Stoney doesn't even kill the engine. Keep in mind, it's December 21st in Cleveland and it's as cold as the north pole. Crackheads are tapping on the windows to be served. It's a cold night but it's about to get warm, I mean *real hot*, for this Houston duo.

Stoney drops the duo at granny's. Though he knows the bedtime hour is 9pm. He knew papa wouldn't want them to get caught going to Pearl's. He drops Ajay at Chill's, Rob at home and goes home at dawn.

After Church, on Nina's birthday, mama Jo has a big dinner. All the families pitch in and everyone attends. Nina is allowed to open her gifts marked, *birthday only*. Her and Ebony always receive 2 gifts from everyone. It's only fair, since everyone else receives a separate birthday and Christmas present. Some say this is where Ebony gets the reputation for being a spoiled child. Because she would always have twice the gifts as everyone else, on Christmas day. Her and Kenny, once he was born, was always labeled, *spoiled rotten*.

After dinner, the crew go decorate the club, for the Christmas Eve party. Everyone except Nina and Tank. They're going to the movies to see *New Jack City,* then to the motel. Chill has hooked them up for Nina's birthday. Tank hasn't gotten his Cleveland license yet but he's still going to drive Tonya's car. The rest of the crew, go decorate while they go to the movies. This time, with their parents permission. They both laugh as they

talk about this being the first, *official* date, they've been on. They've been together for 3 and a half years. Tonight is a date which their parents have actually given them money for. Of course, their parents don't know about the motel room. Nor the birth control pills.

Nina had gotten a prescription for birth control pills through the school nurse, early this fall. They had forged Jo's signature and Lynn pretended to be Jo, when the school called their house for verification. Lynn is home early in the afternoons, now that she's a senior.

After the movie, they go on to the motel room. Which is already equipped with all the necessities they need for a night of romance. Tank has always been openly affectionate with Nina. He isn't the least bit bashful about expressing his love for her or to her. No matter who is around. They communicate more openly, as a couple, than the other 3 couples their age. For instance, they often refer to each other as husband and wife. They talk about their future, their plans to get married and raise a family of their own. At the motel room, they're no different. They talk a lot, about their dreams for the future and the future of the crew. They make love, several times, until it's time to meet up with the crew at the club, around 2:00am.

"And I'm not going to jail tonight, either, Nina boo," Tank says as he laughs and thinks back to the night Chill had gotten the room for Ajay and Ebony.

"No. No you're not, baby," Nina agrees.

They hop in the Sentra and drive to the club to meet up with the crew. First thing they see, is how the 1st Christmas decorations look on their new club. When they get inside of the Chill Spot, they discover that John had come and dropped off Sonya and Shuntay. Joe and Andre are there also. But they don't seem to be as interested in the 2 girls, as they had been the night before. At least, not from Nina's observation.

"Hey Nina! How was the movie?" Ebony asks.

"It was good," she answers, "The crew gotta go see, *Nino Brown.*"

"And how was the side show?" Renee asks as she laughs.

"Much better than the movie, sis," Nina answer as she blushes.

"I guess you see who came to join us?" T-baby asks.

"Oh yea. I was checking that shit out, from the door," Nina says as her facial expression changes to one of disgust.

"Sisters, they're just like a *bad* rash," Rebbie says.

"Uh huh. No matter how many times you get rid of it," Nina starts.

"*It just keeps popping back up, in a different spot*!" All 4 girls say in Unisom as they laugh.

"I know that's right," Renee agrees and laughs.

"At least they got somebody to talk too. Instead of trying to get up on the guys from the crew," Ebony says.

"But Joe and Dre don't even seem to like them ho's anymore. Are y'all *noticing* that?" Nina asks.

"They probably gave it up, already," Rebbie says.

"Probably so. Because I heard my mama telling my aunt Belinda. Granny called and told my daddy, they came in about five something in the morning," T-baby says.

"Now you know granny and papa don't play that," Ebony says.

"And I don't either," T-baby says, "Disrespected my grand's."

"I know that's the truth," Nina says.

"For real!" Rebbie says.

"Nine o'clock is bed time, over there," T-baby says.

"And not nine-oh-one!" Ebony adds, as they all look across the club at the two girls, in anger.

"You know what? Fuck them ho's tonight, y'all. Anyway, it's time for us to take it in, right?" Renee says as she looks at her watch.

"It's almost three o'clock," Nina says as she looks at her watch, which she got at the motel, a birthday gift from Tank.

"Yes, we know you have the time *now*," Rebbie says and laughs.

As they file out, Nina comments on how nice all of the decorations look.

"Well thank you, Nina. Considering you didn't help with it," Ebony says as she laughs.

"Sis, you know I had to have a happy birthday, right?" Nina asks as she smiles back.

"Show you right," Ebony agrees.

The foursome pile into the van with Stoney, Bre, Ajay and Tank, Rob, Jan, Rich and June. Sonya and Shuntay want to squeeze in and are told by Stoney, there isn't enough room for them.

Go figure!

Joe, who's driving his car, offers to take them home and they accept. They're thinking it might be safer to ride with non-crew members. They'll learn later, they would've rather suffered an ass-whipping at the hands of Renee and the girls, then to go through what is about to happen to them at the hands of Joe and Andre.

The next morning, Tonya wakes up with nausea and starts vomiting uncontrollably. Her roommate Terri is concerned for her. She's concerned, so much, she calls Jr's room and asks him to come see about her. He hangs up and within minutes, he's at Tonya's dorm.

Tonya tries telling him the vomiting will subside in a little while. But 20 minutes later, she's dry heaving. Jr is ready to take her to the emergency room. Terri, who is a nursing student, has already given them her diagnosis but Tonya isn't trying to hear it.

"Pregnant?" she asks, "Girl, it's just something I ate, probably. You should've seen all the different foods we was eating at Nina's birthday dinner. I probably mixed something together, that I shouldn't have. I can't be pregnant. I just had my period."

"That don't mean anything," Terri tries.

"It means I'm not pregnant," Tonya says, "Why don't you come to our party tonight?"

They always invite Terri but she never comes. She always has to study.

"Roomy, you know I'm a nursing student. All we do is study and go to class. That's all college is for me," Terri says with laughter.

Tonya agrees and lets her know she's welcome to come, anytime she wants too. Jr sits quietly, watching TV. The girls discuss the symptoms a bit more, while Tonya gets dressed. Jr is filled with nervous energy and has the urge to call his mother, Deb.

"Let me know if I was right," Terri says as Tonya and Jr leave.

Jr drives her to the hospital, where the 1st thing they do is give her a pregnancy test. The test comes back positive. Tonya is pregnant. Jr is nervous about becoming a father but he can't hide his excitement. He's much more excited, than nervous. Tonya feels apprehensive about it. She isn't looking forward to telling her mother. She doesn't even want to, because her mother didn't support her decision to live in Cleveland. Nor to

date Jr. Tonya doesn't see any reason why she'll be accepting of her 1st grandchild being fathered by him, either. Her mother has always loathed the idea of even being a grandmother. Tonya use to talk about wanting kids of her own, one day. Her mother would always say,
"I don't need no snotty nose youngin's running round here, calling me granny." Or something equally appalling.
Tonya actually has more support from Jr, his family and the crew, than she's ever had from her mother in Detroit. Her and Renee are the best of friends. The lack of blood and maternal support is 1 of the biggest things the 2 of them have in common. So who else would Tonya want to tell this news to, other than her best friend, Renee.

Her and Jr leave the hospital and drive directly to Renee and Chill's house. It's the 1st place they both want to go, to share their good news. Tonya sits quietly as Jr reassures her, everything will be okay.

"You don't have to tell your mother, if you don't want too. I will. My mama would love to tell her and she'd be hoping she got ignorant too," Jr says, "I don't want you to stress over it. I got you, baby."

As they turn onto Chill's street, they notice police cars and 2 ambulances in front of mama P's house. Most of the crew are outside. Jr parks on the curb, in front of Chill's house. Him and Tonya jump out and run over to see what happened. Chill, Renee and Ajay are already over on Pearl's driveway, along with Lynn, Nina, Ebony, Tank, Jb, their parents and younger siblings. Other members of the crew are arriving.

"What's going on, man?" Jr asks Chill.

"Them girls from Houston got fucked up, last night," he says.
He goes on to tell Jr, apparently Joe and Dre had taken them to another party or somewhere, instead of bringing them to Pearl's house or taking them to granny's. The 2 girls had been sexually assaulted by at least, 6 guys each and beaten in the process. He tells Jr the police have questioned everybody and though none of them was involved, the officers told them they may need more statements from them, later.

"Damn, that's fucked up," Jr whispers, "If they went around them fools, acting like they was with our crew. Then I believe they got a raw deal. Any negativity to the crew and I'm killing Joe and Dre. This is *fuck shit.*"

"Yea, man. I know. But look here. We don't know shit, alright?" Chill whispers, "We told them we didn't see who they left with, so its gonna

be on them to tell it. The crew is not involved and we are not getting involved. This ain't our shit."

"You think they told them folks who it was?" Jr asks.

"Don't think so, cause these muafuckaz still sweating us," he says. The 2 ambulances pull away from the curb with sirens blaring. The police question all of the crew, once more. Even grandparents Brown and Jones and the crews parents give statements. The crew stick to their story. No one knows who the 2 girls had left the party with. Soon, the police leave going to the hospital to talk with the duo, while the crew gathers at Chill's house.

Today, they're all going to put up decorations for Kenny and put all of his presents under his tree. But before they start, Jr and Tonya tell them the news of Tonya's pregnancy. The crew are supportive, as they knew they would be. Even though the pregnancy wasn't planned.

Tonya starts to feel more excited about the pregnancy after she shares the news with her crew. She decides to let Jr handle her mother, if he so desires. She's just going to handle the being pregnant part. They're 19 and college sophomores now.

"So Ton, when is your due date?" Renee asks.

"August thirtieth."

"Hey, it might have my birthday," Jan says.

"Or mine" Bre says.

"Yea because most of the time, your first baby is born late." Renee offers.

"It might be early, like August fourteenth," Jr says, wishing his 1st child could be born on his birthday.

"Nah, man. You didn't get it in there, soon enough," Chill says and they all laugh.

"*I'm gonna be an auntie*!" Bre sings and rubs Tonya's flat tummy. During all of the excitement about the baby, the crew seem to have forgotten the tragedy that had taken place shortly before daybreak.

"Y'all know this happens in three's, right!" Renee says, "So we better be careful, you young ladies and gentlemen."

She's referring to the crew members who are still in grade school.

"Y'all better be taking those pills because it *seems* like its a spring fever going around here, lately," Chill says.

"Three of those ho's, the other night, was pregnant," June says,

"Why would they even come to a party, *our party* at that and pregnant."

"That ho Angie, jinxed me," Tonya says.

"The way you was whipping her ass, it probably rubbed off on you," Rich says and laughs.

Tonya laughs too, as she calls her roomy to tell her she had the right diagnosis.

Afterwards, the crew sort through decorations and talk about babies and all. Chill notice Stoney, Rob and Ajay are eerily quiet. After the guys take the outside decorations and go out on the porch, Stoney decides they should tell the other guys about their encounter, 2 nights ago in the van, around the way at the deserted baseball field, with Shuntay and Sonya. Just in case their DNA shows up in some test. Even though they all used condoms. Stoney starts the confession. Ajay and Rob add to it.

Big mama and granny go to the hospital with Pearl, Jo and Sandy, to check on Sonya and Shuntay. Officers are questioning them and trying to come up with a lead on who could had done this. The girls only know the first names of a couple of guys. After the female officers are done with their questioning, they allow the rape counselors to talk to them. The counselors and the examining physician asks them about their sexual encounters in the past 7 days. Their lab work shows evidence of numerous partners. Even more than the 6, the girls had told the 1st response officers about, out at the scene. Shuntay and Sonya are embarrassed to mention the night in the van. Because they know the counselors will figure they'd been willing participants with the guys, last night also. They decide not to tell them they had willingly shared 3 guys, 2 nights ago. On several occasions, for that matter. After the questions are done, big mama can take them home.

In the car, Pearl tells them they have to call to inform their parents. Both girls beg her not to make them call. But Pearl knows someone has to call their families because it's the responsible thing to do.

"If anything like this ever happened to Ebony or any of our girls, I would definitely want to be told," Pearl says, "Any parent would want to know if their child was injured, in *any* kind of way."

Shuntay is angry with Pearl because she isn't willing to do the *irresponsible* thing.

She's a goodie two shoes, just like her stuck up ass daughter.

She's already thinking of what revenge she can do to Ebony. That revenge will be against Ebony, through no fault of hers or her mother's. Shuntay is feeling very salty.

As soon as they arrive at granny's house, big mama and Pearl call Houston and speak with both of their mothers. They tell them of the incident. Their families insist they come home and not stay until January, when big mama, poppa and Ebony are returning. Pearl and Sandy get the girls things packed while Jo gets their tickets upgraded to a flight leaving this evening. Sonya and Shuntay still don't want to leave, even after all that's happened. They know their families are feeling they had, most likely, put themselves in this predicament by being so promiscuous. This isn't the 1st time something like this has happened to either girl. Their other instances weren't quite as severe and didn't involve as many guys. But each of them had been raped. They didn't tell the officers or the counselors about that either. In each of their cases, there had been 2 guys. With 1 of the guys, in each case, being none other then Raymond White. *Sweet Ray*, along with a different guy, had forced the 2 of them to have sex, on separate occasions. Raymond had told them he did it because, *"They liked it like that, anyway."* The 2 occurrences had never been reported because Raymond convinced both girls that he was really interested in having a relationship with them. And that it would never happen again. The fact that it hadn't been reported, is probably why Ebony nor her grandparents know about it. It had taken place, long before Ebony moved to Houston. By the time she moved there, it was old news and not even discussed anymore. Ebony *will* find out about it. And even though she had nothing to do with this traumatic experience her teammates went through in Cleveland, somehow Sonya and Shuntay will hold her personally responsible for it. They'll seek revenge on her, in the very near future.

Pearl and Jo have to work this evening, so Sandy and Rena take the 2 girls to the airport. Their flight leaves at 5:15pm. They will arrive back in Houston around 10pm central. Raymond will have the story, the 2 rats decide to give him, by midnight.

The guys finish the decorations on the house, just before dusk. The females have trimmed the tree, finished wrapping the gifts and placed them under the tree for Kenny. There are gifts for everyone. When all the decorating is done, they hang out at Chill's for a few hours, going over last minute plans for the Christmas Eve party. Chill and the guys had finished the discussion on the van incident, before coming inside. They vow to keep it between them. However, Chill warned them that if Sonya and Shuntay told the police about it, then the cops will be harassing them again. Therefore their females will find it out, anyway. He leaves it up to them as to how they want to handle it and the subject is closed.

The guys go do their shopping together and return to Chill's, afterwards. Everyone goes home at 10 o'clock. They're saving their energy for the big party, tomorrow night. Stoney drives Bre, Jan, Rob and June. Rebbie, Rich and T-baby get rides to their houses too, before Stoney takes it in. Jr and Tonya go back to his private dorm room. Tank and Jb walk Nina and Lynn to Jo's house, where they chill for an hour or so. Ebony kicks it with Ajay, up in his room at Chill's. He walks her home, later. Chill and Renee place the gifts under the tree from each other. Then after checking to see that Kenny is tucked in tight, they go to bed. When Ajay returns, he looks in on Kenny before turning in for the night.

The next day is Christmas Eve. June shows up at Chill's with his sister, Brittany. Her and Ajay's sister, Erica are going to baby-sit lil Kenny. When Bre comes in, she has her younger brother, Bruce with her. He's going to attend his 1st crew party. He'll be 13 on New Year's Day. The crew figure it's time to introduce him as part of the crew. Especially to those attending their parties, who may not have known it, otherwise. Bruce is excited to finally get to hang out with his older siblings Jr and Bre plus the entire crew. Because in the past, he was always stuck with the smaller kids.

Later, at The Chill Spot, after about an hour or so into the party, Rob stops the music and they all sing happy birthday to Ebony and Nina. Ebony gets a chance to open all of her birthday gifts. The party goes off without much interference.

Joe and Dre show up. They seem paranoid, at first. Until they find out the 2 girls from Houston are long gone. They decide to mingle. Chill has a talk with them, immediately. He tells them, as far as he knows the cops don't have any leads. But him and his crew prefer it if they leave their party. Him nor his crew can support what they had done, regardless of how trifling Sonya and Shuntay was to Ebony and her girls. They still didn't deserve what they had done to them. Joe and Dre leave immediately. They

know Chill. If he didn't want them there, then they were best to leave. Before him and the crew enforced the request for their departure.

Ebony and Nina enjoy their party to the fullest. The foursome sing together for the first time in over a year. The rest of the crew do their usual thing and the partygoers love it. They end the party at 2:00am because Chill and Renee have to play *Santa Claus. Plus* Brittany and Erica have to get home and go to bed. Ebony's girls help her put her gifts in Tonya's trunk. Ajay already has his license and he's keeping Tonya's car tonight. He's getting his *own car* in a few days. The Detail shop will have it the week after. He's made plans for him and Ebony, for Christmas. Nina and Tank ride home with them. The rest of the crew go home too. Jr and Tonya take Bruce home. Stoney and Bre pick up Brittany and take the rest of the crew home. The Christmas party is at Stoney's house, tomorrow night.

Chill brings Kenny's bike in from the shed and with the help of Ajay, Tank, Ebony and Nina, him and Renee put all of the other toys together. Lynn and Jb come over after taking Erica across the street and putting her back to bed. The 8 of them assemble everything. The 4 guys test all of the battery powered items to assure they're working properly. They manage to have a little fun, in the process.

By 4:30am, all of the toys are assembled and sitting next to the tree for Kenny to see, at first light. That's when the crew prepare to leave. Ajay wants Ebony to stay the night but he knows she can't.

"When I get my spot at the U," he says with a smile, "I'm not bringing you home at night."

"I'm not gonna be mad at that," she says and smiles back.

Him, Tank and Jb walk Ebony, Nina and Lynn home. It had started to snow, earlier. Now the ground is white and beautiful, the way Ebony has always remembered it at Christmas time. She reminisces on how her, Tank and all of their crew would look forward to that first blanket of snow, every year. They would race to build the biggest snowman and make snow angels all over each of the crew members lawns. They use to have major snowball wars on their street and they kept score, for years. Big Paul use to keep up with it and if her memory serves her correctly, her uncle Greg's team has the lead. Her and the other kids never really cared about the score. It was just loads of fun and a chance for the kids and the adults to bond.

"Say, twin. We missed this last year, ha?" Tank asks.

"Uh huh. But it's okay because God has blessed us with a white Christmas, this year, for sure! And it's freezing too," she says.

"All the crew is out and together again!" Jb yells with his arms extended to the sky.

"We're gonna make the best of it too, right baby?" Lynn asks as she hugs him.

He agrees and hugs her back. They stumble and nearly fall down, from intoxication. The others laugh at them, as Tank picks up a hand full of snow and makes a snowball.

"You'd better not!" Nina screams just before the snowball smashes into her face.

She screams again as she makes a snowball of her own. Ebony grabs some snow too.

"You wanna play rough?" Nina asks, trying to imitate *Al Pacino* in *Scarface*.

"Say hello to my little friend!" Ebony says in the same voice, as she hits Tank with her snowball.

At that same moment, she's hit by a snowball from Ajay. She screams and scrambles to find a fort.

"Oh, its on now!" Lynn shouts.

She joins the girls and Jb joins the boys. John and Al, who are still up late playing Santa, step outside after hearing all of the commotion. They observe their youth playing in the snow together. They give each other a nod, then go join in on the 3 girls side. They was getting slammed.

Pearl and Jo take a final break from cooking and come out. They join in on the boys side. John, Pearl, Jo and Al, Jb, Lynn, Ajay and Ebony, Tank and Nina are having a snowball fight, at 5:00am, Christmas morning. It isn't long before a police car, patrolling the area, pulls up. When they see it's only parents and their children having fun, they shake their heads, laugh and leave. Finally, Pearl and Jo say it's enough and suggest they go in, dry up and go to bed. Ebony and Nina walk toward their side doors. Then all of a sudden, the rest yell, *"Happy birthday!"* and pelt them with snowballs. Nina and Ebony scramble to their side doors, screaming as they duck inside. Using the storm doors as a shield. But they're already soaked and chilled to the bone.

"That's alright, sister. We'll get back," Nina says.

"I know that's right. One at a time, just like always," Ebony agrees, "We'll get all of 'em."

Before the parents take it in, Jo ask Ajay to please come and sleep in his own room tonight. She wants her whole family to wake up together for Christmas day. Ebony and Nina watch from their shielded positions, as Jo and Ajay hug each other. Jo holds his hand and they walk toward her house. Ebony and Nina smile at each other. Just before Ajay walks inside, Ebony goes over and kisses him on the cheek. Jo smiles at her and she smiles back. Tank kisses Nina goodnight, with a little peck on the lips. But Jb and Lynn are engaging in a long wet kiss, until Pearl and Jo notice them and tell them to, "Break it up!"

They all laugh. They're so busy laughing, they don't notice Ebony when she picks up a hand full of snow.

"Merry Christmas, Anthony!" she yells as she smashes the snowball on the side of his face.

She runs inside instantly, as he gives chase. Tank tries to pull her back outside but Pearl and Jo say, "No!" and "It's over for now!"

Ebony laughs while Ajay promises to get her back. Just before closing the doors, Ebony says to Nina, "One down, sister!"

"And seven more to go, kid!" Nina yells back.

Then they close the door and their fathers lock up the houses.

In both homes, everyone gets ready for bed, including Ajay. He sleeps in his own bed for the first time in 5 weeks.

CHAPTER 11

THE WAY IT IS!

Ebony sleeps until T-baby wakes her up at 11am. T-baby and her family have come to celebrate Christmas day with the crew. Ebony gets up, gets dressed quickly and joins the others downstairs. Grandparents Jones and Brown are already here, as is Brenda and her family. They exchange gifts, then sing happy birthday to Ebony.

After a wonderful Christmas dinner, Ebony and T-baby go to Nina's house to exchange more gifts with her and Rebbie. All of the crew gather for their day long celebration of Christmas.

Ajay wakes up to eat with his family, at about 2:00pm. He gets dressed and comes downstairs to eat and open his gifts.

"Merry Christmas, Anthony," Ebony says with a smile.

"You said that already. Remember?" he asks with a sly grin.
He hasn't forgotten that last snowball she crammed into his face, earlier.
While smiling, he says, "Same to you and happy birthday too."
She can see it in his smile, he's plotting on something. Just by the expression his face carries. Nevertheless, she gives him, his 2 beautifully wrapped gifts. He opens them, right away.

"Oh yes! I really like these, baby girl. Thank you!" he says with excitement and a kiss on her cheek. While smiling, he adds, "These two are yours but you know the drill, right?"
She isn't going to receive her gifts from him until later tonight. He has something special planned for their 1st *official* date. He will allow her to have her gifts then. But she has to question him anyway.

"Oh that's not fair. Why not?" she asks, "Why can't I open my gifts, right now?"
Her interest in what's inside of the boxes is too much for her to hide.

"Because I said so. That's why not!" he says as he jokes with her.
Then he says, "Nah, for real. It's because I have a surprise for you."
He smiles again and looks at her. His face holds no expression or hint.

"Alright. Just give them to me and I'll wait until you tell me, I can open them," she tries.
He gives them to her. But he can see that she's about to burst from curiosity. She knows Ajay and whatever it is he's planning, will be *worth* the wait. Seeing that she's giddy with curiosity, about the gifts, he decides to hold on to them until later. When she can *actually* open them. He takes them, under protest from her and puts them in the trunk of Tonya's car.

By 4:00pm, the crew are at Chill's house and together again. They've exchanged gifts and everyone wishes Ebony and Kenny a happy birthday. They all play with Kenny's toys, along with him and all of their younger siblings. Their younger siblings had come over to share their toys with Kenny and to join in on his birthday celebration.

Later, the kids go outside to ride their bikes. Each of the youngest kids got a new bike for Christmas. Their street looks like *Tour De France,* once Erica, Pam, Jesse, Roo and Brittany, Kim, Sam Jr, Greg Jr and Steven, Reaper, Ally, Archie Jr and Lil Kenny get out there. The James twins, Brandon and Brina, are out there with their training wheels too. They have to stay on the sidewalk to avoid being run over. It's a very cold Christmas day but everyone is still having a great time. Tank resumes the snowball fight. This time, all 3 generations join in, along Lou Robinson and her family, minus Marsha, as well as a few other neighbors. The snowball war is massive and consumes the entire block. They have a great time, for hours.

By 7:00pm everyone is cold and exhausted. Stoney is hosting the Christmas party at 9pm. The crew has to go home and get dressed in their new Christmas gear. They'll meet up at Stoney's later. Ajay gets his new warm-up suit and Reebok sneakers, his gifts from Ebony and heads back to Chill's. The foursome get dressed at Ebony's house. They're wearing the matching outfits their mothers got them for Christmas. They love to dress alike. They always get matching outfits from their mothers, in their favorite colors. Ebony had no idea Ajay had asked their parents for permission to take her to the movies. Not until Tank comes upstairs to get her.

When her, Tank and her girls come downstairs, her parents and Ajay's parents are waiting for her in the living room and so is Ajay. He looks very handsome.

"Ebony, baby. We're giving y'all our permission to go to a movie together, tonight. Okay?" Pearl says with a smile, "And not, *all* night."

"Yes ma'am. Okay," she answers with a confused look on her face. She looks at Ajay. He's checking out how nice she looks in her new outfit.

"Can y'all be responsible enough to stay out of trouble?" Jo asks, "If we allow you to go to the movies and on to the party, afterwards?"

"Oh, yes ma'am. We can," Ajay says before his mother can finish her sentence.

"I guess it's settled then," big John says as he lights his cigar.
He passes 1 to Al, as the 2 men sip Cognac and watch *NBA* Basketball.
Al is lighting his cigar when he adds, "Y'all just get home at a decent hour, this time-"
Nina interrupts him, saying, "Okay, we will. Oops. I'm sorry, daddy," she apologizes immediately for butting in.
Al nods his head, signaling he's said all he wants to say.

"We'll need for all of you to get home, before dawn, this time," Pearl says, as she smiles and heads into the kitchen.
She has to get ready for the bid wiz game, she's hosting for the parents and grandparents at 9:30pm.

Ebony, Ajay, Tank and Nina, Rebbie and T-baby, leave out the door together, heading back to Chill's house. That's where Jb, Lynn, June and Rich are waiting for them.

Ajay and Ebony leave at 8:30, in Tonya's Sentra, heading out on their date. During the drive is when he informs her, they aren't actually going to see *New Jack City,* tonight. Instead, they're going back to the motel. She blushes as she looks over at him. She leans over and gives him a big kiss on the cheek. She's excited about having him all to herself again. But she wonders if she'll be able to handle him, any better than the last time. She knows in his eyes she's perfect in bed, so everything's okay with her. Ajay promises her, they'll go see the movie on another night, before she leaves. Nina and Tank had raved about *New Jack City,* so much, all of the crew are planning to see it together as soon as possible.

When the crew arrive at Stoney's house, he's in the middle of a business transaction which seems tense. Chill observes the tension between his partner and a guy known as lil Jake, from west Cleveland.

Chill *quickly* intervenes. He solves the problem or so he thinks and has Jake and his boys to move on about their way.

"What was up with that nigga, Stone?" Chill asks.

"He was trying to jimmy with me, on a loan. You know I wasn't having it. He had to come correct or get gone. Cause that's the only way Stoney deals. You know what I'm saying?"

They agree, put it aside and join the others inside.

Meanwhile, lil Jake and his boys drive off, upset that their plan had fallen through. They intended to *jack* Stoney for his product, cash and then some. They didn't know he was hosting a party tonight. Nor that all of those folks was going to arrive when they did. Unfortunately for them, the crew are always around. Their robbery attempt has been temporarily foiled. But unbeknownst to Stoney and the crew, they're planning to try again. Chill makes a comment to Stoney about the fact that he doesn't trust Jake.

He says, "We're not fucking with him. That was the last transaction for that nigga. That shit ends *tonight*, partner. I don't trust that nigga, man."

Stoney agrees with him and the issue is settled and closed. The crew go on with their party, as more and more guest arrive to celebrate with them.

At the motel, Ajay had asked for the same room they had before Ebony left for Houston. *Room 111.* She mentions to him that it might be bad luck to get the same room.

He says, "I haven't had nothing but good memories about this room. All the bad shit, I blocked it out," he says and smiles, "I'm just looking forward to making some new memories with you."

Naturally, she smiles too. Her heart tells her everything will be okay, as they head into the room.

I live in Houston, already. What else can my mama do to punish me?

He has the room stocked adequately, as he walks her inside and tells her to get comfortable. He goes back to the car.

When he returns, he has her gifts. Hidden in his other hand is a handful of snow. When she reaches for the gifts and he hands them to her, he drops the snowball down her back. She lets out a loud shriek, as he holds her down. She screams and giggles. He won't allow her get up to remove the snow. She has to lay there until it melts, while he's kissing on her.

After she wrestles with him, for several minutes, he finally lets her up and hands her the gifts. He tells her to open them, right away. She does.

In the large box, there's a satin warm-up suit, similar to the 1 she gave to him. In the smaller box, is a gold rope chain. She smiles at him and tells him she loves her gifts. He's gotten her exactly what she wanted.

"I love them, Anthony. I can tell you read *all* of my letters."

"Of course, I did. And the gifts will get better, every year," he promises as they smile at each other.

"Will you put this on for me?" she asks, "I wanted a *dukie* chain."

"Uh huh. Turn around. I'll fasten it," he says, "I love giving you what you want, Ebony. I learned that from my daddy. He said that's how he keeps my mama smiling and sleeping in the same room with him."

They laugh. He fastens the clasp and kisses her on the back of her neck.

"Thank you," she says with a smile, "You look great in your gifts."

He's wearing the *Michael Jordan silk* warm-up suit and leather *Reebok* pumps, endorsed by *Dominique Wilkins* of the *Atlanta Hawks,* she had given to him, earlier.

"Thank you, baby girl," he says and laughs, "That was real sweet."

He's a slam dunk fanatic and those are his 2 favorites players, in the league. He can tell she wants to take off her wet blouse. He chuckles as she tries to keep it from touching her back. He still won't let her take it off.

"Do you want me to put on my warm-up suit?" she tries.

"No baby, not right now," he says and smiles, "Actually, I wanna see that *other* suit."

"Oh, okay. What suit is that?" she asks as she smiles and pretends not to know what he's talking about.

He clarifies, "Your *birthday* suit. The one you wore fifteen years ago, today."

He chuckles. He knows that she's aware of what he means but he can't stall, anymore. He wants to see her body, so he starts to undress her.

"Lets get you out of these wet clothes, baby," he say, as he grins.

As he slowly removes her last item of clothing, her panties, they kiss long and hard. He slides out of his clothes and they both lay nude, on the bed. He lights up a blunt and they quench their thirst with beer, before indulging in each other.

Their evening is filled with heated passion. He smothers her lips, neck and nipples, with wet kisses. He feels so good inside of her and as usual, her body lets him know it. When she explodes in ecstasy, he coaches her through it with the demanding phase, "Yes, baby girl. *Get* it wet."

"Oh Anthony, baby!!!!" she yells as she holds him, very tight. She reaches her climax. Minutes later, when he reaches his, she clinches her knees to his sides and digs into his back. He churns into her sweet nectar until he stirs to a slow grind. He had a very energy consuming climax and has very little air left, in his lungs, when it's done.

"I can never handle you," she whispers, breathless, "I never can." She's breathless and he is too. They hold each other very tight.

"You do me *good*, baby," he whispers back, "You do me, just fine." He's panting and trying to catch his breath, before he kisses her again.

Ebony and Ajay share 3 *very* physical episodes of hot lovemaking. Only breaking to smoke *ganja* and sip some more beer to cool off.

It's approaching the 1:00am hour and the party at Stoney's house is jumping. Everyone's having a ball and there has been no unwanted guest, showing up to set the females temperatures at blazing. At this party, everyone is invited and in the festive spirit, while flaunting their new gear and many gifts. The most talked about gifts, of *this* Christmas, are the 2 engagement rings given to Renee and Tonya. Chill and Jr had gone all out and made the matrimonial commitment to their significant female.

Ajay and Ebony show up shortly after 1:00am. They're glowing and visibly exhausted. The crew tease them, for another hour.

"Ebony, did you see what Santa gave Renee and Tonya? Nina asks.

"No. Where are they?"

She searches the room for her big sisters. She spots Renee down the hall and goes directly to her.

"What did you get from Santa, big sis?" she asks.

"Just *this*!" Renee answers, holding her left hand out and flashing her truly visible, solitaire diamond ring.

"Oh *snap*!" Ebony shrieks, "That's the bomb, Renee! I'm so happy for y'all. I know I'm gonna be in the wedding, right?"

"Sis, now you know the whole crew will be representing, like usual," Renee says, "It's gonna be a double ceremony. Tell her, home girl," Renee says to Tonya, who's exiting the bathroom.

"Oh yes baby! It's going down, just like *that*," Tonya says as she flashes her rock for Ebony to admire and it's an identical twin of Renee's.

"Alright now! Just tell me when to get my dress ready, okay?" Ebony says, as they all laugh and join the others in the living room.

Ebony shows everyone her warm-up suit and chain. She's wearing both of her gifts from Ajay. She checks out all of their gifts too.

"How was your birthday?" Bre asks.

Jan giggles and cuts a joke. "More importantly. How was the *movie*?"

"It was *real* good," Ebony answers and returns the giggle.

"Girl, it's hard to believe you're fifteen, already," Stoney says as he passes a blunt to Ajay.

"I guess I just look young for my age," Ebony says and laughs.

She's in pigtails, after their sweaty sessions at the motel.

"Uh huh. What happened to all those curls you had today?" Stoney asks as him and the others laugh.

"I got 'em in my pocket," Ajay says laughing while Ebony blushes.

"Come on, Ebony," Stoney says, "I didn't get my birthday dance."

He pulls her to the dance floor and starts her dancing, with the crew guys.

"Oh, how are you *playing*, man?" Ajay ask as he smiles.

"Come on, Player" Stoney says, "You've been dancing with her, all night. Haven't you? If not, you're slippin. And I know you ain't slippin!"

Him and everyone, who hears that comment, laughs loudly.

"You're right, man," Ajay says as he laughs, "It's alright, bro. You can go ahead. It's cool."

"You're in love, crew," Stoney says, "I done told you, already."

Ajay, Bre and Jan laugh, as Jb comes over with another blunt.

"Ebony still looks like she's ten years old. Except for her height," Jb says, while the 4 of them stand next to the dance floor and pass his blunt. Ajay stares at his lady and smiles. She catches his smile and returns 1 of her own. Chill cuts in on Stoney, for his dance with the birthday girl. Ebony has to dance with every guy in the crew before she can exit the dance floor.

When she's finally done, she gets a cold beer from T-baby, who has 1 waiting for her.

"I know you're ready for this," T-baby asks.

"Hell yea, cousin. I'm as hot and thirsty as a slave, right now!" Ebony says and laughs as she sucks down 4 ounces of her single, right away.

"Damn, *girl.* You put that pass the neck, in one swallow," Rebbie say, as she joins Ebony and T-baby, next to the dance floor.

"I was thirsty," Ebony says and they all laugh.

"Let me get a shot of that, kid," Nina says as she comes off the dance floor.

Ebony shares with Nina while Rebbie goes and gets each of them another one. Stoney and Bre slip into his bedroom to be alone while everyone else starts to wind down and pair off for their marathon of slow dancing.

The 4:00am hour approaches and the crew prepare to leave. They file out to their vehicles and pair off, to get their last minute kisses. Stoney and Bre come outside to his van. He's taking her, Jan, Rob and Bruce home. Ajay drives Ebony, Nina and Tank home. Chill and Renee take Jb, Lynn, Rich and T-baby. Arthur rides with Jr and Tonya as they take June and Rebbie home, before heading to CSU apartment. Jr is an Omega man now. Crew member and frat, Arthur or money shot as they call him because he studies film and photography, lives at the University apartments, better known as, *The U.* He lives in the same complex where Ajay, Jr and Tonya are planning to lease in , come early spring. It's also where Jr and Tonya will stay for the remainder of Christmas break. Ajay stays at Chill's, this morning. Instead of going back home and Ebony stays with him. Pearl had a party last night. Ebony knows she won't be snooping into her room, too early. Because she'll be sleeping in too.

Stoney arrives at Brad Sr and Deb's home with Bre and Bruce, in the van. Bruce hops out quickly and heads inside, while Bre sits in the van for more alone time with her man.

"This was the nicest Christmas I've had in a long time," Stoney says as they sit on the driveway.

"It *was* pretty cool, ha?" Bre says, "All the kids got bikes. Remember when we all got bikes? Our families got it going on."

"Y'all are the only family I have. Seems like," he says, very sincerely "And misses Green, across the street from me."

His mother moved to Columbus with her new husband, Jason Carr, about 2 years ago and took his 2 younger sisters with her. Stoney, who's birth name is Cheston Coleman, has never really known his father. The last he heard about Chester Lee Coleman is that he was somewhere in California, in

prison, serving a life sentence for murder. Stoney and Bre plan to visit him when she finishes school. Stoney lives in Cleveland and other than the crew members who stay with him from time to time, he lives alone. His mother visits, maybe twice a year and brings his 7 and 6 year old sisters. Stoney was legally grown when she moved. He wanted to stay in Cleveland with Chill, Rob and the crew. His mother left him with the house, the van and the furniture. He's partner's with Chill at the detail shop and the new club. Through hard work, he has managed to save a nice lil grip to take care of himself and his crew, if the need arise. He just turned 21, in October. Even though Bre is only 16, he loves her very much. She's very strong and street wise, due to her association with the crew and her parents. They teach their offspring the game, from day one. Any time Bre and Stoney disagree on something, it's when she's kicking it with homeboys outside of the crew, same as the other guys in the crew. Even though it would be strictly business and innocent, Stoney sometimes seemed to feel threatened by the possibility of some other guy receiving attention from her.

"Take the incident at the spot, that night after your first game," he recalls, "I wasn't worried, you would hook up with them niggaz, like I told you. I guess I was just feeling alone. I usually do, when it gets close to the holidays. You mean a lot to me. If it wasn't for you and the crew, I would probably have given this shit up, along time ago."

"Given what up, baby?"

"Everything. Just life, you know? Baby, it's hard to go on smiling, when you feel like your own mother chose a man over you. I mean, y'all in the crew, like the ones who's grandparents kicked this shit off, will never know what abandonment feels like. Because this unit is *so* strong. That's what attracted me. Not the street shit. But the family love. It overwhelmed me. And with your parents accepting our relationship and cosigning it, lets me know they see the good in me and accept me too. I get a card, every now and then, from my own mama or a phone call. A visit. But not that real connection, all of y'all have. Plus your whole family includes me in it too. The crew are here for me, like *my family* should be. That's why I would give my last for this crew and my life too, if necessary. I told you, when I did those three months in county, at the beginning of eighty nine, mama didn't even know I was locked up. Until I got out and called her. Then she came running up here to visit."

"That was a *long* three months," she says, "I was miserable. We had just taken our relationship to the physical level. Then you went behind them walls. It was hard for me. I know it was rougher for you."

"Tell me about it. You was there for every visit. That meant a lot to me. That's why I give you anything you want. Because you looked out on me, when my own mama didn't," he says, "You and my crew."

"So you feel like, if I leave you, I would be abandoning you, the way she seems too? Is that why you tripped about them schoolboys?" she asks while smiling.

"I guess so. It's alright though, baby. Breanna, I know without a doubt, you're loyal to me, in the ways that count. And I would never want you to be lonely, if something happens to you and me. You have too much living to do, baby," he says in an almost whisper.

"Well, there's no need to talk about *that* shit, Stone. Because you're not going *anywhere*. I won't let you," she says and laughs, "You're mine, Stone. You're mine until I get old and crusty, with a bend in my back and breast that hang to my knees."

They both laugh hard. It takes several minutes to overcome that comment.

"That's cool," he finally says, "I'm not trying to go nowhere. But on your eighteenth birthday, I'm giving you a diamond. It can mean, whatever you want it to mean. I just want you to have one."

"Oh wow! You've got me tripping, Stone," she says, "I did want one. But I figured I better not say anything. Because I know I don't wanna get married, *right now*. But I like those rings, they got. A whole lot!"

"I tell you what," he says with a smile, "You don't have to wait for it. When you come by the house, later, I'll give it to you."

"You got it already?!" she asks in amazement.

"It's under my nightstand, still in the box," he reveals, "I put it under there, in case you went plundering. I didn't want you to stumble up on it."

"I am gonna get you, man," she says as she hugs and kisses him.

"You already got me, Breanna. I wanna marry you and have some babies," he answers immediately, before they kiss again.

She says, "I wanna marry you too. The babies have to wait for the degree."

He acknowledges her wishes to finish college. He agrees they'll wait. They kiss again, as Brad Sr turns the porch light off, which is Bre's signal.

"Well, I have to go in," she says.

"Alright, baby," he says, "I love you and I'll see ya."

She kisses him, over and over. She doesn't want to get out of the van but she knows she has too.

She says, "I love you too. In a minute, hubby."

They get out and close the doors. Stoney walks her to the door and kisses her, once more. He waits until she's safely inside, before going back to his van. He gets in, closes the door, backs out and pulls away.

He arrives home at 5:30am. He gets out, locks the van, sticks his pistol in his waistband and walks to his front door. He's still intoxicated, as he fumbles with his keys, then unlocks his door.

As soon as he steps inside, he's hit in the back of his head with a blunt object. He falls to his living room floor. He's dazed but still conscious enough to see 2 guys standing over him.

"You shorted me, nigga. How you gonna fuck over me?"

It's lil Jake and his boys. They've come back to rob him. They hadn't been stiffed on their purchase, at all. Robbing Stoney had been their plan, all along.

"Nigga, you paid for a zone. You got a zone," Stoney says as he tries to get to his knees.

They begin kicking and hitting him as a 3rd guy parks the car and runs in.

At Chill's house, he's having trouble relaxing. He tells Renee about the incident at Stoney's, before the party.

"We'll never trust that nigga, Jake. We're not dealing with that fool, no more," he says.

"You think they're gonna try something?" Renee asks.

"I don't know. But I'm about to call him and tell him to head this way. Or I'm going over there."

Chill grabs his cell phone and calls Stoney's house. After he gets no answer, he calls his pager. He gets no answer from there, either.

Stoney is weak but he manages to pull his pistol from his waist. He fires off 2 shots, into 1 of his attackers. Another attacker, pulls a pistol, stands over Stoney and fires 2 shots into his chest. Him and the 3rd assailant ramshackle the house but find nothing to take. They give up and make a break for it. Two of them have to carry their wounded partner to the car. They rush him into the back seat, jump in and speed away.

Inside the house, Stoney is critically wounded but still breathing. He manages to crawl to the phone and dial *911*. He tries to talk but he can't make his voice clear. The operator dispatch units to his address, from the computer.

"Sir, there are officers and EMS on the way," the dispatcher says. He doesn't hear her. He has passed out.

Chill hops in his Blazer. He wants to get with Stoney and make a plan of action for Jake and his boys. Just in case, they come back. He heads to Union avenue to speak with Stoney, face to face. All the while, his gut is churning. He's feeling uneasy, as he drives.

The medical team arrives, along with the police. Stoney is still unconscious. The paramedics work to revive him. Finally, after several minutes, he regains consciousness. They put him on the stretcher.

"Sir, do you have any family? Was anyone else in the house with you?" the EMS technician ask, as they roll him to the ambulance.

"Bre...., Breanna," he struggles.

"*Breanna, sir*? Who is she?" the technician asks.

"Will...son," he tries.

"Breanna Wilson? Is that your family, sir?"

"Yes," he whispers, as he coughs up blood and slips back into unconsciousness.

They rush him to emergency and leave Bre's name with police, at the scene.

Chill pulls up, just after the ambulance leaves. He see the police cars at Stoney's house. He pulls in front of Mrs. Green's house, hops out and heads over to where an officer is standing.

"What's going on?" Chill asks. "My business partner lives here." The officer is hesitant to give Chill any information. Chill is very impatient and insists on knowing what has happened. Or he's going inside the house and see for himself.

The other officers are questioning the neighbors but only Mrs. Green cooperates. She says she saw a black and white, 4 door car. But she isn't sure of the make.

TIME TO LEARN-RELOADED-Time Will Reveal-part 1

"It could've been a police car but it had no lights on top," she says. Another officer finds Bre number, in an address book on the floor. He shows it to the officer Chill is with. They ask Chill about Breanna Wilson. He tells them, she's family and Stoney's girlfriend. But his patience is gone.

"Where is Stoney?" he asks again.

The officer tells him, Stoney has been taken to the hospital. But he doesn't tell him anymore than that. Chill listens to the other officer, as he calls Brad Sr and Deb's home.

"*Hello*," Deb says as she wakes from an intoxicated sleep, after last nights bid wiz tournament at Pearl and John's house.

She's extremely groggy, as she sits up in bed.

"This is officer McDaniel of the Cleveland Police department. I'm trying to locate a Breanna Wilson. Please ma'am."

"*Police? This is her mother. May I help you?*"

"Ma'am, we responded to a shooting call, this morning, on the west end of Union avenue. We found a man critically wounded. He managed to give the paramedics, your daughters name, before he lost consciousness. We need to know if she can meet us at the hospital. Please," McDaniel says.

Chill has to force himself to stand there to find out where Stoney was taken, while Deb panics on the other end of the phone.

"*Oh my God! Is it Stoney!?! Is he alright?!?*" she asks, scrambling out of bed.

"What's his name, ma'am?" McDaniel asks.

"*Cheston Coleman. But we call him Stoney. Is he alright?*" she asks again.

Chill gives them all of Stoney's information and they still refuse to tell him anything. Chill has no patience left. He wants to know what has happened to his partner and best friend. He decides to go home to get another pistol and to alert his crew to the fact, that Stoney has been shot.

He's most likely at East General.

He heads back to his house. The officer is still on the phone with Deb.

"Ma'am, he's alive but he's lost a lot of blood. Please meet us at East General hospital, as soon as possible. Okay?"

"Okay. Let me get dressed!"

They hang up the phone. Deb wakes Brad Sr and tells him. They go to Bre's

room and wakes her up. They tell her the news. She starts to scream, frantically, as she scrambles for her shoes. She's still wearing her clothes from the party. Deb and Brad Sr try to calm her down, as they put her shoes on, for her and get her to the car. They rush to Stoney's side.

Chill makes it home and grabs another pistol, first thing. He tells Renee, who never went to sleep. He wakes Ajay and tells him. Then has him to call Rob and Jr, while he goes to get Jb and Tank. Ajay gets up. He's instantly angry. Chill told him to get dressed, before he headed across the street. He needs to get his brothers together and find out who shot Stoney.

It's 7:15am and the staff have Stoney stabilized, momentarily. They're taking him to surgery. Bre needs him to know she's there.

"Can I see him, please?" Bre cries.

"Sweetie, he's very weak," the head nurse says.

Tonya's roommate, Terri Edwards, is there doing student nursing. She acts as a liaison for the hospital, since she knows the family. She escorts Bre into the room. Stoney is still unconscious as Bre talks to him.

"Hey, baby," she whispers, "Hold on, Stone. Baby, please. Don't you give it up now. I'm here with you, just like always. You can't let go. Fight it, Stone. Please. Please, fight for me."

She's pleading with God and Stoney, for him to make it.

Out in the lobby, Deb calls Belinda to tell her where they are and what happened. She tells her to alert the family and tell them to come, immediately.

"Girl, no! Oh my God! Let me get Jan up. Deb, we'll be there," Belinda says as she wakes Jan and tells her.

Jan hops up and throws clothes on. She cries and worries, for Bre. Sam Sr and Belinda try to reassure her that only God's will can be done and to just pray. They call Rob before leaving home. He tells them, Ajay had just called him and he needs a ride. He wants to be close to Jan. He can hear her crying. Sam Sr is going to swing by his house and pick him up, on his way to the hospital.

While waiting for them, he calls Chill. Chill can't really talk but he tells Rob, they'll talk at East General and to meet him and Ajay there.

Ebony had gone home, prior to Chill's discovery. Renee takes lil Kenny to mama Jo's house and tells her why she needs to leave him. Jo tells

her to go on and she'll inform the rest of the crew. Renee hugs her and leaves.

Jo calls granny and ask if she can bring Kenny to her. Granny says they'll come get him and they'll be there, momentarily. Jo gets Lynn and Nina up and tells Lynn to call everyone else. Lynn does and finds out they already know. And like, Jr and Tonya, they're in route to the hospital and so is Arthur. Lynn makes sure everyone is contacted, while getting dressed. Nina has gone to get Ebony. They call T-baby and Rebbie.

When Jan and Rob arrive at the hospital, Stoney is in surgery. Bre is standing, just outside of the door which leads to the operating room.

"He woke up and smiled at me, Jan," she says as Jan hugs her.
They both cry while Rob leans against the wall, in silence, waiting for the guys to start arriving. He's both numb and angry.

At 7:25am, Chill's Blazer and Jr's car, pull into the parking lot. They rush in and find Bre. Bre and Jan are still standing together, supporting each other. They cry and pray to God to let his will be done.

"How is he?" Chill asks Rob.

"He's still in surgery and we waiting to hear some-" Rob tries but stops speaking, as his voice cracks from the urge to cry.
Renee and Tonya comfort Bre, who's still clinging to Jan, as the rest of the crew are getting closer to the hospital.

"Come on, ma! We're going *too* slow," Lynn says to mama Jo.
Granny and big mama had arrived to keep Kenny and the other kids. Jo and Pearl are heading to the hospital and bringing Jb, Lynn, Tank, Nina and Ebony. Archie Sr is bringing Rebbie and T-baby while Brian Sr picks up Rich to ride along with him and June. All the parents are trying to make certain their child gets to the hospital. They understand how close this crew are and they understand the family bond and loyalty too. They've been here before. And was the same way with their own crew. They still are too.

When Pearl and Jo arrive, they see Archie and Brian going in. They catch up to them and run into the emergency room doors, together. They're going to find Bre and the rest of their crew.

Bre is still outside the operating room doors, praying, crying and leaning on her girls. The doctors comes out of the operating room and comes to where her and the girls stand, with Terri Edwards. Jr, Chill,

Ajay and Rob join them, so they can hear the results of the surgery.
The lead surgeon says, "Miss Wilson, we did all we could do. But mister Coleman had lost a lot of blood. Both bullets punctured, *both of his lungs*. I'm sorry to tell you............, we were unable to save him."

As Lynn and the others come around the corner, they hear Bre scream out at a horrific pitch. It's absolutely, *bone chilling*.

"Oh God no! No please, no! No! No! No!" she screams as she collapses against Jr and Chill.
Ebony turns the corner and freezes in her tracks, when she sees Ajay drop to his knees and cry out. She starts screaming, instantly. In seconds, everyone is crying. At the same time, all of their parents are trying to comfort them but they're overcome with grief, themselves. Some of the hospital staff try to comfort them too. It's very chaotic and extremely sad, at this moment. Bre's screams have become silent. Her mouth is stretched to it's full potential. But no sound is coming out of her. She soon passes out.
Cheston "Stoney" Wayne Coleman is officially pronounced dead at 8:15am. Thursday, December 26, 1990.

This moment in time will live on in both agony and infamy, with this crew, for the rest of their days on earth. On this bone chillingly, cold day which follows Christmas, the death of 1 of their soul mates will be a bookmark in their lives, forever. It will serve as a reminder of what the largest pitfall is, for the things they chose to involve themselves in.
Death!
And even though death is the only thing guaranteed after birth, certain paths taken in one's life can act as an accelerant to permanent cessation. This crew is no stranger to death. It's something most of them are familiar with and/or have experienced, on an up close and a personal level. Whether death comes to a family suddenly or expected, there is only 1 recourse. Eventual acknowledgement and then acceptance. For there is no cure. In an instant, 1 of the crew is dead. Stoney has been taken from them, when not more than 4 hours had past since they were all together, at his Christmas party, in his home. That home is now a crime scene. The home he'd been ambushed in, by at least 3 assailants. That's all the police have. There *has* to be more to this story and Chill is about to find out. He leans against the wall and watches, in horror, as his crew family grieves the loss of their beloved

brother. He begins to reflect on the past week, like he'd done earlier. He's searching his mind for answers to who might've taken the life of his best friend and business partner. The only name that enters his head is, *lil Jake*. And Chill won't rest until he gets justice for Stoney. He knows this, already. There are a few questions which come to his mind.
Was this random? Or was this step one of someone's plot to take out my crew? My family? Was this Old Jake Johnson? Most likely! No one else has beef!

He has to first, acknowledge the tragedy. Then stubbornly, he accepts it but he wants revenge. And he has no doubt that his crew does too. He doesn't want the perpetrators of this grief, to get an hour older. But first, he has to say goodbye to his brother. He turns and walks to the nurse's station.

"May I see him, please?" he asks softly.

"Yes sir. Of course, you can," the duty nurse replies.

Chill follows her through a door which leads to the room where Stoney's lifeless body lay. He remembers the 2 times he walked through these doors to view his mother and then, his father. He feels numb as he walks through the valley of the shadow of death, which is his life on a daily basis. He feels numb to the pitfall, his brother had just faced. He takes a deep breath and walks through the double doors, slowly behind the nurse. This is surreal. 1 by 1, the crew follow him. They reach the room where Stoney lay. His soul's final destination has already been bided for and decided on. Rigor mortis is still to come. He's still warm. They all surround the bed for a moment of silence, at Chill's request. Their parents wait, just inside the doors.

For Ebony, this is unfamiliar. She has never been this close to *human* death. The lose of her pet is the closest she's been to this finality. She can't even grasp the situation and Stoney was like an older brother to her.
How can he not be coming by Chill's house, later today? Who is Bre gonna pair up with? Oh My God!

She thinks of Bre and the pain she must be feeling, with her man gone.
What if that was Anthony, laying there?

She begins to cry. She can feel it now. She feels helpless. So empty. So useless. She starts to feel sick to her stomach.
Oh God, why?

But then, she knows she can't question God's will. Death is the end. The finale. The final ride. She takes the feelings which stir in her, right now. And vow to use them as a shield to help her protect her loved ones. If they truly love her, they won't do things to accelerate death. For death, is something that not even the *sweetest* smile can reverse. She has to convince Ajay to leave the street life and bring the rest of their crew, along with him.

They all join hands, as Chill says a prayer for Stoney. And they're still crying, softly, as he says, "Amen."

Ajay stands at the end of the bed, staring at Stoney. He's unable to move.

"Come on, baby," Jo says to him, "We need to let the staff in here." She puts her arm around him. The others start to slowly file out of the room, as Ajay backs slowly away from the bed. He's mumbling something, incoherent. It's very low and no one can understand what he's saying. Jo backs up with him, until they're outside in the hallway and the double doors swing back and forth in front of them. They all watch, through the windows, as the staff places the white sheet over Stoney's face. *He's gone.*

Ajay turns and walks away, with tears rolling down his face. Ebony goes after him and the others come too. They walk out of the hospital and into the parking lot. Chill catches up to Ajay and grabs him by the arm. It seems as though it wakes him from some place deep.

"Hey, bro. Let's get the guys together at the crib," Chill says.

Ajay looks into his eyes for the second it takes, for them to go telepathic. He stares at Chill as they seem to share the same thoughts. Then they cosign each others thoughts. Ajay nods his head, affirmative. Each of them tell the crew to meet at Chill's house.

Inside the hospital, Bre's parents sign papers to take responsibility for Stoney's final rest. Then they all leave the hospital.

By 10:30am, the 17 member crew are at Chill and Renee's house. Bruce isn't here yet. Everyone else is still numb. No one says anything, initially. Then out of the blue, Bre finds the strength to speak.

"He told me, just this morning, that we was the *only* family he's got. He said, if it wasn't for us, he would've given up on life a long time ago. It was like he *knew* something was about to happen. The way he talked..., he was telling me. He told me, no matter what happens with me and him, he wants me to be happy. And he appreciates me for sticking by him. Even when his mama didn't. Its like he *knew*! How am *I* suppose to be *happy*?" She starts to cry again.

"They say you can feel when death is on you," Jan adds.

"I feel like that, sometimes," Rob says.

"All the time," Jb adds.

Then the room is quiet again as they reminisce about Stoney and their lives.

"Right about now, is when he would say something funny and have all of us cracking our sides," Jr says.

"True that, man," Tank says.

"He was set up," Chill says softly.

"Come on wit it man," Rich says, "Tell me what you got."

"What's up, big C?" June asks.

Chill says, "Last night, when we first got to his crib. That nigga *Jake* was there, with two more niggaz, to make a buy. He was acting like he wanted to buy large quantity, *right*? But he didn't have that kind of paper. I believe they was there to do Stoney something, *then*. They was casing his house."

"You figure they was trying to see what he had, ha?" Jr asks.

"Hell yea," Jb offers, "Why else would they ask, how much he'd get off a key for? If a nigga can't afford it? He told me what went down."

"Stoney told me too," Tank says, "He said the nigga only got a zone. And they was pooling ends to score *that*. Why else would he be asking about a key, unless he was planning some fuck shit?"

"I stepped in and just told Jake. The only thing he was gonna leave wit, is whatever he could pay for. And crew ain't frontin him, shit. That's when they got the zone and rolled out. I told Stoney then, I didn't trust that nigga and crew wasn't fucking with them, *no more*. That shit stayed on my mind, all night. I told Stoney how I felt. He wasn't worried about em trying shit because they know he got crew. But I didn't think about the possibility of them watching his house to see if any of us stayed behind. I couldn't even lay down. I had to go back. But it was *too* late. The cops was already there. If I had gone back, as soon as I got Renee home, I would've been there to intercept them coward ass niggaz. But I didn't pay attention to my gut."

"Baby, they did the buy from what color car?" Renee asks.

"Black and white, Impala" Chill answers somberly.

"Terri, *Tonya's roommate*, told me and Tonya she heard a cop at the hospital saying, misses Green saw two guys and they was carrying a guy

to a black and white, four door car. They put him in and drove off," Renee says.

"Y'all think them niggaz took him somewhere, shot him and brought him *back*?" Jr asks.

"*No*. They said, misses Green said *'the ambulance came about 20 minutes later and no one else had been there, after that car sped away.'* That's how Terri told us," Tonya adds.

"So who was they carrying?" Tank asks.

"One of they own. Had to be," Rich adds.

"Stoney must've got one of them, before they got him," Jb says.

"Stoney was shot twice. But *didn't* y'all say, the cops said misses Green heard *four shots?*" Chill asks Renee and Tonya.

"Right!" They say.

"Uh huh. Let's go see misses Green, man," Jr says.

The guys get up and walk outside to the Blazer and the Cutlass. They get in and drive to Union avenue to see Mrs. Green.

When they arrive, she lets them in and leads them to the living room. Ajay stares out of her picture window, to Stoney's house, across the street. Which is now marked off with police tape. The van still sits, parked in the driveway, where Stoney had parked it. Investigators are still on the scene. Ajay turns to listen to what Mrs. Green witnessed. Chill is trying to explain to her who they are. She tells him she knows them all. She's seen them over there and knows they are Stoney's family. She knows they are there to find out what she saw and she's willing to tell them.

"Y'all had some party over there, last night. I do declare. I always liked Cheston. He was a nice young man. Anytime I needed *anything,* he would come over and help me. He kept my yard up for me too. That girlfriend of his, Breanna, she would come over and help me clean my house and all," she says.

She goes on to describe how she had gotten up to her cup of coffee. Soon after, is when she saw Stoney come home.

"When he went in his door, someone ran in, *right* behind him. Then another one went in. That's when that black and white car come up on the sidewalk, parked and a third guy ran in," Mrs. Green says, "Then I heard two gunshots and I picked up the phone to call the police. While I was on the

phone, I heard two more shots. When I went back to my window. And I was right there where Ajay is standing," she says, pointing to Ajay, "That's when I saw them. The two guys, carrying the third guy to the car. They put him in and drove away, *very* fast."
Then she expresses her deepest sympathy to the guys, for the lost of Stoney. She cries, as she thinks about the relationship she had with him too.
"He was like a grandson to me. He looked out for me, real nice," she says, "He use to bring me money or he would send Breanna with it. And food too. He said it was because he knew my fixed income wasn't enough. I'm gonna miss him, so much."
She wipes her eyes with her handkerchief. The guys thank her for sharing the complete story with them, of what she'd witnessed. She hadn't told the police all of it. Because she didn't trust that they would really do anything. The crew lets her know, they'll look out on her, now that Stoney has passed on. She will never have to worry about, *not* having enough.

They walk outside, as more of the investigating team are arriving at Stoney's house. They walk over to find out if they have any new leads. The officers tell them the same story, the girls had gotten at the hospital. The crew know more than the cops know. But they don't offer the cops any information. They know it was Jake. Now, all they have to do is find out if anybody from Jake's clique had been taken to the hospital, with 2 gunshot wounds. Then they'll have their 2nd guy. They go back to Chill's house to call up some folk, *they know,* on the west side of town.

Rob calls Andre. The same Andre from the party, at the club, the night Sonya and Shuntay was raped. Dre owes them a favor for not giving him and Joe up to the police. When Rob asks him, if he knew of anybody getting shot over their way, Dre answers, right away.

"Oh yea, man. That nigga Danny Washington got popped twice in the head. I heard he was over y'all way, somewhere. I wanted to call y'all and see if y'all did that nigga. But I didn't know if it was cool to call. These niggaz over here trying to keep it on the hush. Why? What's up?" Dre asks.

"Is he dead?" Rob asks.

"Not yet. But that muafucka is critical *though*. Joe told me, he's in a coma at West General," Dre says.

"That's the nigga that drive that gray *B-M-W*?" Rob asks, trying to get more information on the car without alerting Dre, that he is.

"Nah, man. Danny got that Impala. Black and white. It almost look like a damn squad car. Except he got rims on that bitch," Dre says.

"Alright. That's not who I'm talking about. Anyway, stay up. And holla at me if you hear any thing else, alright? I'll holla at you later," Rob says and they hang up.

Rob tells the crew, "*Bingo*. Danny Washington. Dead ass, *Eddie's* brother. That nigga in a coma at West. Two shots to the skull."

"I'm finishing his ass on off," Ajay says, "Just like his brother."

Until now, he hadn't said anything. Ebony sits next to him and watches with worry in her eyes. She wants to talk to him about leaving the game. But his head isn't even in the same stratosphere as hers. She wants them to leave the street life and they're about to go *deeper* into it. Ajay wants a plan of action now.

"We need to discuss what we're gonna do," he says to Chill, "I want some get back. We needs to come up with a plan."

"Oh, we're about too. *Believe that*," Chill answers.

Then Ajay turns to Ebony and tells her to come upstairs with him. She does. She wants to talk to him alone.

But once they're upstairs, inside his room, he says,

"Listen to me. I want you to go home."

"Why? No, baby. I wanna stay," she tries.

"Look here. Don't make me say something to you, that's gonna hurt your feelings, alright? I don't wanna say anything that'll come out the wrong way. Just do what I tell you to do. Nina and all the girls are leaving too. Even Renee and Tonya. It's not just you. Y'all go help mama and them, with the arrangements and stuff. The guys need to talk alone. That's what we're gonna do. Do you understand?" he asks calmly.

"I need to talk to you, baby," she tries.

"Not now. Later. Okay? Go home."

She knows his mind is made up.

"Be careful, please," she pleads, "I can't live through what Bre is going through, right now," she finishes as her eyes well up with tears.

He doesn't even react to what she's just said. He's numb to his own feelings. Much less hers.

"I *am* careful. Just go home. I'll get with you later."

"I love you," she says.

"Then do what I tell you to do, okay?"

"Alright. I'm going," she says as she cries, "You better come back."

"I will. Come on. I'll call you when I get done talking," he says.

"Can I have a kiss?" she asks.

"Ebony, I'm not in the mood, right now," he says.

Then after seeing the desperate look on her face, he gives her a peck on the lips. "Alright. Now go home," he says again and she leaves with the girls.

After the females are gone, the guys mull over the facts they've gathered, so far. They have the driver's name. It's Danny Washington and he's in a coma. He won't be going anywhere. They figure Jake is the 2nd suspect because he was riding in the black and white Impala, the night before. And he's old man Jake Johnson's grandson.

"Now, we have to find out who the third nigga is," Jr says.

"We will," Chill says, "But look here. We have to be *smart* about this shit. We've got to use our heads, like we know how to do. Because when we go back and get them niggaz, our shit has to be low key."

"Man, I wanna bust them niggaz ass, right now!" Rich says, very agitated.

"No, man. We gotta let things cool down, a lil bit, first," Chill says.

"*What*?" Tank questions.

"Tank, listen," Chill says, "I want these niggaz, just as bad as any man in this room. Stoney helped me form this crew. Him and Rob was the only one's old enough to hang out at our parents parties, when I turned thirteen. My own father picked Stoney and Rob to be crew. And all of your fathers cosigned him. You know that's the only way a male, who's not blood, can be crew. So nobody wants to kill these muthafuckaz, more than I do. Because that's our brother. My *ace*! But don't forget to use your head and not just your heart. Think about it. *Everybody* knew Stoney was crew."

"So they know we're gonna retaliate," Jb adds.

"Uh huh and them folks gonna be watching too," Rob says as he recognizes the point Chill is trying to make.

"Sho you right. But we're gonna let the cops work the case, for a minute. While we pay our brother his last respects. The last thing we want, is for somebody to get locked up and not be able to see Stoney laid to rest," Chill says as he shakes his head.

He's still finding it hard to believe he's having this conversation.

For clarity, Ajay asks, "Alright, man. So in the meantime, we just lay low and let the cops think we're letting them handle it? While all the time, we're working it underground, right?"

"You got it, Ajay. And remember, now especially. Nobody from the crew is to roll, *anywhere* alone. Always take, at least one other person with you," Chill says.

"That goes for the females too," Rob says, "If this wasn't some random shit. If these niggaz really are trying to move on crew, they might be looking to try to take out one of our girls too."

"They took my mama," Chill says in a very low voice.

"I'm ready to take these muthafuckaz to war!" Rich says as he stands and walks across the room to the window. He adds, "I just wanna kill a bitch ass nigga wit my bare hands!"

Ajay adds, "True that. And in time, we will. But right now is when we get our battle plan together. Lets network all the muthafuckaz we know. Y'all know we can get at a lot of people, as far as letting the streets talk to us. Let them find out shit and report it back to us. Let them do the leg work and think we're just grieving. All the time, we'll be putting our shit in motion. I know y'all can feel what I'm saying."

He's already in a contemplative state of mind. He's going to get even.

"We're feeling you, Ajay," June states, before turning to Chill and saying, "So for right now, we're just gonna keep it neutral. To the *outsiders*, that is."

"Just appear to be clueless to who actually did this shit," Rich says.

"When all the time, we're just gathering info," June says.

"So when the best opportunity do come, we can go in, take care of business and come out cleaner than a muafucka," Rich says, now realizing this is the smartest plan.

"Now y'all wit me," Chill says.

"We go in, catch wreck and bounce back to chill mode, without any nigga even knowing we was there," Ajay breaks it down.

"Like we always do it," Tank adds as the rest nod in agreement.

"Bottom line is. These niggaz violated. They murdered one of our brothers. We're gonna bury, at least three of theirs. And that, my brothers, is the way it is," Chill says and that ends the discussion.

Jb gets on the phone and calls Lynn. He tells her to inform all the girls that they have to roll thick, from now on. And not to be anywhere alone. Not even at home.

In the meantime, Deb and Belinda have reached Stoney's mother, Jackie, in Columbus. They inform her of her son's death. She will arrive this evening to start making funeral arrangements. All of the females are at Bre's house to be as much support for her, as they can be. While they wait for mama Jackie, Bre tells them more of her final conversation with Stoney. She tells them about the ring he has taped to the bottom of his night stand.

"Do you think it's still there?" Rebbie asks.

"I don't know. They might've taken it. Mama said they trashed the house," she answers.

She hasn't stopped crying since hearing that Stoney had been shot.

"Well, I tell you what we can do," Lynn says, "We can all go over there with his mama, when she gets here. We can look for it."

"Yes. We can do that," Jan says.

They all want her to have it. Because that will be the last thing he can give her. With him being gone, they know it's important for her to have this memento. Jan puts her arm around Bre, who can't stop crying. 1 by 1, all of the girls begin to comfort each other, once more. Renee gets a page from Chill. She uses mama Deb's phone and calls him back.

"Y'all can come back this way, whenever you're ready," Chill says.

"Alright. Let me leave some number's with mama Deb, so Stoney's mom can contact us when she gets in. We'll tell you about it, when we get there," Renee says and they hang up as Chill settles back in his recliner.

"Was baby girl with them?" Ajay asks Chill.

"Yea. They're all there and fixing to roll back this way," he says.

"Cool," Ajay says as he lights up a blunt, "Let me smoke one for my brother."

The females are back at Chill's by 7:30pm. Not long after, Bre gets a call from Stoney's mother.

"Hello, miss Jackie. This is Breanna. How are you?"

"Not to good, right now, baby. How are you doing?" Jackie asks.

"Not well, at all," Bre replies.

Jackie has a lot of questions. All of which Bre answers, as well as she can.

Bre tells her they need to go over to the house. Jr will drive them over to pick up Jackie, so they can all go to Stoney's house, together.

Bre, Jan and Lynn ride with Jr, Chill and Renee. The others crowd into the Blazer and Tonya's car. The foursome stay at Chill's house with lil Kenny. Big John and Al are watching Chill's house, from theirs.

Jackie contacts the police, so they can have someone there to let her go in the house, to get whatever she needs for her son's burial.

Once in the house, the crew begin to look for clues. Anything which will help them get another step closer to finding out who the third guy is.

Bre goes into Stoney's bedroom and sits on the bed. She thinks back to the early morning hours, when they had made love. Right here on this bed. Her eyes survey the room, which is in disorder and fall upon the night stand. It sits next to the bed. The lamp had been knocked to the floor and the drawer was pulled out, onto the floor, with all of it's contents strewn over the floor, around it. But the night stand itself, remains in place. She stands up and slowly flips it over onto it's side. Jan and Lynn come into the room. A small black square, velvet box is taped in the front right hand corner, on the bottom of the night stand. Bre removes the duck tape and retrieves the box. Then sits back on the bed, as tears remain in her eyes. Jb and Rob walk into the room as she opens the box.

Rob whispers, "He wanted to give you that, yesterday. But he wasn't sure how you would've reacted."

Jb sits down on the bed, next to her. The guys knew about the ring but they also knew Stoney was nervous about giving it to her.

"He didn't want you to feel like he was rushing you into any kind of situation, that you might not have been ready to commit too," Jb says.

"I would've said yes," Bre whispers as she breaks down again.

Lynn sits by her side and comforts her while Jb takes the ring from the box.

"Here you go, Bre," he whispers as he slides the ring on her finger.

She continues to cry as she stares at the ring.

Jackie comes into the room to look through the closet. She sorts through it's contents, asking them which suit they like for him and oblivious to the warmth the room's occupants shared with her son.

"I wonder if he would want me to put him in one of these?" Jackie ponders aloud, as she looks through his closet at his many suits.

"Mama Jackie, we're gonna take care of that," Chill says when he comes into the room.

"We've already decided, we're gonna get a suit for him," Rob says.

"Oh baby, you don't have to do that," Jackie says, "He's got all of these nice suits in here."

"Yes ma'am, we do," Jb says, "He's our brother. He would do the same for us."

"He would wanna go out in style and we're just gonna make sure that he does," Chill says as the others agree.

Jackie smiles and says nothing else. Then the officer comes into the room to see if they're about done. They are. On the officer's request, they move to the outside of the house.

The crew goes to check on Mrs. Green and Bre assures her, they will be in touch with her, at least once daily. And that Stoney had left something for her. She tells Mrs. Green she will bring it by real soon. When they're done talking to her, they all load into the vehicles and drive away.

The next few days are spent making funeral arrangements. Bre kept the largest quantities of money and valuables which Stoney owned. For safe keeping, she kept them in the steel safe at her mother and father's home. She's going to secure the funeral arrangements, even though the entire crew have put more than $10,000 into a burial fund. She gives the funeral director another $16K. Any balance, she tells them, should be returned to the crew. The service has been set for New Year's Day. *Wednesday, January 1, 1991.*

During the service, all crew members speak on Stoney's behalf. Most of them are barely able to complete their speeches, without breaking down. As they finish their written speeches, they fold it and put it in his coffin. They include 1 other memento, they want him to take to the grave. Their fathers say a few words and their mother's sing, *Hard To Say Goodbye,* at the crews request.

Later, at the cemetery, while Mrs. Tucker, the pastor's wife, sings *Precious Lord Take My Hand,* the funeral director's lower Stoney's casket into the ground. The crew weep openly, as each tries to comfort the other. Pastor Tucker gives the closing remarks. Then all except the crew, walk to their cars. The crew stay behind to say their final words. Then each of them drop a white carnation on his coffin top. Before they turn to walk away, they each say, "*In a minute*," as if Stoney had said, "*See ya.*" They take photo's with his casket, before they walk to Chill's parents plots and pay respects to them too. Then they get into their vehicles and proceed to Breanna Wilson's house, where the repasts is being held.

At the house, Bre takes Stoney's 2 sisters into her room. She gives each of them $200 from Stoney's money. She knows he would want them to have it. Later, she'll set up escrow accounts in each of their names, at the Cleveland Bank and Trust. Their accounts will mature when they each turn 18 years old. She'll also open an account for Mrs. Green and use the $8000 Stoney kept for her. The crew will make monthly deposits and make sure she wants for nothing. Bre still has Stoney's pagers and his product. She'll get with the crew and move that, later. His van is registered in her name. Jackie says she should keep it. The house is in Jackie's name. She ask Bre if any of the crew want to live there. She wants it to stay in the family, as well. Jr and Tonya are in need of a place. Especially with the baby coming, later this year. The crew agree to take responsibility for the house. They'll do the paperwork, at a later date. Bre can use the balance of the monies, the crew donated, to upgrade the house, before her brother and future sister-in-law take occupancy.

Today is also her younger brother, Bruce's 13th birthday. He joins the crew at Chill's house. They play cards, listen to music, sing songs and mostly, reminisce about Stoney. It's snowing heavily outside, as the crew, once again 18 strong, sit around at Chill's house. They're going to spend the night together. In their hearts and minds, Stoney is here too.

CHESTON WAYNE "STONEY" COLEMAN
OCTOBER 20, 1969-DECMBER 26, 1990
AGE-21 YEARS OLD
"STONEY! MAY HE REST IN PEACE!"
JANUARY 1, 1991.
Always Crew!

THE END OF PART ONE!

Find the READER'S GUIDE FOR
The TIME WILL REVEAL series
By Black Coffee
On website: www.truesrelatepublishing.com

What to read next in the series?

"MORE THAN 4 ADMIRERS- "The Threat To A Legacy" short story 1"

Description:

Do you think everyone loves the crew and everyone, of the Black race, wants them to prosper? *Really*?
The crew have enemies dating back to the 1st generation. But who wants the crew to lose? Who's life's work had it become to dismantle the Cleveland crew? Those questions are yet to be answered.

It's a fact that every generation has at least 1 man who stands out as the best leader. One who is strong in his convictions, unwavering in his decisions and truly in control of any relationship, he's apart of.

Both Allen Saul Williams and Allen Devante' Jackson Sr were leaders in the Civil Rights Era. Big John and big Al are both viewed that way, in the 2nd generation. But in the 3rd generation, there are two, as well. Big Chill is the *named* leader of the 3rd generation. There was an attempt made on his life in 1993, while the man seen as his sibling had to be away, bettering himself in college. But was Chill really the main target? Or was the hit on him, meant to be a mental weight on Anthony "Ajay" Jackson?

Many view Ajay as the key to prolonging the crews dominance into the new millennium. And they would be absolutely correct. An attempt on his life was made, the following year. Of course, it was unsuccessful. But afterwards, a powerful man made his presence known and he moved his money and his prominence around to establish an invisible shield around the crew. His name is Bert Parkwood. According to papa Brown, grandpa Logan and poppa Jones, he is the modern day, Jeb Baker.

Find out the answers and much more in: "MORE THAN 4 ADMIRERS" "The Threat to a Legacy" Time Will Reveal short story #1 by Black Coffee.

Join us on FACEBOOK for the discussion questions:
Group: "Black Coffee's Crew Nation" or Fan page: "Black Coffee's Books"

If you were charged more than $25(US dollars) and shipping & handling was not included in the price, please contact us at one of the following websites immediately:

[Black Coffee's websites]

www.blackdollone.com or www.truesrelatepublishing.com

On Twitter:

http://twitter.com/AuthorBlkCoffee

On INSTAGRAM: AuthorBlkCoffee

All books available in print and eBooks

Nook and Kindle

Be sure to pick up the sequels to this Time Will Reveal Series

Time To Grow-RELOADED-Time Will Reveal part 2
Time To Love-RELOADED-Time Will Reveal part 3
Time to Know-RELOADED-Time Will Reveal part 4
Time To Feel-RELOADED-Time Will Reveal part 5
The Making of AJAY- "Every Man"-RELOADED (PRINT ONLY)

(Time Will Reveal- short stories)

#1 MORE THE 4 ADMIRERS-RELOADED
#2 MR. WRONG AND THE RATS-RELOADED
#3 THE CREW'S PRIORITY(TBA)

And more of the Time Will Reveal series to come!

Time To Show-Time Will Reveal part 6 [Late Fall 2013]
Ajay and Ebony 1-Time Will Reveal 7-Time To Give(TBA)
Ajay and Ebony 2-Time Will Reveal 8- Time To Live(TBA)

Look for these future releases by Black Coffee

The Foe, The Friend-Poetry [print & audio](TBA)
The Organization-part one, All By My Lonely [TBA]
The Organization-part two, Still By My Lonely(TBA)

www.ingramcontent.com/pod-product-compliance
Lightning Source LLC
LaVergne TN
LVHW020659110826
845149LV00012B/2047

* 9 7 8 0 9 8 4 4 7 0 1 0 5 *